THE JACK

THE COCKY KINGMANS
BOOK FIVE

AMY AWARD

Copyright © 2025 by Amy Award

All rights reserved.

No part of this book may be reproduced in any form or by any electronic or mechanical means, including information storage and retrieval systems, without written permission from the author, except for the use of brief quotations in a book review.

Cover Design: Leni Kauffman

THE JACK*SS IN CLASS

He's the campus king with a no girlfriends rule.

But he's about to break it for the most irritating, sassy-mouthed woman he's ever met.

Flynn Kingman's senior year plan is simple: class, getting drafted in the first round, and no romantic complications. Until he chases a rogue baby donkey across campus and meets Tempest Navarro—the one woman immune to his charm.

Tempest Navarro is hiding her bestselling romance novels, anxiety, and a baby donkey in her sorority house. Nope, nothing to see here. Especially not for a jock that's too hot for his own good. Why does he have to be in her Shakespeare class, saying smart things, and driving her insane?

When they're forced together by a university tutoring program, verbal sparring turns to undeniable attraction. Especially when Tempest's emotional support donkey, her meddling sisters, and a whole lot of Kingman siblings are all conspiring to push them together at every turn.

This steamy sports romance features a protective football player with hidden depths, a curvy heroine owning her talents and learning to take up space, an emotional support donkey with perfect timing, and that Bridgertons-meets-American-Football family that'll make you wish you were a Kingman.

CONTENT NOTE

This is a book of fluff.

We need fluff; it's the insulation from the harsh world around us. Don't let anyone make you feel ashamed for reading fluffy romances.

It's important to me to have representation of marginalized communities in the media, and I do that by showing fat women getting happy ever afters without ever having to lose weight.

But fluff and representation doesn't mean there isn't any conflict. The heroine does face a world that has made her feel like she's not enough, and that includes some external fatphobia.

There is also talk about loss of a parent and a spouse, in the past. Our Cocky Kingmans were raised by a single father, and life without their wonderful mother is a fact of their existence and has shaped their lives.

I've worked very hard to create an emotionally nuanced story in a the kind of world I want to live in, that includes diversity, equity, inclusion, and accessibility for all kinds of people. I've had help from diversity readers with carefully crafting this story for you to escape into, kick your feet, and feel good. But if you feel I've misrepresented or caused harm, please let me know so that I can do what I need to learn, fix, and be better.

What I can promise you is that my books will always hold a space that is free of physical violence against women including sexual assault. That just doesn't exist in the world I create in my mind.

And finally, I love to write about funny animals and pets. No pets will ever be harmed or die in any of my books.

I like to cry on draft day and at touching Super Bowl commercials, not in my romances.

wink

*For all the readers who think you aren't loveable.
I know you've hidden yourself away, you protected that spark deep inside your heart, the one that burns with the light of your true self.
It's time to let that spark ignite.
The real you is exactly what the world needs.*

Titania:
> Methought I was enamour'd of an ass.
> – *A Midsummer Night's Dream*, Act 4, scene 1

FUN TIMES WITH FLYNN

FLYNN

ootball, adoring fans, especially the sexy ones who wanted to get in my pants, and a cheering stadium. This was my kind of fun.

"Dragons on three." I pumped my fist in the air, and the crowd of students packed into the quad echoed my enthusiasm. "One... two... three..."

"DRAGONS!"

The responding roar was exactly what I lived for. Game day energy, but without the pressure. Just pure school spirit and academic excellence. Which, yeah, sounded ridiculous, but this whole pep rally was the athletic department's way of proving we weren't just dumb jocks. Hence the "Brains and Brawn" banners everywhere and the fact that I'd just had to rattle off my GPA to the crowd, which of course included my father, former National Championship coach of the Denver State Dragons football team.

"Speaking of brains," my twin brother, Gryff, muttered

beside me, "explain to me again why we're doing this instead of prepping for the combine?"

"Because Coach says we need more positive PR for the football team." I elbowed him in the ribs, nearly knocking him off our makeshift stage. "Especially after Xander's InstaSnap went viral."

"I told you that wasn't my fault." Gryff moved to elbow me back, then froze. "Uh, Flynn? Is that a baby donkey... wearing a purple and gold jersey?"

"What? No." I followed his gaze to the edge of the crowd where... "Holy shit, that is a donkey. In a jersey. With... are those wings?"

A tiny gray donkey stood at the edge of the crowd, sporting both a Denver State Dragons jersey and what appeared to be sparkly dragon wings attached to a tiny harness. The wings actually fluttered in the breeze, which was both weird as shit and adorable. It was being led through the crowd by a one of the players from the DSU women's soccer team.

"Freddie," our younger brother Isak called out from where he was filming the rally for his FaceSpace followers. "What are you doing with a bonkey?"

"Isn't he cute?" She beamed up at us, practically bouncing as she walked. The donkey followed docilely at her heels, its oversized ears twitching beneath what might have been a tiny dragon horn headband. "He's my sister's, and she is busy studying. So, I thought he needed some school spirit."

"You stole your sister's donkey to bring it to a pep rally?" A tall girl with wild curls pushed through the crowd, grinning. "Classic Freddie move."

"Artemis," Gryffin's whole face lit up at the sight of his best friend. "Done crushing souls at rugby practice?"

"Never done crushing souls, Kingman," she said and flexed dramatically. "But I took a break to see this disaster in the making. Why is it always the football players up on stage, hmm?"

"Because we win shit," I said. Like the Snoop Cat bowl. Which brought money and fame, and did I mention the money, into the school.

Artemis slugged me in the arm which garnered nothing more than a snicker from my twin. "Uh, so do the rest of us, jackass. No offense, baby donkey."

"Ladies and gentlemen." The assistant athletic director grabbed the mic, oblivious to the barnyard animal in our midst. "Please welcome our beloved mascot... Drake the Dragon."

The crowd cheered as our mascot bounded onto the stage in his oversized dragon costume. He did his usual hype dance, spinning and...

His head fell off.

The fuzzy green dragon head rolled right off the stage.

Directly toward the baby donkey.

"Oh shit," all three of us Kingman brothers said in unison.

The donkey's eyes went wide. Its ears shot straight up. And then...

"¡Ay, no! Wait." Freddie's cry was drowned out by the sound of tiny hooves on pavement as her sister's donkey took off like a shot through the crowd, sparkly wings flapping wildly.

"I got it." I vaulted off the stage, because obviously this

was what I did. I protected, defended, and made my team look good. That's the mission when you are team captain.

"I bet I catch it before you yahoos," Artemis called out, already sprinting after the donkey.

"Hey, who you calling a yahoo?" Why did women always call me that?

"You're on," Gryffin shouted, hot on her heels.

"This is definitely gonna go viral," Isak yelled, phone held high as he chased after all of us. "Best Scholar-Athlete rally ever."

The things I did for this school. The things I did for this team. And now, apparently, the things I did for random baby donkeys in dragon costumes.

For a tiny donkey, that thing could move.

"Left, go left," I yelled as our sparkly-winged fugitive darted between students' legs, causing a chain reaction of dropped books and spilled coffee. "Gryff, cut him off at the student center."

Gryff had already been moving in that direction before the words were out of my mouth. Twin telepathy strikes again. It was no myth, and damn fucking useful in football and foot chases after donkey-bats out of hell.

"On it." He split off toward the historic brick building, while Artemis vaulted over a bench and took the path past the fountain.

"You crazy little donkey, come here." Freddie was surprisingly fast for someone so tiny, her soccer training showing as she wove through the growing crowd of spectators.

"What's the donkey's name?" Isak called out, still filming everything.

"I don't have a clue." Freddie ducked under someone's arms.

Because that was clearly our biggest problem right now was not knowing this little terror's name. Not the fact that there was a mini donkey in a Dragons jersey running wild across campus while half the student body filmed it on their phones.

The donkey banked hard right, its tiny wings flapping as it headed straight for the science building. A group of students emerged from the doors, arms full of project boards from what looked like chemistry.

"No, no, no." I put on a burst of speed. Those project boards definitely looked explosive.

"I got him." Artemis lunged, hands outstretched.

The donkey pulled a spin move that would have made our running backs jealous.

Artemis crashed into Gryffin, who'd been coming from the other direction. They went down in a tangle of limbs, and I heard my brother's distinctive wheezing laugh.

"Dude," Isak zoomed in on them with his phone, "this is better than the time Trixie's rooster crashed Chris's surprise birthday party."

"Focus." I jumped over my brother and his best friend, who were still trying to untangle themselves. "That donkey's heading for the coffee shop."

The outdoor seating area of Dragon's Brew was packed, because it was one of those sunny sixty-degree Colorado days in January. Dozens of students sat at the scattered tables, most of them wearing headphones and staring at laptops or textbooks. None of them had noticed the chaos heading their way.

"Look alive people, incoming," Freddie yelled in warning.

A few heads turned. Someone screamed, or maybe laughed. A half dozen coffee cups went flying.

I had a brief flash of tomorrow's headlines. KINGMAN BROTHERS DESTROY CAMPUS IN DONKEY DISASTER.

Dad would laugh. Coach would not.

The donkey's wings flapped faster as it wove between the tables, surprisingly graceful for something with hooves. It was heading straight for a girl curled up in one of the oversized armchairs in the corner. She hadn't looked up from her book once, despite the chaos around her.

"Watch out," I called, already envisioning the lawsuit. "There's a—"

The girl turned the page of her book, then held that same hand, palm out, right into the path of mass donkstruction.

The donkey skidded to a stop.

Just... stopped. Right in front of her chair. Then stuck its tiny gray nose directly into her palm like it was getting pets from its favorite person in the world.

What the actual—

"Thank god." Freddie caught up to me, doubling over as she tried to catch her breath. "Tempest, I can explain. Don't kill me."

Tempest. The girl in the chair must be Freddie's sister. The one who owned a yet unnamed pet donkey.

The one who still hadn't looked up from her book.

"Got it all," Isak announced triumphantly, finally lowering his phone. "This is going to break my record for views. Artemis, that fall was epic."

"Shut up, mini-Kingman." Artemis and Gryffin joined us, both covered in grass stains. She punched Gryff, in the chest this time. She should have been a boxer instead of a rugby player. "Your tackling form needs work."

"Excuse you, I am a Heisman nominee. I have perfect form." Gryff rubbed his rock solid chest, grinning. "You're the one who missed the donkey."

"Pretty sure we all missed the donkey." I gestured to where the little troublemaker was now contentedly leaning against mystery girl's, Tempest's chair, wings drooping. "Nice defensive moves, though. Both of you."

A crowd had gathered around us, phones still out. Instead of the academic excellence PR the athletic department had wanted, we were about to go viral for chasing a winged donkey across campus.

Not exactly the senior year legacy I'd been going for.

I'd met a lot of beautiful women in my life. Came with the territory of being a Heisman-nominated linebacker for a D1 school. But I'd never met one who completely ignored me while casually taming a runaway donkey.

"So," I cleared my throat, trying to get her attention. "That's your donkey?"

She turned a page in her book. Actually turned a page. Without looking up.

"No," she said, her voice low and smooth. "Currently, that's Freddie's donkey because they borrowed without asking. Isn't that right?"

"Don't be mad, Tempest." Freddie dropped down to sit

cross-legged next to the chair. "Look how cute he is in his jersey. I thought he'd love the pep rally."

"Hmm." Another page turn. The donkey had settled completely now, sitting at her feet like an oversized gray puppy, its tiny wings drooping.

"I'm Flynn," I tried again. "Flynn Kingman."

"I know who you are." She still didn't look up, but I caught the slight curl at the corner of her mouth. "Everyone knows who you are."

"And you're Tempest..." I waited for her to fill in her last name.

"Yes." That was it. Just yes.

Behind me, I heard Gryff trying not to laugh. Jerk.

"Your donkey just crashed our pep rally," I pointed out, wondering what it would take to get her to actually look at me. "Almost took out half the chemistry department."

"Again, not my donkey at this particular moment." She reached down to scratch behind its ears, her book never wavering. "Though I suppose I should reclaim him before he decides to join one of the athletic teams. Those are some impressive moves he's got."

Was she making fun of me?

"Better moves than some of your running backs, boys," Artemis chimed in, dropping into the chair next to Tempest's. "You should bring him to one of the women's rugby team practices, Freddie."

Now, Artemis was definitely making fun of me as she fucking flirted with Freddie while I couldn't even get Tempest to look at me.

"¡Mira!" Freddie held up her phone. "Isak's video

already has ten thousand views! The donkey's wings look so cool when he runs."

"Fantastic." Tempest's tone suggested it was anything but. "I can't wait to explain this to the farm sanctuary."

"I can help with that," I found myself offering. "I mean, I can explain that it wasn't your fault. Or his fault. It was just a series of unfortunate—"

"Events?" She actually looked up then, one eyebrow raised. Her eyes were dark and sharp behind black-framed glasses, and they saw way too much. "Did you just quote Lemony Snicket to me, Flynn Kingman?"

"I... might have." I hadn't meant to. "I have a little sister who reads a lot."

"Hmm." Those eyes stayed on mine for a moment longer than was comfortable, like she was reading something she didn't quite believe. Then they dropped back to her book. "Well, thank you for the offer, but I can handle the sanctuary staff. And Freddie can handle cleaning out the stalls for the next month as penance."

"What? No." Freddie flopped dramatically across her sister's legs. "Tempest, no. I have games, and practice, and studying."

"Should have thought about that before you borrowed him without asking." But Tempest's free hand dropped to smooth her sister's hair, the gesture automatic and affectionate. "Also, you're crushing my book."

"I'll help her," Artemis offered, grinning. "I love animals. And watching Freddie suffer."

"Aww, that's our Artie," Gryffin laughed. "Always looking out for the downtrodden, but cute AF soccer players of the world."

"Someone has to." Tempest's voice held a note of steel under the casual tone. "Since her big sister clearly can't keep her out of trouble."

Ouch. Self-burn. Those were rare.

I tried one more time, not sure why I was still trying except that something about this girl fascinated me. "The boys and I are doing our gaming live stream on Saturday. You should come. Bring the donkey. Fairly sure those wings make him lucky, and trust me, you need all the luck you can get."

"Video game night?" She actually looked up at that, one eyebrow raised. "With the boys?"

"Afraid you can't handle a little competition?" I hadn't mentioned that my brothers' girlfriends Penelope and Willa joined us most weekends. Because I was gonna win this girl over with my best smile, the one that usually got me exactly what I wanted. "Or just afraid of losing?"

"Pass." She turned another page. "But thanks."

"She has plans," Freddie stage whispered. "Very important plans that involve her fav—ow."

Tempest had pinched her sister's leg.

"Right." I rocked back on my heels, weirdly disappointed. "Well, if you change your mind..."

"I won't." She finally glanced up again, and this time there was something almost kind in her expression. "But have fun with the boys."

She went back to her book before I could respond. The donkey looked between us, gave a tiny snort, and snuggled closer to her chair.

Even the livestock was ghosting me. That was new.

"Come on, lover boy." Gryff clapped me on the shoulder. "We gotta get those 40-yard dash times down before the combine. Artie, you coming to run sprints?"

"Can't." Artemis stood, stretching. "Got a date with a pretty bio-chem major. But save me a spot at game night tomorrow?"

"Sure. As long as you know you're going down."

I let my brother pull me away from the coffee shop, but I looked back once, twice, and maybe a third time. Tempest had shifted in her chair, making room for both Freddie and the donkey to lean against her legs while she read. She looked... content. Like the chaos of the last twenty minutes hadn't touched her at all.

"Stop staring," Gryff muttered. "She's not interested."

"I wasn't—"

"Sure." He grinned at me. "Just like I'm not interested in watching Artemis tackle all those thick-thighed rugby girls."

"Shut up." I shoved him ahead of me. "Let's go practice. Maybe the donkey will show up and give Xander some competition for his spot in the draft," I said, even as we headed for the field, and I definitely forgot all about that tiny-winged donkey and a girl who wouldn't look up from her book.

I had approximately fifteen weeks until graduation, and that gave me and my one girl for two-weeks plan a good seven more college women's beds to get into. And there were plenty of DSU Dragonette's who would squeal for a chance to let me give them beard burn between their thighs.

Plenty to whom I was more interesting than a damn book.

Although, I doubted any of them would have a donkey.

SECRET AGENT BONKEY

TEMPEST

"Mija, please tell me you're taking more business classes than those literature classes your papá talked you into."

I adjusted my laptop screen, buying time before answering my mother. The wi-fi at the remote clinic where she was stationed for the Doctors Without Borders mission was sketchy at best, but her disapproval came through in perfect HD.

"Literature is my major, Mamá." I held up my planner, showing her my color-coded schedule. "Ves? I'm still taking all the practical classes you wanted. Including a minor in business marketing, just like you suggested."

"Ah, yes," Her whole face lit up. "At least that's something useful."

My stomach gurgled even though I wasn't the least bit hungry. What I needed here was a subject change. "How is Papá's book coming along?"

"He works at that tiny desk in the camp office for hours. Something about the Shakespearean histories and their political relevance to modern humanitarian crises." Her expression softened. "He reads me passages in the evenings. I don't understand half of it, but it's nice having him here."

She laughed, and then her face shifted to one of amused disdain. "Oh, I almost forgot to tell you. One of the nurses from Boston brought the most ridiculous book with her. Some trashy romance novel based on—you won't believe this—a Shakespeare play. *The Taming of the Shrew*, but with a hockey player and the coach's daughter. Can you imagine? Your father and I had quite the laugh over it during dinner."

My spine turned to stone. My book. The one that had been a huge break out, changing my whole life. Publishing it was supposed to just be for funsies. But then it hit several best seller lists and poof, there went my carefully planned life.

"Sounds... interesting," I managed to say while my insides went all spikey and sharp.

"Interesting? It's absurd." She waved her hand dismissively. "If you're going to adapt the greatest playwright in history, at least do it with some dignity. Your father was appalled at how they butchered his beloved text. Though I must admit, he stayed up late reading it, purely for academic critique, of course."

Oh, yes. Mamá could diagnose and treat any medical condition, but she'd never understand pursuing literature for its own sake rather than as a stepping stone to something practical.

"How terrible," I managed. "That he's not getting enough sleep, I mean."

"You would never do such a thing, mija." She beamed at me. "I raised you to be smarter than that. Speaking of which, how are your law school applications coming along? The program at Georgetown has an excellent focus on international law. Or, with your literature background, you could specialize in intellectual property, something practical with your oh-so-useful liberal arts degree. I'm sure you could get into the law school at DSU como tu hermana."

Ah, yes, the be more like your successful older sisters part of the conversation. Great.

A loud bang saved me from having to answer. My bedroom door flew open, revealing my roommate, Parker, in all her purple-haired, caffeinated glory.

"T, you have to see this. You're not going to believe what your—" She froze, spotting my laptop screen. "Oh, sorry Dr. Navarro. Didn't know you were having mother-daughter time."

"Parker." Mamá's smile turned slightly strained. "How lovely to see you. Still studying... computers?"

"Cybersecurity," Parker corrected cheerfully. She flopped onto my bed, making my laptop bounce. "But I'm branching into ethical hacking. Way more fun."

I bit back a smile. Parker knew exactly how much that kind of talk bothered my mother, which was precisely why she did it. It was also why she was the perfect person to help keep my literary alter ego safely anonymous online.

"How... innovative." Mamá's lips pursed. "Tempest, mi vida, I should go. I've got a surgery consult. But think about what I said about DSU. And please do something with your hair before you go anywhere today."

I resisted the urge to touch my messy bun, which was the easiest thing to do with all my hair. It was a Saturday for goodness' sake. "Yes, Mamá."

"Good. Don't forget to call your abuela on Sunday. Te quiero." The screen went dark before I could reply. I was saved from her seeing my eyeroll. I talked to Abuela more than I did anyone else in the family.

"Dude." Parker sat up, already pulling out her phone. "You need to see this. Freddie just made you FlipFlop famous."

"What?" No, no, no, no. The horrible sensation of spiders crawling up and down my spine, underneath my skin shivered through me. I grabbed her phone. We'd worked so hard to keep everything about my books anonymous. How had Freddie found out? "Can you take it down? How many people know who I am?"

"Calm down, your secrets are still safe and secure." Parker's grin was evil. "Freddie just filmed your unnamed donkey friend, put him in a Dragons jersey and tiny wings, and set him loose at the scholar-athlete rally. Where he was chased across campus by half the football team. Including Flynn Kingman."

I just about collapsed with relief. "I already knew that. Don't scare me that way."

The video started playing. There was my sibling, looking way too pleased. There was the baby donkey, his little wings flapping as he ran. And there was Flynn Kingman, DSU's golden boy, vaulting over a bench like some kind of romance novel hero...

Not that I would ever read romance novels. Or write them. Or had possibly just outlined a scene eerily similar to this for my next book.

"I'm actually going to kill them this time. I'm going to kill them and that kid Isak," I muttered. "Then you for scaring me half to death that someone had found out."

"You can't." Parker was still scrolling. "You love me and she's your special little she/they enby. IDK about Isak. Also, this is comedy gold. Look, someone set it to the Chariots of Fire theme. Oh, and there's a remix with—"

"Park." I dropped my head into my hands. "The sanctuary is going to fire me when they see this. Then what am I going to do to keep my therapist happy?"

She'd told me to get a hobby to keep my anxiety at bay. All work and no play and all that. I would admit, cuddling baby animals did seem to keep my panic attacks at bay.

"Please." She bumped my shoulder. "They think you're the best thing since sliced bread, especially since your donations mean they don't have to spend all their time fundraising anymore. Besides, this is great publicity for them. Look how happy he is in his little outfit. But I have to ask..." She paused the video. "Why exactly did Freddie have tiny dragon wings just lying around?"

"Because it's Freddie." I peeked through my fingers at the screen. "Though I have to admit, they do suit him."

"They really do." Parker switched to another app. "Also, not to stress you out, but your book just hit number two in Italy, and your agent's been blowing up your secure email all morning. Want me to run interference while you do damage control the donkey situation?"

I groaned and fell back on my bed. Some days I wasn't

sure which was harder, keeping my writing career a secret from my family and the rest of the world, or keeping my siblings from causing chaos in my carefully controlled life.

Today, it was definitely a tie.

At least I had Abuela. Except she and Abuelo had been in Mexico almost the entire year.

An hour later, I pulled my new-to-me-but-used-so-no-one-would-suspect-I'd-paid-cash-for-anew-car - Lexus SUV - into the sanctuary's gravel parking lot, glancing in the rearview mirror at my passenger. The baby donkey lay curled up in the back, his tiny wings slightly crooked from the day's adventures, looking about as innocent as a donkey who'd just caused campus-wide chaos could look.

"Don't give me that face," I muttered. "We're still having a talk about appropriate behavior on campus."

But as I turned off the engine, I realized something was wrong. People were running across the yard. I could hear shouting, and was that... a geyser of water?

"Stay," I told baby donkey, not that he would actually listen to me. I jumped out of the car and jogged toward the main barn, where water was literally pouring out the side door.

"Get the gates," someone yelled. "The goats are loose."

A streak of white shot past me, followed by what looked like every volunteer on staff, all trying to corral our small herd of escaped, very wet, very panicked goats. If they weren't going by at the speed of light, I'd tell them I could relate.

"Maria?" I called out, spotting the sanctuary director

as she ran past, phone pressed to her ear, other hand gripping a bucket.

"Can't talk—yes, I need emergency plumbing service right now—no, I can't wait until—Trixie, grab that chicken."

The whole scene was chaos. Water streaming everywhere, animals escaping in all directions, volunteers slipping in the mud as they tried to help. And in the middle of it all, Maria was trying to coordinate everything at once.

"Where do you need me?" I asked, already rolling up my sleeves.

Maria pressed her phone to her chest. "Tempest. Thank god. The water main freaking burst. We've got to clear the barn before, –no, I will not hold for your supervisor." She went back to arguing with the plumbing people while gesturing toward a group of panicked cows.

I dove in, helping herd animals to dry ground, making quick decisions about which pens could still be used far enough away from the flooding. It was like trying to organize a library where all the books had legs and opinions.

It didn't take long before I was freezing, soaked, muddy, and helping Trixie load chickens into her hatchback. She had a whole setup at home. A fancy coop she called the Millenhen Falcon that her fiancé had built her, though I'd never met the guy. All I knew was that he apparently thought her hilarious obsession with punny chicken names was adorable.

"Come on, Hennifer Lopez," Trixie cooed, somehow managing to cradle three chickens at once. "Your vacation home awaits."

I caught another escapee and passed it to her. "How many can you take?"

"As many as needed." She settled the chickens into their makeshift travel crates. "Luke Skycocker and the girls will love having company."

I trudged back to my car, remembering I still needed to tell Maria about the donkey's social media debut.

She was by the fence, still on the phone, but now arguing with someone about emergency foster placement.

"No, I understand your process, but I have thirty-seven animals who need—yes, I know you require home visits, but—"

Baby donkey chose that moment to let out a tiny bray from the back of my SUV. Maria glanced over, then did a double take at his wings.

I opened my mouth to explain, but she just waved a tired hand. "Whatever you need to do, honey. I trust you. I've got to figure out where to put these sheep and—no, sir, I am not being unreasonable."

She hurried off toward a new crisis, leaving me standing there with a baby donkey who needed a place to stay and absolutely no plan whatsoever.

I looked back at him. He looked at me, those big brown eyes somehow even bigger than usual.

"Okay," I sighed, climbing back into the driver's seat. "I guess you're coming home with me. Temporarily. Just until..." Until what? And honestly, where was I going to take him?

There was no way I was going to hide a donkey in a sorority house.

It only needed to be until the barn was fixed. But I had

no idea how long that was going to be. I popped onto the sanctuary's website and made a quick, but big, donation. My shiny new accountant said I could write it off.

I could take him...home. We had the space. My sisters would freak, except Freddie, of course. Until she had to scoop donkey poo. It wasn't like I wanted to move back to Casa Navarro, even for a few weeks. Not even for an adorably cute baby donkey. I loved my family, but they were a lot. Especially when I was the odd middle sister out all the time.

Abuela wouldn't mind watching baby donkey. Despite her glamorous telenovela star facade, she was the one who I inherited my love of animals from. But she wasn't back for another few weeks.

Donkey stuck his nose between the front seats, his wings rustling.

The sorority house was totally not a good idea, but I'd have to figure out how to make it work.

"Don't look so smug," I told him, but I was already mentally calculating how many bales of hay I could fit in my room without our house mother noticing. "This is just temporary. And we're taking those wings off before anyone sees you."

He brayed again, softer this time, like he knew he'd won. Reminded me of a certain cocky football player I knew. Maybe I should drop baby donkey off with him and they could strut their stuff together.

I texted Parker from the parking lot behind the Kappa house.

> Me: Need help. Don't ask questions.

> Parker: I've got the shovel and I know where we can stop to get columbines to plant over the body.

> Me: Actually, do ask questions. Many questions. Like how much trouble we'd get in if we temporarily housed farm animals in our room.

> Parker: ...

> Parker: Is this about the FlipFlop donkey?

> Parker: OMG IT'S ABOUT THE FLIPFLOP DONKEY

> Parker: I'M COMING DOWN

One minute later, she stuck her head out our second-floor balcony instead. "Please tell me you have him."

"Shh." I glanced around the dark parking lot. "Yes. But we have a problem."

"Only one?"

I popped open the back of my Lexus. Baby donkey looked up from where he was curled on the bed of towels, his wings now definitely crooked from the day's adventures.

Parker's eyes went wide. "He's so much cuter in person. But also... bigger than I expected."

"Yeah." I ran a hand through my hair. "So about that..."

"Ladies?" A voice called from the front of the house. "Is someone out here?"

Mrs. Henderson. Our house mother. The woman

THE JACK*SS IN CLASS

who'd once written someone up for having one of those pretty blue Beta fishes and had developed a love of random room checks.

"Quick." Parker tossed down a bright red rope. "Like we practiced."

"We've never practiced this," I whisper shouted back.

"Yeah, but I've been reading a lot of heist novels lately. Same principle."

The donkey chose that moment to let out a tiny bray.

"Was that..." Mrs. Henderson's voice got closer. "Is there an animal out here?"

I grabbed the rope and started tying it around the donkey's middle, thanking every deity I could think of that I'd done that shibari class for research on my second book. "Parker, if you let him fall on me..."

"Please." She disappeared from the balcony. A moment later, the rope started moving upward. "I once hacked the dean of students' laptop for fun. I think I can manage some basic pulley physics."

I steadied the donkey as Parker hauled him up, praying he'd stay quiet. He seemed more interested in watching the ground get farther away, his tiny wings fluttering like he was trying to help.

"Hello?" Mrs. Henderson rounded the corner just as Parker grabbed the donkey and they tumbled onto the balcony. "Miss Navarro? What are you doing out here?"

"Just..." I gestured vaguely at my muddy clothes. "Getting some things from my car. Volunteering at the sanctuary. You know how it is."

She sniffed. "You smell like barn."

"Yes." I tried to look apologetic. "I was going to shower right now, actually."

"See that you do." She gave me one last suspicious look before heading back inside. I swore that woman had it out for me this year.

I waited until she was gone, then sprinted for the side entrance. Taking the stairs two at a time, I burst into our room to find...

Parker sitting cross-legged on her bed, feeding the donkey what appeared to be her secret stash of fruit snacks.

"First of all," I closed and locked the door, "those aren't good for him. Second..." I looked around our small room. "Where is he going to sleep?"

"Already figured it out." Parker pointed to the corner where she'd somehow constructed a makeshift pen using a random shower curtain rod, some command hooks, and what looked like every blanket we owned.

"The balcony can be his outdoor space during the day. No one ever looks up there anyway, and we'll get some fake plants or something to block any lookie-loos. And I've got three of my noise machines, white, brown, and pink noise, ready to rock to cover any suspicious sounds. Ooh, this is the perfect excuse to get that sleep sounds app I've been wanting to try."

Never before had I been thankful Parker was an insomniac.

I stared at her. "You did all this in the five minutes it took me to get upstairs?"

"I told you. Heist novels. Well, actually romantic suspense. What's a heist without a little smut, you know?"

She scratched behind the donkey's ears. "Also, I maybe already had some contingency plans in place. You know, in case we ever needed to hide something... or someone in our room."

"Why would we ever need to—" I stopped. "You know what? I don't want to know."

The donkey had finished the fruit snacks and was now investigating Parker's laptop, his tiny wings leaving glitter on her keyboard.

"So," Parker grinned at me. "Want to tell me why we're harboring a fugitive farm animal?"

I sank onto my bed, suddenly exhausted. "The sanctuary's flooding. Everything's chaos. Maria was dealing with emergency foster placements, and I just... I couldn't let him get sent away somewhere."

"Hmm." She studied me for a moment. "And this has nothing to do with a certain bearded football player who spent his afternoon chasing said donkey across campus?"

"What? No." I grabbed my shower caddy, needing something to do with my hands. "I barely know Flynn Kingman."

"And yet you knew exactly who I meant." She wiggled her eyebrows. "You know, this could make excellent research for your next book. Hot football player, secret donkey-sitting, forbidden—"

"We are not having this conversation." I headed for the door. "Just... keep him quiet until I get back. And no more fruit snacks."

"Fine." Parker was already pulling out her phone. "But we're definitely talking about the fact that you're blushing. Also, we need to name him something epic.

Something that captures his true spirit of chaos and glitter."

I left her scrolling through baby name websites, the donkey peering over her shoulder at the screen.

My donkey problems would have to wait. I needed to space to think, and the best place to do that was a long, hot destinkifying shower. Then I could come up with a plan, and possibly a miracle.

Behind me, I heard Parker's delighted laugh, followed by the distinct sound of more fruit snacks being opened.

Make that definitely a miracle. Something like one of those Hail Mary passes.

MUCH ADO ABOUT FLIRTING

FLYNN

"*D*ude." Gryff rewound the video for approximately the hundredth time. "Look at your face when the donkey does that spin move. You got absolutely schooled. Better hope the scouts don't see that."

I threw a protein bar at his head. "Pretty sure you're the one who ended up on your ass with Artemis."

"Worth it." My twin sprawled deeper into our ancient living room couch, his feet propped on a stack of League combine prep guides. "Besides, that clip only has, like, ten million views. The one where Artie and I collide? Fifteen mil and counting. Every scout's probably showing how badass I am at taking a hit to their teams now."

"You're both idiots." Isak looked up from where he was editing the footage for his InstaSnap. "The best part is clearly when the donkey's wings start flapping right before he hits top speed. I've already got three workout supplement companies and an energy drink wanting sponsorship deals to use it."

The rest of us would make our millions with our pro football contracts, but for all I knew, Isak probably already had enough money to retire with the way he lined up sponsorships.

My phone buzzed and I turned the screen for Gryff and Isak to see. "It's Pen. She says we're catching a ride on Kelsey's jet for the big Bowl. Jules is with us too. Dad is flying out with the boys on the Kingman jet."

Crazy that we didn't all fit on the jet anymore. Our family had grown last year. Well, not officially yet as the Dec and Chris were waiting for the off-season to get married. We better be getting a tropical vacay out of wedding season.

"Four Kingman brothers in one very big Bowl." Isak shook his head. "Plus the biggest popstar in the world. The media's going to lose their minds. And I am here for it."

My phone buzzed again. This time it was a video from Hayes recreating the donkey's spin move during Bowl practice, much to the offense of the Mustangs' amusement.

"See?" I held up the phone. "The donkey's got skills."

"If Hayes uses this as an end zone dance, it'll definitely go viral. Baby DK is gonna make me and your girlfriend rich."

I smacked Isak on the back of the head. "I don't do girlfriends."

Isak smirked at me. "Did you guys sign up for tutoring yet? Coach is asking."

"It's the second day of the semester," I protested. "I

haven't even been to my Tuesday-Thursday classes yet. We don't even know if we need tutoring."

"Doesn't matter." Gryff pulled up the athletic department email on his phone. "Says here all team captains have to participate. 'Setting a leadership example' and all that."

"Fine." I grabbed my laptop. "But I've only got three classes. Doesn't give me a whole lot of choices."

"We've got Shakespeare." Gryff scrolled through his schedule. "We could request the same tutor, make it easier to study around combine prep."

"I heard we've got a visiting professor from Cambridge. It can't be that bad." Besides, I liked a good story. I wasn't some dumb jock. I read a lot. Mostly sci-fi and fantasy. "Guy wrote plays about love and sword fights. I got this."

Gryff rewound the donkey video yet again. "What's up with that girl? The one who just held out her hand and the donkey went right to her? She's like a freaking wizard or something."

"Who, Tempest?" The name slipped out before I could stop it.

Both my brothers' heads snapped up.

"First name basis already?" Isak's grin was pure evil. "Interesting."

"It's not—" I started to protest, but Isak was already pulling up her InstaSnap.

"Tempest Navarro," he read. "English major. Member of Kappa Alpha Tau. Oh, and look at that, she volunteers at the same animal sanctuary Trixie does."

"Bet that's where she got the donkey," Gryff added helpfully.

"Drop it." I grabbed my combine prep guide, needing something to do with my hands. "I've got a no girlfriends rule. No more than two weeks with a girl ever, and I'm not wasting time trying to get into the pants of anyone who isn't interested. Enthusiastic consent or I don't want it."

"Sure." Gryff didn't look convinced. "That's why you've watched this clip forty times staring at her and not the donkey."

"I have not—"

My phone buzzed again. This time it was Jules.

> Julinator: Saw the donkey vid. Very smooth. Try looking at the book she's reading instead of just staring at her boobs, jackass. Might give you something to talk about...

I groaned and shoved my phone in my pocket. When your baby sister was giving you dating advice, you knew you were in trouble.

Not that I was interested in dating Tempest Navarro.

Two-week rule with women who were into me, and not looking for a commitment. That was the plan. It was a good plan. A plan that had never failed me.

"Dude." Gryff's voice broke into my thoughts. "You're staring at the video again."

I was. But this time I noticed something I hadn't before.

The book in her hand was a well-worn copy of *Much Ado About Nothing*.

The same play on my book list for Shakespeare class.

Huh. I knew what I was reading tonight.

Gryff and I walked into the English building the next day more than prepared. No one could accuse the Kingmans of being dumb jocks.

The thing about being an identical twin was that you got used to people staring. The thing about being an identical twin who also happened to be co-captain of a D1 football team that won Bowl games was that you learned to ignore all that attention.

Mostly.

"Ten bucks says he asks us to sit on opposite sides of the room," Gryff muttered as we entered the lecture hall.

"Twenty says he makes us wear name tags." I scanned the rows of seats, trying to look casual when I spotted Tempest in the third row from the back. She had her nose buried in a book again, or rather an e-book. Damn. Made it harder to see what she was reading when there was literally no cover to spy on.

Gryff caught my glance and grinned. "Well, well. Look who's here."

"Shut up."

"Make me." He headed straight for the empty seat next to her.

Traitor.

I slid into the seat directly behind Tempest, while my twin dropped into the desk to her left. She didn't look up, but I saw her fingers tighten slightly on her Kindle.

"Great turnout today," Gryff said loudly. "Must be

because of the reading material. I hear *Much Ado About Nothing* is quite the comedy."

Still no response from Tempest, but the rest of the class was watching us like they were at a tennis match. Or maybe a football game.

"Indeed." I leaned forward, close enough to see that she was reading something called *Curvy Temptation*. "Though personally, I've always thought Beatrice and Benedick had the right idea. Start with antagonism..."

That got me a tiny head tilt. Progress.

"Mr. Kingman." Dr. Whitmore's crisp British accent cut through the pre-class chatter. "And... Mr. Kingman. How lovely. I don't suppose you'd be willing to sit on opposite sides of the—"

"Called it." Gryff held out his hand. I slapped a twenty in it.

"We're good here, Professor." I gave him my best responsible-student smile. "Wouldn't want to disrupt your seating chart."

"I don't have a..." He trailed off, looking between us. "Which one of you is—"

"Flynn," we said in unison.

His eyes narrowed. Tempest's shoulders shook slightly.

"Well." Dr. Whitmore straightened his jacket. "Let's begin, shall we? We're discussing *Much Ado About Nothing*, which I assume you've all read?" His gaze landed on me. "Mr. Kingman?"

"Which one?" Gryff asked innocently.

Tempest tipped her head to the side like she was about to look back at me, but then changed her mind. It was enough for me to see her press her lips together, fighting a smile.

"The one behind Miss Navarro." Dr. Whitmore's tone could have frozen hell. "Since he seems so interested in Beatrice and Benedick's antagonistic courtship."

"Oh, you mean the way they use wit as a defense mechanism?" I didn't look up from where I was doodling on my notebook. "Creating verbal barriers to avoid emotional vulnerability while simultaneously proving themselves intellectual equals? That antagonistic courtship?"

Silence.

Complete silence.

Tempest turned around slowly, her dark eyes wide behind her glasses.

"I..." Dr. Whitmore blinked. "Well, yes, actually. That's quite—"

"Though personally," Gryff cut in, because we'd been tag-teaming class discussions since kindergarten, "I think it's more about their fear of being publicly vulnerable. They're both performers, living up to everyone's expectations of their roles."

Okay, that was a little pointed. Asshat.

"Like the way Benedick has to maintain his reputation as a confirmed bachelor," I added, glaring at the back of Gryff's head.

"While Beatrice gets to be the clever one who's above it all." Gryff nodded at Tempest, who was still staring at me like we'd all started speaking in tongues.

"Until they realize," Gryff cut in before I could get

another word in edgewise, "that those roles are actually trapping them."

Dr. Whitmore opened and closed his mouth several times. Like some kind of British codfish.

"Though the public performance aspect is really driven home in the party scene," I continued, mostly because Tempest hadn't looked away yet and her shocked expression was doing funny things to my chest. I mean, well below my chest. Like in my pants. My heart had nothing to do with this. "Everyone wearing literal masks while acting out metaphorical ones?"

"Mr. Kingman." Dr. Whitmore had found his voice. "That's... quite an interpretation."

"Which Mr. Kingman?" Gryff asked.

I bit back a grin as our professor visibly reconsidered his life choices.

Tempest was still watching me, her expression somewhere between irritated and intrigued. I winked at her, and instead of the cute kind of blush I was used to getting for my attention, she huffed out a sigh, rolled her eyes, and turned back around.

Gryff grinned at me like the dickhead that he was.

I threw my pen at his head.

"Right then. For the rest of you who aren't such a fan of the bard, let's get into the text. Please open up to act two, scene two, and discuss how the ruse..."

I leaned forward as Dr. Whitmore began to drone as English professors were want to do. Tempest was apparently also tuning out, because she'd sneakily turned her Kindle back on. Oh, ho. Not only was this book a romance novel, it was a really fucking dirty one.

THE JACK*SS IN CLASS

. . .

Wasn't that a fun tidbit of information for me to file away?

She moved her finger to flip the virtual page, but her hand froze when I leaned forward and whispered in her ear. "Wait a second. I'm not done with that page yet."

That Kindle got flipped over faster than the speed of light. Tempest didn't even turn around to glare at me this time.

Hmm... time to cool my jets. Aside from having some fun poking at her and the good doctor for thinking I wouldn't have done the reading, I wasn't interested in her. Or her curves.

I glanced down and absolutely did not spend the rest of the class fixated on the way her ass didn't quite fit on these stupid tiny desks. These things weren't made for big football players, or lush asses like hers.

Our hour and fifteen minutes of Shakespeare finally came to an end, and I stood up stretching. My phone buzzed just as Tempest was doing her best speed-walking escape from class.

"Congratulations," Gryff read from his screen. "You've been matched with your academic success partner for the semester—"

"Carajo." Tempest stopped dead in the doorway, staring at her own phone.

I grinned, coming up behind her. "Looks like fate wants us to spend more time together."

"Fate has nothing to do with it." She spun around,

waving her phone. "This is ridiculous. You clearly don't need tutoring."

"Team captain," I reminded her. "Setting an example as an athlete scholar and all that."

"Right." Her eyes narrowed. "And your extremely detailed analysis of Beatrice and Benedick's emotional defense mechanisms was just what? Lucky guessing?"

"I contain multitudes."

"You contain something." She turned to go, but Gryff blocked the doorway.

"Sorry," he said, not looking sorry at all. "Getting a text from Artie. Very important. Can't move."

Tempest's phone buzzed again. "I have to get to my next class."

"I'll walk you." Didn't really matter if I was late to my next class, did it?

"I think I can make it two buildings over, but thanks."

No way. Maybe fate was conspiring in my favor. "Marketing Analytics with Professor Calloway?" I asked innocently.

She froze. "How did you—"

"What a coincidence." I shouldered my bag. "Me too. We can walk together."

"I'm off to the weight room," Gryff called after us as Tempest started powerwalking down the hall. "You two crazy kids have fun."

I caught up to her easily, my longer stride matching her quick steps. "So, how's our mutual friend doing?"

"I don't know what you're talking about."

"You know, about yay high." I held my hand at waist level. "Gray. Sparkly wings. Excellent footwork."

"The wings were temporary."

"Ah, so you admit there is a donkey."

She shot me a look that could have melted steel. "There was a donkey. At a pep rally. That's all."

"Named..."

She frowned at me and kept on walking.

"Is it Donkey McDonkface?"

That got me the smallest twitch of her lips. "No."

"Sir Brays-a-Lot? I grew up with a goose named Sir Honksalot. He was cool as shit."

"No."

"Eeyore 2: Electric Boogaloo?"

She actually snorted at that one, then immediately tried to cover it with a cough.

"Come on," I wheedled. "Give me a hint. Wait, is it Shakespeare themed? Bottom? No, no, Donklet, Prince of Denmark?"

"You're ridiculous." But she was fighting a smile now.

"I am also your new tutoring assignment." I held the door for her as we entered the business building. "So really, this is a trust-building exercise."

"This," she gestured between us, "is you wasting both our time. You don't need a tutor."

"Maybe I just want to spend more time discussing literature with a beautiful woman." She was fucking beautiful.

She yanked open the door to the business building before I had a chance to get it and hold it open for her. I tried again as we entered the classroom. "How is nameless bonkey doing? After his brush with fame?"

Something flickered across her face. Worry? Guilt?

"The donkey is fine." She took a seat near the front. "And his name is not Donklet."

"Fernando Lamas? Ooh. Tell me you're friends with a llama too."

"No."

"Wanna be friends with my goose?" Sir Honksalot was, like, a thousand years old, and he wasn't mine, but she was going to say no, anyway.

"Stop."

"I know a hilarious rooster."

She pulled out her marketing textbook with what seemed like unnecessary force. "Flynn. One jackass in my life is enough."

I dropped into the seat next to her, ignoring her glare. She'd just called me a jackass and I wasn't the least bit insulted. Most women practically fell at my feet, which was exactly the way that I liked it.

But verbally sparring with Tempest was more fun than I'd had in... years. Okay, so she wasn't on the slate to be one of my two-week girls. Didn't mean I wasn't going to have just as much fun poking the bear, or rather donkey, this semester.

Real life started in just a few short months once I was drafted, graduated, and started playing in the pros. Might as well make the most of my last semester.

"Your life is definitely not full enough. I volunteer as tribute to help you fix that."

"Mr. Kingman," Professor Calloway's voice cut through the pre-class chatter. "How nice of you to join us. I trust you've done the pre-reading?"

"Of course." I pulled out my own book, but not before

catching Tempest's surprised look. "Chapter one: Marketing Analytics in the Digital Age. Did you want to discuss the case study on data-driven decision-making, or should we start with the ethics of predictive modeling?"

Tempest's textbook slipped off her desk.

I caught it before it hit the ground, unable to resist leaning close as I handed it back. "You know, if you keep looking shocked every time I know something, people might start to think you're operating under some unfair stereotypes about football players."

She wasn't quite smiling, but she wasn't glaring either. And she hadn't moved away when I'd leaned close to return her book. Which meant I could get in one more poke at her.

"I got it," I whispered as Professor Calloway started class. "It's Donkey Hoetee de la Donkey, isn't it?"

This time she did smile, just a little, before firmly opening her textbook.

This semester was going to rock.

BATPHONES AND BOYS

TEMPEST

"**S**up?" Parker spun away from her laptop and sucked on the straw of her ever present iced coffee. At this point, she should just mainline it. "How was your day? Make any life-altering decisions? Hide any farm animals? Get assigned to tutor any hot football players?"

I dropped my bag and stared at the corner of our room. "Why is there a kiddie pool on our balcony?"

The two of us had worked out a temporary schedule so we could get to classes and extra-curriculars without ever leaving baby donkey home alone. And honestly, the brunt of the donkey-sitting so far had fallen on Parker's shoulders since a lot of her classes were virtual.

I think she'd managed by consuming an inordinate amount of caffeine.

"Brilliant, right?" She bounced up to demonstrate. "Love me some same-day Zon delivery. I figured out that if we put puppy pads in it and surrounded it with hay, it makes a perfect donkey bathroom. We still gotta do some serious big boy pooper scoops, but better than our room smelling like a barn."

It was better, and what was more, with the kinds of things a house full of fifty-five sorority sisters ordered online, I'm sure no one looked twice at a kiddie pool, puppy pads, a collapsible shovel, and a block of hay arriving on the front porch.

Baby donkey looked up from where he was munching hay, his makeshift wings from yesterday were back on, and decidedly crooked. So fricking cute.

"That's..." I couldn't decide whether it was genius or insane. "Actually kind of brilliant." Until we got the inevitable January cold snap and snow. But hopefully the sanctuary would be back up and running by then.

"And..." She grabbed her phone. "I made him social media accounts. InstaSnap, FlipFlop, the works. He already has thirteen-thousand followers."

"You what?" Someday I was either going to strangle Parker for her love of social media, or thank her for it. I hadn't decided yet. I wouldn't even have accounts at all if she didn't basically post to all of them on my behalf. But it was all part of her grand strategy to make sure no one associated the close-to-real-life version of me with the best-selling romance author version of me.

"Look." She shoved her phone at me. "I called him @BabyDragonDonkey, since you still won't decide on his name, and people are obsessed. The video of him doing the spin move around Flynn Kingman has, like, a million views now."

"Parker." I pressed my fingers to my temples. "We're trying to keep him secret."

"No, we're trying to keep him from getting caught in our room. His social media presence is totally separate. Oh, oh, oh." She clicked to another screen. "And get this. I've been messaging with this gamer guy who says he can get us sponsorship deals. Some protein powder company wants Baby Dragon Donkey to be their mascot for their Bowl ad. Something about 'the strength of a dragon in the body of a donkey.'"

I sank onto my bed. "Please tell me you didn't agree to anything."

"Not yet. This guy's kind of annoying actually. Keeps sending me memes and asking if Mystery Donkey's mommy is single." She wrinkled her nose. "But he does have, like, three million followers, and has a ton of sponsorship deal on his livestreams, so, I guess he knows what he's doing."

"No sponsorship deals." I grabbed her phone and scrolled through the accounts she'd made. The donkey doing his little wing flap. The donkey investigating Parker's gaming setup. That was probably the one that got the gamer guy's attention. The donkey wearing a tiny graduation cap Parker had apparently crafted while I'd been in class.

They were actually kind of adorable. But still. "We can't draw attention to him. He's supposed to be at the sanctuary."

"I've made sure that no one can tell where he is in the vids, literally or virtually." Parker took her phone back. "And, the sanctuary's account already followed us. They seem cool with it though. Even shared the original video."

The donkey chose that moment to bump his head against my leg, looking for treats.

"Don't give me that look, you poor, nameless cutie patootie." I told him. "This is exactly the kind of chaos I was trying to avoid."

"This is our last semester and you're going to live a little if it's the last thing I do." Parker's grin turned evil. "Did you happen to get an email about that tutoring thing your mother made you sign up for?"

It was supposed to make my law school applications look good. And, of course, reflect well on the family since my papá was in line to be head of the English department at DSU when ancient Dr. Dillamond finally retired.

Not that I needed to look good on any applications. Because I hadn't started filling any of them out.

I groaned and fell back on my bed. "I don't know what you did, but I already feel the need to murder you for it. Unless, of course, you somehow got me out of it."

Then I wouldn't have to spend any more time than was absolutely necessary with annoying Flynn Kingman.

"No, but I did hack the academic success program database this morning. Had to make sure they paired you with someone hot."

"Parker."

"What? Like you weren't hoping for a meet-cute with a secret genius who'd totally get your romance novel career?"

I sat up so fast I got dizzy. "First of all, Flynn Kingman is not a secret genius."

"So you admit he's hot?"

"Second of all," I ignored her, "I don't need meet-cutes.

I need to figure out how to hide a donkey, maintain my GPA, keep my family happy, and now apparently prevent you from turning our room into a social media content farm."

"Too late." She held up her phone again. "Look, someone already made fan art of Baby Dragon Donkey. They gave him a little football jersey and everything. Oh, and that gamer guy just messaged again. Says his brother wants to know if—"

A tiny bray interrupted her as the donkey stuck his nose in my backpack, pulling out my marketing textbook.

"No." I rescued the book. "That is not for eating. Unlike some people in this room, I actually need to study."

"Sure." Parker was typing rapidly. "You study. I'll just be over here making our donkey into a famous influencer. Maybe starting a merchandise line. Building his brand."

Parker mumbled something under her breath that sounded a lot like her eternal diatribe about me not letting her build my author brand.

I just couldn't afford to let the world find out. The therapy bills alone...

"He's not our—" I stopped. The donkey had settled next to my bed, his crooked wings rustling as he dozed off snuffling his way into adorable little baby donkey snores.

Parker's phone dinged again. "Ooh, the gamer guy wants to know if Mystery Donkey takes modeling requests. Says his team captain has some ideas for—"

Gamers had team captains? Maybe DSU had an e-sports team. Huh.

"No." I pulled out my Shakespeare notes, trying to think of anything I could possibly tutor Flynn and his surprising comprehension of Renaissance literature on. I wasn't telling the school, or my mother, I couldn't tutor the captain of the football team. "No modeling. No sponsorships. No team captains."

"Fine." She turned back to her laptop. "You're going to have to name him eventually. The internet wants to know."

The donkey's ears twitched in his sleep. I leaned in to snuggle his cute face and whispered, "And your name shall be..."

Nothing. I had nothing. This was worse than writer's block. Because I couldn't use any of the hilarious suggestions Flynn had just tossed out, my brain matter was on creative overload.

My phone buzzed.

Wait. Oh, shizznit.

Not my regular one that I carried around with me. No, this was the super-secret sneaky phone. Parker and I looked at each other, looked at the phone as it buzzed again, and dove for it.

"Batphone alert," she squealed and snatched it from my grasp. I blamed that on the fact that I had a cute donkey resting against my lap and clearly couldn't move for fear of waking him.

"Holy donkey balls, Temp..." She stared down at the phone and licked her lips like her mouth had suddenly gone dry.

My agent only used the phone for big, important stuff. Usually we just emailed.

Parker slowly handed me the phone like it was made of fairy dust and cookie crumbs.

> Gloria Horne: FlixNChill just threw an offer on the table. And they want all the books. Including the one you haven't finished yet. Call me.

And now I was the one licking my lips searching for the moisture Gloria's message had just evaporated. I just stared at my phone, my tutoring plans forgotten.

> Me: In class. Can't call. Give me deets?

> Gloria Horne: They're thinking eight episodes per book. But the way you've structured the series, they need to introduce each of the players in the club. Which means we need book 5 finished... yesterday.

I was on chapter three. Okay, chapter one. But I had ideas for chapters two and three. And there were supposed to be six books in the series.

> Gloria Horne: Also, their marketing team wants you to do author interviews when they announce.

My stomach dropped. No, that didn't even come close to the feeling. It dropped all the way out of my body, bounced on the floor a couple times, and rolled under the bed to hide with the dust bunnies.

> Me: We discussed this. No public appearances.

> Gloria Horne: Darling, you can't stay anonymous forever. Your books are too big now. The readers want to know who wrote their favorite love stories.

Sometimes I missed the simplicity of self-publishing, back when I could control every aspect of my career. Back before my little stories about love and sexy times had somehow turned into an international best-selling series.

Back when no one cared who I was, what I did, or what I looked like.

> Me: My mother is a surgeon who thinks romance novels are "trashy garbage" and my father's a Shakespearean scholar who just laughed at a romance adaptation of his beloved plays.

> Gloria Horne: And when you're making multi-seven figures from the FlixNChill deal, merchandising, and even more backlist royalties because of the ridiculous amounts of publicity you're about to get, you can buy them... I don't know, a private hospital wing and a first edition folio to make it up to them.

She thought buying my mother's love would do anything? She didn't know my family. Because it wasn't just my parents who were going to judge me. My mother was nothing compared to what would happen when my abuela found out I'd been hiding something this big from the family.

> Gloria Horne: When can I get pages of the new book? Football player and nerdy girl trope is a personal favorite of mine.

The universe had a twisted sense of humor sometimes.

> Me: I need more time.

> Gloria Horne: Two weeks. Then I need at least a partial manuscript.

> Gloria Horne: And seriously consider the publicity angle. Maybe start small. InstaSnap, FlipFlop, any kind of social media presence. Build up to the big reveal.

Right. Because I didn't have enough social media chaos in my life already. But Parker would pee her pants to launch socials for my pen name.

> Me: Two weeks for pages. Still no to the publicity.

> Gloria Horne: For now. But darling? The world's going to know about Miranda Milan eventually. Might as well be on your terms.

I turned the Batphone face down, trying to ignore the way my hands were shaking slightly. Miranda Milan... the mysterious romance author who wrote about love and family and happy endings, felt extremely far away from Tempest Navarro, the good daughter who was supposed to be applying to law school instead of wasting time on frivolous literature.

"You good?" Parker asked without looking up from her laptop where she'd pretended not to watch every reaction I had to the conversation on the Batphone. "You're doing that thing where you forget to breathe."

"I'm fine." I ran my fingers along that swirl of soft fuzz right on baby donkey's forehead, staring at him like he held all the answers to life, the universe, and everything.

"Uh-huh." She still didn't look up. "But also...I want you to note, that you aren't currently having a panic attack, and... that's good. Give yourself a pat on the back for that."

She was right. I could still literally feel the dread right smack dab in the middle of my chest, but I could breathe. I could swallow. My heart wasn't racing. My brain wasn't fritzing out into fight-or-flight mode.

I could... think.

"Yeah. Thanks. I... I'm not...not freaking out. But I'm not okay. I just need some time to think."

I carefully scooched out from beside the sweetly snoring donkey and grabbed my notebook. The one I did all my plotting in. "Mind donkey-sitting a little bit more today? I'd like to hit the library."

"I know that look. It means you have a book idea." She waggled her eyebrows. "If it happens to involve tying up a sexy football player and your, ahem, heroine having her way with him, I'm all for it."

"That happened in book three with the baseball player. I'm not doing the same thing again." I slipped on my jacket and gave the donkey another scritch between the ears.

"Too bad. That was hot." Parker shook her head, faux disappointed. "Oh, and that gamer guy messaged again. Says his brother wants to know if you've picked a name for the donkey yet."

The library steps appeared blissfully quiet and people-free. Probably because we were two days into the semester and no one was ready to get back to studying yet. Exactly what I'd hoped for. Because I didn't need anyone looking over my shoulder at these notes.

I didn't even usually let this notebook out of the lock and key safety of my room. But the library had a certain magic to it for me, and I needed that right now.

"Oh em gee, Flynn." A blonde in a Denver State cheerleading jacket was practically bouncing down the steps. "You're hilarious. Come on, it's so cold out here, I'm nipping out. Let's go grab coffee or..."

Of course. I hitched my bag higher on my shoulder and prepared to slip past Denver State's golden boy and his admiring fangirl.

"Sorry, babe." Flynn's voice carried clearly in the evening air. "Can't. Got a study date with my tutor."

I froze mid-step.

"Your tutor?" The blonde's voice rose slightly. "But you're, like, really smart."

"He is, isn't he?" I muttered under my breath.

"There she is now." Suddenly Flynn was beside me, one hand landing warm on my shoulder. "Ready to dive into some Shakespeare?"

The blonde looked between us, her perfect ponytail swishing. "Oh. I didn't realize..."

"Tempest's brilliant." Flynn's hand was still on me, slowly creeping across my back. "I'm lucky she agreed to help me."

I shrugged off his hand. "I didn't agree. I was assigned."

"Even better." He grinned down at me. "Fate."

"That's not—" I started, but blondie was already backing away. She gave me an interesting look that, if I didn't know better, was jealousy. Nothing to be jealous of. Guys like Flynn Kingman weren't ever interested in me.

"Well, have fun studying." She gave a little wave. "Text me later?"

"Can't." Flynn was already steering me toward the library doors. "Probably be at this for hours. Shakespeare's complicated, right, tutor?"

I waited until the other woman was out of earshot. "What are you doing?"

"Getting tutored?" He held the door for me with an exaggerated flourish. "Unless you'd rather go over Beatrice and Benedick's antagonistic flirtation techniques out here?"

"There's nothing to tutor you on. We don't even have homework yet." I tried my best to speed-walk to the area with the study carols, but I should have remembered that Flynn could keep up. He had earlier today too.

"Consider this a preview." He followed me into the quiet of the library. "Besides, you still haven't told me the bonkey's name."

"That's because—"

"Is it Eeyore-udite? Get it? Because he's clearly very smart, running circles around the football team like that..."

I bit the inside of my cheek to keep from smiling. "No."

"Sir Francis Bacon Bits? No wait, that would be better for a pet pig."

"Do you ever stop?"

"Not when I'm winning." He dropped into the chair next to mine as I tried to set up at an empty study table. "Come on, one hint? Is it literary? Historical? Sports-related? Does it involve puns?"

I pulled out my notebook, but kept it firmly shut, determined to ignore him.

"It's definitely pun-related, isn't it?" He leaned closer, lowering his voice. "I bet it's awesome. I bet it's the best donkey name in the history of donkey names."

"No."

But I was smiling now, despite my best efforts not to.

And Flynn definitely noticed. Dammit.

FOR A GOOD TIME CALL...

FLYNN

*I*t was a good thing I basically already had enough credits to graduate, because if I had more than the three classes this semester, my combine prep practice schedule would be wrecked. I could have just skipped this last semester like a lot of guys who were a shoe in for the draft did.

It wasn't like I was going to go get some job with my business degree. I'd done a lot of marketing to make sure my pro ball player brand was on point.

But no Kingman went onto the pros without a degree.

Did give me a whole extra semester at DSU with a light load, which meant time to play the field for a few more months. But week one of the semester was already down, and I didn't have anyone on the line for my first two-week round. But it was Saturday, and I was on the way to hit the gym, then headed to...

I spotted her right away, sitting at a corner table in the campus coffee shop, hunched over what looked like three different textbooks. The sunshine streaming through the window caught the shine in her messy dark hair, making it shimmer. Today she was wearing a dress covered in tiny book spines, and I was staring far too hard. Trying to read the titles printed on the fabric, of course.

Change of plans. Poking at the grumpy girl who was ready to shoot me down again was way more fun.

I put the hood on my sweatshirt up and headed inside to quietly order two cups of coffee. They poured those at the register and I waited so no one would call out my name. I didn't need her spotting me and bolting.

Her nose was so buried in the notebook she was writing in, she didn't notice me until I stopped at her table, coffees in hand. "Fancy meeting you here."

She didn't even look up. "Following me now, Kingman?"

"You caught me. I have spies all over campus reporting your location to me at all times."

That got her attention. Her head snapped up, dark eyes narrowing. "Why would that not surprise me?"

"Surprise." I pulled out the chair across from her. "About this tutoring thing."

"I already told you it's a moot point." She returned to her books, clearly dismissing me. "The tutoring program is to help students who need it. You clearly don't."

I let out a big grin. "Was that a compliment hidden in there somewhere? Did you just admit I'm smart?"

"Don't let it go to your head, Kingman. I'm not totally convinced you didn't just memorize all that jazz you said in class from some study guide."

"I think, if you'll recall, it was a duet with Gryff."

Her lips twitched, but she maintained her serious expression. Progress.

"Look," I said, leaning forward. "We both have to do this tutoring program thing. But what if we just... did our homework in the same space? No actual tutoring required."

She raised an eyebrow.

"We sign off online saying when and where we meet. You don't have to teach me anything, I don't have to pretend I need help, and we both get credit for participating in the program." I spread my hands. "Win-win."

"And what do you get out of this arrangement?"

More time sparring with you. "Coffee?"

She snorted, but I could see her considering it. Time to sweeten the deal.

"I'll buy your coffee for the semester too."

Wrong move. Her expression went from considering to closed-off in an instant.

"I can buy my own coffee, thank you very much." She started gathering her books, her shoulders tensing. "I don't need anyone to take care of me."

"Whoa, wait." I held up my hands in surrender. "That came out wrong. I wasn't trying to...I mean, I know you can afford..." I was making it worse. I took a breath.

"Let me try again. No coffee bribes. Just two people, doing their homework, occasionally acknowledging each other's existence. Maybe even having a conversation that doesn't involve cute fuzzy livestock making people spill their coffee all across campus."

She paused in her packing. "The donkey chaos was your fault. You were chasing him."

"Partially my fault," I corrected. "But I seem to recall that if someone hadn't lent a certain four-legged troublemaker to the soccer team for a pep rally, I wouldn't have had to chase him through half the campus."

"If someone hadn't decided to show off his..." she waved her hand in a circular motion in my direction, "football... skills in front of the entire student body, he probably wouldn't have gotten so freaked out and run all the way through the quad."

"See? We're already great at conversation." I gestured to her books. "Come on. What's the worst that could happen?"

She sat back down, but her expression remained skeptical. "You actually do your own homework?"

"Shocking, I know. But yes. How do you think I maintain my eligibility to chase balls around a field?"

Another lip twitch. "Fine," she said finally. "But I have conditions."

"Name them."

"No trying to charm me. No asking personal questions." She ticked them off on her fingers. "And absolutely no....looking at my notebook, umm notes. Keep your eyes on your own paper."

I filed that last one away for future reference. "Counteroffer. Charming is my natural state so I can't help it, and I accept the notebook mystery. But I reserve the right to ask exactly three personal questions per study session."

She considered this for a long moment. "Two questions. And I can veto any I don't want to answer."

"Deal." I stuck out my hand.

She shook it, her soft small hand disappearing in mine.

"This doesn't mean we're friends."

"No, of course not." I opened up my backpack and pulled out my own books and settled in.

Her groan was music to my ears. "Now?"

"What? Like I've got something else to do?"

We settled into a surprisingly comfortable silence, just the scratch of pens and occasional sips of coffee. I tried to focus on my marketing assignment, but I kept getting distracted by her.

She had at least four different colored pens spread out on the table, all these colorful tabs, and she was using them systematically as she made notes in the mysterious notebook. Every few minutes, she'd smile at something she was writing, this small, secret smile that made me want to know what was so funny.

Finally, I couldn't help myself. "Good part?"

She glanced up, like she'd forgotten I was there. "What?"

"In the play." I nodded toward her book. "You keep smiling."

A faint blush colored her cheeks. "Oh. It's just *As You Like It*. Rosalind and Orlando are..." She trailed off, then straightened like I'd caught her doing something... naughty. "It's a classic example of early modern theatrical comedy."

"With all the best parts," I said. "Love at first sight, gender-bending disguises, forest adventures, multiple couples getting together in the end."

She stared at me.

"What?" I grinned. "You're not the only one who's done the reading list."

"No, it's just..." She tilted her head, studying me like I was a puzzle she couldn't quite solve. "Most people don't get excited about Shakespeare. They think it's boring or too highbrow."

"That's because they forget he wasn't writing for highbrow audiences. I mean, yeah, he had the nobles up in the balcony, but he was really writing for everyone. The groundlings paid to stand there and watch for hours." I thought about Jules and her romance novel collection. "It's kind of like how my sister and soon to be sister-in-law talk about romance novels."

Her pen stilled. "Romance novels?"

"Yeah. Jules, my sister, she's always telling me how romance gets dismissed as frivolous, because it's mostly for women, by women, about women, but it's actually this huge genre that appeals to all kinds of readers. And my brother's fiancée, she runs this book club, and her members are, like, doctors and CEOs and stuff, but they all love these books because they're fun and engaging and..." I noticed her staring again. "What?"

"Nothing. Just... surprised you know so much about romance novels."

I shrugged. "Hard not to when you live with a teenager who won't shut up about them. Actually, I'm fairly sure Jules was just freaking out about some super-popular romance novel based on a Shakespeare play, but with hockey players or something. Wouldn't stop talking about it at family dinner last week. She kept saying she can't wait to see what the author writes next."

Something flickered across her face—surprise? panic? and was that a slight smile when I mentioned the author's next book?—but before I could be sure, her phone buzzed. She grabbed it immediately, frowning at the screen.

"Everything okay?"

"I have to go." She started shoving books into her bag. "There's a... situation I need to handle."

"Anything I can help with?"

"No." She said it too quickly, then tried to smooth it over. "No, thank you. It's just... a thing. At my place. Which is... somewhere you definitely can't go."

I raised my eyebrows. "That's not suspicious at all."

"Shut up, Kingman." But there was no heat in it. She hesitated, half-standing. "Same time Thursday?"

"I'll be here." I watched her hurry away, nearly colliding with a chair in her rush. Only after she'd disappeared did I realize I hadn't used either of my two questions for the day.

Somehow, I had a feeling she'd planned it that way.

I packed up, feeling a little off kilter. The campus rec center was exactly where I needed to be. A good workout always cleared my head, and after that... study session, my head definitely needed clearing. I checked my phone as I pushed through the doors, finding a text from Gryff.

You missed training, jackass. Whoever she was, must have been hella cute.

What he was really saying was that she'd better have been worth it.

She was.

This was ninety percent of the reason why I didn't do girlfriends. They were a distraction. But everyone knew Kingmans played better when we were getting laid. It was why the Mustangs were going to win the big Bowl this year. All four Kingmans on the team had a woman in their bed.

In their lives.

In their hearts.

That was a bit much for me. I didn't need to be in love. Ever. I just needed to have some fun. That way nobody got hurt.

Time to focus on football and forget about the way Tempest's eyes lit up when she talked about Shakespeare, or how she didn't simper or giggle or—

"Oh my god, Flynn. I didn't know you worked out here."

I looked up to find Brittany from my business capstone class walking over, followed by two other girls I vaguely recognized from the department. We'd probably had classes together sometime in the last four years.

All three of them were wearing matching pink workout sets that had definitely never seen a drop of sweat.

"Hey." I switched on my media smile, the one that made headline writers call me 'charming' instead of 'cocky.' "Just getting in some work to prep for the combine next month."

"That's so amazing." Brittany twirled her ponytail. "You're going to get drafted so high. I just know it."

"First round for sure," one of her friends chimed in.

A semester ago, this would have been exactly what I wanted. Easy conversation, obvious interest, clear expectations. My two-week rule was practically famous on campus. Everyone knew exactly what they were getting into with me.

But now all I could think about was how Tempest had rolled her eyes when I'd mentioned playing pro ball. Not dismissively, like she didn't care about football, but like she wasn't impressed by it either. Like I'd need to bring something more to the table than just my future draft prospects.

"Thanks." I adjusted my gym bag. "But I should probably—"

"We're about to do a spin class," Brittany said quickly. "But maybe after, we could get smoothies?"

She was pretty. They all were. And they were exactly the kind of girls I usually dated. Ones who knew the score, wouldn't get attached, perfect for my no girlfriends rule.

Unlike Tempest who had just flat-out refused to be charmed by me.

"Can't today." I gestured vaguely toward the weight room. "Serious training schedule."

"Oh my god, you're so dedicated." Brittany's friend—Kirsten? Kylie?—stepped closer. "That's so hot."

I waited for the usual rush of blood to my dick from female attention like this. Nothing.

No, what got my engine revving was Tempest's unimpressed "you actually do your homework?" And how much better it had felt to surprise her, to prove her assumptions wrong.

"Thanks." I took a step back. "But I really need to—"

"Here." Brittany made a motion for me to pull out my

phone. "Let me give you my number. You know, in case you want company during your next workout."

I let her put her number in my phone, more out of habit than interest. She'd probably tell her friends I was playing hard to get. They'd probably find it exciting.

And I was bored to death right now.

Two weeks with Britt would be easy. Like a habit. My brand, practically. Everyone knew Flynn Kingman didn't do relationships. Didn't do complications. Didn't do real feelings. Just fun.

For a good time, call Flynn.

But watching the pink-clad trio head toward their spin class, giggling and glancing back at me, my usual fun times with Flynn held absolutely no appeal.

At the end of this semester, my whole life was going to change. I had to hit the real world, and while I was looking forward to playing in the pros, it wasn't going to be the same as this easy, comfortable life I'd been living.

I wasn't going to be ready if the only prep I did was for playing ball. I needed to change things up in my life too. Maybe just for this semester, I abandoned my rules. Just to see if I could get past Tempest's defenses, get her to actually like me instead of just tolerating me.

Not like I was going to fall in love with her. Or her with me.

Just getting her to let me kiss her would be a challenge. Into bed, would be practically impossible.

I smiled as I headed for the weights. I'd always loved a good challenge. I ate impossible for breakfast.

In fact... I was really good at eating a lot of things. That was something else I'd love to surprise her with. And it would definitely be more fun than I'd ever had with any of my two-week flings.

BABY DONKEY SITTERS CLUB

TEMPEST

I speed-walked across campus, mentally cursing Flynn Kingman and his annoying habit of being... not annoying. It would be so much easier if he was just another dumb jock who thought Shakespeare wrote greeting cards. Instead, he had to go and be perceptive and intelligent and actually understand my favorite play.

And that thing about romance novels? About how they're like Shakespeare, writing for everyone? I had lit professors who didn't make that connection. But Flynn just casually drops it into conversation, like he isn't completely upending everything I thought I knew about him.

Plus, he had to mention my book. Well, he didn't know it was my book. But still. The way he talked about it, like it was something worth reading, something his sister and sister-in-law were excited about...

Parker's text buzzed again.

> Parker: Donkey EMERGENCY is escalating!!! Get home NOW!!!

Right. Focus. Donkey crisis first, Flynn Kingman crisis later.

I pushed through the sorority house doors and took the back stairs two at a time. The last thing I expected when I burst into my room was giggles and coos.

Bettie, the president of the sorority, did something very unpresidential. She squealed and grabbed me into a big hug. "The secret donkey mamá."

I froze in her arms, my heart stopped, started again, and sped up to near panic speed. At least six of my sorority sisters were crowded into my room, all of them seniors, all of them staring at the baby donkey who was currently being hand-fed carrots by my roommate, Parker.

"I'm so sorry," Parker said, though she didn't look particularly sorry. "He got excited when Bettie came to borrow my economics notes and started making these little happy noises and—"

"He's so cute," Hannah reached out to scratch behind his ears. "Why didn't you tell us you were harboring a farm animal, most illegally? We could have helped."

"I..." I looked from face to face, waiting for someone to be angry, to threaten to report me to the house manager. Instead, I found only delighted grins. "It's temporary. The animal sanctuary flooded and—"

"Ohmygod, is this the one from the viral video?" Alice, our rush chair, pushed forward. "The one Flynn Kingman was chasing at the pep rally?"

"The very same." Hannah grinned. "I saw the two of you together at the coffee shop." She waggled her eyebrows at me.

"Nothing happened." I dropped my bag and shut the door quickly. "We were just studying."

Hannah's grin widened. "There was definitely flirting."

"There was... negotiating. About tutoring." I tried to sound stern, but it was hard when the baby donkey had noticed my return and was making his way over, stumbling a bit on his gangly legs. "Which isn't happening, by the way."

"Because he doesn't need it," Bettie said. "I have business econ with him. He's actually really smart."

"I know." The words slipped out before I could stop them.

Six pairs of eyebrows shot up.

"Not that it matters," I added quickly. "Look, about the donkey—"

"We're already working on it." Alice held up her phone, showing a color-coded spreadsheet. "Parker's been doing all the donkey-sitting while you're in class or at the sanctuary, and vicey-versa, but we can totally take shifts so you two can have social lives too."

"I can't ask you to—"

"You're not asking. We're telling." Bettie stepped forward, putting her hands on my shoulders. "Tempest. Love. Light of my life. You cannot keep a secret baby donkey in your room without letting us help. It's, like, against the sister code or something."

"Is there a sister code about adorable livestock?"

"There is now." She steered me toward my bed and sat

me down. "Now. Tell us everything. Starting with why Flynn Kingman was flirting with you over coffee."

"He didn't—" I started, but the donkey chose that moment to rest his head on my knee and look up at me with those big brown eyes. "Fine. But first we need to figure out how to keep this quiet. If Lindsey finds out..."

Lindsey was a junior, and the house manager. She would definitely not approve of our newest resident.

"On it." Hannah pulled out her own phone. "I made a group chat. Operation Baby Donkey Sitters Club is officially a go."

I looked around at their eager faces, feeling something tight in my chest loosen. I'd been so worried about keeping secrets, the donkey, my writing, my general existence, that I'd forgotten what it was like to let people help.

"Okay," I said finally. "But we need some ground rules."

The donkey brayed softly, as if in agreement, and the room dissolved into giggles.

Some secrets, it turned out, were better shared.

"Okay, so we need a schedule." Alice was in her element, already creating a shared calendar on her phone. "Parker can't keep skipping her internship shifts at the computer lab."

"I've got Tuesday afternoons free," Bettie offered. "I can do donkey duty between classes."

"I can take Thursdays," Hannah added, already typing in the group chat. "My last class ends at two."

"And I've got Fridays covered," Alice said. "As long as you don't mind him sitting in on rush committee meetings."

I pictured the donkey helping select next year's pledge

class and had to bite back a laugh. "Are we sure this is going to work?"

"Please." Parker waved a hand. "Between all of us, we've got enough engineering, computer science, and business majors to plan a lunar landing. We can handle one tiny donkey."

The donkey, as if sensing he was being discussed, abandoned his investigation of my backpack to waddle over to Bettie. She immediately melted.

"Look at that face. How could anyone say no to that face?"

"Mrs. Henderson could," I pointed out. "And would."

"Then we don't let her find out." Hannah was still typing. "I've got noise canceling equipment from my music production class we can use. And Alice already has the perfect excuse for extra traffic to your room."

Alice nodded. "Rush planning meetings. No one questions why the committee needs to meet so often. Especially not after last year's glitter incident."

Everyone winced. We'd all agreed never to speak of the glitter incident again.

"And," Parker added with a sly grin, "if anyone asks why Flynn Kingman keeps coming around, we can say he's helping with the athletics recruitment initiative."

I choked on air. "Why would Flynn be coming around?"

"Oh, honey." Bettie patted my hand. "We all saw how he looked at you in that video. And Hannah said he was definitely flirting at the coffee shop."

"He wasn't—" I started, but my phone chose that moment to buzz.

Six heads immediately craned to read over my shoulder. It wasn't like it was going to be Flynn. He didn't even have my number. Not sure why I was thinking it was going to be him, or why I was blushing like I was caught doing something naughty.

"Not flirting, huh?" Hannah smirked.

"It's just my family group chat." I clutched my phone to my chest, but it was too late. The damage was done.

"Ladies," Bettie announced with the air of someone opening a chapter meeting, "I believe we need to add Operation Get Tempest a Social Life to our agenda."

"No," I said firmly. "No operations. No agendas. No Flynn."

The donkey brayed, clearly disagreeing with me.

Traitor.

The knock at the door made us all freeze. The donkey, bless his heart, chose that moment to sneeze.

"Tempest?" My eldest sister's voice carried through the door with all the authority of a Victorian governess. "Why aren't you answering your phone?"

"Catalina?" I whispered in horror. Then louder, "Just a minute."

The sisters sprang into action like a well-rehearsed ballet. Hannah and Alice whisked the donkey into Parker's closet while Bettie grabbed a bottle of air freshener, and Parker opened the door to our balcony. I opened the door just wide enough to slip out onto the landing our rooms connected to.

Catalina stood there in her signature pristine white suit, carrying what looked like color-coded designer Tupperware and a crisp canvas bag with books and flowers printed on it. I think the bag... and maybe the food containers were Spate Kade.

She wrinkled her nose. "Why does it smell like a barn covered in fake lavender?"

"New air freshener." I tried to block her view of my room. "What are you doing here?"

"You've missed three Sunday dinners." She thrust the stack of food containers at me. "Mamá's in Ecuador, Papá's with her working on his book, and you're avoiding family dinner. Someone had to check if you'd been devoured by your literature textbooks."

"I've been busy with—"

"Senior year, yes, I know." She looked me up and down, taking in my coffee-stained sweater and messy bun. "Though apparently not too busy for..." She gestured vaguely at my entire existence.

From inside my room came a suspicious thump, followed by Parker's too-loud laugh.

Catalina's perfectly sculpted eyebrows rose. "Do I want to know?"

"Just study group." I hugged the food containers closer. "Thanks for the food. I'll come to dinner this Sunday, promise."

"Wait." She pulled something from her bag. "I brought you this too. Since you're always quoting Shakespeare like Papá, I thought you might enjoy a... modern interpretation."

My heart stopped. There, in my sister's manicured hands, was my first book. The one based on *The Taming of the Shrew*. Maybe, possibly, probably, I'd gotten a little of the inspiration for the heroine from my own sharp-tongued, quick-tempered eldest sister. The same one who was narrowing her eyes at me right at this very moment.

"Have you read it?" she asked. "Everyone at my boutique is obsessed. They all want me to read it. Says I'll relate to the main character."

Another thump from my room, followed by a sound that was definitely not human.

"What was that?" Catalina tried to peer around me.

"Studying." I grabbed the book. "Thanks, Cat. Really. I'll try it."

"Try to tame that hair too," she said, already turning to go. "Oh, and Freddie says to tell you she's sorry about something involving wings? I didn't ask. I've learned not to ask with her."

She turned on her heel and if the flooring hadn't been carpet, her heels would have clacked to announce her every step. I waited until she disappeared down the stairs before sagging against the door. When I went back inside, I found five sorority sisters and one baby donkey all trying to look innocent.

"Oh my gosh," Hannah said, peering at the book in my hands. "Is that the hockey romance based on *The Taming of the Shrew*? It's book one in that spicy rom-com series and I just finished book three."

"You've read them?" My voice came out squeakier than intended.

"Are you kidding? We all have," Bettie chimed in. "I already finished that one. I stayed up all night to see how it ended. The scene where the hero has to reorganize the heroine's entire closet as punishment? Iconic."

My stomach twisted. I'd worked hard on making that

scene as a subtle a nod to my older sister and her infamous closet organization system.

Parker caught my eye and gave me a tiny shake of her head. Right. Stay calm. Act normal.

"I'll have to check it out," I managed.

The donkey chose that moment to headbutt my knee, either offering comfort or demanding attention. Knowing him, probably both.

"Your sister's so polished. But also intense," Alice said, watching me scratch behind his ears. "Like, channeling Victoria Beckham intense. Don't hate me, but I'm not sad we only see her a couple times a year, even if she is a KAT alum."

I snorted before I could stop myself. "You have no idea. Although she's less Beckham and more..."

"Posh Spice?" Parker suggested with a knowing grin.

The room went silent. Then everyone started giggling.

"Oh my god." Hannah's eyes went wide. "Freddie is so Sporty Spice, and Rosalind is definitely Scary Spice. You totally have all the Spice Girls as your siblings, don't you?"

"No?" But I was already laughing too. "Maybe? Don't you dare tell them I call them that."

"Your secret's safe with us." Alice patted the donkey's head. "All your secrets are."

If they only knew. Looking around at their smiling faces, I almost wished I could tell them everything. But as I set my sister's gift on my desk, watching the late afternoon sun glint off the gold foil cover, I wondered how many secrets one person could keep before they all came tumbling down.

"Okay, I've got class. Who is donkey-sitting?" Parker

grabbed her backpack and gave baby donkey a scritch between the ears.

"It's definitely my turn, and I could use the quiet study time." By which I meant I didn't want anyone around while I worked on my manuscript

Baby donkey got a parade of coos and cuddles as everyone filed out. Parker was the last to leave, pausing at the door. "You sure you don't want company for your shift?"

"No, it's fine." I gestured to my laptop. "I've got some writing to do. Better to focus without an audience."

Once I was alone, I collapsed onto my bed, the donkey curling up by my feet. My phone buzzed with the family group chat.

> Freddie: EMERGENCY FAMILY MEETING

> Catalina: What now?

> Freddie: Abuela comes back in 2 weeks!!

> Ophelia: That's not an emergency.

> Freddie: She's been gone for half a year! We need to plan something epic!

> Rosalind: No glitter bombs this time.

> Freddie: That was ONE TIME.

> Catalina: We're not letting you plan anything involving pyrotechnics either.

> Me: Or livestock.

> Freddie: You're no fun anymore, T.

> Freddie: Also, I said I was sorry about the donkey thing.

> Ophelia: What donkey thing?

> Catalina: Don't ask.

> Rosalind: Can we focus? Some of us have actual work to do.

My phone buzzed again, this time with a text from an unknown number.

> Unknown: Same time, same place on Thursday?

I frowned. Had to be Flynn. How did he get my number? And why did that make my stomach do a weird little flip?

The donkey nudged my hand, leaving a tiny glitter smudge from his wings on my palm. I still needed to figure out how to get those off without hurting him.

> Me: How did you get this number, Kingman?

> Flynn: Parker. I like her. For tutoring purposes only, obviously.

> Me: I'm not tutoring you.

> Flynn: Study purposes then.

I glanced at the color-coded schedule Alice had created. Thursday after Shakespeare was my donkey-sitting shift.

> Flynn: Actually nvm. Combine workout on Thursday.

I definitely didn't feel disappointed. Not even a little.

> Flynn: But I can do Friday. I've got weights in the morning, so after that?

> Me: How do you know I'm not already busy? And I'm not hanging out with a stinky jock.

> Flynn: Like I don't already know your schedule? But fine, are you free on Wednesday? I promise to shower and douse myself in jock-scented body spray.

> Me: Fine. But skip the spray. Coffee shop?

> Flynn: Unless you're scared to be seen with me in public.

> Me: In your dreams, Kingman.

> Flynn: Probably.

I nearly dropped my phone. Before I could process that, the family chat erupted again.

> Freddie: MARIACHI BAND

> Catalina: NO

> Ophelia: What about a nice dinner? I'll cater from the restaurant.

> Freddie: While we all love Las Barditas food, just a dinner is BORING. This is AbuelaNovela we're talking about. We need DRAMA!

> Rosalind: I have classes to study for and don't do drama.

> Me: Dinner sounds good.

> Catalina: With NO surprise entertainment.

> Freddie: You're all crushing my creative spirit.

I set my phone down and picked up the book Catalina had brought, running my fingers over the gold foil letters of my pen name. She'd even bought the special edition.

"What am I doing?" I asked the donkey.

He just blinked at me, then went back to methodically destroying a throw pillow one tiny, baby donkey bite at a time.

Baby Donkey had the right idea. One problem at a time.

First, find the donkey a home outside of the sorority house. Maybe even a forever home. And a forever name.

Then figure out how to keep my agent happy without exposing my identity with —eek— press.

Then deal with my family, school, graduation, what to do after graduation, deal with Mamá...

Then maybe, possibly, figure out why Flynn Kingman's text messages made me want to simultaneously smile and throw my phone out the window.

Or maybe I'd just ignore that last one entirely.

HOT FOR TUTOR

FLYNN

I was fifteen minutes early to our faux tutoring session, which was probably some kind of record. Usually I rolled into stuff exactly on time, a habit that drove Gryff crazy. But lately I'd been finding reasons to show up early to the quad's coffee shop. No mystery why. Just the slim chance of catching Tempest alone, without her walls up.

Today that strategy paid off, but not in the way I'd hoped.

I heard her voice before I rounded the corner, whispering, but sharp with frustration. "I can't just drop everything and fly to L.A. next week. I have commitments here."

Slowing my steps, I lingered by the wall. I wasn't trying to eavesdrop, but something in her tone made me pause. I'd never heard Tempest sound rattled before.

"You don't understand," she continued, her voice dropping. "It's complicated. The timing is impossible... No, I'm not being difficult. You're the one who promised I could maintain my pri—"

She cut off abruptly. I peered around the corner to see her pacing the length of one of the private study rooms across from the coffee shop, one hand pressed to her forehead. Her dark hair was piled in a messy bun, and she wore an oversized DSU Dragons sweatshirt that made something in my chest tighten.

And my pants. Because now I was imagining her wearing my jersey and... nope. Shit. If I went any farther with that image, I'd need to hide one hell of a woody behind my books.

"Listen, can we table this until after spring break?" She sighed, shoulders slumping. "Yes, I know it's a huge opportunity. Yes, I know these people don't wait around... Fine. Send me the details. I'll figure something out."

She ended the call and dropped into a chair, pressing her face into her hands and halfway to hyperventilating. The gesture was so unguarded, so unlike her usual composed self, that I felt like I was intruding on something private. I waited a few seconds, then deliberately scuffed my shoes against the floor as I approached.

Tempest's head snapped up, her expression smoothing over so fast it was almost scary. "You're early."

"Showered extra fast, just for you," I lied, dropping my bag on the table. I'd postponed my weightlifting to this afternoon. "Everything okay?"

"Fine." She was already pulling out her color-coded study materials, spine straight as a ruler. "Let's pick up where we left off in class with *Othello*."

I sat across from her, studying the tight set of her jaw. "You know, it's okay to not be fine sometimes."

Her hands stilled on her notebook. "What makes you think I'm not fine?"

"Just a feeling." I kept my tone casual, though there was nothing casual about the way my pulse kicked up when she finally met my eyes. "Also, because that's not your Shakespeare notebook, and it's upside down."

She glanced down at the notebook and gulped, then swept it back into her bag.

A flush crept up her neck. "That's... nothing. You agreed to no questions about my notes. Pretend you never saw it."

Like that was going to happen. "Already forgotten."

She narrowed her eyes at me, but there was a hint of a smile playing at the corners of her mouth. "Why do I think you've got a memory like a steel trap?"

The way she kept searching my eyes said that she was legitimately worried I was going to rat her out on whatever was in that notebook. Or question her about it, and she wanted to hide something. Something important to her.

She actually looked like she was on the verge of a panic attack. While it was way more fun to poke at her than I wanted to admit to, seeing her meltdown was not on my fun-times-with-Flynn list.

The best thing I could do for her right now was find a way to put her at ease. Or...even better, give her something more fun to think about. I leaned forward, closing the space between us, and gave her my absolute best come-hither look. "That's not the only thing I've got that's steely."

Her eyes flicked down to my lips and back up. Got her. She wasn't worried about the notebook anymore. "You'd better mean your blue eyes, football boy."

"There she is," I said, and watched a reluctant smile break through her worry. "Since we're friends—"

"We're not friends."

"Study buddies, then."

"Mandatory academic partners," she countered.

"Whatever you want to call it." I spread my hands. "Point is, if you need to talk, or vent, or just sit here and not study for a while... that's cool."

For a moment, something flickered in her dark eyes. Vulnerability, maybe, or longing. Then she squared her shoulders. "What I need is to get through Act Three, so I can finish my paper. Tell me you at least know what you're writing yours about."

The words were sharp, but I caught the teensy-tiny tremor beneath them. Something was definitely up with her, beyond the mysterious phone call. But pushing wouldn't get me anywhere. I'd learned that much about Tempest Navarro in the past few weeks.

"I do. So let's get down to Shakespeare." I pulled out my annotated copy of the play, dog-eared and coffee stained. "But whatever it is that's got you stressed, I'm sure you've got this. And if you don't, I know people. Say the word, and we'll be there with shovels, and tarps, and pickup trucks, and picnic baskets."

Her hands relaxed on the actual Shakespeare notebook she'd pulled out and she took a normal breath instead of the rapid ones she was taking up until now. "Picnic baskets?"

Small victories. I'd take them where I could get them. "If we're digging holes for...whatever we might need six-foot-deep holes for, then we need snacks. Growing boys and all that."

"You're...a lot."

She had no idea.

"Now," I said, flipping to the right page, "let's talk about why Iago's such a dick."

That startled a laugh out of her, a real one, rich and warm, and something in my chest expanded. Making Tempest laugh felt like winning the game. Better, maybe.

Which was exactly the kind of thought that should have sent me running for the hills. Instead, I found myself hoping I could make her laugh again before the hour was up.

I was so screwed.

Two hours later, right when we were in the middle of battling over whether the feminist leanings in Shakespeare's works meant the writer behind the plays was actually a woman or not, Tempest's alarm on her phone went off.

She sighed and turned the alarm off. "I have somewhere else I need to be."

Did she look disappointed?

Maybe that was just me projecting. How was it that the only dates we'd been on were the legit studying kind, and I was more into Tempest than any two-week girl I'd ever taken out a dozen times on all kinds of fun and creative dates.

No. Ridiculous. I could think of a lot more fun things I'd like to do with Ms. Navarro. Under Ms. Navarro, between Ms. Navarro's thick, thick thighs.

Yeah. That was more like it.

"Okay, I'll walk you home." I swept my books into my bag and slung it over my shoulder.

Tempest was slower to pack up. "Who said I was going home?"

I grabbed the door and held it open for her. "Ah, trying to make me jealous with your hot date?"

"If you count a date with a baby donkey, hot, then sure. I can see how you might find yourself competing against farm animals for dates."

We headed down the stairs and I stayed a step behind just to watch the sway of her hips and the way her round ass jiggled in all the right ways. "Oh, yeah. How is Baby Donk doo doo doo doo da doo?"

She shook her head but I saw the second smile of the afternoon. "Great, now I'm gonna have that song stuck in my head."

When we walked out the front door, a chilly wind hit us both in the face. Gotta love Colorado winter. If you don't like the weather, just wait a minute.

"See you later, Kingman."

Shit. I'd just been dismissed. But...she did say she'd see me later. I could hardly wait.

For a full minute I watched her walk away and fully contemplated following her. Desperate much, Kingman.

Nope. Time to hit the gym like I was supposed to this morning. We had a lot of work to do before the combine and next week would be a short week since we were headed to watch the boys in the big Bowl game.

I still couldn't shake the image of her face when she'd shoved that notebook away. Everybody got stressed, especially in their senior year of college, facing down the real world in only a few months' time. But my delicious Tempest was usually so unflappable. I'd seen her face down our professor in a heated debate about Hamlet's mom last week.

But this was different. This wasn't academic stress. This was something else, something that made me want to fix it, even though she'd probably murder me for trying.

The weight room smelled like sweat, rubber, and ambition. I was supposed to be focusing on my bench press form. My numbers were good, but they needed to be great if I wanted to impress at the combine. Instead, I kept thinking about that notebook Tempest had tried to hide.

"Your left side's dropping," Gryff chastised while spotting me. "And you're doing that thing with your face."

I racked the bar and sat up. "What thing?"

"That thinking thing." He tossed me a towel. "The one where your forehead gets all scrunchy and you look constipated."

"Fuck off." But I wiped my face, avoiding his too-knowing grin. Having a twin meant never getting away with anything. "I'm focused."

"Yeah? What's your target for the three-cone drill?"

"Uh..."

"Exactly." He dropped onto the bench next to me.

"Spill it. What's got you more distracted than that time Hayes convinced you his cat could read minds?"

"Seven of Nine Lives totally knew what I was thinking."

"Seven is a demon in a fur suit, and you're changing the subject."

I stood and started adding more plates to the bar, mostly to have something to do with my hands. "It's nothing. Just this paper for Shakespeare."

"Bullshit. You could write Shakespeare papers in your sleep." Gryff's voice took on that annoying sing-song quality that meant he thought he had me figured out. "This is about your hot tutor."

"She's not my tutor." The plates clanged louder than necessary. "We're study partners."

"Right." He snorted. "Come on, man. I've seen you quote Romeo and Juliet in your sleep."

"That was one time, and I had the flu with a fever of a hundred and three, and we'd just watched Leo and Claire in that romantic disaster."

"The lady doth protest too much, methinks."

I pointed at him. "You're not allowed to quote Shakespeare at me. That's not a thing we do."

"Fine." He held up his hands in surrender, but his eyes were dancing. "Heard some of the guys saying some of the KAT girls are going to be at the hockey house party this weekend."

My grip tightened on the weight I was holding. "Who's talking about Tempest?"

"Oh, it's Tempest now?" His grin widened. "Not 'that

annoying know-it-all' anymore? And I didn't say anything about her."

I deliberately set the weight down before I did something stupid like throw it at my brother's head. "You're reading way too much into this."

"Am I? Because I distinctly remember you saying, and I quote, 'That girl is a menace to society and my sanity.'"

"That was weeks ago."

"More than...two weeks ago. That's exactly my point." He leaned forward, elbows on his knees. "Look, I get it. She's smart, she's gorgeous, and she doesn't take any of your shit. But you've got the combine coming up, and after that, the draft. You sure this is the time to break your two-week rule?"

"I'm not breaking anything." I grabbed my water bottle, suddenly needing something to do with my hands. "And my rule has nothing to do with this. We're just studying."

"Uh-huh." Gryff stood, stretching his arms overhead. "So you won't mind if I make a move on her?"

The water bottle crinkled in my grip. "What?"

His laugh echoed through the weight room. "Wow. You are so screwed."

"You stay away from her, you hear me, little brother?"

"We're twins."

"I am still four minutes older than you."

"Yeah. But no wiser." He clapped me on the shoulder. "Come on. Let's get back to work. You can pine over your not-tutor later."

I flipped him off, but followed him back to the bench. He was right. I needed to focus. The combine and my

THE JACK*SS IN CLASS 87

future in the pros were what I should spend my time caring about. I couldn't afford any distractions right now, no matter how intriguing they might be.

Even if they had surprisingly sexy reading glasses and a laugh that made my chest feel too tight.

Shit. I really was screwed.

Two days later, I slid into my usual seat in Shakespeare class, hyperaware of Tempest's presence to my right. She hadn't shown up for coffee yesterday, and her texts about rescheduling our study session had been weirdly formal. Like she was pulling away.

"Today," the professor announced, "we're discussing the nature of deception in *Othello*. The way secrets eat at the soul of not just the deceiver, but those around them."

Tempest shifted in her seat, and I caught the same tension in her shoulders I'd seen during that phone call.

"Partner up," Williams continued. "Discussion prompt is on the board. Ten minutes."

Usually this was when Gryff would turn to us with his shit-eating grin, but today he was already pivoting to talk to the hockey player he had a crush on behind him. Subtle, bro. Real subtle.

"Guess you're stuck with me," I said to Tempest, turning my desk to face hers.

"Joy." But the corner of her mouth moved in a decidedly smile direction.

"So." I tapped my pen against my notebook. "Deception and secrets. You have any thoughts about those lately?"

Her eyes narrowed. "What's that supposed to mean?"

"Just that you're good at analyzing hidden motives in literature. Makes me wonder what you're hiding."

"I'm not hiding anything." But her hand drifted to her bag, where I bet that mystery notebook was stashed.

"See, that right there?" I leaned closer, lowering my voice. "That's exactly what Iago would say."

"Did you just compare me to the villain?"

"Nah. You're way prettier." I grinned at her eye roll. "Come on, Tempest. I know something's up. You've been weird since our study date the other day."

She tapped her pencil on the desk at the rate of a bunny on speed. "We should focus on the assignment."

"Fine. Let's talk about how Othello's real tragedy isn't the deception itself, but his failure to trust the people who actually care about him."

That landed. I watched her throat work as she swallowed. "Some secrets aren't about trust. They're about protection."

Hmm. That had me scooting my chair closer. "Protection for who?"

She met my eyes then, and something in her expression made my chest tight. "Everyone."

Before I could push further, the professor called time. Tempest turned back to face front so fast she almost gave herself whiplash.

I spent the rest of class watching her take notes, her handwriting getting messier every time the professor talked about the weight of carrying secrets. When the bell rang, she was packed and halfway to the door before I could even stand.

"Hey." I caught up to her in the hallway. "You coming to the hockey house tonight with your sorority sisters?"

"Parties aren't really my thing."

"Because you'd rather hide in your books?"

She stopped walking. "I don't hide."

"Prove it."

"That's your play? Really?" She shook her head, but I caught the ghost of a smile. "Questioning my courage?"

I shrugged, trying to look casual even though my heart was hammering. "If the book jacket fits..."

"You're impossible."

"Is that a yes?"

She shouldered her bag, already turning away. "It's a 'we'll see.'" But this time when she walked away, her hips had a little extra sway to them.

"Smooth," Gryff said, appearing at my shoulder. "Real smooth."

"Shut up."

"You know your rule doesn't actually work if you spend every minute thinking about her, right?"

I watched until Tempest disappeared around the corner, that notebook-sized mystery still tucked in her bag. "Rules schmules, bro. Rules schmules."

PONG CHAMPIONSHIPS

TEMPEST

I'd just queued up "That'll do, Pig" when someone pounded on my door.

Mierda. The only people who knocked were the ones not in the Baby Donkey Sitters Club.

If it was House mother Henderson checking to make sure I was actually staying in to answer the safety sister phone, I was going down fast and hard.

Baby Donkey was sleeping hard, and barely even pricked up his ears. Maybe if I arranged some stuffed animals around him, she wouldn't notice.

Yeah, right.

Before I could have a full-on panic attack, the door swung open and three faces peered back at me. Parker, Hannah, and Alice stood there barely containing their giggles. Phew.

"Emotional support tacos," Hannah announced, holding up a grease-stained paper bag. "No arguments."

I waved them in, reaching for the bag where the smell

of Cluck U's street tacos wafted through the air. "I'm on safety sister duty tonight."

"No, you're not." Alice flopped onto my bed. "Bettie's taking over. She said, and I quote, 'If Tempest spends one more night in those ridiculous slippers watching farm animal movies, I'm calling an intervention.'"

I looked down at my fuzzy pink slippers. "What's wrong with my slippers?"

"Everything," all three of them said in unison.

Parker grabbed a taco. "You have been extra stressed lately."

Because my agent wouldn't stop hounding me about meetings in L.A., my deadline was looming, and Flynn Kingman had started looking at me like I was a puzzle he wanted to solve. But I could only tell Parker about two of those things.

"It's just senior year stuff." I held out my hand for a taco from the bag, hoping food would stop the interrogation. "And being on call is important. You know how many creeps show up at hockey parties. We shall leave no sister behind...or intoxicated and alone."

"Which is exactly why you should come." Hannah started rummaging through my closet. "Safety in numbers."

"I have reading to do."

"You always have reading to do." Alice tried to steal a bite of my taco, but I quickly shoved the rest in my mouth. "But lately you've been practically hermitted away. Is this about Flynn?"

I choked on my extra big bite. "Whrr?"

It took me a minute to finish chewing and swallow. "No. Why would you—"

"Because he's been looking at you like you're his next meal," Hannah said from inside my closet. "And you've been looking back."

"I have not."

Parker snorted. "You totally have."

Traitor.

"I just..." I glanced over to where the notebook hidden under my Shakespeare texts poked out. "I don't have time for distractions right now."

"Distractions are exactly what you need." Hannah emerged with a pair of heels Catalina had given me, some jeans that I thought were a bit too tight, and a flowy white shirt that I didn't know why I even bought. "You're wound tighter than Mrs. Henderson's bun. When's the last time you had fun?"

"I have fun."

"Watching movies about talking farm animals doesn't count." Alice grabbed my slippers and tossed them under the bed. "Come on, T. One night. If it sucks, you can come home and watch all the pig movies you want."

"But—"

"No buts." Hannah threw the jeans at me. "Get dressed. You're going to have a drink, dance with your sisters, and maybe flirt with a hot football player who clearly has a thing for you."

"Flynn doesn't have a thing for me."

Three skeptical faces stared back.

"He doesn't," I insisted. "We just study together."

To be honest, no guys ever had a thing for me. Flynn was just a big flirt. It didn't mean he was actually into me.

"Right." Alice rolled her eyes. "Because Flynn Kingman, who could probably quote the entire works of Shakespeare in his sleep, needs a study partner."

I opened my mouth to argue, then closed it. There was no use arguing with them. Let them think what they wanted to.

"Fine." I grabbed the clothes. "One hour. But only because I don't trust any of you to play a proper game of beer pong." All those long summers at Abuela's with the neighbor kids had given me a lot of weird gaming skills.

Parker bounced off the bed. "That's my girl. Now, since Flynn's going to be there..."

"This isn't about Flynn."

But as my sisters descended on me with hair styling torture devices and makeup that would make Abuelita proud, like a pack of well-meaning wolves, I thought of the way he'd looked at me in class today. Like he could see right through me.

That was exactly the problem.

The hockey house looked exactly like every party house in every college rom-com movie or romance novel I'd ever written, or read, as far as anyone here knew. Red Solo cups, sticky floors, and enough sexual tension to fuel a trilogy.

I cataloged the classic romance novel scenarios playing out around me. By the beer pong table, a classic enemies-to-lovers was brewing between the hockey captain and the women's soccer team goalkeeper. Near the kitchen, there was a friends-to-lovers slow burn happening with two guys who clearly hadn't figured out they were gone for each other yet. And in the corner... oh, that was definitely the setup for a drunk-confession-of-feelings that would lead to the inevitable morning-after-regret subplot.

"Stop analyzing and start having fun," Hannah said, pressing a cup into my hand.

"I'm not analyzing." I was totally analyzing. But when you spent most of your time crafting meet-cutes and orchestrating perfect kisses, you could see the story beats everywhere.

Like the way Flynn Kingman had just walked in.

If this were one of my books, this would be the moment where the heroine's breath caught, where time slowed down and the rest of the party faded away. And okay, maybe my breath did catch a little, because Flynn in fitted jeans and a vintage DSU Dragons t-shirt was the kind of visual that deserved its own chapter.

"Your writer face is showing," Parker murmured as she passed by.

I schooled my features. I did not have a writer face. But I did have a problem, because Flynn had spotted me and was now making his way over with the kind of swagger that belonged in the climax of a romance novel, not a college party that smelled like stale beer and hockey gear.

In my books, this would be where the sexual tension finally boiled over. Where the hero and heroine would have their big moment, leading to either a passionate declaration or an epic misunderstanding that would fuel the third act conflict.

But this wasn't one of my books. This was real life, where I had secrets to keep and a career to protect, and absolutely no business noticing how good Flynn's shoulders looked in that shirt.

"You came." His voice had that low, gravelly quality that I definitely hadn't used as inspiration for my latest hero's voice. Definitely not.

"Don't sound so surprised." I took a sip from my cup to hide whatever my face was doing. "Some of us can actually be spontaneous."

"Spontaneous?" He raised an eyebrow. "You probably did a cost-benefit analysis before coming here."

He wasn't wrong, but I wasn't about to admit it. "Maybe I just needed a break from farm animal movies."

He glanced around. "How is our mutual friend? No partying for him tonight?"

"The sanctuary's still flooded," I said, trying to keep my voice casual. "But he's safe and settled."

Flynn's eyes narrowed. "Settled where, exactly?"

Shoot. In my books, this would be the moment where the heroine accidentally reveals too much, setting up future complications. But I was smarter than that. "Somewhere safe."

"Uh-huh." He was giving me that look again, the one that said he was putting pieces together. "And this somewhere safe wouldn't happen to be closer to campus than the sanctuary, would it?"

Double shoot. I took a long sip of my beer to avoid answering. If this were a romance novel, this would be the part where the mysterious secret created delicious tension. But in real life, juggling secrets just made me feel like I was one miss-step away from disaster.

A cheer went up from the beer pong table, drawing my attention. The hockey captain had just sunk a dramatic shot, and the goalkeeper was trying not to look impressed. Now that was the kind of scene that sold books.

"Earth to Tempest." Flynn was watching me with that intense look again, the one that made me feel like he could read every thought running through my head. "Where'd you go just now?"

Nowhere safe to admit to. "Just wondering how many of these parties end up being someone's origin story."

His laugh was unfairly attractive. "You think too much."

"You don't think enough."

"Prove it." He nodded toward the beer pong table. "Play me."

And there it was. The classic challenge that would drive the rest of the chapter. In my books, this would be where the heroine would say something witty and flirtatious. Where she'd rise to the challenge with perfect confidence because she didn't have a secret identity to protect or a business meeting in L.A. to worry about.

But I wasn't my heroine. I was just me, trying not to stare at Flynn's mouth.

Then again... sometimes the best way to hide was in plain sight.

"Hope you're ready to lose, Kingman."

Flynn lined up six cups in a triangle at each end of the

table, but instead of heading to the keg, he pulled out bottles of water.

"Water pong?" some guy in a hockey jersey called out. "Come on, Kingman. Live a little."

"Not tonight, Morris." Flynn's tone was light, but had an edge I hadn't heard before. "I'm DD."

"You're always DD," Morris grumbled, but backed off.

Interesting. I filed that away as Flynn filled our cups with water. In my romance novels, this would be where the heroine discovered the first crack in the hero's carefully constructed facade. But before I could analyze it further, Flynn sank his first shot directly into my front cup.

"Ladies first." He smirked as I lifted the cup. "Don't worry, I'll go easy on you."

I drained the water, took aim, and sank the ball straight into his back center cup. "Please don't."

His eyebrows shot up. "Okay, where did that come from?"

"You spend enough summers with an Abuelo who is ultra-competitive, you pick up a few things." I lined up my next shot. I lined up my next shot. "The local ambassador's kids organized underground tournaments every weekend. High-stakes games."

"This Abuelo sounds like a very interesting grandfather."

"Yep." Another perfect shot. "Though my abuela pretended not to know about the tournaments. Just like she never knew about the poker games, the salsa lessons, or that time I helped smuggle a neighbor's chihuahua past the security guards during a quinceañera, Abuelo Leo made sure we had the competitive edge in everything from poker to beer pong."

Flynn's laugh was surprised and genuine. "There's a story there."

"Many stories." I watched him sink another shot. "Most of them involving schemes with my sisters, questionable decision-making, and... let's say creative problem-solving."

"I love me some questionable decisions, and I can be very creative." Every single word of that dripped with innuendo. Way more than should be possible. Except, of course, for Flirty Flynn.

That's all this was. Him flirting. Because he could. Because that's what he did all the time.

A small crowd had gathered to watch us play. I was aware of the whispers. But I was more interested in the way his shoulders tensed every time someone walked past with a drink, the careful way he positioned himself between me and the rowdier part of the crowd by setting himself on that side of the table.

"My turn," he said, after I missed my first shot. "Though I'm starting to think I've been hustled by a secret beer pong champion."

"Water pong champion," I corrected. "And the night's still young."

His eyes darkened at that, and something hot unfurled in my stomach. If this were one of my books, this would be where the sexual tension peaked, where the hero and heroine's playful competition turned into something more.

But before either of us could say anything else, Morris stumbled back over with a pitcher of beer. "Time to make this kiddie game interesting."

"I said no." All playfulness vanished from Flynn's voice. He stepped between Morris and the table, suddenly every inch the linebacker he was on the field. "We're good with water."

The shift in his demeanor was so sharp it made me catch my breath. This wasn't just about being designated driver. This was something deeper, something that put the steel in his voice and the shadow in his eyes.

If this were my novel, this would be the moment where the heroine realized there was more to her love interest than she'd thought. Where she saw past his carefully constructed image to the complex man underneath.

Damn it. I was not allowed to think of Flynn Kingman as a love interest.

"Everything okay?" I asked softly as Morris stumbled away shaking his head.

Flynn's expression smoothed out, but I caught the lingering tension in his jaw.

"Always." He picked up the ball. "Ready to lose?"

I studied him for just a moment. He didn't want to be pushed on what that was all about. He just wanted to have fun.

I could be fun. Okay, not normally, but I'd had more fun with him since the beginning of the semester than I had in the rest of my three and a half years at college.

I held up the ping pong ball and smiled. "Bring it on, Kingman."

But as we fell back into our rhythm of shots and

banter, I couldn't shake the feeling that I'd just glimpsed something important. Something real.

And that was dangerous. Because real meant complicated, and complicated meant exactly the kind of distraction I couldn't afford right now.

I sank my next shot without looking. "Your turn."

I was two shots away from beating Flynn Kingman at his own game when a girl in a crop top stumbled into our space.

"Flynn." She grabbed his arm, nearly falling over. "I wanna go home. Like, right now."

Something flashed across Flynn's face, concern mixed with resignation. "Sasha, where's your roommate? Weren't you supposed to—"

"Please?" Her mascara was smeared under her eyes, but that didn't stop her from dancing her fingers up the front of his shirt. "I just... want you to take me home."

And just like that, Flynn's entire demeanor changed. The playful competitor disappeared, replaced by someone harder, more serious. He set down the ping pong ball and pulled out his keys.

"Rain check?" he asked me, but he was already steering Sasha toward the door, one hand steady on her elbow.

If this were a romance novel, this would be the moment of misunderstanding that drove the characters apart. The scene where the heroine watched the hero leave with another woman and jumped to all the wrong conclusions.

But I wasn't that kind of heroine. I was the kind who knew better than to get invested in the first place.

"Whatever." I turned away, ignoring the tight feeling in

my chest. "Hey, Hannah, what's that I heard about Jello shots?"

As I walked away, I heard Flynn call my name. But I was done being the girl who waited around for the hero to choose her.

They never chose me anyway.

FUCK, I NEEDED THIS

FLYNN

I watched until Sasha made it safely inside her apartment building, waiting for her to text her roommate like she'd promised.

I texted Gryff while I waited for her roommate's message.

> Me: Don't give me shit. Give me information. Is Tempest still there?

My phone lit up, but with the confirmation from Sasha's roomie that she was safely tucked into bed.

Good. One more person who wouldn't end up causing a late-night police visit to someone's family.

Gryff's text finally came back.

> Gryff: She's here. Don't think she's going anywhere until she's done getting lit.
> You'd better get your ass back pronto.

Tempest? Drunk? While I didn't stand for drunk

driving, I didn't have a problem with anyone wanting to blow off some steam with a few drinks. Lord knows, she needed to blow off some steam, but I didn't see her getting sloppy drunk.

She was too careful. Wound too tightly. Keeping secrets that she was taking pains to hide. Getting drunk meant loose lips.

And she didn't want any of her ships sinking.

The drive back to the hockey house felt longer than it should have. That look on her face when I'd walked away...fuck. She probably thought I'd blown her off for another girl, which... hell.

But I had to fulfill my duty as designated driver. Even for the likes of Sasha, who never learned her lesson. Not when she'd had that look I knew too well. The one that said she needed to get out before she did something she'd regret. Not when she'd been too drunk to drive herself. Never that.

A car swerved in the lane ahead of me, and my hands tightened on the wheel.

Even if Tempest was still at the party when I got back, she probably wouldn't want to finish our game. Hell, she probably wouldn't want anything to do with me now.

Which should have been fine. That's what I wanted, right? Keep things casual. No expectations, no attachments, no chance of the kind of soul-crushing loss that could bring a strong man to his knees. I'd seen what that looked like, watched my dad try to rebuild a life around a Mom-shaped hole in our family. Some wounds never really healed.

Except I couldn't stop thinking about the way Tempest's smile reached all the way to her eyes when she sank that perfect shot. Or how she'd lit up talking about her adventures with her sisters and her grandparents at their villa in Mexico. Or how she hadn't pushed when I wanted to play beer pong with water.

"Get it together, Kingman," I muttered, turning onto Greek Row. Music thumped from the hockey house, bass vibrating through my chest as I parked. Through the front window, I could see bodies moving, red cups raising, another Friday night in full swing.

Please still be here.

I hadn't meant to think it. Didn't want to examine why it mattered so much. But I killed the engine and couldn't deny the way my pulse kicked up at the possibility of finding her in the crowd.

I could handle more than two weeks with Tempest. I'd already accepted that. But anything deeper? That was a different kind of risk. The kind that ended with someone shattered beyond repair.

I headed for the front door and all I could think about was the way Tempest's laugh had wrapped around me like a promise I was terrified to keep.

The party had hit that sweet spot between chaos and catastrophe by the time I got back inside. Music thundered through the floorboards, and the crowd had thinned just enough that I could scan faces without having to wade through a mosh pit of drunk college students.

No sign of Tempest at the beer pong table. Or in the kitchen. Or—

"Looking for your girl?" Gryff materialized at my elbow, wiping at his lips. I knew that look. He'd been making out with someone. Which is exactly what I was usually doing at parties like this too. I'd scan for who, but I was already looking for someone.

"Not my girl." I stood on my tiptoes and didn't see Tempest anywhere. I did see fucking Xander, skulking away. He was the last guy I wanted around my...friends.

"Right. That's why you're doing that thing with your jaw."

"What thing?"

"That clenched, cave-man thing. Like you're about to grab her by the hair and drag her back to your—" He cut off with a grunt as my elbow found his ribs.

A burst of familiar laughter drew my attention to the living room. Tempest was perched on the arm of the couch, surrounded by her sorority sisters, and a slew of male admirers. Her cheeks were flushed, her dark hair wild, and she had a shot glass in her hand.

Shit.

"Oh yeah," Gryff said, following my gaze. "She's been doing shots since you left. Something about writing her own ending? Not sure what that means, but the girl can drink."

Double shit.

As I watched, she threw back another shot, then immediately reached for a second one. Hannah, or maybe it was Alice, I couldn't keep her sisters straight, tried to intercept, but Tempest was faster.

"Didn't peg her for a party girl," Gryff mused.

She wasn't. I'd had to goad her into even considering a

party. Which meant this was my fault. Because I'd walked away and made her think…

"Down boy," Gryff said as I started forward. "Let her have some fun. She's got her sorority sisters with her, and they're a stronger force than a steel chastity belt that's got a whole bevy of locks."

But I'd been to too many parties like this in my almost four years at this school not to recognize when someone was spiraling. Especially someone who clearly wasn't used to drinking like this.

I made it halfway across the room before Tempest spotted me. Her eyes narrowed, and she deliberately reached for another shot.

"I don't think you wanna do that, sweetheart," I said, closing the distance between us.

"Don't wanna do what, jackass?" Her words had the careful precision of someone trying hard to sound sober. "Don't wanna have fun? Don't wanna let loose? Don't assume the great Flynn Kingman might actually…" She stumbled as she stood, and I caught her elbow before she could fall.

"Hey." I steadied her, trying to ignore how right she felt under my hands. "I came back."

"To save another damsel?" She tried to pull away, but ended up swaying into my chest instead. "Sorry, this damsel's busy getting distressed all by herself."

Christ. How many shots had she done?

She spun away from her sisters and directly into Brad Mitchell from the rugby team.

"Flynn," Brad called out. "Your study partner's been teaching us Espanol."

Tempest draped herself against Brad's arm, deliberately not looking at me. "Díle, Brad. ¿Qué significa 'arrogante'?"

"Arrogante," Brad repeated proudly, butchering the pronunciation. "It means football player."

Thank you, four years of high school Spanish, two in college, and the occasional sexy Spanish-speaking babysitter. I bit back a smile as Tempest moved on to her next victim.

"Ricky." She collapsed onto the couch next to the soccer captain. "Enséñales cómo se dice 'tiene el trasero increíble pero no tiene huevos.'"

Ricky, who definitely spoke Spanish, shot me an apologetic look before turning to the group. "It means... uh... football players are great study partners."

Liar. She'd just announced to half the party that I had an incredible ass but no... guts.

"No, no, no." Tempest wagged her finger at Ricky. "En español, por favor repíteme—"

She proceeded to teach a group of increasingly confused hockey players how to say what I was quite sure translated to "pretty boy who runs away from feelings." All while shooting me these little glances to make sure I was watching.

That's when she noticed me staring and her eyes narrowed. With a lot of effort, she pulled herself up off the couch and walked right up to me. "If you're here to play hero again," she said, poking my chest, "I don't need saving. I have sisters for that."

"What you need is water."

"What I need," she announced to the room at large, "is

for certain football players to stop telling me what to do like... like..."

"Like what?"

"Like that." She gestured at my face, then grabbed my beard and gave it a little shake. "All concerned and focused and... and Flynn-like."

Several of her sisters laughed. I shot them a look, and Hannah made a "what can you do?" shrug.

"Come here." I sank into one of the oversized armchairs, hoping to at least get her sitting down before she fell down.

"No." But she swayed a little. "You're not the boss of me, Flynn Kingman."

"Never said I was."

"Good. Because I am a strong, independent woman who doesn't need..." She stumbled slightly, catching herself on the arm of my chair. "Doesn't need..."

"A hand?"

She glared at me, but there wasn't much heat in it. More like the way a grumpy kitten might glare at someone who'd interrupted their nap.

But kittens didn't wear sexy-as-fuck heels, which she turned on and clacked her way into the kitchen where she grabbed a bottle of water. With much aplomb, she twisted the cap off and took several long gulps, just as much spilling down her face, down her throat, disappearing behind her shirt, but no doubt going right into that cleavage.

Fuck, and now I was jealous of a bottle of water.

I spent the next hour sitting in that damn chair,

watching her flit around the party from group to group like a little drunk butterfly. At least she'd slowed down on the fruity vodka drinks. But that also meant eventually she'd run out of steam.

I'd be right here, ready to take her home. Hers, not mine. And probably along with her gaggle of sorority sisters. I wasn't the kind of guy to take advantage of a drunk girl. Guys who did that were gross at best, and fucking criminals as far as I was concerned.

I gripped the armrests when she walked up to Gryff. I was about to tear the arms of this chair right off when she caressed his cheek, wiggling her fingers through his facial hair. But then she gave him a little baby slap and stuck her tongue out at him.

Gryff laughed, took her by the shoulders and spun her until she was facing me. "I think that's the Kingman you meant that for."

He gave her a little shove, and she stumbled her way right toward me. I geared up for a brand new confrontation with her, mentally preparing myself for a bigger slap than what Gryff had gotten. Hopefully I'd get the caress first though.

But without warning, she sort of... collapsed. Right into my lap.

I froze. Every muscle locked up as she curled into me, her head tucking perfectly under my chin, her lush ass filling my lap perfectly.

"Tempest?"

"Shh." She pressed her face into my chest. "M'comfortable."

Jesus Christ.

My arms moved without my permission, wrapping around her. She was soft and warm and felt so damn right against me that my chest physically ached.

"Fuck," I breathed, more to myself than to her. "I needed this."

She hummed something that might have been agreement, her fingers curling into my shirt.

The room had gone suspiciously quiet. I looked up to find at least six phones pointed our way, and both Hannah and Alice wearing identical knowing grins.

"Don't you dare," I mouthed at them.

Parker just wiggled her phone at me and mouthed back, "Blackmail material."

Great. She was totally going to blame me for this.

But Tempest shifted against me, making this little contented noise, and I couldn't bring myself to care. Let them take their pictures. Let them spread their rumors. Right now, all that mattered was the girl in my arms and the way something in my chest had finally settled, like a key clicking into a lock I hadn't known was there.

"You smell good," she mumbled into my shirt. "Like... like my hero would smell."

"Your what?"

But she was already pushing herself up, her eyes wide. "I think... I need air."

That was my cue. Time to move this to the back porch before I had a vastly different kind of mess on my hands.

"Tempest." I ducked my head to meet her eyes, which had gone slightly unfocused. "Let me get you some water."

"Let me get you some water," she mimicked, then

immediately pressed a hand to her mouth. "Oh. That wasn't nice. Guess I'm a mean drunk. But at least I'm not a bully like you..."

Bully?

Fuck me. Did she really think I was a bully? I thought we were having fun poking at each other.

Double fuck.

She trailed off, her face going pale, and I knew that look. I'd seen it on enough rookie partiers.

"Okay, time to get you that air." I wrapped an arm around her waist, guiding her toward the back door. To her sisters, I added, "I've got her."

Hannah, wait, right, got it now, definitely Hannah this time, gave me a look that promised creative dismemberment if I screwed this up. Tempest's roommate, Parker, gave me two thumbs up and a smile, but then she narrowed her eyes and flashed the two finger I'm-watching-you signal. I respected that. These girls looked after their own.

The back porch was mercifully empty. Tempest pulled away, yanking her arm from my hold, but then promptly slid down to the ground and pressed her forehead to the glass of the sliding door.

"The world's spinny," she muttered.

"That tends to happen when you try to drink an entire spring break's worth of alcohol." I sat next to her, close enough to catch her if she toppled over, but not so close that she'd feel crowded. "Want to tell me what that was about?"

"You," she poked me in the chest, "left. With sexy Sasha."

She lifted her head to glare at me, but the effect was somewhat ruined by the way she had to squint to focus. "Which is fine. You can leave with whoever you want. I don't care."

She very clearly cared. And if she were in better shape, I'd be fucking delighted.

"I took Sasha home because she was drunk and needed a safe ride." I kept my voice gentle. "That's all."

"Oh, right." She blinked a few times. "You're sure back fast though. Quickie?"

Even drunk as shit, she was still filled with sass. No one but my brothers and one very bratty little sister sassed me. I liked it. Too much.

"Nope. When I take a woman to bed, there's nothing quick about it. I like to take my time to tease, taste, make you tremble."

"Pfft." She leaned against my arm, losing her fight against consciousness. "I don't tremble."

"Then you haven't had the right man in your bed."

She didn't say anything to that, and for a second, I wondered if she'd passed out. "You really just took her home cuz she was drunk and asked for a ride?"

"Yep."

"That's... actually really nice."

"Try not to sound so surprised."

"But you're not nice." She waved a hand vaguely. "You're all... muscles. And beard. And two-weeks-only-no-girlfriend rules. And stupid perfect eyes that see too much. Nice guys don't look like you."

Jesus. Drunk Tempest was going to kill me.

I was going to kill whoever told her about my two-week rule. But I was also hoping she wouldn't remember it tomorrow.

"I'm plenty nice," I said, fighting a smile. "I even brought you water."

I pulled a bottle from my pocket, that I'd grabbed on our way to the back porch, and held it out. She stared at it like it might bite her.

"You planned this," she accused. "You knew I'd get drunk and need water."

"Yes, that was my grand plan. Get you drunk by... leaving the party completely. So I could then rehydrate you."

"Shut up." But she took the water, and some of the tension in my chest eased. "Your face is stupid."

"You just said my eyes were perfect."

"They can be stupid and perfect." She took a sip of water, then immediately made a face. "Everything's wobbly."

Before I could respond, she slumped sideways, her head sliding from my arm to my chest. Every muscle in my body locked up.

"You're warm," she mumbled.

Christ almighty.

I should move her. Should get her sisters to take her home, put some distance between us before I did something stupid like bury my face in her hair or pull her into my lap or—

She nuzzled closer, and my brain short-circuited.

"This is nice," she sighed. Then, so quietly I almost missed it, she said, "My hero would totally do this."

"Your what?"

But she was already out, breathing deep and even against my chest. Except for that cute little snuffle-snore she just made.

I'd pick her up, get her sisters, and drive them home... in a minute.

SPICE GIRLS HANGOVER

TEMPEST

My pendejo of a phone wouldn't shut up.

I cracked one eye open, immediately regretting every life choice that had led to this moment. Especially the fancy fruity flavored vodka. And the beer pong. And... oh god.

Flynn's lap.

I'd sat in Flynn Kingman's lap. In front of everyone. A lot of the night was a blur, but I remembered that.

My phone buzzed again. Twenty-seven notifications, all from the Baby Donkey Sitters Club group chat. With growing horror, I opened the first message.

It was a video. Of me. Downing two shots. At the same time.

Kill me now.

The next message was worse. A photo of me curled up in Flynn's lap like some kind of drunk sorority cat, his arms wrapped around me, looking down at me with an expression that made my chest hurt.

"You're alive." Parker's whisper stabbed directly into my brain. "How's the hangover?"

I pulled my pillow over my face. "I'm dead. This is my ghost. January whatever the day is will now be known as the true Dio de las Muertos. Please delete all social media immediately and find me in the afterlife."

"But then how would we preserve the greatest moment in KAT history? When Tempest Navarro, queen of control, decided to teach the entire rugby team Spanish insults about Flynn Kingman?"

I peeked out from under the pillow. "I did what now?"

"Oh, it gets better." The bed dipped as Parker sat down. "You called him arrogant in front of everyone. Then something about his... assets? Ricky refused to translate that part, for which I later made out with him to reward his act of service. And then you fell asleep in Flynn's lap."

"You did what? And I did nawwwwt."

Parker held up her phone, showing me the incriminating photo. "You absolutely did. And then Flynn wouldn't let anyone else take you home. Hannah, Alice, and I had to help him sneak up the back stairs to our room since you were completely out. He carried you the whole way, got you tucked in with water and Advil by your bed."

Oh no. No, no, no.

A soft bray from the corner of the room interrupted my spiral of mortification. I lifted my head, slowly, because the room was still spinning, to see my secret roommate watching me with concerned brown eyes.

"Hey, baby," I whispered. "Come here. I'm okay. I'm...okay."

The donkey clip-clopped over to my bed and pressed his velvet nose against my cheek. For a baby animal who'd been basically abandoned at birth, he had remarkable emotional intelligence.

"He was worried about you," Parker said. "Kept making these little sounds whenever you stirred in your sleep."

"Flynn?" It was against every rule in the book to even have a man upstairs at the house, but to have one spend the night? That was a conduct unbecoming a sister offense that could get one booted.

I shot upright, then immediately regretted it as my head threatened to explode. "What? Flynn spent the night? He knows?"

"Relax. He did not spend the night."

"But he knows about the donkey being in our room?" I was going to throw up.

"He was a little distracted making sure you were okay. Maybe he didn't notice." She handed me a bottle of water. "Seriously, Temporino. What happened last night? That wasn't like you."

I flopped back into my pillows, wishing they would suck me up.

"I remember him leaving with some girl, and then..." I pressed the cold bottle to my forehead. "It's all kind of fuzzy after that."

"You mean Sasha? The one he drove home because she was too drunk to drive?" Parker's voice was gentle. "He came right back. Looking for you."

The donkey nudged my arm, clearly picking up on my

distress. I scratched behind his ears, grateful for the distraction.

"It doesn't matter. I made a complete fool of myself. Teaching Spanish insults to half the athletic department? Falling asleep on him? God." I put my pillow over my face but winced at the movement. "I'm never leaving this room again."

"They weren't all insults," Parker said with a smirk. "I distinctly remember something about his incredible—"

I threw my pillow at her.

The donkey, thinking this was a new game, grabbed the pillow in his teeth and started prancing around the room.

"No, baby, don't!"

Too late. He knocked over my backpack, spilling books everywhere. Including my romance novel plotting notebook.

Great. Because this morning needed one more reminder of all the secrets I was juggling.

"So," Parker said, rescuing my notebook before it could become donkey breakfast. "What are you going to do about Flynn?"

"Nothing. I'm going to avoid him until graduation or death, whichever comes first."

"Tem..."

"Nope. Not discussing it." I pulled the covers over my head. "I'm just going to lie here and wait for the earth to swallow me whole."

The donkey made a disapproving sound and head-butted my shoulder through the blanket.

"Even the donkey thinks you're being dramatic."

Parker tugged the covers down. "Come on. You have Sunday dinner with your sisters, and if you don't show up, they'll come looking. You know how Catalina gets."

I groaned. She was right. And showing up hungover to family dinner was still better than letting the Spicy Girls storm the sorority house looking for me.

"Fine." I sat up slowly. "But first I need to figure out how to delete about fifty photos and videos from the group chat."

"And feed your secret emotional support donkey."

"That too." I scratched the donkey's ears as he snuffled hopefully at my pockets for treats. "At least you still respect me, right buddy?"

He promptly sneezed in my face.

"Rude."

A couple hours later and at least I was showered and dressed... and sober.

I slid my sunglasses back on before stepping into the delicious smells of the Navarro family kitchen. If anything could cure a hangover, it was Ophelia's pozole. The scent was already making me feel better. It was her look and the Spice Girls Inquisition I knew was coming that had me turning a little green.

"¿Qué diablos?" She squinted at me over a simmering pot of something that smelled amazing and also like it might make me throw up. "Are you hungover?"

"No."

"She's lying," Freddie called from the living room, not looking up from what appeared to be game film on her laptop. "It's all over the DSU underground FaceSpace. Our sweet sister went wild."

"Jesus." Catalina abandoned her critic's position at Ophelia's elbow to snatch my glasses off. "You *are* hungover. You never drink."

"I drink," I protested, squinting against the afternoon light streaming through the bay windows.

"Wine with dinner doesn't count," Rosalind said, sitting all prim and proper at the kitchen island with her ever-present phone. "Neither does that time you had half a margarita on New Year's and declared yourself tipsy."

Freddie's grin turned wicked. "Want to tell us about your Spanish lessons last night?"

I groaned, dropping my head onto the cool granite counter. "Can we not?"

"We absolutely must." Cat pulled up a stool next to me. "What happened to my sensible sister who makes Mamá proud with all her responsible choices?"

"Maybe she finally snapped," Freddie suggested. "It's about damn time."

"Or maybe," Rosalind said meaningfully, "it has something to do with a certain football player who carried her home."

I lifted my head. "How do you know about that?"

"Please." She stirred whatever heavenly torture was in that pot. "I still have my sources at the KAT house. Someone texted me the video."

"Which video?"

"Several." Freddie finally looked up from her laptop. "But don't worry, the one of you teaching the rugby team to say ' Kingman tiene un trasero que no para' is my favorite."

I was never drinking again.

"Remember when she used to be fun?" Ophelia asked no one in particular.

"Nope." Ros shook her head and crossed her arms.

"Yes," Catalina wagged her finger. "When we all spent summers at Abuela's villa Oaxaca, Nerdy Spice here was fun."

Oh mierda. Catalina knew. Of course she did.

"Before Mamá decided we needed to 'develop our interests into sustainable careers' or whatever and sent us to academic summer programs."

"You mean before she wanted alone time with Papá," Ophelia corrected.

"Can you blame her?" Freddie waggled her eyebrows. "Have you seen the way she looks at Papá in his professor tweed? Or when he tells her he wants to play doctor with her later when he thinks we aren't listening?"

"¡Cállate!" we all shouted, throwing dish towels and oven mitts at her.

Ophelia set a steaming bowl of pozole in front of me. "When's the last time you really relaxed, Tem? And don't say 'when I'm reading' because we all know that's just like Papá, work disguised as pleasure, Miss Literature Major, following in his footsteps."

I stared into my bowl, stomach churning for reasons that had nothing to do with my hangover. If they only knew how much work it really was. I picked up my spoon, mostly to have something to do with my hands. "Can we talk about something else? Like Abuela's welcome home party?"

"Nice try." Catalina sat across from me. "But we're not letting this go. Something's up with you. You're stressed, it looks like you're not sleeping. Don't think I haven't noticed those ojeras you try to hide, and now you're getting drunk at frat parties?"

"Hockey house," I corrected weakly.

"Not the point." She reached for my hand. "Go back to Oaxaca for spring break. Abuela would love it, and you clearly need the escape. Mamá won't even know, she's too busy with her clinic in Ecuador to track our whereabouts."

"I can't. I have... commitments."

"What commitments?"

If they only knew. The book deadline. The meetings in L.A. The secret baby donkey living in my room.

"Spring break at Abuela's villa would do you good," Ophelia said. "Remember that time we helped the magician sneak into her gated community when she wanted to surprise us with a birthday party?"

Despite everything, I smiled. "And that poker tournament she and Abuelo Leo organized for the neighborhood kids?"

"Where you won three hundred dollars off the ambassador's son?" Freddie laughed. "Abuelo always bragged about that to his friends."

"Or about the salsa lessons from AbuelaNovela's former co-star," Ophelia added with a waggle of her brows.

"Or the time Freddie and Abuelo Leo took—" Catalina cut off as my phone buzzed.

I glanced at the screen, then immediately wished I hadn't.

> Flynn: How you feeling today?

"Interesting," Rosalind said, reading over my shoulder. "Very interesting."

I turned my phone face down. "It's nothing."

Four sets of skeptical eyes stared back at me.

"Okay," Catalina said slowly. "Now we definitely know something's wrong. The Tempest I know would have at least three clever responses to her rom-com movie hero in the flesh at the ready."

She wasn't wrong. But the Tempest they knew wasn't hiding multiple secret identities while nursing the worst hangover of her life.

"Spring break at Abuela's villa," Catalina said again. "Promise you'll think about it? She's been asking for you specifically. Says you're the only one who appreciates her telenovela marathons. And it would get you away from all..." she gestured vaguely at me, "...this."

I nodded, mostly to make them stop looking at me like that.

My phone buzzed again. And again.

"Aren't you going to answer him?" Rosalind asked.

"Nope." I took a careful sip of pozole. I needed some regenerative nutrition if I was going to make it through the rest of this family...life. "I'm going to pretend last night never happened and avoid him until graduation."

"Bold strategy." Freddie closed her laptop. "Especially since you have class with him tomorrow."

Oh donkey balls. I did. And our fake-tutoring study sessions after.

My sisters exchanged looks that definitely meant trouble.

"Don't," I warned.

"Don't what?" Ophelia asked innocently. "Don't point out that you're obviously into him? Don't mention how he literally carried you home? Don't—"

I threw a tortilla at her head.

"Violence." She ducked, laughing. "See? This is why you need a vacation. You're getting aggressive in your old age."

My phone buzzed a fourth time.

"At least read the messages," Ophelia said softly.

I shook my head. Some things were better left unread. Like drunk texts, party photos, and whatever Flynn Kingman had to say about my behavior last night.

But as my siblings launched into planning Abuela's welcome home party, including every extended family member we had in a hundred mile radius, a donkey piñata and an AbuelaNovela shaped cake, my brain wouldn't let go of what those messages might say.

Not that it mattered. I had enough complications in my life without adding six feet plus of football player with annoyingly perfect biceps to the mix.

Even if he did have un trasero that wouldn't quit.

One that I couldn't face right now. And for the first time in my entire academic career, I skipped class.

And I skipped our regular study session. And ignored Flynn's texts. It was better that way.

Because I did not want to admit to...anything even close to maybe, possibly, a tiny bit of developing feelings for him.

I knew better. Flynn Kingman was a flirt. He had more notches on his headboard than was reasonable, and I doubted he even wanted to add me to them. I'd read that kind of romantic plotline, and it didn't have an HEA.

Unrequited love was my least favorite trope.

So I'd continue to ignore him for a few more days until I could remember who and what I was. Then at least that part of my life would go back to normal. I needed some normalcy.

I was hoping I would find it at the farm animal sanctuary. I loved baby donkey, but he needed a real home.

The main barn was in shambles and the sanctuary's small barn smelled like mildew and broken dreams. None of the animals that had to be evacuated were going to have a new home for at least another month. Minimum.

"I know, buddy." I patted Supersweet, the ancient black and white pig who was currently sharing his temporary pen in the only dry corner of the barn. "This isn't ideal for any of us."

Supersweet snuffled my pockets for treats, reminding me so much of his baby donkey cousin currently hiding in my dorm room that my chest ached.

"Thanks to a certain anonymous contribution, the new barn will start going up next week," The sanctuary owner said, leaning against the stall door.

"I can help more," I offered. "If that will get the animals back home sooner."

"Absolutely not." Her tone left no room for argument. "You've done more than enough, taking in our littlest resident. Speaking of which, how's he doing?"

"Getting bigger. And louder." I smiled.

And harder to hide. But I couldn't tell her that since she had no idea I was keeping a farm animal in my sorority house.

"You know you can bring him back here. We'll figure something out."

I gestured at the water damage. "No, no. He's fine where he is for a little while longer. I know the other barn is already overcrowded with the rescued animals."

"We'll figure something out," she repeated, but we both knew it wasn't that simple. "I'll leave you to commune with Supersweet's nature. At least she loves all this mud."

The sound of boots on gravel should have been going away from me, but someone was approaching. And it had me tensing, but it was just one of the volunteers bringing fresh hay. I'd been jumpy all morning, half-expecting Flynn to materialize every time I turned around.

Not that he would. I'd skipped both our Shakespeare and marketing classes, and our study session. He had no reason to—

"There you are."

I closed my eyes. Because of course. Of course Flynn Kingman would track me down at the one place I felt safe. Of course he'd look unfairly good in a worn DSU hoodie and jeans. And of course Supersweet would immediately abandon me to investigate this new treat-dispensing possibility.

"Traitor," I muttered as Supersweet pressed her nose into Flynn's palm.

"You missed class." Flynn scratched Supersweet's ears like he'd been doing it his whole life.

"Observant of you."

"I was worried."

Something in his voice made me look up. He was watching me with that same expression from the party photos. The one I couldn't quite decipher.

"I'm fine." I turned back to the water line. "Just busy."

"Too busy to read your texts?"

"My phone died."

"For a week? Also, it's literally buzzing in your pocket right now."

Damn it.

"Look." He stepped closer, still absently petting Supersweet. "About the party. I think we should talk about—"

"We really shouldn't."

"I was a jerk."

That made me turn. "What?"

"When you called me arrogant. And a bully." He ran a hand through his hair. "You weren't wrong."

"I called you what?" The words slipped out before I could stop them.

His eyes narrowed. "You don't remember?"

"I... parts of Saturday night are a little fuzzy."

"Just parts?"

"Most parts." I focused hard on a spot just past his left ear. "Okay, fine. All parts after you left with that girl."

"I came back."

"So I've also been told."

He was quiet for a moment, just scratching at Supersweet's ears.

A moment passed where we just watched the enormous and adorable pig try to nose his way into Flynn's pockets.

"I, umm," I said slowly, surprising myself, "I don't actually mind when you're being... what did I apparently call you? Arrogant?"

His mouth quirked. "Among other things."

"It's kind of nice." I focused on Supersweet's snuffling, avoiding Flynn's eyes. "Having someone who challenges me. You know, intellectually."

"Yeah?"

"Yeah." I took a deep breath. "I shouldn't have skipped our study sessions."

When he didn't immediately respond, I risked a glance at his face. He was watching me with an expression that made my chest tight.

"Tempest..."

"Not that I'm admitting you're right about Iago's motivations," I added quickly. "Because you're definitely not."

"Actually, about our study sessions..." He ran a hand through his hair. "I'm going to have to miss the next couple."

"Oh." Something cold settled in my stomach. An all too familiar rock.

"The big Bowl stuff with my brothers. We're headed out to LA early. There're all these media appearances, family events, meetings with scouts while I'm out there..."

"Right. Of course." I turned back to the water line, pretending to measure something. "That makes sense. Have fun with all that."

"When I get back—"

"Supersweet needs her afternoon feeding."

"Would you just—" He reached for my arm, but I stepped away.

"I'll see you around, Flynn."

I waited until his footsteps faded before looking at Supersweet. "Don't give me that. Whatever happened to 'We listen and we don't judge?' You'd have done the same thing."

Supersweet snorted in what was definitely disapproval.

SCHOOL OF JULES

FLYNN

The suite buzzed with pre-game energy as Gryff and Isak argued over the last of the nachos, but I couldn't focus on anything except my phone. I'd sent Tempest three texts in the past hour, each one carefully crafted to seem casual. Like I wasn't thinking about her every five seconds.

> Me: You watching the game?

> Me: Wouldn't want to miss the commercials. That's the best part. Especially if they're tear-jerkers.

And finally, the most recent.

> Me: How's our favorite four-legged friend?

No response. To any of them.

"Earth to Flynn." Gryff elbowed me in the ribs. "You in there?"

I pocketed my phone and tried to look interested in whatever football talk I'd missed. "Yeah, sorry. Just thinking about the draft."

It wasn't entirely a lie. The draft was definitely on my mind—especially since getting picked up by the Mustangs would mean staying in Denver. Staying near her.

God, what was wrong with me? I was in a VIP suite at the fucking Bowl, watching four of my brothers about to play in the biggest game of their lives, and all I could think about was whether Tempest was ignoring my texts on purpose.

"The draft?" Isak's eyebrows shot up. "Since when do you worry about anything?"

He had a point. Fun brother didn't worry about shit. As far as they knew. Fun times with Flynn was practically trademarked in my family. Nothing got to me. Even all the pressure that came with the captain-of-the-football-team spot I shared with Gryff hadn't changed that. But lately...

My phone buzzed and I grabbed it so fast I nearly dropped it. Just the Sport Network app with a game notification. Damn it.

"Okay, what's her name?" Jules appeared at my elbow, a knowing smirk on her face.

"What? There's no—I don't—" I stumbled over the denial, which was basically admitting guilt to my baby sister. Jules could smell relationship drama like a shark smells blood in the water.

"Uh-huh." She grabbed my arm and dragged me over to the snack table, away from the rest of my gossipy family. "Spill."

I busied myself loading up a plate with wings, buying time. Through the suite's sliding windows, I could see our brothers warming up on the field. Chris was running plays with Hayes, Ev, and the offense, while Dec worked with the defense. This was what I should be focusing on. I hoped to join Dec on the field next season.

"Flynn." Jules's voice had that same stern tone Mom used to use when she caught us in a lie. God, she reminded me of her. "You've checked your phone seventeen times in the past twenty minutes. I counted."

"It's nothing," I insisted, but even I didn't believe myself. "Just my Shakespeare tutor—"

"Uh, but you love two fiction genres...sci-fi and Shakespeare." Jules's eyes lit up. "Oh my god, you're flunking your class to get with your tutor? You're disgusting."

"I'm not flunking anything," I corrected quickly. "We're in a peer tutoring program. And I don't like her. She's stubborn and sarcastic and completely immune to my charm and—" I stopped, realizing I was only digging myself deeper.

Jules batted her eyelashes at me, grinning all innocent like. "Go on."

I sighed, dropping into one of the plush chairs with my mountain of wings. "It doesn't matter anyway. She's so not interested."

"The great Flynn Kingman, struck out?" Jules perched on the arm of my chair. "This I have to hear."

"I didn't strike out," I protested. "I haven't even... I mean, we're just..." I shoved a wing into my mouth, frustrated. "I don't know what we are. She's different."

"Different how?"

"She's not like the girls I usually... date." The words came out before I could stop them. I didn't so much date, as...fuck.

Jules's expression shifted from teasing to serious. "You mean because she's plus-size?"

"What? No, that's not—" But Jules cut me off. How did she know that Tempest was a thick girl anyway? She had to have some kind of spy network.

Besides, I'd slept with plenty of thick and curvy girls. Hadn't I? I frowned.

"But she's beautiful." The words came out automatically, because they were true. Tempest was gorgeous, with her curves and her smile and the way her eyes lit up when she talked about...anything.

Jules smacked me on the back of the head and gave me her patented you're-a-dumbass glare. The one where she expected us to realize what dumbassery we'd done and to fix it immediately.

"Hey. What the hell was that for, brat?"

"I thought I raised you better than that, big brother. Have you legit fallen prey to the idea that being fat and being beautiful are mutually exclusive?" She glared at me. "Because I have very specific ways to reeducate you that involve death and dismemberment."

Oh fuck. I'd just made my beautiful baby sister feel less than, and I deserved whatever punishment she meted out.

I set down my food, did the same with hers and then wrapped her into big bear hug. "I swear I didn't mean it like that, princess. You know I think all women are beautiful. And I'm sorry if how I acted or what I said made you feel anything different."

"Okay. I won't taint your Cheerios with the most vile additives I can come up with," Jules gave me a squeeze, and then punched my arm, a little harder than I expected. "And by that, I mean I won't pee in them. I'll forgive you, even if you are a total horndog who never dates anyone longer than two weeks."

"I'm not liking how you know so much about my love life." But I couldn't argue. It was true. I'd never wanted anything longer than a fling. Until now.

The suite erupted in cheers as something happened on the field, but my phone buzzed again and this time it actually was a text from Tempest.

> Tempest: The donkey says hi. Now stop texting me and watch your brothers win.

I smiled stupidly at my phone.

"Oh brother," Jules sighed, but she was smiling too. "You are in so much trouble."

She had no idea.

The first quarter flew by in a blur of spectacular plays. Chris was on fire, connecting with Hayes for two massive gains, and Declan's defense was crushing it. But during the first commercial break of the second quarter, the energy in our suite shifted.

"Here we go," Trixie said, practically vibrating with excitement. "The KnightWear commercial is up first."

I'd heard about these ads but hadn't paid much attention to the details. Something about body positivity and our brothers' partners. But after my conversation with Jules, I found myself watching with new eyes.

The KnightWear ad started with Everett talking about Mom. My throat tightened. It always did when anyone mentioned her. But this was different. He was talking about how she'd taught us about self-acceptance, about seeing beauty in everyone. The camera panned across people of all sizes wearing sexy pajamas, sharing their stories.

"Your brother's a good man," Dad said quietly beside me. I turned to find him watching the screen intently, his eyes suspiciously bright. "Your mother would be proud."

Before I could respond, a loud snort came from the neighboring suite. "What is this touchy-feely crap?"

My jaw clenched. Dad's expression darkened, but before he could move, Jules grabbed his arm. "Don't. We've got something better coming."

She was right. A Swoosh commercial aired next, featuring Kelsey Best, popstar extraordinaire who was about to join our family as Declan's wife, singing about self-love and acceptance. The camera showed people of all shapes and sizes making heart symbols with their hands, including my family members.

"Did you know about this?" I asked Gryff.

He shook his head, grinning. "Nope. But it's pretty awesome."

More jeers floated over from the next suite, but they were drowned out by the cheers in ours. I found myself thinking about Tempest, wondering if she was watching these ads too. Wondering what she thought about them.

My phone buzzed.

> Tempest: Okay, these commercials are actually making me cry a little.

I smiled, typing back quickly.

> Me: Wish I was there to wipe those tears away for you.

The moment I hit send, I realized how much I meant that. I wanted more than to have a fling, or get in her pants. I wanted whatever this was between us, to be something real.

"Earth to lover boy," Gryff elbowed me. "Chris just threw a touchdown while you were making googly eyes at your phone."

I looked up in time to see the replay. Chris to Hayes, beautiful spiral, perfect catch. The suite erupted in cheers.

"Sorry," I muttered, shoving my phone in my pocket. "I'm watching."

"No, you're not," Gryff said, but he was smiling. "And that's okay. It's kind of nice seeing you actually care about someone for once."

"I care about people," I protested.

"Yeah, for exactly two weeks." He gave me a knowing look. "This is different though, isn't it?"

Before I could answer, another round of crude comments floated over from the next suite. Something about "lowering standards."

Dad stood up silently, his jaw clenched. Even after all these years, he still had that look that could send even the toughest among us, scurrying to their room, or to do their chores and homework. Without a word, he strode toward the door.

"Dad?" Jules called after him, worry clear in her voice.

But he didn't respond. The suite fell silent as we heard him knock on the door next door.

"Should we..." Gryff started, but Jules shook her head.

"Trust me, those jerks are about to learn why Dad was voted meanest defensive player in the League."

A few minutes later, Dad returned, looking satisfied. The neighboring suite had gone suspiciously quiet.

"What did you say to them?" I asked.

Dad just shrugged, but there was a glint in his eye that spoke volumes. "Just reminded them about good sportsmanship and respect."

I pulled out my phone again, started typing to Tempest about how my dad had just possibly terrified some corporate executives into silence, but stopped myself. For once in my life, I didn't want to play this cool or funny. I wanted her to know I took this stuff seriously.

Chris was leading another drive down the field, and this time I was going to actually watch my brothers play.

But as the game wound down, I was itching to reach back into my pocket and check to see if she'd texted back.

The Mustangs' victory set off a chain reaction of chaos in our suite. Gryff and Isak were practically hanging out the windows screaming while Jules jumped up and down shouting something about dynasty status. I was right there with them until my phone buzzed.

> Tempest: Tell your brothers congrats on the win. It was more fun to watch than I expected.

My heart did a stupid little flip. She'd been watching. Really watching.

> Me: Wish you were here to see everyone freaking out.

I added a picture of Gryff and Isak basically climbing over each other trying to get a better view of the field.

> Tempest: Some of us are watching from the comfort of our beds, surrounded by homework, like responsible students.

> Me: Responsible shmesponsible.

"Mom would have loved this," Dad said to all of us in the suite. His eyes were fixed on the field where Chris, Hayes, Everett, and Declan were being mobbed by teammates and press. "Especially those commercials."

She was still making an impact on all of our lives, even after all these years without her.

The lot of us headed out of the suite. The girls and Dad were headed to the field, but Gryff and I were tasked with taking Isak and Jules back to the hotel before we hit the after party.

As we walked toward the elevators, Marie Manniway sidled up next to Dad. "Now seems a suitable time to ask for favors. Would you mind showing up to the KAT house on campus next Monday? The National Chapter president just emailed and the DSU girls are being honored with the April De la Reine Award. I'll be there, of course, but I thought you might like to go too."

My head snapped up. KAT house? As in Kappa Alpha Tau? As in Tempest's sorority?

"Of course," Dad nodded. "April loved being a KAT at University of Los Angeles. She'd be delighted our local girls are getting the award. Wouldn't miss it."

"Wait," I tried to sound casual. "Mom was in that sorority?"

"Damn straight she was." Dad's expression softened the way it always did when he talked about Mom. "Chapter president. Changed a lot of minds about what beauty looked like and how the media could be harmful to young adults. They created this service award in her honor."

The universe was literally handing me an opportunity on a silver platter. "Mind if I come with? You know, for... family support?"

Dad raised an eyebrow, and I thought he was going to call me out. But he just nodded. "Sure. Could use the company."

My phone buzzed again.

> Tempest: Being responsible is sexy.

I grinned. She was definitely flirting back.

"What's got you smiling like that?" Jules appeared at my elbow, eyeing my phone suspiciously.

"Nothing," I said quickly, shoving it in my pocket. "Just... happy for the win."

After hitting the field to celebrate with a boys and an appearance at the afterparty Pen had organized for the team, it was back at the hotel for those of us who weren't yet Mustangs.

Gryff sprawled across his bed, flipping through channels until he found the post-game coverage. I was only half paying attention until they started discussing the commercials.

"In an unprecedented move, both KnightWear and Swoosh debuted body-positive ads featuring members of the Mustangs' organization," the announcer said. "Social media reaction has been—"

"Don't." Jules snatched the remote, and changed the channel. "Nobody needs to see what the trolls are saying."

"They were about to say how great the response was. You're making us miss it."

Jules threw some popcorn at me. "Get a clue, Flynn. They were definitely about to say something about promoting unhealthy lifestyles and obesity."

"But... I thought...the commercials...society is being more body positive, aren't they?" Just having the commercials on at the Bowl was proof of that. "It's only dickheads like the Flabby Fit guys that don't get it."

Jules rolled her eyes at me. "Look, you're fit and good-looking and have been since you were, like, five. The only comments anyone has ever made about your body is how well you can play football."

Uh. She wasn't wrong. Except I wasn't going to tell her about how I had definitely overheard women talking about how hot they found my body.

"I'm not even eighteen and I get insanely negative

comments about my body every day." She shook her head. "It's exhausting. But I've got a great support system around me, even if you're completely obtuse sometimes. I know I'm enough. A lot of women can't say the same."

Isak folded his arms and glared at the TV. "I will happily stomp on anyone who even thinks about saying crap like this to you, princess."

"You all don't see it, because you don't have to. This is just a smidge of the shit we deal with about our bodies. Those commercials today were revolutionary. They meant something. They mattered."

The three of us stared at her like she'd grown tentacles out of her hair. I didn't know she went through any of that, and I wanted to tackle and beat the parts of the world that thought it was okay to make a women feel bad about herself.

"And this is why none of you have girlfriends. Pay better attention, jackasses."

Fuck. Were the same things happening to Tempest? Jules put the Sport Network on, but I barely noticed. I was thinking about how Tempest always deflected compliments with sarcasm. How she kept everyone at arm's length with her wit. How she seemed surprised every time I sought her out.

I needed air and headed for the balcony. The LA lights sparkled below, but all I could think about was Denver. About getting back to campus. About proving to Tempest that I could be more than just the guy with the two-week rule.

"It's different this time, isn't it?" Gryff joined me, leaning against the railing.

I didn't bother pretending not to know what he meant. "Yeah. But I think I screwed it up before it even started."

"Nah." He bumped my shoulder. "You're just finally playing in her league instead of trying to get her to play in yours."

My Tempest was in a league of her own.

And with her, I was playing in the pee-wees.

But if there was one thing I knew how to do, it was up my game. Come class next week, I was going to be on the varsity get-the-girl team.

OPERATION GET TEMPEST A DATE

TEMPEST

*A*fter our chapter meeting, the seniors retreated back to our room for an emergency meeting of The Donkey Sitters Club.

"Um, guys?" Hannah raised her hand like we were in still in our weekly chapter meeting. "What are we going to do about the awards ceremony next week? The whole first floor is going to be full of alums and guests."

We'd found out in our meeting that our chapter was being honored with the April De la Reine Leadership Award. It was kind of a huge deal.

"Oh god." Parker flopped back on her bed. "There's going to be so many people here. And you know Lindsey's going to want to give house tours."

"Can we move him somewhere else for the day?" I asked, watching the donkey methodically destroy one of my throw pillows. I couldn't even be mad about it.

"It's kind of amazing we got this award," Bettie said thoughtfully. "I mean, April De la Reine was such a badass. Did you know she actually lived in Denver?"

Alice looked up from her phone. "Once a sister, always a sister. Even if she was in the University of LA chapter."

"And her husband is coming to present it." Hannah bounced a little. "Bridger Kingman. In our house."

"Do you think he'll bring any of the boys?" Bettie asked, waggling her eyebrows at me. "I heard he brings family sometimes to these appearances he does on campus."

"Maybe Flynn will come," Parker said innocently. Too innocently. "Since he's already spending so much time with our Tempest."

I threw my remaining pillow at her. "We're not spending time together. We're being forced to do this tutoring thing."

"But KATman is coming up..." Bettie sang. "And you know the rules—every senior needs to ask someone."

That was not a rule. Bettie was worse than even Abuela when to trying to get me to date.

"I've never had a date to KATman and I don't intend to start now." I focused on scratching behind the donkey's ears. "Besides, Flynn Kingman doesn't do real dates. Everyone knows about his two-week rule."

I hadn't known about it until the party. That was one of the only things I did remember.

"But you're already breaking all his rules," Alice pointed out.

"That has nothing to do with me."

"Sure." Parker grinned. "Just like he wasn't totally flirting with you at the coffee shop, and the library, and during the Bowl game."

"Can we please focus on the actual crisis?" I gestured

to the donkey, who had given up on the pillow and was now investigating Alice's shoes. "Like how we're going to hide a baby farm animal during a major award ceremony where alums and guest will be filling the first floor?"

"Fine." Bettie sighed dramatically. "But this KATman conversation isn't over."

"Actually..." Hannah's eyes lit up. "I might have an idea about the donkey. You know how the basement storage room has that outside entrance? The one we use during move out and move in?"

As she outlined her plan, I tried super hard not to think about Flynn Kingman, or KATman, or the way he had texted me all throughout the Bowl game.

I failed miserably at all three.

And I continued to fail throughout the week, especially in the classes I had with him. I had no idea how I was going to make it through this study da—no, no, it wasn't a date—this study session that I'd both been dreading and couldn't stop thinking about.

Should I ask him to KATman?

No.

I'd never had a date before. But it was different for seniors. It was our last hurrah. All eyes were on us. A senior without a boyfriend at the dance was...weird and pathetic. Catalina had taken her now husband her senior year.

I stared at my laptop screen, trying to focus on the scene I was writing. My hero was just about to finally kiss the heroine after weeks of verbal sparring and denied attraction, but the words wouldn't come.

Probably because in exactly seven minutes, I had my

own verbal sparring match scheduled with Flynn Kingman.

After the way I'd dismissed him for ditching me for the Bowl with his family, which I knew was ridiculous of me, I'd thought things might be different between us. Because I was the one who made it weird.

The text exchange during the Bowl had been an olive branch I didn't know I'd wanted. And yesterday in class, he'd acted completely normal, if you could call anything about Flynn Kingman normal. Still charming, still frustrating, still way too attractive for my peace of mind.

"The course of true love never did run smooth," I muttered, then immediately wanted to smack myself. I was not in love with Flynn Kingman. I was barely tolerating him for the sake of my mother's expectations that I tutor an athlete.

Even if he had been surprisingly sweet, and smart, and funny...

"Working on something interesting?"

I slammed my laptop closed so fast I nearly knocked over my coffee. Flynn stood there, looking unfairly gorgeous in a DSU Dragons hoodie and that smile that probably got him out of speeding tickets.

"Homework," I said quickly. "Very boring homework."

"Must be some homework." He dropped into the chair across from me. "You were smiling at your screen."

Had I been? Damn it.

"I was thinking about the donkey," I lied. "He ate...something, and has the worst donkey farts right now."

Flynn's eyes lit up. "I would pay to see your face when you smelled that."

"Oh, yes. I would very much like you in particular to get to smell Sir Ass-tronaut's stink bombs."

He laughed, and something warm unfurled in my chest. I squashed it immediately. Flynn Kingman did not need to know he could make me feel warm and fuzzy.

"Tempest, oh my god, what a coincidence."

I closed my eyes briefly, praying I was hallucinating. But no, there was Parker, with Hannah right behind her, both wearing identical looks of faux surprise. I was being stalked by my own sorority sisters. And they were going to make my life hell.

"We were just talking about KATman," Hannah said, pulling up a chair without being invited. "You know, the biggest social event of the KAT house year?"

"And wondering who our Tempest might bring," Parker sing-songed oh so sweetly. "Since she's been spending so much time with a certain football player..."

I was going to murder them both. Slowly. With their own KAT badges.

"Really?" He drew the word out way, way too long.

Flynn's eyes darted between them and me. "I haven't heard a thing about it."

"Oh, it's so much fun," Hannah gushed. "Everyone dresses up, there's a live band, we vote one of the senior's boyfriends KATman of the year, and all the sisters are required to bring dates—"

"We are not required to bring dates," I cut in. "That's not a thing."

"It's totally a thing," Parker stage-whispered to Flynn. "She's just being difficult."

Flynn was watching this exchange with far too much interest. "Difficult? Our Tempest?"

Our Tempest? When did I become our anything?

"We should really start studying," I said loudly. "That essay on *Twelfth Night* isn't going to write itself."

"Right." Parker's grin was pure evil. "Studying. Very important. We'll leave you to your... academic pursuits."

But they didn't leave. They went to a nearby table where they could very obviously watch us while pretending to be on their phones.

"So," Flynn said after a moment. "KATman, huh?"

"Don't."

"Don't what? I'm just making conversation about this amazing social event that's apparently coming up soon. Just how soon is soon?"

"We're here to study." I pulled out my book. "Unless you'd rather talk about dances than pass this class?"

"I'm definitely going to pass this class." He leaned forward, lowering his voice. "But I'd rather talk about why you're blushing."

"I'm not—" My phone buzzed. A text from Parker.

> Parker: ASK HIM.

"Everything okay?" Flynn asked.

"Fine." I shoved my phone in my pocket. "Just sorority stuff. Now, about that essay..."

Oh no. No no no. He could not look at me like that, all

sincere and vulnerable. Not when I was trying so hard to keep my walls up.

"Flynn—"

"Tempest," Bettie's voice cut through the coffee shop like a knife. Our chapter president had impeccable timing, as always. "Just the person I needed to see."

I froze. If she was here about the donkey...

"Bettie, we were just..." Parker started, but Bettie waved her off with a wink.

I really was being stalked by my sisters. Stalked and harassed. My life probably would be easier if I just asked him.

"Actually, I need to discuss some details about the awards ceremony with everyone in the senior class. When you have a moment?"

"Uh, yeah, sure," I managed. That had to be code for donkey hiding plans.

Flynn's eyes narrowed slightly. "Ceremony?"

"Just sorority stuff," I said quickly. "Nothing interesting. Now, about that essay..."

He let me change the subject this time, but there was something different in the way he was looking at me. Like he was trying to solve a puzzle.

"Okay, so for the essay—"

"What were you really writing? Before I got here?"

Gulp. What was with everyone being all up in my business today? "I told you. Homework."

"See, normally I'd believe you because you're basically a walking library card. But you're doing that thing with your nose."

I froze. "What thing?"

"That little scrunch you do when you're deflecting." He mimicked the expression, and I had to fight back a laugh.

When did he start noticing things like that?

"Maybe I just have allergies," I said, but my heart wasn't in the deflection.

"Maybe." His smile was softer now, less cocky and more... something else. Something dangerous. "Or maybe you have secrets, Tempest Navarro. And now I know your tell."

Well, shit.

"Everyone has secrets, Flynn." I checked my phone and nearly cursed. Alice just got her grade on her bio-chem project and it wasn't good. She needed to head out to make her professor's office hours. "Speaking of secrets, I need to go. Sisterhood stuff."

"We've haven't even started our essays yet." He leaned back, crossing his arms. But he was enjoying the way I was flustered.

"Some of us have responsibilities beyond looking pretty and sacking quarterbacks."

"You think I'm pretty?"

"I think you're impossible." I started packing up my laptop. "And I really do have to go."

"Go to dinner with me tomorrow to make up our study time." The request, or command, came out casual, but there was nothing casual about the way he was watching me.

My heart did a stupid little flip. "That's not part of the tutoring arrangement."

"Maybe I'm tired of arrangements."

For a moment, I was tempted. I kept pushing him

away, and he kept trying. He was the last guy I expected to do that, especially when no other guy had. I was very, very tempted.

But that way lay madness. And probably heartbreak.

"Maybe another time." I turned to go, then stopped. "But Flynn?"

"Yeah?"

I bit my lip, but that didn't keep the words from coming out. "Ask me again, sometime."

I left him sitting there, a slow grin spreading across his face. And if I put a little extra sway in my walk because I knew he was watching?

Well, that was my secret to keep.

When I got back to the house, Alice slapped a remote for the speaker into my hand. "He won't eat the hay unless someone plays Taylor Swift or Kelsey Best," Hannah reported during our daily status meeting. "And he only likes the old country albums."

"Our donkey is a Swiftie?" Parker came in right behind me and looked delighted. "And a Bestie? That's badass."

"Our donkey is about to get us found out," I reminded her. "Who needs to eat his dinner and take a nap so I can study?"

The dinner happened, studying not so much. But it wasn't like I didn't know most Shakespeare plays backward and forward. But I also had marketing, mythology lit, and my senior thesis class on Herman fricking Melville. Not to mention I was miles behind on my chapters.

I could only put off my agent, and FlixNChill, for so much longer.

Somehow I made it through the rest of the week without a panic attack. And I'd never admit it to anyone but baby donkey, but Flynn's texts were keeping me going.

The morning of the awards ceremony, my phone buzzed with a text from Flynn.

> Flynn: You haven't named the bonkey yet, right? Because I got it for sure this time.

I smiled despite myself.

> Me: I doubt it.

Because unless he said Houdonkini, the great disappearing farm animal, he'd be wrong.

> Flynn: Since I haven't seen hide nor hair of our furry friend for weeks, you should call him Houdonki. Get it? Like Houdini, because he's completely disappeared.

First of all, what the heck? How did he do that? And second, Houdonki was better than Houdonkini. But still not the right name for my favorite confidant.

"Are you sure he's secure?" I whispered, peering down the basement stairs for the hundredth time.

"For the last time, yes." Parker adjusted my collar. "The outside door is locked, he has hay and water, and Hannah set up that tablet playing farm animal videos to keep him calm."

"He does love his YouTube," Alice added, straightening the welcome banner.

I took a deep breath. We could do this. Just get through the ceremony, but then I really had to figure out a more permanent solution for our four-legged friend.

"Tempest," Catalina's voice carried across the foyer. "¿Qué pasa, hermanita?"

My eldest sister swept in, immaculate as always in her black blazer trimmed with gold to match our sorority colors, with Rosalind right behind her. They'd both been active in the chapter during their college years, which was why I'd pledged KAT in the first place.

"What's wrong?" Rosalind's eyes narrowed. "You look guilty."

"Nothing's wrong." I forced a smile. "Just nervous about the ceremony."

"Since when do you get nervous about anything?" Catalina raised a perfectly shaped eyebrow.

She had no idea. Before I could answer, Bettie called out, "Let's go, ladies."

A stream of alums and guests flowed through the front doors. I lost track of how many hands I shook, how many congratulations I accepted. Everything was going perfectly until—

"Dad, this is amazing." A familiar voice cut through the crowd. "Mom lived in a house like this at University of Los Angeles?"

I froze. No. No way.

But there he was. Flynn Kingman, looking devastating in a suit and standing next to his father. In my sorority house. Where I was hiding a donkey.

"Ooh, who's that?" Catalina nudged me. "Wait, isn't that—"

"No one," I said quickly. "Just a guy on the football team who is in my Shakespeare class."

"Just a guy?" Rosalind's way too observant eyes turned predatory. "The way he's looking at you suggests otherwise."

I risked a glance. Flynn was indeed looking at me, a slow smile spreading across his face. The same smile he'd given me in the coffee shop the other day when I told him to ask me out to dinner again sometime.

"Ladies and gentlemen." The National Board President tapped her glass for attention. "If you'll all gather in the main room..."

Everyone began migrating toward the ceremony space. I tried to slip away to check on the donkey one last time, but Catalina linked her arm through mine.

"Oh no, hermanita. You're staying right here where we can watch whatever this is."

The ceremony started with the usual formalities. I barely heard them, too aware of Flynn standing off to the side, occasionally whispering something to his father. Every time I glanced back, he was watching me.

"And now," the national president continued, "I'd like to share some history about April De la Reine's impact on our organization..."

A muffled sound came from below. My heart stopped. No one else seemed to notice, but Flynn's head tilted slightly.

Then he moved, quietly slipping toward the back of the room.

No no no.

I couldn't follow him without drawing attention.

Couldn't text him without being obvious. Could only sit there, heart pounding, as he disappeared into the hallway.

Maybe he just had to use the bathroom?

Another sound, louder this time. Like a very distinctive bray.

Mierda. A very unpleasant rush of pins and needles ran along the back of my neck.

"Are you okay?" Catalina whispered. "You look like you're about to throw up."

Before I could answer, there was a crash from the basement. Then the thunder of hooves on stairs.

"Holy donkey balls," Flynn's voice rang down the hallway.

And then chaos erupted as a baby donkey wearing a KAT bandanna burst into the ceremony, followed by a very startled-looking Flynn.

"Is that..." Rosalind's eyes went wide. "Tempest, why is there a donkey in the sorority house?"

"Would you believe it's our new mascot?" I managed weakly.

The donkey trotted straight to the podium and began nibbling on the national president's dress. Well, at least he had good taste in fashion.

If I knew how to faint on command, I would. Right now. But knowing my life, I'd swoon right into the arms of Flynn Kingman.

KINGMANS IN THE HOUSE

FLYNN

I was trying my best to pay attention to the president lady's talk, but something kept niggling at my attention. No way she actually had that donkey in the house, right?

So I quietly moved toward this strange sound that was suspiciously familiar. Like the bray of a certain farm animal I knew. When I opened the door, I don't know what I was expecting, but it wasn't a scared and bolting baby donkey wearing a KAT bandanna.

I'd faced down three-hundred-pound offensive lineman and stared into the bright lights of Sports Channel cameras, but nothing prepared me for the fastest feet west of the Mississippi, galloping through a room full of sorority sisters, their alumnae, and my father, right in the middle of the award ceremony that was supposed to get me in deeper with Tempest.

The national sorority president was finishing her speech about Mom's legacy of embracing life's chaos with grace. But all eyes in the room swung toward me, once again, chasing a baby donkey. My dad watched with his signature stone-faced WTF expression. The one that had terrorized two decades of college athletes.

"Flynn Kingman," the National KAT President, snapped as the donkey knocked over the display featuring Mom's old KAT photos. "Of all the nights for one of your infamous Kingman disruptions—"

Behind her, Mrs. Henderson, the house mother, turned an alarming shade of purple. Tempest stood frozen in horror, and I knew I had to do something. Fast.

Think, Kingman. The same instinct that helped me read plays on the field kicked in. Only this time, instead of protecting my quarterback, I needed to protect Tempest.

I lunged for the donkey, but the little escape artist sidestepped me with surprising agility. Defensive training since I was five, and I was being outmaneuvered by a baby farm animal.

"Dr. Sterling," Tempest said, clearly trying to maintain her composure as I circled the refreshment table trying to knab the little stinker. "I can explain—"

The donkey darted left, snatching a cucumber sandwich. Little bugger wasn't scared, he was hungry.

The national president adjusted her designer glasses with a perfectly manicured finger. "I'm waiting."

Another grab, another miss. The donkey was making me look like a rookie. This didn't bode well for the combine. If any of the scouts saw me now, I'd never get drafted.

"You see," she squeaked, "I've been volunteering at the animal sanctuary."

The donkey brayed victoriously and knocked over a crystal punch bowl. "And their main barn flooded."

"Young lady," Dr. Sterling cut Tempest off, "this is completely unacceptable. In my thirty years with KAT—"

"He's mine," I blurted out and finally snagged the baby donkey, getting the bandanna and using it like a collar. I also grabbed another cucumber sandwich and led my hungry friend to position myself between Tempest and the president. "I convinced some of the sisters to help me temporarily house him. They had nothing to do with this."

Tempest's head snapped toward me, her eyes wide. I gave her a subtle wink before turning back to face judgment.

"And you thought a sorority house was an appropriate location for livestock?" Dr. Sterling's voice could have frozen hell.

"No, ma'am." I flashed my most charming smile and blinked up at her. "But I only recently found out my mother was a KAT at UCLA, and I hoped because of their reputation for philanthropy, they'd take pity on me and my poor, homeless, orphaned, adorable baby donkey."

"Just like your mother," Dr. Sterling said, and despite her stern tone, I caught a glimmer of something softer in her eyes. "April could turn any momentous occasion into an adventure. Though even she never managed to smuggle livestock into an award ceremony in her honor."

Dad cleared his throat. "To be fair, Vicky, there was that incident with the mariachi band and the piglet during finals week when she was a junior."

"Bridger Kingman, don't you dare bring that up right now."

"Ma'am? Did you... know April De la Reine personally?" Tempest asked.

"She was my 'lil sis." She smiled, clearly remembering good times. "I was a bridesmaid at their wedding."

The donkey slipped right out of that bandanna and trotted over to my father, who until now had been watching the scene unfold with his arms crossed. To everyone's surprise, the animal pressed its head against Dad's leg like an oversized puppy. A muscle twitched in Dad's jaw, the closest thing to a smile he showed in public.

"She was quite the prankster," Dr. Sterling said softly, her stern facade cracking slightly. "Always getting into scrapes, but her heart was in the right place."

Dad cleared his throat. "The apple doesn't fall far from the tree, it seems." He reached down absently to scratch behind the donkey's ears. "Though this is a new level of chaos, even for a Kingman."

Aha. I knew what to do.

"Dad," I started, "I know it's a lot to ask—"

"No." His voice carried the same authority that had commanded football fields for twenty years. "Absolutely not. I have neighbors, Flynn. Respectable people who don't expect livestock next door."

Uh, that was bullshit. Trixie and Chris lived next door and had the noisiest rooster on the planet who woke up the whole damn neighborhood most mornings.

The donkey looked up at him with big, soulful eyes. Dad's hand stilled on its head.

"Sir," Tempest addressed my dad, her voice quiet but determined. "We'll find another solution. I promise—"

"One week," Dad interrupted, and I could have sworn I

saw the ghost of a smile as the donkey nuzzled his hand. "You have until next weekend to figure something else out. And you'll both be responsible for its care." He fixed me with the look that had launched a thousand wind sprints. "This doesn't interfere with your combine prep, understood?"

"Yes, sir."

"Well," Dr. Sterling said, looking at the donkey now contentedly leaning against my father's leg, "I suppose this is a fitting tribute to April in its own way. She always did say college was about more than just grades and rules."

She turned to Mrs. Henderson. "We should overlook this incident. After all, the April De la Reine Leadership Award is meant to honor sisters who think creatively and make a difference in unexpected ways—though perhaps next time, we'll stick to less... furry forms of philanthropy."

Mrs. Henderson deflated like a popped balloon.

I felt Tempest's hand brush against mine, a silent thank you that sent electricity up my arm. I resisted the urge to grab it, to pull her close and promise that I'd always have her back.

"Right," she said, straightening her shoulders. "Let's get this chaos machine to his temporary home before he decides to redecorate the whole house."

"Lead the way, Queen Titania." I grinned, then turned to my father. "Think Declan will bring his truck over to help with the move?"

Dad pulled out his phone, his expression softening almost imperceptibly. "Already texted him. Your brother says he's bringing Wiener the Pooh for moral support." He paused. "God help us all."

The donkey brayed in what sounded suspiciously like agreement.

The thing about having seven siblings is that crisis management becomes a spectator sport. Within fifteen minutes of Dad's text, my brothers had turned Operation Donkey Evacuation into a full-scale production.

"I still say we dress him up as the Dragons' mascot," Isak said, filming everything on his phone. "No one questions the mascot."

Declan, who'd shown up with his fiancé's dachshund, shook his head. "And risk another head-falling-off incident? Did you learn nothing from the pep rally?"

"Boys," Dad's voice carried across the KAT house lawn. "Less commentary, more action."

I turned to Tempest, who stood next to me watching my family's chaos with wide eyes.

"Sorry about... all of this." I gestured to where Hayes was attempting to coax the donkey with organic carrots while Everett consulted Wiki How articles about livestock transport. This is what the off-season looked like to my family.

"Don't be," she said softly. "I'm not used to people helping like this, and honestly, it's kind of entertaining. Definitely good for a, uh, story later."

Something in her voice made my chest tight. Before I could respond, Gryff jogged up with Declan's truck keys dangling from his finger.

"Got the getaway vehicle," he announced. "Though

Declan says if there's any damage to his precious truck, you're running suicides until the combine."

"Noted." I caught the keys. "Where's Chris? We could use him to quarterback this situation."

"He stayed behind with Jules and Trix to prepare a place in the backyard for BadonkaDonk to hang out in this week. But they said to tell Tempest that Luke Skycocker sends his regards to his fellow farm animal revolutionary."

Tempest's laugh caught me off guard—a real one, not the guarded chuckle I usually got. I wanted to hear it again.

"Okay, people," Dad clapped his hands, every inch the coach taking control of his team. "Here's the play. Flynn, you and Tempest lead our friend here to the truck. Declan, you and Gryff provide blocking. Hayes, you're on lookout for any curious neighbors. Isak..." He sighed. "Try not to make this go viral."

"No promises, Dad."

I turned to the donkey, who had finished the carrots and was now eyeing Wiener the Pooh with great interest. The dachshund, to her credit, stood her ground.

"Ready?" I asked Tempest.

She squared her shoulders. "Lead the way, quarterback."

"I'm a linebacker."

"I know." Her smile was small but real. "But right now, you're calling the plays."

We made it approximately ten feet before everything went sideways. A car alarm went off down the street, spooking both the donkey and Wiener the Pooh. The dachshund took off running, which the donkey apparently took as an invitation to play chase.

"Pooh, no." Declan sprinted after his dog.

"Bonkey, no." I grabbed for the lead rope, but it slipped through my fingers.

What followed was five minutes of pure chaos as a baby donkey chased a dachshund around the KAT house lawn, with the entire Kingman family in pursuit. Except of course, Isak, who stood on the front steps recording the whole thing and laughing so hard he had to sit down.

"Your family," Tempest said beside me as we watched Declan dive and miss his dog for the third time, "is absolutely ins... umm, interesting."

"Yeah." I was used to this chaos, but even for us, this was laughable. "But we get results."

As if on cue, the donkey stopped to investigate a bush, allowing Hayes to finally grab the lead rope. Wiener the Pooh, sensing the game was up, trotted back to Declan looking mighty pleased with herself.

"Show off," Declan muttered, brushing grass off his jeans.

Loading the donkey into Declan's truck proved surprisingly anticlimactic after that. Dad had already laid down rubber mats, and Hayes, who had somehow charmed the baby donkey, got our four-legged friend settled with minimal fuss.

"I'll drive," Dad announced, plucking the keys from my hand. "Flynn, you drive my car and follow. Tempest, you're welcome to join him. The rest of you..." He surveyed his sons with the look that had launched countless wind sprints. "Shoo. We got this. I know you all were here to feed the gossip mill."

My brothers dispersed, except Isak who was both still filming and somehow flirting with the KAT sisters who'd come out to watch. I pointed Tempest to my dad's car, which he never, ever let any of us drive, so this was extra weird. At least it was cool.

Tempest kept her eyes on the passing streets, but her hand found mine in the darkness. I intertwined our fingers, hoping she couldn't feel my pulse racing.

"Thank you," she whispered, so quietly I almost missed it.

I squeezed her hand. "Anytime, my queen. Though next time, maybe we stick to smuggling something smaller and easier to hide... like chinchillas or oh, I know, let's leave animals out of it all together and start a sex toys smuggling business."

Her laugh, soft and real, mixed with the night air. "Dildos and vibrators aren't illegal, and I don't think we need to smuggle them either in or out of a sorority house."

Hot damn. Now I was imagining her with a room full of a whole menagerie of sex toys. Fuck me. Was it hot in here?

Normally, this was the part where I made my move. Got myself two weeks of blissful sexy times romps in the sheets. Sitting there, in my dad's vintage mustang, trailing behind a criminal donkey, flirting with a girl who kept surprising me, my heart didn't pitter pat. It didn't skip a beat. I wasn't twitterpated.

What I was would be much worse.

I was in serious trouble.

Because this felt a lot like falling, and I swore I'd never do that.

I couldn't.

We pulled into my old neighborhood in Thornminster, and seeing my dad's house and the Kingman family home through Tempest's eyes made it feel different somehow. Manicured lawn, same Denver Mustangs and DSU flags, same rose bushes Mom had planted that Dad still maintained with precision.

"This is where you grew up?" She stood in the driveway, taking in the sprawling two-story that had somehow contained eight kids and more chaos than should be legally possible.

"Home sweet home." I helped the donkey down the truck ramp we'd borrowed from Hayes. Through the backyard gate, I could hear Chris and Jules bickering about proper hay storage while Trixie played mediator.

Dad cleared his throat. "Your siblings appear to be making a mess of my yard."

"It's what we do best," I said, just as Jules shouted, "Flynn, tell Chris he's arranging the hay bales wrong."

"Sorry about..." I gestured vaguely at the chaos. "All of this."

"Don't be," Tempest said softly, and something in her voice made me look closer. She was staring at Mom's roses, illuminated by the porch lights, with an expression I couldn't quite read.

The donkey chose that moment to discover those same rosebushes.

"No," Dad and I shouted in unison, but Tempest was

faster. She stepped between the donkey and the flowers with a grace that stopped both of us in our tracks.

"Hey there, little one." Her voice was soft but firm. "Those aren't for eating." She pulled what looked like a granola bar from her pocket. "This is much better."

The donkey considered its options, then delicately took the treat from her hand.

"You've done this before," Dad said, and it wasn't a question.

"I volunteer at a farm sanctuary." She shrugged, but I caught the hint of pride in her voice. "Animals respond to calm energy."

"Hmm." Dad studied her with the same intensity he used to evaluate potential recruits. Then his expression softened as the donkey bumped against his leg again. "That'll do, donkey. That'll do."

From the backyard, Jules called out, "Dad, Chris is being impossible."

"Speaking of impossible..." Dad sighed. "I better go supervise before they undo all of Trixie's organizing. Flynn, show our guest what they've set up." He headed toward the gate, then paused. "And Miss Navarro? I assume you'll be here early to help with his care?"

"Yes, sir. I have an eight o'clock class, but I can come right after."

"Good. Flynn's free from nine to noon. Between combine prep sessions." He disappeared into the backyard before I could protest being scheduled like a rookie.

"Your father's quite the commander," Tempest said, amusement coloring her voice.

"You have no idea, my queen." The nickname slipped

out without thought, inspired by her regal handling of the chaos. When her cheeks flushed pink, I decided to keep it.

We rounded the corner to find Chris and Jules had actually done a decent job setting up a sheltered area with fresh hay and water. Trixie was adding some finishing touches, including what looked suspiciously like fairy lights.

"For ambiance," she explained, not at all sheepishly. "Every creature deserves a little magic."

After a quick tutorial on the setup from Trixie, I drove Tempest back to campus. She was quiet, but I caught her smiling at nothing more than once.

"I can't believe your whole family dropped everything to help," she said as I pulled up to the KAT house.

"That's what Kingmans do. We're ride-or-die, even for criminal donkeys." I turned to face her. "And definitely for people we care about."

Her breath caught, and for a moment, I thought about closing the distance between us. About finally finding out if her lips were as soft as they looked.

"Flynn..." The way she said my name did dangerous things to my heart rate.

A tap on the window made us both jump. Parker, Tempest's roommate, waved apologetically.

"Sorry." Her voice was muffled through the glass. "But Mrs. Henderson is doing one of her infamous random room checks in ten minutes and she's already suspicious about the donkey thing."

Tempest sighed, reaching for the door handle. "Duty calls."

"Hey." I caught her hand before she could leave. "See you at nine-ish tomorrow, my queen?"

Her smile was worth every second of chaos we'd endured. "Don't be late, Kingman."

I watched her disappear inside, already counting the hours until morning. Because for the first time since I made my two-week rule, I wasn't looking for an exit strategy.

I was looking for a reason to stay.

MUD WRESTLING CHAMPIONS

TEMPEST

I didn't register the cold until I was halfway to the Kingman house. February in Colorado wasn't known for its mercy, and I'd rushed out after my morning class without bothering to check the weather. Now, power-walking from my car past frost-kissed lawns in Thornminster's nicest neighborhood, I pulled my jacket tighter and wished I'd remembered gloves.

The Kingman house looked different in daylight, less imposing, more lived-in. A forgotten football rested by the front steps. Wind chimes tinkled from the porch. It looked like a home, not just a house, and something in my chest tightened at the thought.

Before I could knock, the front door swung open. Coach Kingman stood there in running clothes and a Denver Mustangs cap, a travel mug in his hand.

"Miss Navarro." He checked his watch. "Nine o'clock exactly. Punctual."

"Good morning, sir." I tried not to shiver. "I hope the donkey didn't cause too much trouble overnight."

A noise that might have been a laugh escaped him. "Less than any one of my children on a good day. Flynn's out back already. Coffee?"

I blinked. "Yes, please. Thank you."

He gestured me inside, and I followed him through a house that was simultaneously exactly what I'd expected and nothing like I'd imagined. Sports trophies competed for space with framed family photos. A massive bookshelf held everything from playbooks to Shakespeare to romance novels, the latter probably Flynn's little sister's influence. The kitchen was enormous, clearly designed to feed a small army of athletic men.

Coach handed me a mug featuring a cartoon dragon wearing a football helmet. "Milk's in the fridge if you need it. Flynn takes his mostly milk, two sugars."

"I—" I started, but he was already heading toward the door.

"Early meeting at the university. Back by noon. Tell Flynn I expect those combine drills completed by three."

And then he was gone, leaving me holding two mugs of coffee in a stranger's kitchen, wondering how exactly my life had led to this moment.

I found my way to the back deck, where I discovered exactly why Flynn hadn't answered the door. He stood shirtless in the middle of the yard, attempting to coax our donkey away from what appeared to be a freshly planted section of garden. Morning sunlight glinted off his shoulders, highlighting muscles that belonged on a Greek statue, not a college senior.

I nearly dropped both coffee mugs.

"Come on, buddy," Flynn was saying, "those are not for

you to eat. Dad will actually murder me if you eat his herbs."

The donkey looked thoroughly unimpressed by this logic and continued munching on whatever poor plant had caught his interest.

I set the mugs down on the deck railing and cleared my throat. "Need some help?"

Flynn spun around, and the smile that spread across his face did dangerous things to my heart rate. "My queen arrives." He gestured dramatically to the donkey. "Your subject is misbehaving."

"And you're..." I gestured vaguely at his lack of shirt, hoping the morning chill explained my flushed cheeks. "...cold?"

"Hay emergency." He grabbed a towel draped over a nearby chair and wiped his hands. "Little guy knocked over his feeder and somehow managed to get hay everywhere. Including down my shirt." His eyes sparkled with mischief. "But if the view's distracting you, I can put it back on."

"I'm not distracted," I lied, sounding unconvincing even to myself. I held out his coffee like a shield. "Your dad made this for you."

"Ah, the Coach Kingman seal of approval—coffee delivery service." He bounded up the steps to the deck, taking the mug with a grateful sigh. "You're already doing better than most of my teammates. He usually makes them fetch their own."

We stood side by side at the railing, watching the donkey happily destroy what I now recognized as a winter herb garden. Up close, I could smell Flynn's soap and something warmer beneath it. It was unfairly distracting.

"Should we rescue those plants?" I asked, desperate for something to focus on besides the completely unnecessary dimple in his right cheek when he smiled.

"Probably." He didn't move. "But they're just herbs. Dad loves to cook. We ate sooooo much spaghetti growing up." He took a sip of coffee, his expression softening. "Besides, look how happy he is."

The donkey did indeed look blissful, ears perked forward as he systematically eviscerated what might have been basil.

"Your dad's going to kill us both," I pointed out.

"Nah." Flynn's shoulder brushed mine as he leaned against the railing. "Dad's got a soft spot for giant balls of fluff. We had so many dogs growing up. He thought if he called them all Bear, we wouldn't notice it wasn't the same dog for... twenty years," he added with a grin.

"So that's where we're setting the bar? As long as your father likes me more than your childhood pets, we're good?"

"Trust me, my queen, you're leagues ahead of Bear the Third. That dog ate Dad's championship ring."

I nearly choked on my coffee. "What?"

"Yep. Dad took it off to do dishes one night, Bear decided it looked tasty, and three extremely uncomfortable days later..."

"Okay, stop." I laughed, holding up a hand. "Too much information before I finish my coffee."

His smile turned softer, more genuine. "You have a great laugh, you know that?"

THE JACK*SS IN CLASS

The sudden shift caught me off guard. "I—thank you."

A comfortable silence fell between us, broken only by the occasional happy snuffle from the donkey. Flynn still hadn't put a shirt on, and I was running out of willpower to look elsewhere.

"So," I said finally, "what's the plan for today's donkey care?"

"Well, we need to reinforce his pen, refresh his water, give him a good brushing, and figure out why he keeps escaping to eat Dad's herbs when he has perfectly good hay." Flynn ticked each item off on his fingers. "Also, Dad reminded me four hundred and forty-two times that this is only lasting a week, so we should definitely brainstorm exit strategies."

"I have an idea about that. I'm really hoping my abuela might take him in when she gets back next week." I smiled at the thought. "She's kind of a force of nature. Former telenovela star, never met an animal she didn't love. Between her drama and your donkey's escape artist tendencies, they'd make quite the pair."

"Telenovela star?" Flynn's eyes lit up. "That's amazing. No wonder you have such a flair for the dramatic."

I shoved his shoulder playfully. "Says the man who creates campus-wide chaos on a weekly basis."

"It's a gift." He winked, and my stomach did a completely unauthorized flip. "Come on, let's save what's left of Dad's herbs before he revokes my key privileges."

We made our way down to the yard, where the donkey greeted me with an enthusiastic bump of his head against my hip. Flynn disappeared into the shed and returned with brushes and a repaired hay feeder.

I brushed baby donkey and Flynn knelt to secure the feeder. The morning light caught in his hair, turning the edges golden. "This little guy has about ten times the personality per pound."

As if to prove the point, the donkey stretched his neck out and gently tugged on Flynn's hair.

"Hey," Flynn laughed, gently extracting himself. "I'm trying to help you here, ingrate."

I allowed myself a small smile at the sight of six-foot-something of college football star being bullied by a miniature donkey. "I think he likes you."

"Story of my life. The ones I'm not trying to impress love me, and the ones I am..." He looked up at me, his expression suddenly serious. "Well, jury's still out on that one."

My heart stuttered. "Flynn—"

Before I could finish whatever dangerous thing I was about to say, the donkey spotted something beyond the fence and took off at surprising speed, dragging his lead rope with him.

"No," we both shouted, lunging after him.

What happened next was pure chaos. The donkey circled the yard, kicking up mud. Flynn slipped, grabbing for my arm to steady himself but succeeding only in pulling me down with him. We landed in a tangled heap of limbs and laughter, covered in Colorado's finest February mud.

"Sorry," Flynn gasped, still laughing. "I was trying to be heroic."

"How's that working out for you?" I couldn't stop giggling, even as I felt mud seeping into my jeans.

He propped himself up on one elbow, looking down at me with an expression that made my breath catch. "I think my heroism might need some work."

"Just a bit," I agreed, suddenly very aware of how close his face was to mine, how easy it would be to close that distance.

His eyes dropped to my lips. "Tempest—"

"FLYNN!" A voice from inside the house shattered the moment. "HAVE YOU SEEN MY PURPLE CONVERSE?"

Flynn closed his eyes, looking pained. "And that would be my sister."

"The infamous Jules?"

"The very same." He stood, offering me a hand up.

As he pulled me to my feet, the donkey trotted back, looking entirely too pleased with himself. Flynn sighed, tugging gently on the lead rope.

"Come on, troublemaker. Let's get you sorted before you cause any more problems." He glanced at me, mud-splattered and disheveled, and his smile returned. "Though I have to admit, chaos looks good on you, my queen."

Despite the cold, the mud, and the runaway donkey, warmth spread through my chest. This boy was dangerous in ways I hadn't anticipated.

Jules bounded onto the deck, her purple-streaked hair pulled into a messy bun. She stopped short when she saw us mud-covered and standing awkwardly apart.

"Well, well," she said, eyes darting between us with laser-like assessment. "I was looking for shoes, but it seems I found the entertainment instead."

Flynn gestured to the donkey. "This one's fault. Don't even start."

"I'm Jules," she said, completely ignoring her brother and extending her hand to me before realizing it was pointless given my mud-caked state. "And you must be the Shakespeare girl who's been driving my brother insane."

"Tempest," I managed, suddenly very aware of how I looked. "Nice to meet you."

"You too." Her smile was genuine but calculating, like she was solving a puzzle. "I've heard so much about you that I was beginning to wonder if Flynn had made you up."

"Jules," Flynn warned.

"What? It's true. Gryff, and Isak talked about nothing but 'Tempest this' and 'Tempest that' at game night at Hayes's house the other day." She leaned against the railing. "Though they failed to mention you're exactly the kind of badass who'd roll around in mud with a donkey and my brother."

"It wasn't intentional," I said, feeling heat creep up my neck.

"The best mud fights never are." Jules grinned. "Come on, I'll find you something to wear." Before I could protest, Jules had linked her arm through mine and was steering me toward the house, mud be damned. "Flynn, deal with your escape artist while we handle the fashion emergency."

"I don't want to mess up your floors," I started.

"Please. This house has survived eight athletes and countless man-child disasters. A little mud is nothing."

She pulled me through a side door that led to a laundry room. "Strip down to whatever you're comfortable with. I'll grab you some clothes."

She disappeared before I could respond. I peeled off my mud-caked jacket and jeans, grateful I'd worn decent underwear. Jules returned with a stack of clothes and a towel.

"The sweats are Flynn's because, yes, he still does his laundry at home, so they might be big, but they'll work. The t-shirt is mine." She handed them over with a critical eye. "So you're the tutor who doesn't need to tutor Flynn because he's secretly a Shakespeare nerd."

I laughed despite myself. "Pretty much."

"And you're the girl with the viral donkey and secret writing sessions in the library."

My head snapped up. "What?"

Jules's smile turned knowing. "Flynn mentioned you're always writing something. Said you slam your notebook shut whenever he gets too close." She perched on the washing machine. "I do the same thing when I'm writing fanfiction my brothers would be traumatized to read."

"I'm just... taking notes," I said lamely.

"Sure." She nodded, clearly not believing me. "Just like I'm 'just studying' when I have six tabs of AO3 open."

I pulled on the sweats, which were indeed too big but soft and comfortable. As I tugged the t-shirt over my head, I noticed it featured the art from a dragon-shifter paranormal romance novel.

"You like romance?" I asked, gesturing to the shirt.

"Love it. It's basically all I read." She sighed happily. "I'm obsessed with this dragon-shifter series right now.

I'm a sucker for forced proximity trope. Like... there's only one bed? Hell, yeah." Her eyes sparkled mischievously. "Know anything about that trope?"

I swallowed hard. "I might have read a few."

"Although, I'm a bit distracted by this sports romance series." She jumped down from the washing machine and gathered my muddy clothes. "The author is super secretive about their identity, which of course has everyone freaking out trying to find out who they are. Everyone in my plus-size book club has theories about who it could be."

My throat went dry. "Really?"

"Mmhmm. The books are based on Shakespeare plays, but with, you know, sexy times." She winked. "The newest one's coming out soon. I have it preordered, but also notifications set up for her InstaSnap account and FlipFlop and everything."

"Sounds... interesting," I managed.

"You should check it out. I think you'd like it. The heroines are all smart women who don't take any crap from the heroes." She started the washing machine. "Speaking of which, my brother isn't giving you any trouble, is he? Because I can totally take him down if necessary."

"No," I said, surprised by the protectiveness in her voice. "Flynn's been... unexpectedly nice."

Jules studied me for a long moment. "He's different with you. Usually he's all charm and swagger, but with you, he's more... himself." She shrugged. "It's weird. Good weird."

Before I could process that, Flynn appeared in the

doorway, still shirtless but significantly less muddy and a little wet. Looking like that, he wasn't the only one who was going to be wet.

"Jules, are you interrogating my guest?"

"Of course." She grinned unrepentantly. "Someone has to vet the first girl you've actually liked in... ever."

"I like plenty of girls," Flynn protested.

"For exactly two weeks," Jules shot back. To me, she added, "You've already outlasted his usual expiration date, which means you're special."

But also... "I'm not, we're not—"

"That's enough," Flynn said, but there was no heat in it. "Dad called. He's picking up lunch on his way home and wants to know if you're staying, Tempest."

The invitation hung in the air. Jules looked at me expectantly.

"I should probably get back to campus," I said, though part of me wanted to stay. "I have a deadline for... a paper."

"Let me drive you back when your clothes are done," Flynn said, disappointment flashing across his face before his easy smile returned.

"I can take her," Jules offered. "I'm heading to the library anyway. We can get to know each other better." She waggled her eyebrows at Flynn, who looked mildly terrified.

"That's okay," I said quickly. "I have my own car."

"Next time, then." Jules's smile was determined. "Because there will be a next time."

I had no doubt about that, and honestly, I was looking forward to coming back to the Kingmans'. Which is not something I ever thought I'd think. It was probably a really bad idea to let Flynn get into my heart. Uh, I mean his family.

One more sister was definitely not what I needed. Even if I really liked her, and her older brother.

Mierda.

HE FELL FIRST

FLYNN

The door hadn't even closed behind Tempest before Jules pounced.

"So that's the girl who's gotten under your skin." She folded her arms, grinning at me like she'd caught me stealing cookies. "Gotta say, big brother, you've been holding out on us."

I grabbed a clean t-shirt from the laundry pile. "There's nothing to hold out on."

"Please." She rolled her eyes with the dramatic flair that only a teenage girl could perfect. "I haven't seen you look at anyone like that since... ever."

"Like what?" I pulled the shirt over my head, grateful for the momentary escape from her scrutiny.

"Like she hung the moon and stars and possibly invented football."

I snorted. "You've been reading too many of those romance novels."

"And you," she pointed at me accusingly, "have been

breaking your stupid no girlfriends, I only date someone for two-weeks rule. Admit it."

Baby donkey brayed from the backyard, as if adding his agreement. We would be having a talk about manners and how to be a better wingman later.

"Don't you have somewhere to be?" I asked, heading back outside to check on our four-legged troublemaker. "The mall? A friend's house? Literally anywhere that isn't here interrogating me?"

Jules followed, undeterred. "First of all, nobody goes to *the mall* anymore, and this is way more interesting than anything and everything else that I have to do. Flynn Kingman, campus player extraordinaire, tripping over himself for a girl who doesn't even seem impressed by his football skills or status as an upcoming first-round draft pick."

"She's just... different." I grabbed the brush we'd dropped earlier and started grooming the donkey, who had finally tired of destroying Dad's herb garden.

"Different how?"

I thought about Tempest's laugh, the way her eyes lit up when she talked about literature, how she kept pushing back against my charm until I had to be real with her.

"I don't know," I lied. "She's just not what I expected."

Jules hopped up on the fence, watching me with a smirk that was far too knowing for a high school senior. "You know what I think?"

"I'm sure you're about to tell me."

"I think she's exactly your type, but you never knew it because you've been dating the wrong girls."

I focused on brushing a particularly stubborn knot out

of the donkey's mane. "And what type would that be, Dr. Ruth?"

"Smart. Independent. Doesn't take your crap." She ticked off on her fingers. "Has her own thing going on that has nothing to do with you or football. Oh, and she clearly loves animals, which means she's not a sociopath."

"Low bar there, princess."

"You'd be surprised." She swung her legs, studying me. "So when are you seeing her again?"

"We're going to be connected at the donkey hip this week. We're figuring out what to do with this guy," I nodded toward the donkey, who had decided my shoelaces were tasty. "Tempest's grandmother gets back next week and might take him in, until the sanctuary is able to rebuild their barns."

"Cool, so family introductions already. Moving fast."

I shot her a patented shut-your-face-brat look. But fucknuts. I hadn't thought about that. I hadn't ever gotten to the meeting-someone's-family stage with any woman. "It's not like that."

"Sure." She grinned, but her expression turned more serious. "You know, it wouldn't be the worst thing if it was like that."

Something in her tone made me stop brushing, but I stared into the abyss of brown fuzz instead of at my overly perceptive little sister. "What's that supposed to mean?"

Sigh. I gave her a quick sideways look just in time to catch her shrug. She suddenly found her fingernails fascinating. "Just that... I don't know. You're always so careful not to get attached to anyone. Even more than the rest of the guys."

"I'm not—"

"You are." She cut me off. "Just because you let someone into your heart doesn't mean they're going to... hurt you."

"I don't think Tempest is going to hurt me." Because I wasn't actually letting her into my heart or whatever other mushy-gushy stuff teenage sisters dreamed up when they read too many romance novels.

"Right." She slugged me in the arm." Well, you should know that even if you do get your heart broken or something, you'd survive, you know?"

Why was Jules The Kickass being so gentle with me right now? It was totally unnerving me.

"Just like Dad survived Mom dying."

The brush stilled in my hand.

Did he?

We didn't talk about Mom often, especially not like this.

"Low blow, Jules."

"Not a blow. An observation." Her voice softened. "I just think maybe it wouldn't be the end of the world if you let someone in. Especially someone who looks at you the way she does when she thinks no one's watching."

My head snapped up. "How does she look at me?"

Jules's smile returned, smug now. "Like she's trying really hard not to look at you at all."

Before I could respond, my phone buzzed with a text from Dad.

> Dad: On my way with the food. Gryff joining. Drills at 2.

I showed Jules the text. "Dad's bringing lunch. You sticking around?"

"Nah." She hopped off the fence. "I really do need to find my purple Converse. I'm meeting friends at the library." She started toward the house, then paused. "Flynn?"

"Yeah?"

"That donkey needs a name. A real one. It's weird calling him 'the donkey' all the time."

I glanced at our four-legged friend who was now contentedly munching on the hay I'd laid out. "I've been trying to guess his name for weeks. Tempest won't tell me."

"Maybe she hasn't named him yet." Jules tilted her head, considering. "He seems like a Fernando to me."

"I already suggested that." I grinned. "Along with about fifty other names."

"Well, keep trying." She gestured between me and the donkey. "You two have a lot in common. Both stubborn as hell and in desperate need of Tempest's attention."

Christ, she knew me way too well. "Hilarious."

"I know." She blew me a kiss and disappeared inside, leaving me alone with a nameless donkey and thoughts I wasn't ready to examine too closely.

By the time Dad returned with enough sandwiches to feed his defensive line, I'd finished reinforcing the donkey's pen, patched the hole in the fence he'd somehow created overnight, and was working on a more secure gate latch.

"Looks good." Dad surveyed my handiwork, handing me a bottle of water. "Though I still expect those combine drills done this afternoon. Lots of teams are interested in the two of you this year."

I always assumed we'd somehow both get drafted to the Mustangs like every Kingman before us.

"Yes, sir." I took a long drink. "Sorry about the herbs."

He shrugged. "Plants grow back." He watched the donkey, who was now napping in a patch of sunlight. "Interesting girl, that Tempest."

I nearly choked on my water. "You talked to her for all of two minutes."

"Sometimes that's all you need." He leaned against the fence. "She reminds me of your mother."

The comparison startled me. "How?"

"April was a challenge too." A rare smile crossed his face. The one that was specifically for memories of Mom. "First time I met her, she pretended we weren't flirting our asses off."

"What happened to the love at first sight story?"

His smile widened. "I fell first, and harder. The best way to go, kid."

I absorbed this information, trying to reconcile it with the scattered memories I had of Mom. She'd died when I was six, leaving behind impressions more than concrete memories—her laugh, the smell of her perfume, the way Dad's face lit up when she entered a room.

The way he hadn't lit up again for years after she died.

"She would have liked Tempest," Dad continued. "She

always appreciated people who weren't impressed by superficial things."

"We're just friends," I said automatically.

Dad gave me a look that said he wasn't buying it. "If you say so." He pushed off from the fence. "Gryff's inside. Says he's got news about the combine."

My twin was sprawled across the couch in the family room, demolishing a sandwich the size of his head.

"About time," he said when I walked in. "I've been waiting forever."

"It's been fifteen minutes, drama queen." I grabbed my own sandwich from the kitchen counter. "What's this news?"

Gryff's face split into a wide grin. "The LA Bandits are sending their head scout specifically to watch us."

My stomach did a weird flip. The Bandits were a top-tier team, three-time Bowl champions. Getting on their radar was huge.

"Both of us?" I asked.

"Yep. They're looking to rebuild their defense, and want to protect that slow-ass quarterback they won't let go of." He paused dramatically. "Imagine both of us getting drafted to the same team. We'd never have to split up."

We'd played side by side our entire lives. The thought of continuing that in the pros had always been our dream, but it also seemed impossible given how the draft worked.

"That would be..." I searched for the right word. "Badass."

"Right? And it's LA. Sun, surf, celebrities." Gryff wiggled his eyebrows.

I nodded, trying to match his enthusiasm. LA would be incredible for our careers. The coaching staff was legendary, the facilities top-notch. And yet...

"What about Denver?" I asked. "Any word from the Mustangs?"

"Sure, of course they're interested too. We're legacies, man. But there is no guarantee. More teams recruiting us, the better." He studied me. "I thought you'd be more excited."

I was. Or I should be. But suddenly there was a new variable in the equation I hadn't considered before.

"I am excited," I assured him.

"But?" Gryff's eyes narrowed. "This doesn't have anything to do with a certain Shakespeare-loving donkey owner, who lives here in Denver, does it?"

"No," I said, too quickly.

My twin's expression turned smug. "Holy shit. It does." He leaned forward. "Flynn Kingman, are you actually considering a girl in your future plans? A girl who's not a two-week fling?"

"I'm considering my career," I corrected, even as something twisted in my chest. "The Bandits or the Mustangs, or wherever we get drafted, would be amazing. And even better if we get to play together in the pros."

Gryff watched me for a long moment, then nodded slowly. "Again...but?"

"No buts." I took a bite of my sandwich, chewing longer than necessary. "Tell me more about what the scout said."

He let me change the subject, launching into details about combine expectations and draft projections. I listened and nodded in all the right places, but part of my mind kept drifting to Tempest, to mud fights and coffee on the deck and the way her laugh made everything else fade away.

LA was a long way from Denver. A long way from her.

"Earth to Flynn." Gryff snapped his fingers in front of my face. "You in there?"

"Yeah, sorry." I shook my head to clear it. "Just thinking about the drills Dad wants us to run."

"Sure you were." He smirked. "Anyway, they want to fly us out to LA after the combine to see the facilities. All expenses paid. How cool is that?"

"Very cool," I agreed, and tried to mean it.

Because it was cool. It was everything we'd worked for. Everything I'd dreamed of since I was old enough to hold a football. Of course I knew we might not get to stay in Denver forever. This was home, but I was ready to go wherever offered me the best deal and let me play a good game.

And I'd lied about no more "buts. It suddenly felt like I might be leaving something behind that I hadn't counted on.

The donkey's bray from the backyard seemed to answer my unspoken question.

Some things were harder to walk away from than I'd ever expected.

By the time we finished the combine drills, sweat had soaked through my second t-shirt of the day, and my muscles burned in that satisfying way that meant progress. Dad had been merciless, running us through cone drills, ladder work, and explosive starts until even

Gryff, who never complained about training, was groaning.

"Good work," Dad said, checking his stopwatch. "Your three-cone time is improving."

"Thanks." I gulped from my water bottle, willing my heart rate to slow. "Still need to shave off another two-tenths."

"You'll get there." He clapped me on the shoulder. "Get cleaned up. I've got something to do at the university tonight."

As he headed inside, Gryff collapsed dramatically onto the grass. "I think my legs have officially detached from my body."

"Lightweight," I teased, though my own quads were trembling.

"Worth it though." He grinned up at me. "You're doing it again."

"What?"

"That thing where you're physically here but mentally you're somewhere else." He pushed himself up to sitting. "Or with someone else."

I ignored him, pulling out my phone instead. No missed calls, but a text notification caught my eye.

> Tempest: Hope your dad didn't murder you over his herbs becoming a donkey buffet.

A smile tugged at my lips before I could stop it.

"See? That right there." Gryff pointed accusingly. "Your whole face changes when she texts you."

"Shut up." I turned away, already typing a response.

> Me: I'm alive, barely. Dad actually thought it was funny. Says the herbs needed pruning anyway.

I hesitated, then added one more thought.

> Me: Sorry my baby sister harassed the hell out of you.

Her response came almost immediately.

> Tempest: No apology necessary. She told me about her romance novel collection while we waited. Your sister is... interesting.

I laughed, which earned me another knowing look from Gryff.

> Me: That's putting it mildly. She likes you though.

> Tempest: How can you tell?

> Me: She grilled me about you after you left. That's practically a declaration of love in Jules-speak.

Gryff hauled himself to his feet. "I'm gonna shower. Tell Tempest I said hi."

I flipped him off without looking up from my phone, where another message had appeared.

> Tempest: Do you think your dad will be okay for a few more days? Abuela gets back this weekend, and I'm *almost* sure I can talk her into donkey duty until the sanctuary can take him back.

> Me: He's actually warming up to the little troublemaker. Found him sneaking apple slices to him earlier.

> Tempest: No way.

> Me: Way. But don't tell him I told you.

I hesitated, then pulled my head out of my ass and typed back.

> Me: Tomorrow after Shakespeare? For more donkey-sitting purposes, of course.

The three dots appeared, disappeared, then reappeared. My heart did something stupid while I waited.

> Tempest: It's a date.

Then immediately her next message appeared.

> Tempest: I mean, not a date date. A donkey-sitting arrangement. You know what I mean.

I grinned at her flustered backtracking.

> Me: I know what you mean. But just so you know, if you ever want to make it a date date, I wouldn't object.

This time the three dots appeared and disappeared several times. Finally she replied one more time.

> Tempest: See you tomorrow, Kingman.

Not quite a yes, but definitely not a no. Progress.

I headed inside to shower, unable to wipe the smile off my face. The LA Bandits, the combine, even the mud on my shoes, none of it seemed to matter as much as seeing Tempest tomorrow.

The longer I let this go on, the more screwed I was. And I didn't even care. These past two months were way more fun than two weeks I'd ever had with any other woman.

A PRAYER TO SAINT WHOSIEWHATSIE

TEMPEST

I spent thirty minutes that morning telling myself that my outfit choice had nothing to do with Flynn Kingman. The blue sweater that hugged my curves instead of hiding them was practical for winter in Colorado. The jeans that actually fit my ass instead of trying to disguise it were just comfortable. And if I'd spent an extra few minutes on my hair, letting it fall in soft curls instead of my usual messy bun, it was only because I was tired of Parker's comments about me looking like "academic despair personified."

None of it had anything to do with Flynn's text from last night that I'd reread approximately fifty times before falling asleep.

If you ever want to make it a date date, I wouldn't object.

"You're staring at your phone again," Parker observed, leaning against our doorframe. "Just text him back and put yourself out of your misery."

"I already did," I muttered, shoving the phone in my bag. "We have Shakespeare in twenty minutes."

"And you just happened to dress like that for Shakespeare?" She grinned. "Not for the hot football player who sits behind you and has been flirting and trying to get your attention hard core for weeks?"

"I dress for myself," I insisted, though my cheeks burned. "Besides, we're going to take care of the donkey after class. These are practical clothes for donkey-sitting."

"Right. The low-cut sweater that shows off the girls at their best is essential for optimal donkey care." She rolled her eyes. "Just admit you like him."

"I'm late," I said, brushing past her.

Her laughter followed me down the hallway. "You can run from me, but you can't hide from your feelings."

I arrived at Shakespeare class five minutes early, sliding into my usual seat and pulling out my color-coded notes. I was outlining my thesis for our midterm paper when the room's energy shifted, that subtle change in atmosphere that always accompanied the Kingman twins' entrance.

"Morning, my queen." Flynn's voice was low as he slid into the seat behind me, the faint scent of his cologne making my pulse jump. "Sleep well?"

I turned slightly, keeping my expression neutral. "Well enough. You?"

"Dreamed about a stubborn English major and her escape artist donkey." His blue eyes crinkled at the corners as he smiled. "So, better than usual."

Before I could respond, his twin dropped into the chair beside him, looking between us with obvious amusement.

"Don't mind me," Gryff said. "Just pretend I'm not witnessing this flirtation attempt disaster."

Flynn kicked his brother's chair. "Don't you have someone else to annoy?"

"And miss this entertainment? Not a chance." Gryff leaned forward, and flicked his eyes between us, like he was expectantly waiting for us to perform for him. He grinned, the expression so similar to Flynn's yet, somehow totally different. I would always be able to tell the difference between them.

Flynn cleared his throat and scowled at his brother. "Don't you have notes to review or something?"

"Nope." Gryff settled back in his chair. "All caught up. Free to observe your painfully obvious crush in action."

Flynn's default mode was flirt. Didn't mean he had a crush on me. No one ever did. I wasn't the type of girl guys crushed on. And I needed to remember that. Especially around someone like Flynn. Or actually, just around him.

Heat crept up my neck and I busied myself with my notes, but not before catching Flynn's glare and was...was that a pink slash of a blush across his cheeks? It was. There was something oddly comforting about seeing the golden boy of DSU as flustered as I felt.

Dr. Whitmore swept into the room, saving us from further awkwardness. "Today we're continuing our discussion on disguises and mistaken identity. Shakespeare was fascinated by the concept of hidden selves and the gap between who we present ourselves as and who we truly are."

I sank lower in my seat, hyperaware of the notebook with my notes on the first draft of the new book.

No one seemed to notice, which was exactly how I liked it. The professor continued. "I want you to discuss with your neighbor, what disguises do we wear in our daily lives in the twenty-first century and which characters from Shakespeare have similarities to your discoveries?"

Flynn leaned forward, his breath warm against my ear. "I know what disguise you wear."

My heart stopped. "What are you talking about?"

"This serious academic facade," he murmured, his voice low enough that only I could hear. "But I've seen you laugh in the mud with a donkey. I know there's more to Tempest Navarro than perfect notes and color-coded pens."

Relief flooded through me. "That's not a disguise. That's just... a different side of me."

"A side I'd like to see more of." His fingers brushed my shoulder briefly, the touch sending sparks down my spine. "Your move..." he winked at me, "I mean turn."

See? Flirt mode on twenty-four-seven. His brother was wrong.

For once, I was grateful when Dr. Whitmore called the class back to attention, because I had no idea how to respond to the raw honesty in Flynn's voice.

"I think there're a lot of people in our modern day that hide behind a mask. Most people don't want their true, authentic selves to be seen. Because then they'd also see our flaws and fears."

"I'm an open book, sweetheart."

"No you aren't. You wear cocky like it's armor." I motioned to his chest as if he was actually wearing a chest plate. "Flirting is your shield and sword."

I expected him to retort with some kind of sexual innuendo about his sword. But he looked right into my eyes and said, "And what if I'm not flirting with you? What if every single thing I say and do, is because I genuinely like you and want to get to know you?"

Holy patron saint of women losing their hearts to sexy, sincere football players. Whoever that saint may be, protect me and my heart from this onslaught.

"Donkey duty calls," Flynn said as we filed out of the classroom. "My car or yours?"

"Mine," I said automatically. I needed home turf, and to be in control here. Because everything about Flynn was making me feel so chaotic. "I have some treats for him."

Gryff snorted. "Treats for a donkey. You two are something else."

"Everyone needs a treat sometimes," Flynn replied to Gryff, but he was looking at me. Where was Saint Whosiewhatsie when you needed her?

I gulped and managed to squeak out, "Especially poor homeless donkeys with no one to love them."

"Uh-huh. Keep telling yourself this is all about the donkey." Gryff clapped his brother on the shoulder. "Have fun, kids. Don't do anything I wouldn't do."

"That leaves everything on the table," Flynn called after him, then turned back to me with a grin. "Shall we?"

Everything? Eek.

Twenty minutes later, we pulled into the Kingmans' driveway.

"Dad's at the university until this afternoon and Jules is at school," Flynn said as he unlocked the front door. "We've got the place to ourselves."

The words hung in the air between us, loaded with possibility. Like... everything.

"Great," I managed, adjusting my backpack. "More quality donkey time."

He led me through the house toward the back deck. Without the chaos of yesterday, I could appreciate details I'd missed. Family photos lining the hallway, a wall of achievement certificates, a bookshelf stuffed with an eclectic mix of titles.

"Wait." I stopped short, examining the bookshelf more closely. "Is that—"

Flynn followed my gaze and grinned. "Yeah, Jules has been collecting them since she was, like, twelve. Dad says we've spent enough on romance novels to fund a small country."

My heart stuttered as I spotted several familiar spines. Like three of my own books. I forced myself to keep moving, throat suddenly dry.

"Your sister has a lot of books," I said, hoping my voice sounded normal.

Flynn shrugged. "She claims they're feminist literature disguised as smut. Her words, not mine."

"She's not wrong." The words slipped out before I could stop them.

He raised an eyebrow and there was an all too knowing gleam in his eye. "Read a few yourself?"

"I'm a literature major, so it's mandatory that I'm well read," I hedged, grateful when we reached the back door and the conversation naturally shifted.

The donkey greeted us with an enthusiastic bray, trotting to the fence when he spotted me. His little wings from the viral video days were long gone, but someone, Jules, probably, had tied a jaunty bandanna around his neck.

"See?" Flynn crossed his arms, watching the donkey prance around. "Total favoritism. I spend all morning before class mucking out his pen, and he acts like I don't exist the moment you show up."

"He just knows who provides the best treats." I pulled a carrot from my bag, breaking it into bite-sized chunks.

"So that's your secret." Flynn's shoulder brushed against mine as he leaned closer, the contact sending warmth through my body despite the February chill. "Here I've been trying to win him over with my charm, and all I needed was produce."

"Charm only gets you so far, Kingman." I fed a chunk to the eager donkey, acutely aware of Flynn watching me instead of the animal. "Sometimes substance matters more."

His eyes met mine, suddenly serious. "Substance is my middle name."

We worked side by side, refilling the buckets with water and snacks for later. The donkey followed us like an oversized puppy, occasionally bumping against my leg for attention. Flynn's proximity, the way his hand would brush mine when passing tools, how his eyes lingered when he thought I wasn't looking, had my skin tingling.

"Have you talked to your grandmother about taking

him?" Flynn asked, changing the subject as he latched the pen gate.

"She gets in on Saturday. I showed her pictures when we Facetimed a couple of days ago, and she already loves him." I smiled, remembering Abuela's rapid-fire excitement over video chat. "She's abducted our welcome home party and is making it a party for him."

"A party? For a donkey?"

"Welcome to the Navarro family. We celebrate everything. When my sister Rosalind got her braces off, Abuela hired a mariachi band." I shrugged at Flynn's incredulous look. "She's... theatrical."

He leaned against the fence post. "So am I invited to this donkey party?"

The question caught me off guard. "You want to come?"

"Well, yeah." He looked almost shy. And I definitely did not find that the cutest thing I'd ever seen in my life. "I've gotten invested in this little guy's welfare. Plus, it seems only fair that I meet your family since you've met mine."

"My family is a lot," I warned. "Four sisters, my grandmother who acts like she's eternally on a telenovela, and probably a dozen other aunts, uncles, and cousins who'll show up. It'll be chaos."

"I have seven siblings," he reminded me with a grin. "Chaos is my comfort zone."

I pictured Flynn at Abuela's welcome home party, surrounded by my family, subjected to a literal Spanish Inquisition from my sisters, Abuela, and a smattering of tios and tias. At least Mamá wouldn't be there to judge him.

Judge Judy had nothing on Dr. Luz Navarro.

"Fine," I conceded. "But don't say I didn't warn you."

"I'll consider myself warned." His smile widened. "So, since we've finished donkey duties in record time, want to grab lunch? There's a great sandwich place down the street."

My heart did that stupid fluttery thing again. "Is this that date date thing?"

"Depends." His eyes held mine, suddenly intense. "Is this you saying yes?"

I opened my mouth to respond, but my words caught in my throat as he took a step closer, deliberately closing the space between us.

"Tempest," he said softly, my name almost a question on his lips.

Time slowed, just like in the movies, and he reached up, gently tucking a curl behind my ear, his fingers lingering against my cheek. His touch sent electricity racing from my face, down to my heart, and then straight between my legs. Ridiculously, I found myself leaning into his palm, wanting this connection, wanting it to be real.

"I've been wanting to do this since you calmed a rogue donkey without even looking up from your book," he murmured, his eyes dropping to my lips. "Will you let me?"

He was going to kiss me. Flynn Kingman was going to kiss me, and despite all my walls and rules and reasons to keep him at a distance, I wanted him to. In less than a whisper, I forced out a "yes.

His head dipped lower, and I could feel his breath

warm against my lips, the faintest tickle of his beard so close to my face, my eyes fluttering closed...

A sudden, sharp tug yanked me backward, nearly sending me stumbling. The donkey had grabbed the hem of my sweater between his teeth and was pulling with surprising strength, braying indignantly.

"Hey," Flynn steadied me with his hands on my waist. "Let go, you little terror."

The donkey refused, tugging harder until I was forced to take a step away to avoid being dragged across the yard.

"I think someone's jealous," Flynn laughed, though there was frustration beneath his amusement.

Donkey gave a little kick and a hee-haw directed at Flynn, then trotted away triumphantly, looking entirely too pleased with himself.

"He's never done that before," I said, breathless from more than just the surprise. "I think he might actually be jealous."

Flynn's hands went back to my waist, his thumbs tracing small circles that made it hard to think. "Can't say I blame him. I don't want to share you with anyone else either."

The intensity in his gaze made my knees weak. The moment stretched between us, charged with possibility.

"Flynn—" I started, not even sure what I was going to say.

A series of loud, demanding brays broke the moment for a second time. We both turned to see him pawing at the ground, clearly distressed about something.

I walked over to see if there was something actually

wrong with him. Donkey positioned himself between me and Flynn, glaring at him with what could only be described as donkey disapproval.

"Unbelievable," Flynn muttered. "Cockblocked by a donkey. What do you even call that? Donkblocked?"

Heat rushed to my face at his blunt assessment. "Flynn."

"What? It's true." He shook his head, smiling despite his obvious frustration. "This guy is definitely jealous."

The donkey snorted, apparently satisfied now that he had reclaimed my attention. If I didn't know better, I'd think Puck had enchanted my little donkey friend to act up just now. Which, honestly, I needed the respite. I felt more like a drunken midsummer's night reveler than anything else.

And I didn't know how to do this. Any of it.

If anyone could talk me through how the hell to act around guys, it was my sorority sisters. I needed that talk sooner rather than later. Definitely before any kind of date, or any sort of kissing. Even if I did want to know if his beard would feel scratchy or soft on my skin. Would I get beard burn? "I'm gonna take a rain check on that lunch. I've got some, umm, sorority stuff to take care of."

He studied me for a moment, then stepped aside and motioned me toward the gate that led out of the yard. Flynn opened it, carefully blocking the donkey's line of sight. Before I could react, he pressed a quick, soft kiss to my forehead.

"Just so we're clear," he murmured against my ear, "I'm not giving up that easily. Not even for a jealous donkey."

The warmth of his breath sent shivers down my spine, and I found myself leaning toward him again.

"And just so we're clear," I whispered back, surprising myself with my boldness, "I might not want you to give up."

Holy. Shit. I couldn't believe I just said that out loud.

His smile was brighter than the late February sun overhead, and for a moment, I forgot about all the reasons this was a bad idea. My secret career, his future in the League, our completely different worlds.

The fact that I'd never in my life had a boy, or a guy, or...a man pay this kind of attention to me, ever, had me more than flustered. I didn't know how to feel or what to think.

The fact that I'd never been kissed.

I drove home, my skin still tingling from that little peck on the forehead. Something fundamental had shifted between us. A line had been crossed, even without the kiss the donkey had so effectively prevented.

And despite all my careful plans and compartmentalized life, I wasn't sure I wanted to step back to the other side.

"He almost kissed you?" Parker shrieked when I recounted the story to her. "And then the donkey interrupted? And then he kissed you but on the forehead? That's some romance-novel-level drama right there."

"It wasn't that dramatic," I protested, though my racing heart disagreed. "And it was just a moment."

"A moment that involved Flynn Kingman, campus heartbreaker, looking at you like you hung the moon." She flopped back on her bed. "Face it, Tempest. You're the heroine of your own romance novel now."

Was I? You'd think I'd know how to act and what was supposed to come next if that was the case.

My agent chose that moment to light up my secret phone again.

> Gloria Horne: FlixNChill execs confirmed for March 15-17 in LA. Need you to confirm ASAP.

Spring break. Right when I could plausibly get away without raising suspicion.

Right when things with Flynn were getting complicated. Not like I thought he and I were going to spend spring break together or something.

I stared at the text, feeling the weight of my separate lives pressing in. The practical, serious student who made her mother proud. The secret romance author on the verge of her big break. And now, apparently, the girl who caught Flynn Kingman's interest despite all odds.

Something had to give. I just wasn't sure what, or who, I was willing to sacrifice.

And for the first time in as long as I could remember, I didn't want to give up any part of me. I didn't want to hide, I didn't want to have a mask. Not with him anyway.

The rest of the world was another story.

THE STARS SMILE DOWN

FLYNN

"Blue or green?" Jules held up two button-down shirts, her critical gaze sweeping over me as I sat on my bed scrolling through Tempest's latest texts.

> Tempest: Abuela just landed. She's already asking about "el chico guapo con el burro." Fairly sure that means you.

I smiled at my phone, ignoring Jules until she snapped her fingers in front of my face.

"Earth to lover boy. This is important. First impressions with abuelitas are make-or-break."

"Since when are you an expert on Mexican grandmothers?" I grabbed the green shirt from her hand. "And why are you so invested in my wardrobe?"

"Since I dated Miguel from the soccer team." She snatched the shirt back. "His abuela is the family gatekeeper. One wrong move and you're dead to them." She thrust the blue shirt at me instead. "This one with the dark jeans. It makes your eyes pop without being too try-hard."

I took the shirt, surprised by her certainty. "Does Dad know you're dating this Miguel? Or at all?"

"No, and you're not going to tell him or I'll make you wish peeing in your Cheerios is the worst thing I ever did to you. Got it?"

Hell hath no fury like a sister who's been tattled on. I raised my hands in surrender.

"Trust me." She flopped onto my bed, watching as I changed shirts. "So I think your Shakespeare tutor is secretly writing a romance novel. She was making some notes on her phone when you were doing donkey things."

"Don't be weird. Tempest is an English major. I'm sure it's just something for a class," I said, though some things clicked into place. Tempest's secretiveness about her supposed notes, her nervousness when I mentioned romance novels, the way she'd reacted when she saw books on our shelf.

"Nope. It's definitely a book." Jules sat up, eyes gleaming. "I'm going to figure out if she's published anything. I have my ways."

"You keep your Google Fu to yourself," I said firmly. "If she's writing something, it's her business to share or not."

Jules smiled smugly. "Look at you, being all protective. You really do like this girl."

I couldn't deny it, so I changed the subject. "Do you know if Dad talked the boys into letting us use the jet to fly to Indiana?"

"I did, and we leave at nine sharp." Dad's voice made us

both jump. He stood in the doorway, arms crossed but expression softer than I expected. "Blue was the right choice, Jules."

"Told you," she gloated.

Dad stepped into the room, examining me with the same critical eye he used to evaluate new recruits. "Meeting her family tonight?"

"Yes, sir." I finished buttoning the shirt. "Her grandmother just got back from Mexico. It's a welcome home party."

His expression grew serious. "Look, Flynn, tomorrow starts combine week. The scouts will be watching your every move. It's important."

Here it came, the lecture about priorities, about focus, about not letting anything distract from football.

Instead, Dad surprised me. "But this—" he gestured vaguely to my outfit, "—this matters too. When I met your mother, I nearly missed a playoff game because her car broke down and she needed a ride."

I stared at him. Dad talked about Mom, but he had his standard set of stories, and reminders. I've never heard this one. "You did?"

"Coach benched me for the first quarter." His smile was tinged with memory. "Worth it, though. April wore this blue dress that matched her eyes, and I remember thinking I'd sit out the whole damn season for another hour with her."

I saw the way he blinked a few extra times and heard the gruffness in his voice talking about Mom. He would never get over her.

If I got too close to Tempest, let her in too far, I wouldn't either.

He cleared his throat. "Point is, football's important. The combine's important. But it's not everything."

"So..." I said slowly, "you're saying I should go to this party? Even with traveling and combine check-in tomorrow?"

"I'm saying don't miss the things that matter because you're too focused on the future." He stood, clapping me on the shoulder, and left Jules and I just staring at each other.

With the two-week rule, I'd managed to avoid the meet-the-family milestone. But as I pulled up with baby donkey to the address Tempest had texted, a sprawling ranch-style house on the outskirts of Golden, my palms were actually sweating.

Music and laughter spilled from the house. Cars lined the driveway and street, confirming that "small family gathering" meant something similar to the Navarros as it did to the Kingmans. Nothing small about it. Which was exactly the way I liked it.

I parked and Tempest emerged from the house. Something in my chest tightened. She wore a green dress that made her dark eyes shine, but her smile didn't quite reach those eyes. She looked beautiful, but guarded, like she was bracing herself.

"You're here," She hurried over, her relief evident as she peered into the trailer. "And our favorite troublemaker made it okay?"

"He's raring to go." I smiled, drinking in the sight of

her. Her nervous flutter made me want to wrap her in my arms and help still whatever had her on edge.

Her shoulders relaxed slightly. "Abuela's more excited to meet him than you, no offense."

"None taken. I know my place in the hierarchy."

A curvaceous woman with dramatically styled silver hair, and I swear to god, wearing one of those golden age of movies feather-lined filmy robe things, emerged from the house, followed by what had to be a dozen family members of various ages. She wore enough jewelry to open a small boutique, and her commanding presence made it immediately clear who was in charge.

"¡Ay, Dios mío! ¡Ahí está! ¡Mi burrito precioso!" She practically floated down the steps, hands clasped in delight.

"That's my abuela, Estrella Ramirez," Tempest whispered, straightening her posture as if preparing for inspection. "Also known as AbuelaNovela."

Abuela Estrella reached the trailer and peered inside, her expression one of pure joy. "Qué lindo. Tempest, mi amor, es perfecto. Exactamente como dijiste." She turned to me, eyes twinkling. "And you must be the footballer who rescued him."

"That's me." I extended the flowers I'd brought to her, which she took with a twinkle in her eye.

"Very nice arms. May I?" She reached out and squeezed one of my biceps. "Tempest, no me dijiste que era tan guapo."

I caught enough Spanish to understand I was being assessed, and that Tempest had apparently neglected to mention I was "tan guapo"— so handsome.

"Gracias, Señora Ramirez," I replied, offering a slight bow. "Es un placer conocerla."

Abuela's eyebrows shot up, and Tempest's mouth actually dropped open.

"Habla Español." Abuela clapped her hands in delight. "Tempest, why didn't you tell me he speaks Spanish?"

"I didn't know," Tempest said, looking at me with new eyes.

I shrugged. "Just the basics. Been taking it since high school. This is Denver, lots of Spanish speakers, seemed dumb not to learn."

"Humilde y inteligente," Abuela nodded approvingly, and handed the flowers to Tempest. "I like him already."

With everyone's help, we lowered the trailer ramp and guided the donkey down. Baby donkey, perhaps sensing he was the center of attention, stepped fully down the ramp, lifting his head with the dignity of visiting royalty. The crowd let out a collective "aww" as he surveyed his new domain.

What happened next was like watching love at first sight in an old movie. Abuela stepped forward, her hand extended palm out exactly the way Tempest had done the first time she stopped the runaway donkey. The animal looked at her, ears perked forward, then slowly approached, pressing his soft muzzle into her palm.

"Mi corazón," she whispered, her free hand coming up to stroke between his ears. "Mi alma pequeñita."

The donkey leaned into her touch like they'd known each other forever, making soft snuffling sounds of contentment.

Abuela's eyes misted over as she wrapped her arms

around his neck. "Oh, mi precioso. My sweet, sweet boy." She looked up at Tempest. "You were right. He is special. Wait until Leo meets him."

"I told you," Tempest said softly, watching the two of them with obvious affection.

Finally, Abuela turned to address the gathering with the flair of a ringleader announcing the main act. "Everyone, meet the newest member of our family. My beautiful boy. Mi Burrito Petito!"

The crowd cheered as the newly christened Burrito Petito tossed his head, acknowledging his new name.

"Burrito," Tempest repeated, a slow smile spreading across her face. "Why didn't we think of that?"

"Wait. Are you telling me all that time I was guessing epic donkey names, you hadn't given the poor slob an actual name?"

Tempest shrugged and gave a small chuckle, watching as family members began introducing themselves to Burrito Petito as if he were a visiting dignitary. "I couldn't decide on anything."

"Querida, my Tempest." A man who looked to be a similar age as my dad, with the same eyes as Tempest, waltzed out from the backyard, took the flowers, and wrapped Tempest into a huge, enveloping hug. "Only you could make your abuela even more happy than me."

"Tío Pedro," he introduced himself with a warm handshake. In a lowered voice, he stage-whispered like he was telling me a secret that wasn't a secret at all, "I'm the cool uncle and Tempest's biggest fan."

"Flynn Kingman." I returned the handshake.

His eyes sparked with the same mischief I often saw in Tempest's. "Querida, no me dijiste que era tan guapo."

"Tio," Tempest closed her eyes and pressed her hand over her face. "Flynn speaks enough Spanish to know what you just said."

"Well, it's not like he doesn't know he's good-looking." He winked at me. "Now come, I want to hear all about everything you've been working on, and see if your gentleman suitor can keep up with you."

"Tio." Her hand headed toward her face again, but I grabbed it, and pressed a kiss to the back.

"Oh, I can keep up. Let's see what you've got."

What the Navarros had was... a lot. I met Tempest's older sisters, Catalina and Rosalind, first. If I didn't have three very intense older brothers and an even more intense little sister of my own, I wouldn't have stood a chance against them.

"So, Flynn, tell us about your football prospects." Catalina, Tempest's eldest sister, directed the conversation as we were seated around one of the enormous tables in the backyard. Everything about her was polished and precise, from her immaculate white suit to her perfectly articulated questions.

I answered politely, watching Tempest from the corner of my eye. She physically shrunk, hunching her shoulders and slumping down when her sisters took center stage, and her earlier animation faded.

"Tempest never brings boys home," Ophelia said, coming over and ladling more food onto my plate. "Especially not football players."

"This is why," Tempest muttered, but only I seemed to hear her.

"Perhaps you're just scaring them off with the way you dress," Catalina chimed in. "All those baggy sweaters and clunky shoes. Please come to boutique and let me style you."

I noticed Tempest's grip tighten around her fork.

"I think she looks perfect exactly how she is," I said firmly, meeting Catalina's eyes.

A surprised silence fell over the table.

"Well, of course," Catalina recovered smoothly. "We all just think she could enhance her natural beauty with a little effort. Like Ophelia with her cooking, or how Freddie has her Olympic prospects, and Rosalind with her deviously strategic mind. That one is going to be president someday."

Tío Pedro interjected, winking at Tempest. "The real question is whether Flynn here has read anything more challenging than a playbook."

Tempest's mouth quirked up slightly at that. She liked Uncle Pedro. I did too. More than her sisters. I knew family ribbing, and this judgment of Tempest wasn't that.

I turned to address him directly, "Tempest and I met in Shakespeare class. She's been tutoring me, though to be honest, I never needed it. I just like hearing her talk about books."

"A football player who reads Shakespeare?" Rosalind peered at me, looking skeptical. "I find that hard to believe."

"'The fool doth think he is wise, but the wise man knows himself to be a fool,'" I quoted with a slight smile.

"*As You Like It*, Act 5." Everything Jules had ever done to prepare me to deal with sisters was coming in handy today.

Tempest's head snapped up, her eyes wide. She glanced around, clearly checking how everyone else reacted to my challenge.

God dammit. She definitely wasn't used to anyone standing up for her and it had me wanting to throw her over my shoulder and haul her straight out of this party. Family were supposed to be the ones that supported you, not tore you down.

"'We know what we are, but know not what we may be,'" Tío Pedro responded, raising his glass to me.

"*Hamlet*," I acknowledged with a nod. Okay, she had one person on her side. I suspected her abuela was too, but she was holding court at another table. We should have sat with her.

"Well," Rosalind's surprised timbre said it all. "It seems our Tempest has found someone who speaks her quirky little language."

I turned back to Tempest, ready to ask if she was ready to go. I didn't know where, but I'd had enough of this kind of celebration.

"If only she'd find someone who could help her go on a diet," a slightly older woman, probably one her aunts, stage-whispered from down the table. "That dress is at least a size too small."

Tempest's face flushed, her eyes dropping to her plate.

Something incredibly hot and protective surged through me.

"Actually," I said, loud enough for everyone to hear, "I

think Tempest's body is both perfect and sexy as hell." I turned to look directly at her. "I'm hot for her because of her curves, not despite them."

The table fell silent again, but this time Tempest looked up, her eyes meeting mine with a mixture of surprise and gratitude that made my chest tight.

"Bien dicho," Abuela Estrella declared from the other table, her eyes homed in on me. "I knew I liked you, young man. More of my family needs to embrace that energy."

At least half the table had the sense to look abashed by their matriarch's chastisement.

Ophelia stood and grabbed one of the plates stacked with grilled meats. "Who wants more food?"

The conversation shifted back to the party, everyone avoiding eye contact with me and Tempest. She leaned closer to me.

"Thank you," she whispered. "You didn't have to say that."

"I meant every word," I told her quietly.

Something flashed in her eyes, vulnerability, maybe, before she looked away. "They're just used to me being the odd one out. I always have been."

"Their loss," I said simply. "Because from where I'm sitting, you're the most interesting person here. Except maybe AbuelaNovela. Where did she get that outfit?"

Her smile then was small but real, and I realized I'd do just about anything to see it again.

"Why don't you go check on Burrito while I help clear the dishes." She got up, taking my plate and nodding toward the backyard where Burrito Petito was holding court in his new enclosure.

"I can do dishes."

She scrunched up her face and shook her head. "And be subjected to more of my family? I don't think so."

Tío Pedro appeared beside me and jerked his head, indicating for me to follow him. I went, but was going to keep my eye on Tempest.

"She's different with you," he said without preamble.

"Different how?"

"More herself." He studied me thoughtfully. "Tempest has spent her whole life trying to fit into spaces that weren't built for her. Driven enough for her mother, academic enough for her father, fashionable enough for Catalina, strategic enough for Rosalind, social enough for Ophelia, and athletic enough for Freddie." He shook his head. "It's exhausting being everyone's afterthought."

The way Tempest had shrunk under her family's attention yet bloomed under Abuela's and Pedro's spoke volumes. "She's not an afterthought to me."

"I can see that." His eyes were kind but assessing. "She has gifts none of them understand. Things she keeps hidden because they've never been valued."

"Her writing?" The question slipped out before I could stop it.

Pedro's eyebrows rose. "She told you about that?"

"No. But I've noticed." And damn if Jules hadn't been right. "She's talented, isn't she?"

"Extraordinarily." Pride colored his voice. "But don't tell her I mentioned anything. She thinks it's our secret, though I am sure AbuelaNovela knows too. Mamá knows everything."

"I won't say a word," I promised, looking back toward the house where I could see Tempest helping clear the table, carefully maintaining that good girl persona she kept wearing like a mask. "I'd love if she'd let me in."

Pedro clapped me on the shoulder. "Be that safe space for her like you were today, and she just might."

The party was winding down when I finally caught Tempest alone on the back porch, away from the chaos of her family. Burrito Petito had been settled for the night, and most of the relatives had dispersed to various parts of the house.

"Sorry about all that at dinner," she said, leaning against the railing. "My family can be a lot."

I put myself between her and the house, blocking anyone else's view of us. Then I put my hands on the railing on either side of her, and boxed out the rest of the world.

She looked up at me, a flush spreading across her cheeks. "Flynn, I'm not—" she started, then stopped, biting her lip. "I'm not good at this. I'm not used to letting anyone see...me."

I focused on her, so she knew she had all of my attention. "I very much want to see all of you, Tempest."

Her eyebrows rose questioningly, definitely doubting everything I said. Probably everything I'd ever said. My girl wasn't just shy, or stand-offish. She had some deep wounds and it was going to take more than charm to win her over.

I had my work cut out for me. And just like I'd told her Tio Pedro, I was up for it.

Because despite all the rules and my determination not to catch feelings, I was falling in love with Tempest Navarro. Right here, right now, I wanted her to know that. But she never believed anything I said. So instead, I showed her.

I lowered my head and brushed a soft kiss over her lips. "Tell me to stop if you don't want this, Tempest."

Her breath stuttered, but she whispered, "Don't stop."

BETTER THAN IN THE BOOKS

TEMPEST

"*D*on't stop," I whispered. Though I wasn't sure I even heard it myself. My heart thundered in my chest so hard, that I was sure a tornado was brewing inside of me.

Flynn's eyes went all dark, and I watched his gaze drop to my lips again. The entire world went into slo-mo with every centimeter he leaned in closer. One hand came up to cup my cheek, and where I expected sparks, I got a soft warmth like a fuzzy blanket, cup of tea, and a cozy fire. But when his lips finally met mine, his beard brushing against my skin, that heat turned to pure lava. His mouth was impossibly soft yet firm, tentative at first and then more certain.

My first kiss.

I'd written dozens of them. First kisses that sparked fireworks, that melted heroines' knees, that changed lives in an instant. But nothing I'd ever written came close to this reality. The warmth of Flynn's palm against my face. The faint scent of his cologne mixed with a scent all his own. The gentle pressure of his mouth against mine, coaxing me to open for him, rather than demanding. And that beard that made every cell in my body tingle when it rubbed against my skin.

I didn't even know I was a beard girl. Until now.

I was frozen for a heartbeat, overwhelmed by sensations. My brain was fritzing and then my body told it to fuck off and pure instinct took over. My hands found his chest, feeling the solid strength beneath his blue shirt as I leaned into him. His other arm wrapped around my waist, pulling me closer, and a small sound, an actual whimpered little moan, escaped.

Flynn growled or purred or groaned, I didn't even know except that the sound went skittering from my chest, down to my belly and pooled right between my legs. He deepened the kiss, slipping his tongue past my lips, and I followed his lead, letting him show me how our mouths fit together.

Every romance novel I'd ever read or written had attempted to describe this feeling, this dizzy, breathless, alive feeling, but the words I'd so readily relied on my whole life were now completely inadequate.

He broke the kiss way before I was ready, nibbling at the corner of my mouth, teasing me with soft brushes of his lips across mine and his whiskers across my cheek. I kept my eyes closed for a moment, afraid that opening them would somehow break the spell.

"Tempest," Flynn murmured, his voice lower than I'd ever heard it. "Look at me."

I opened my eyes to find him watching me with an expression that made the lightning and lava in my chest send shockwaves to my stomach. This was so far beyond the butterflies I'd written for my heroines. Wonder, heat, and something else I couldn't quite name pooled in his eyes.

"You're fucking delicious, Tempest. That was..." he started.

"My first," I confessed without thinking, then immediately wanted to snatch the words back.

His eyes widened slightly and flashed between mine, studying me for at least a thousand and one years, which was really only a second. I saw a multitude of thoughts and emotions run through his face and swallowed down the fear that he was about to judge me like everyone else in the world did.

"Your... first kiss?"

I nodded, heat rushing to my cheeks with the realization of what I'd really just admitted. "It's weird, I know, but—"

"No," he said, his thumb brushing across my lower lip in a way that made me shiver. "It's not weird. And I don't want you to think I'm some misogynistic asshole who thinks virginity is hot, but, fuck, Tempest. I can't tell you how goddamned turned on I am to know I'm the only man who ever gets to have this with you."

Flynn pressed his forehead against mine. "I want so fucking much to get to be the only man who gets to do a lot more firsts with you."

I had convinced myself that first kisses, and sex, and falling in love weren't actually important to me. I had to because I was sure I'd never get to experience any of them. If they didn't matter, then it wouldn't hurt so much that I missed out when everyone else around me got their cake and had fun eating it too.

But I was wrong.

I was so, incredibly, stupidly, wrong.

Because I was falling in love with the cocky, arrogant, sweet Flynn Kingman. And I was scared out of my mind, and maybe the happiest I'd ever been at the same time.

He wrapped a stray strand of hair from my carefully done party do, and tucked it behind my ear. "I really wish I didn't have to leave right now."

"Do you? Have to leave?" The questions slipped out before I could stop them.

He smiled, and this time, it wasn't that same flirty grin I'd grown so used to. He took a breath and shook his head but then leaned in and kissed me again, briefer this time but no less intense. "I do. But I'll call you from the combine. And text. Probably too much."

"I don't want to be a distraction." Why did I say that? Because my defenses still weren't sure this was real. "But if you really want to... I'll, you know, make sure to have my phone handy."

God, I sounded so dumb. Did kissing kill brain cells? Probably.

Flynn stepped back reluctantly, his hand sliding down my arm to squeeze my fingers before letting go. "I'll see you in a week, my queen."

There was a promise in his eyes that sent those sparks inside burning again.

I watched him walk away, touching my still-tingling lips in wonder. Was this how all first kisses felt, or was it just Flynn?

"Tempeeeeeeeeest," Freddie's voice carried from inside the house. "Abuela wants to know if you're staying the night."

Reality crashed back. I was standing on my family's porch, all of them just meters away, feeling like I'd just been fundamentally altered by Flynn Kingman's kiss.

"Coming," I called, taking a moment to compose myself before heading inside.

But I couldn't stop smiling. "Sorry, Abuela, I can't stay. I've got sorority business I need to get done tonight."

By business, I meant examining every millisecond of what just happened with Parker and a whole lot of leftover dulce de leche cake. I went home and prepared for a deep dig on my feelings.

"Spill it, Navarro."

Parker blocked the doorway to our room, arms crossed, expression determined. I'd barely gotten my foot in the door before she ambushed me.

"Spill what?" I tried to keep my face neutral, but Parker could read me like a romance book.

"Whatever has you looking like that." She gestured vaguely at my face. "You've got this weird glow thing happening, and you're rarely smiling when you come back from your family's place."

"I don't know what you're talking about." I edged past her into our room, dropping my bag on the bed.

"Oh my god." Parker's eyes widened with realization. "He kissed you, didn't he? Flynn Kingman kissed you."

I opened my mouth to deny it, but what came out instead was, "How did you know?"

"HA!" She slammed the door and did a little victory

dance. "I knew it! You've got that just-been-thoroughly-kissed face."

"That's not a thing," I protested, but I couldn't hide the smile.

"It is absolutely a thing, and you are wearing it like a billboard." She plopped down on my bed, eyes gleaming. "So? How was it? Is he as good as he looks like he'd be? Did he use tongue? Wait, hang on."

Parker pulled out her phone, thumbs flying.

"What are you doing?" I asked, suddenly nervous.

"Emergency meeting of the Baby Donkey Sitters Club," she announced. "This is big news."

"Parker, no—"

"Too late." She grinned unrepentantly. "And... sent."

I groaned, burying my face in my hands. "It's not that big a deal."

"Um, Flynn Kingman, campus heartbreaker and your nemesis-turned-crush, kissed you, and you're saying it's not a big deal?" She raised an eyebrow. "Either it was the worst kiss in history, or you're lying."

Before I could respond, there was a rapid knock at our door. Parker bounded over to open it, revealing Hannah, Alice, and Bettie, all wide-eyed and expectant.

"That was fast," I muttered.

"We were already in the common room," Alice explained, rushing in. "Is it true? Did the Flynn Kingman kiss happen?"

I sighed, knowing resistance was futile. "Yes, okay? We kissed. It was nice. End of story."

Except in my romance novels, it was just the beginning and I hoped this held true in real life.

"'Nice' she says." Bettie shook her head, closing the door behind them. "Honey, men like Flynn Kingman don't do 'nice' kisses. They do earth-shattering, life-altering, panty-melting kisses."

"Bettie," I covered my face, which was on fire.

"What? It's true." She sat at my desk chair. "Now give us details. And don't leave anything out."

Surrounded and outnumbered, I surrendered. "It was... my first."

Four pairs of eyes widened in perfect synchronization. The words hung in the air between us. It was one thing to admit I'd never had a relationship, but confessing I'd never been kissed felt embarrassingly juvenile.

"Your first kiss?" Hannah asked gently. "Ever?"

I nodded, suddenly self-conscious. At twenty-two, I was practically ancient to just be having my first kiss. "I know it's—"

"It's sweet," Alice said firmly.

To my surprise, no one laughed. Instead, Hannah squeezed my hand. "That's okay," she said softly. "We've all been there."

"So, how was it?" Parker prompted.

I thought about Flynn's lips on mine, the way his hand had cradled my face, how safe and wanted I'd felt in his arms. "It was perfect," I admitted quietly. "Better than I imagined."

"See? Earth-shattering." Bettie nodded sagely. "The point is," she continued, "we're here for you. Whatever you need. Advice, pep talks, someone to help you pick out date outfits—"

"Or first-time lingerie," Alice added with a wink.

"Oh my god, we are not there yet." I covered my face again.

"But you're thinking about it," Parker teased. When I didn't immediately deny it, she crowed triumphantly. "I knew it."

"I don't know what I'm thinking," I admitted. "This is all so complicated. And terrifying."

"Oh, sweetie." Hannah patted my hand. "It doesn't have to be. You don't have to do anything you're not ready for."

"What Hannah means," Bettie interjected, "is that Flynn Kingman has a certain... reputation."

The two-week rule. I remembered hearing about it at the party, though the details were fuzzy thanks to the vodka. "I know he doesn't do serious relationships. I'm sure this is just another fling for him."

Of course it was. That was why I needed to dissect this with my girls. They'd set me straight.

"Usually," Alice agreed. "But he's been chasing you for months. And I've never seen him look at any girl the way he looks at you."

How exactly did he look at me?

"And he's not usually a first kiss kind of guy," Parker added. "Word is he usually skips to the main event pretty quickly. Is that what you want?"

The implication made my cheeks burn hotter. "We're not... I mean, I haven't..." I took a deep breath. "I've never even had a boyfriend before, much less had sex. Mierda. This is a disaster, isn't it?"

"That's how the best stories start," Hannah said wisely.

But did I want to have sex with Flynn?

Ugh. Very much. Very, very much.

"But now he's gone for a week," I added, unable to keep the disappointment from my voice. "For his football thing."

"Which gives us exactly seven days to prepare for what happens when he comes back," Parker declared.

Oh, gawd. If anyone brought out Barbie and Ken and tried to give me the birds and bees talk, I was going to feed them to Burrito Petito.

"Operation Fun Times with Flynn is officially a go." Bettie clapped her hands. "The combine's on TV tomorrow. I'm declaring it a KAT house viewing party."

"What? No. That's too much," I protested. I wasn't even sure what a combine was.

"Too late." Alice said, tapping on her phone. "And I may have just had 'Team Flynn' shirts made for the senior class."

"You did not," I groaned.

"Oh, but I did." She showed me her screen, where a mock-up displayed a purple and gold DSU Dragons shirt with 'KINGMAN 50' on the back. "They'll be here tomorrow."

I flopped back on my bed, torn between mortification and a strange, bubbling happiness. "You're all terrible."

"You love us," Parker said confidently.

Looking around at their eager, supportive faces, I couldn't argue with that. For all their teasing and meddling, they were the first people besides Tío Pedro and Abuela who accepted me exactly as I was.

"Fine," I conceded. "But no signs. Or body paint. Or anything that would end up on Flynn's InstaSnap."

"No promises," Bettie sang.

Monday afternoon, more sorority sisters than I knew I had gathered in our TV room watching...football players do... things.

"There he is," Parker screamed, pointing at the TV.

The room erupted in cheers as the screen filled with Flynn's face. He stood in a line of players waiting for the 40-yard dash, looking focused but confident in his training gear, number 50 displayed prominently on his chest.

I sank lower in my seat, feeling simultaneously proud and embarrassed by the spectacle around me. True to her word, Alice had distributed "Team Flynn" shirts to way more than the senior class. Someone, probably Hannah, had even made a banner.

"God, he's so hot," a sophomore named Heather sighed from somewhere behind me. "Tempest, you are so lucky."

"We're just friends," I said automatically, though the words felt hollow after that kiss.

The room filled with knowing laughter.

"Sure, honey." Bettie patted my shoulder. "Just friends who make out on your abuela's porch."

"Shh, he's up." Alice hushed the room.

I held my breath as he crouched into position. The camera zoomed in on his face, those blue eyes intense with concentration, jaw set. This was the future professional football star, and potentially my boyfriend.

The whistle blew, and Flynn exploded off the line. Even to my untrained eye, his speed was impressive, his form perfect as he powered down the track.

"4.58 seconds," Hannah read as his time flashed on the screen. "Is that good?"

"For a linebacker? It's amazing," Bettie confirmed, and the room erupted in cheers again.

The broadcast cut to a replay of his run, then to the announcers discussing his performance.

"Flynn Kingman showing why he's projected as a first-round pick," one analyst said. "Great speed, excellent movement skills. He's going to make some team incredibly happy."

"And I'm hearing the LA Bandits are showing particular interest," the other added. "Along with the Denver Mustangs, of course, where Kingman would join his brothers."

LA. The word sent an unexpected chill through me.

My phone buzzed with a text.

> Flynn: Did you see that? Pretty sure I felt you watching.

I smiled, typing back quickly.

> Me: The entire KAT house saw it. Someone may have made Team Flynn shirts.

> Flynn: Please tell me you're wearing one.

> Me: No comment.

> Flynn: I'll take that as a yes. Gotta run, more drills. Miss you.

The last two words made my heart stutter. Miss you. As if we'd been together forever instead of sharing one kiss.

> Me: Good luck. We're all cheering for you.

I almost added "miss you too," but something held me back. This was all happening so fast. One minute we were arguing about Shakespeare, the next we were kissing, and now...

Now what?

My career phone vibrated in my back pocket. Gloria again, confirming my flight for LA during spring break.

Parker noticed my sudden distraction. "You look like someone just told you they killed your fictional boyfriend."

"I'm fine," I lied. "Just thinking."

The broadcast moved on to other players, but my mind remained stuck on Flynn, on LA, on the complicated web I was weaving around myself. Each secret I kept made it harder to be honest, to be vulnerable. And didn't Flynn deserve the truth?

"I'm gonna grab some...water before Flynn is on again," I murmured, slipping out of the room while everyone was distracted by Gryffin's turn on the track.

In the quiet of our bedroom, before I could overthink it, I dialed Abuela's number.

"Mi corazón," her warm voice answered. "How are you?"

"Confused," I admitted. "Can I ask your advice?"

"Of course. Is this about your handsome friend? You know I'm a fan of the footballers."

Despite everything, I smiled. "Sort of. It's complicated."

"Ah," Abuela said knowingly. "Because he kissed you."

"How did you...?" I stopped. Abuela knew everything. She always did.

"The way I see it, you have two options," Abuela said. "You can continue keeping these various parts of your life, school, family, career, love, separate, which means more lies and complications. Or..."

I didn't pretend not to know what she was talking about. She was one of the only people in the world who knew almost all my secrets. Even so, I kept certain parts of my heart hidden away.

"Or?" I prompted when she paused.

"Or you can start letting people in," she said gently. "Not everyone. Not all at once. But maybe it's time to stop hiding yourself away, Tempestina."

"What if he thinks I'm, I don't know, some silly girl with romantic fantasies?" The question was barely a whisper. "What if he realizes I've been lying to him and everyone else?"

"Listen, querida. If this boy can't appreciate your talent and your reasons for privacy, then he's not worth your time anyway."

"He might be worth it," I admitted softly.

"Then trust him with the truth," Abuela advised. "But no matter what you decide, your future is bright, mi corazón, with or without a handsome footballer."

"Though the handsome footballer doesn't hurt," Tío Pedro added in the background. Because of course, he was listening in.

I laughed despite myself. "Thank you both. I love you."

"We love you too, Tempestina. Now go watch your boy run around in his tight pants."

"Abuela."

Her laughter was the last thing I heard before hanging up.

Back in the common room, I slipped into my seat just as Flynn appeared on screen again, this time for shuttle drills. Parker raised an eyebrow at me but didn't comment on my absence.

On screen, Flynn moved with athletic grace, his face a mask of concentration. When he finished, the camera caught him looking directly into the lens for a moment, as if he could see through it to me. He held up his hands to the camera and made a heart with his fingers.

My heart lurched in my chest as the room erupted in squeals and cheers around me. Several sisters turned to look at me, their expressions delighted.

"Oh my god," Parker grabbed my arm. "Did Flynn Kingman just give you heart hands on national TV?"

I couldn't answer. Couldn't breathe. He'd basically just declared his love for me in front of the universe, and here I was, still keeping secrets, still hiding parts of myself away.

Abuela's words echoed in my mind. If he's worth it, trust him with the truth.

I pulled out my phone and opened my texts with Flynn. I sent him the heart hands emoji and then waited to see if he got it and replied.

His response came almost immediately.

> Flynn: Can't wait to see you when I get back. Hopefully in nothing but that Team Flynn t-shirt.

> Me: Me either. I have some spring break plans I want to tell you about later too.

Before I could second-guess myself, I sent a final message.

> Me: I am wearing the shirt now. Maybe I'll wear it to bed tonight too.

I'd written dozens of revelation scenes in my books. Now it was time to write my own.

YOU'LL BE IN MY HEART

FLYNN

"*K*ingmans!"

Gryff and I turned at the same time. We'd just finished our individual drills for the day, and Dad was waiting to analyze our performances with the ruthlessness only a former coach could muster.

The voice belonged to a combine official who was escorting someone who looked strikingly familiar. Tall, athletic build, with the good looks that belonged in the movies more than football.

"Huh," Gryff muttered beside me. "Is that—"

"Yeah, it is," I confirmed, surprised to see the rising Hollywood star in the middle-of-nowhere Indiana. Sure, he played football for Bay State University, and he was good too, but he was a sophomore so he wasn't here for the combine.

Dad stepped forward, ever the diplomat. "Bridger Kingman," he said, extending his hand. "These are my sons, Flynn and Gryffin."

"Fox Daws," he replied, shaking Dad's hand before

turning to us. "You guys looked great out there today. Not that I expected anything less from the Kingman dynasty."

"Thanks." But the combine wasn't a sporting event that attracted celebrities. "Not exactly where you'd expect to find a movie star, even one who is also a tight end for the Dire Wolves."

Fox laughed, an easy sound that matched his laid-back demeanor. "I'm here doing research for a role this summer, and was hoping to talk to Coach Bridger actually."

Dad's eyebrows rose. "What can I do for you, son?"

"I've been cast as Danny Watkins in a movie about his comeback after serving in the Middle East. I know you were drafted along with him." Fox looked genuinely pleased.

Dad nodded. "That guy was tough as hell."

"That's exactly what I'm trying to capture," Fox said, enthusiasm clear in his voice. "My grandparents live in Colorado and I'm headed there for spring break. I was hoping I could stop over for a visit and maybe talk to you about him?"

"Sure, kid. I'd be happy to help."

"And maybe get in a little coaching on the field too?"

This guy was fucking ballsy. I liked it.

Dad folded his arms and gave Fox the patented take-no-prisoners coach look. But there was a smile behind his eyes. "We'll see about that."

I leaned in and stage-whispered, "Be prepared to be puking your guts out by the end of practice."

"Speaking from experience?"

Gryff and I both nodded emphatically. "You know it."

"I'm down. I'm hoping to be right here with the scouts watching me like they are the two of you in a couple of years."

"You're pretty damn good," I said. He was a scorer for the Dire Wolves and I wouldn't be surprised if he'd be in line for a Heisman in the next couple of years, up against Isak, of course. "But there aren't a lot of movie stars in the League."

Fox rubbed the back of his neck. "My agent wants me to focus on movies, but I love the game. Trying to balance the acting thing with school and football has been... interesting."

"Tough choice," Dad said, with the understanding of someone who'd seen plenty of young men at career crossroads.

The official cleared his throat. "Mr. Daws, we should continue if you want to catch the defensive back drills."

"Right," Fox nodded, then turned back to us. "Great meeting you guys."

As he turned to leave, Gryff suddenly smacked my arm. "Dude. Jules."

"Oh, shit." Jules would absolutely lose it if she knew we met Fox Daws and didn't her get anything.

Fox overheard and turned back. "Who or what is a Jules?"

"Youngest of the Kingmans, and a big fan of yours," Dad said dryly. "She makes us watch your movies on repeat."

"Oh, I got you." Fox snapped a quick selfie with the three of us, then typed something into his phone. "Good luck with the rest of the combine, guys. And with the draft."

We watched him walk away, the official already bending his ear about someone else he needed to meet.

"Jules is going to absolutely lose her mind," Gryff grinned. "I can wait to tell Artie either. She made me watch that space movie of his about seven hundred and forty-two times. Maybe now she'll stop complaining I drag her to football games."

I laughed, already imagining her reaction. "Not a chance."

"Alright, enough distractions," Dad said, shifting back to coach mode. "Let's get back to the hotel and talk about those drills."

The hotel suite Dad booked was littered with the detritus of combine prep, protein shake bottles, printed workout schedules, and recovery gear strewn across every surface. Gryff sprawled on one of the beds, scrolling through his phone, while I iced my shoulder.

"The Bandits scout was watching you like a hawk today," Dad said as he entered from the adjoining room, tablet in hand.

"I spotted Denver's guy," I pointed out, "making notes the whole time."

"The Sharks and the Presidents too. Because they all want you. Both of you." Dad sat on the edge of the other bed. "Got calls from a lot of teams today. They're wanting to set up private workouts and meetings."

Gryff sat up, suddenly alert. "They want both of us? Together?"

"There're a few who are looking to slot you individually into their rosters," Dad confirmed. "But Bandits specifically want you both. Their defensive coordinator apparently has this whole vision for deploying you two as a package deal."

A package deal. The possibility of continuing to play alongside my twin had always seemed like a pipe dream given the draft system, but hearing it might actually happen sent a surge of excitement through me.

Denver would mean staying close to home, to family, to our support system.

To Tempest.

The thought caught me off guard. We'd shared one kiss. Admittedly, an incredible kiss, but that shouldn't be enough to influence where I played pro ball.

And yet.

"LA wants to fly you out next week," Dad continued, oblivious to my internal debate. "Tours, meetings with coaches, the works. The other teams are going to work around your classes."

"Spring break," Gryff noted. "Perfect timing for a trip to the beach."

Would Tempest be staying in Denver or heading to some senior year bacchanalia with her sorority sisters? Damn. I wish I'd made plans with her before I left. Not that I'd get to keep them if I was headed to LA.

"Hit the showers. Got dinner with the agents in thirty."

Dad went back to his room, and Gryff threw a pillow at me. "Dude. You were a million miles away just now."

I didn't bother denying it. Gryff knew. Twin telepathy was strong in us.

"It's okay to admit it, you know." Gryff's tone softened. "That she matters."

"She shouldn't though, should she?"

"That's bullshit. Unless this isn't a serious thing. Do not fucking tell me Tempest is just another two-week special. Because I will fucking... I don't know, make Artie sit on you while I fart in your face."

Gryff's chastisement hit harder than it should have. I'd been breaking my own rules since the moment I met Tempest. My two-week limit had flown by weeks ago, and instead of losing interest, I thought about her more, not less.

"I don't know," I admitted. "It's... different. She's different. I...like her. A lot."

My phone buzzed from the nightstand. I reached for it, unsurprised to see Tempest's name on the screen.

> Tempest: The Donkey Sitters Club sends their congratulations on today's performance. Apparently your vertical jump was, and I quote, "absolutely divine."

I smiled, fingers already typing a response.

> Me: I'm more interested in what you thought.

Three dots appeared, disappeared, then reappeared.

> Tempest: It was pretty amazing to see you in your element like that. And...*blush* kind of hot. I'm a bit mad I never went to football games now.

> Me: I can give you your own personal football game when I get back.

She didn't take the bait. Because she was never charmed by any flirting I ever did with her. I needed to step up my game.

> Tempest: It was like your future was right in front of you, and I'm really happy for you.

I swallowed hard. She was right. My future was right in front of me. I just wasn't sure anymore what shape I wanted it to take.

Football, the League, and Tempest. That's what I wanted. And it scared the shit out of me.

But there was only one way I knew how to deal with fear and that was to tackle it head on. And I was an excellent tackle.

I texted Tempest one more time.

> Me: I'm home on Saturday. Let me take you out on a date. A date date. A real one.

Her message took a few minutes and a lot of me watching the dots appear and disappear. What was she writing me, a novel for an answer?

> Tempest: Okay.

I was about to worry over that one word response, until I got the kissy lips emoji one moment later.

The last few days of the combine were bangers, and in

the evenings I planned that date. It had to be fucking perfect.

Saturday night, I caught a flash of movement at an upstairs window, several faces pressed against the glass, quickly disappearing when they realized I'd spotted them. The Donkey Sitters Club was clearly on surveillance duty.

Tempest emerged before I could text that I'd arrived. She wore a deep-green sweater that made her dark eyes seem even more luminous and a pair of jeans that hugged her curves. Her hair fell in loose waves past her shoulders instead of her usual practical but cute AF messy bun.

"Hi," she said simply, a small smile playing at her lips as she approached the car.

I opened the passenger door for her, catching a hint of her perfume as she slid past me, something floral with a spicy undertone that suited her perfectly.

"So," she asked once I was back behind the wheel, "where are we going?"

"Oh no, you're not gonna get it out of me with promises of more sweet kisses." I gave her wink, but my eyes dipped down to her lips and back up, which was a mistake if I wanted to keep my zipper from creating a permanent imprint in my dick.

Tempest gasped and rolled her eyes at me, but it was matched with an adorable smile, which was exactly what I was going for. "I never promised any such thing."

I pulled away from her house and headed up Colorado Boulevard. "Hmm. Are you sure? I'm sure that promise was in your eyes when I picked you up."

"Flynn." She raised an eyebrow at me. I was going to kiss that look right off her face later. "Are you trying to get me to kiss you? Because I was sort of hoping you would do that when you picked me up."

I swerved into a parking lot and stopped short. In two point one milliseconds I had her lips on mine and I cursed the fact I had a newer car with a console between us instead of a bench seat in old classic cars.

"We don't have to go out at all, sweet queen." I may have put a lot of effort into this date, but I'd forgo it all if she was asking what I fucking prayed to the sex gods she wanted from me right now.

"Mmm." Her eyes remained closed, and her thumb stroked along the edge of my beard.

Hell yeah, a few more kisses and we'd be headed right back to my place so we could—

"But don't think for a second you're getting out of taking me out on a proper date in the two days we have together before spring break." Neither of us had talked about our plans for the week.

"As you wish." Twenty minutes later, I pulled up to the Denver Museum of Natural History. The main entrance was quiet, most of the daytime visitors long gone.

"The museum?" Tempest looked confused. "Isn't it closed?"

"To the general public, yes." I came around to open her door. "But not to us. The museum does these special after-hours events, and we're here for their newest exhibit."

A security guard was waiting at a side entrance. He nodded at us as we approached. "Mr. Kingman. Right this way."

We followed him through hushed, dimly lit halls. The

museum after hours had an almost magical quality—the exhibits cast in soft shadow, the usual crowds replaced by stillness.

The guard stopped in front of a set of double doors. "Dr. Sharma is waiting inside. Enjoy your evening."

As the doors opened, Tempest's grip on my arm tightened. Inside was the special exhibition room, and across its entrance was a banner that read, "First Folio: The Book That Gave Us Shakespeare."

"Oh my god," she breathed, stopping in her tracks. "Is that…?"

"The First Folio," I confirmed. "On loan from the Folger Shakespeare Library. One of the original 1623 editions."

She turned to me, astonishment written across her face. "How did you…?"

"Coach's wife sits on the museum board. I asked for a favor." I shrugged, trying to downplay how many strings I'd pulled to get this spot on the list before the exhibition even opened. "I may have mentioned that I know a brilliant literature scholar who would appreciate a private viewing."

A woman approached us, extending her hand. "Ms. Navarro? I'm Dr. Sharma, the curator of this exhibition. I hear you're quite the Shakespeare enthusiast."

"I am," Tempest managed, still looking stunned. "This is incredible."

"Well, you're in for a treat." Dr. Sharma smiled warmly. "We're going to do something very special tonight—something we don't offer to the public."

She led us through the exhibition, where glass cases

displayed various historical documents and artifacts related to Shakespeare and his work. Tempest moved from display to display with reverence, occasionally glancing back at me with an expression of pure wonder.

Finally, we reached the central exhibit, a glass case containing the First Folio itself, open to Hamlet's famous soliloquy.

"Now," Dr. Sharma said, pulling on a pair of white cotton gloves, "how would you like to see it up close?"

Tempest's eyes grew impossibly wider. "You mean...?"

"With proper precautions, of course." The curator handed each of us a pair of gloves. "Flynn mentioned you're writing about Shakespeare. I thought you might appreciate examining some of the typographical features firsthand."

Tempest's brow furrowed and she looked at me like she was about to say something, but she turned to Dr. Sharma instead and nodded. "I'd like that a lot. Thank you."

Once Dr. Sharma finished letting us see as much as we wanted, Tempest turned to me, eyes shining. "Flynn, I can't believe you did this. This is—" She shook her head, seemingly at a loss for words. "Thank you doesn't seem adequate."

"Your face right now is all the thanks I need." I stepped closer, careful not to touch the precious book even with my gloved hands. "I wanted to do something that was just for you."

"Mission accomplished." She laughed softly, looking back at the Folio.

After the Folio was safely back in its case, I led

Tempest to an elevator at the back of the exhibition hall. It took us to the museum's upper level, where a glassed-in balcony overlooked the city and the mountains.

A small table had been set for dinner, complete with candles and a bottle of champagne in an ice bucket. The Denver skyline sparkled against the night sky, the mountains a dark silhouette in the distance.

"Flynn," she whispered, "this is too much."

"Not for you," I said simply, pulling out her chair.

A waiter appeared, uncorking the champagne and presenting the first course, a selection of small plates featuring foods from Shakespeare's era, each with a small card explaining its historical context.

Tempest ran her fingers over the menu card, which had been designed to look like a playbill. "You planned all of this. Why?" she asked, her dark eyes searching mine across the table.

"Because I wanted to show you that I see you," I said honestly. "The real you. Not just the Tempest who aces Shakespeare classes or rescues donkeys, but the one who lights up when she talks about literature. The one who notices details others miss. The one I can't stop thinking about."

Her breath caught, and for a moment, I thought I'd said too much. Then she reached across the table, taking my hand in hers.

"Thank you," she said softly. "No one's ever done anything like this for me before."

"You deserve to be spoiled," I countered, enjoying the way her eyes sparkled at my response.

"Can I ask you something?"

"Anything," I replied, meaning it.

She hesitated, then squared her shoulders. "What's your two-week rule about?"

I tensed, caught off guard. Of all the things I'd expected her to bring up, that wasn't on the list.

"Everyone knows about it," she continued when I didn't immediately respond. "How you never date anyone longer than two weeks. How it's... a game to you."

"It's not a game," I said quietly, setting down my champagne glass.

"Then what is it?" Her voice was steady, but I could see the vulnerability behind her question. "Because I need to know if I'm just another girl you're going to walk away from when your arbitrary deadline hits. Although, I guess I don't know when the timer started."

The truth hovered on the tip of my tongue, heavy and unfamiliar. I'd never explained my rule to anyone, not even my brothers. It had always been easier to let people believe I was just a player, unwilling to be tied down.

But Tempest deserved better than easy.

"After my mom died," I began, the words coming slowly, "my dad was... destroyed. Completely shattered. He tried to hide it from us kids, but I remember waking up at night and hearing him crying in their bedroom." I swallowed hard. "He never really recovered. Not completely."

Tempest's expression softened, but she remained silent, giving me space to continue.

"I was six, but I understood enough. Loving someone that much meant losing them could break you. And that scared the hell out of me." I met her eyes. "The two-week rule started in high school. Long enough for fun, short enough that no one got attached. Especially me."

She didn't say anything but softly squeezed my hand.

"It was... safe." I shrugged. "Until you."

Her breath caught. "What do you mean?"

"I mean we're way past two weeks, Tempest. And instead of looking for an exit, I'm sitting here trying to figure out how to convince you to give me more time."

Something flickered in her eyes, surprise, uncertainty, hope. "But what changed?"

"I did," I admitted. "Or maybe you changed me. I don't know. I just know that when I was at the combine, surrounded by everything I've worked for my entire life, I was thinking about you. About whether you were watching. About what you'd think of LA if I got drafted there."

I reached across the table, offering my hand palm up. After a moment's hesitation, she placed her hand in mine.

"I'm not saying I've got everything figured out," I continued. "But I'm done pretending I don't have feelings for you. That I'm not falling for you."

OPERATION GET TEMPEST LAID

TEMPEST

Flynn's words hung in the air between us, illuminated by the soft glow of candlelight and the twinkling Denver skyline beyond the museum balcony. My heart hammered against my ribs so hard I was certain he could hear it.

I'd spent so long crafting perfect words on paper, dialogue, confessions, declarations of love, but now, faced with the real thing, I couldn't find my voice.

"Tempest?" His expression shifted, uncertainty creeping in. "Was that too much, too soon—"

"No," I finally managed, squeezing his hand where it still held mine across the table. "It's not too much. It's just..."

How could I explain that no one had ever said those words to me before? That I'd written countless versions of this scene but never expected to live it?

"It's just that I'm feeling the same way," I admitted softly. "And that's a little scary to me too."

Relief washed over his face, his blue eyes brightening. "It is?"

"I've never done this before." I gestured vaguely between us. "Any of it. I don't know how."

Flynn stood, circling the table without releasing my hand, and gently pulled me to my feet. "There's no instruction manual," he said, his voice low as he tucked a strand of hair behind my ear. "We'll figure it out together."

He was so close I could feel the warmth radiating from his body, smell the subtle cologne that had been driving me crazy all evening. When his gaze dropped to my lips, I felt my breath hitch.

"Remember those promised kisses?" he asked.

In answer, I rose on my tiptoes and pressed my lips to his.

This one ignited immediately. Flynn's arm wrapped around my waist, pulling me against him as his other hand cradled my face. I wound my arms around his neck, completely lost in the sensation of his mouth on mine, his body pressed to mine. I could feel that bulge in his jeans pressing against my belly, and I wanted so much more.

I danced my fingers down the front of his shirt and to his belt. Flynn grabbed my hand and stilled it, breaking the kiss. We were both breathing heavily, and the look in his eyes made heat pool low in my belly.

"Do you want to get out of here?" he asked, his voice rougher than before.

I nodded, not trusting myself to speak.

The museum curator appeared so quickly I wondered if she'd been waiting nearby. "I hope everything was satisfactory?"

"Perfect," Flynn assured her, his hand finding the small of my back. "Thank you for everything."

Ten minutes later, we were in his car, an electric tension filling the space between us. Flynn's hand rested on my knee, his thumb tracing small circles that sent shivers up my spine.

"My place isn't far," he said, shooting me a glance that made my pulse race.

"Okay," I heard myself say, though a small voice in the back of my mind was screaming that this was moving too fast.

But I silenced it. For once in my life, I didn't want to overthink. I wanted to feel.

Flynn's house was modern and unexpectedly neat for a college athlete. But I barely had time to register my surroundings before his lips were on mine again, his hands tangling in my hair as he backed me against the closed front door.

"You're so beautiful," he murmured against my neck, sending electricity across my skin. "I've wanted this for so long."

I gasped as his hands skimmed down my sides, pulling me closer. The solid warmth of him pressed against me was intoxicating, and I found myself tugging at his shirt, desperate to feel his skin against mine.

"Yo, Flynn, you back?" a voice called from deeper in the house. "We need a tiebreaker on whether camping in *Call of Doody* is a legitimate strategy."

Flynn froze, his forehead dropping to my shoulder with a groan. "You have got to be kidding me."

Voices and laughter suddenly registered from what I

guessed was the living room—lots of voices. Flynn pulled back slightly, keeping his hands on my waist.

"I forgot," he said, looking genuinely pained. "Pre-spring break gaming tournament. The team does it every year."

"The whole team?" I asked, trying to catch my breath and straighten my clothes.

"Feels like it," he sighed, pressing a quick kiss to my lips. "I'm so sorry."

"Flynn," the voice called again. "Is that you?"

"Yeah," he called back, then lowered his voice. "We could still go to my room. They'll be too busy gaming to bother us."

Before I could answer, heavy footsteps approached, and Gryffin appeared in the hallway. His eyebrows rose as he took in our slightly disheveled appearance.

"Oh. Hey, Tempest." His grin was knowing. "Didn't mean to interrupt."

"You're not," I said quickly, heat flooding my cheeks.

"We were just leaving," Flynn added, shooting his twin a look.

"My room's free if you need it," Gryff offered with a wink. "Though fair warning, these walls are pretty thin."

"Shut up," Flynn muttered, grabbing his keys. "Let's go," he said to me.

As we passed the living room, I caught sight of at least eight football players sprawled across couches and the floor, controllers in hand, surrounded by pizza boxes and energy drinks. Several called out greetings as we hurried past.

"So much for privacy," Flynn said once we were back in his car. "I'm really sorry about that."

"It's okay." I squeezed his hand. "But now I'm not sure where we can go."

Flynn gave me a hopeful look. "Your place?"

I bit my lip, considering. My sorority house had strict rules about male visitors, especially after hours. But then again...

I pulled out my phone and texted Parker.

> Me: Need a MAJOR favor. Can you help sneak Flynn into the house?

Her response was immediate.

> Parker: OMG YES!!! Operation Get Tempest Laid is GO!!! Give me 5 min to organize the troops!

"I think we have a chance," I told Flynn, showing him the message.

His laugh was both surprised and delighted. "The Donkey Sitters Club rides again?"

"Apparently so."

Fifteen minutes later, we parked a block from the KAT house and waited for Parker's signal. My phone buzzed with detailed instructions.

THE JACK*SS IN CLASS

> Parker: Mrs. H is in her office. Hannah will create a distraction in the common room at 9:42 EXACTLY. Come in through the kitchen door. Alice will flash the porch light twice when coast is clear. Bettie has lookouts posted on all floors. DO NOT USE THE MAIN STAIRS. Take the service stairs by the pantry. I'll be waiting at our door. GOOD LUCK SOLDIER.

"Wow," Flynn said, reading over my shoulder. "This is some serious black ops planning."

"They're very invested in my love life," I muttered, embarrassed. "Or lack thereof."

"Not lacking anymore," he said, leaning over to kiss me softly.

At exactly 9:42, we saw the porch light flash twice. We sprinted across the lawn to the kitchen door, where Alice was waiting.

"Target approaching," she whispered into her phone. "Initiating Phase Two."

Somewhere deep in the depths of the house came the sound of a crash, followed by shrieks that sounded suspiciously rehearsed.

"That's Hannah," Alice confirmed. "Move now, you've got forty seconds before Mrs. Henderson reaches the noise."

We crept through the kitchen, following Alice's directions to the service stairs. Just as we reached them, footsteps approached from the main hallway.

"Hide," Alice hissed, shoving us behind a large pantry shelf.

I found myself pressed against Flynn in the narrow

space, his arms around me, both of us trying not to breathe as Mrs. Henderson's voice drifted past.

"What in heaven's name is going on in here? Oh my lord. What happened to that vase?"

"Such a terrible accident," Hannah's voice replied, the picture of contrition. "I was practicing my dance routine for the spring showcase and—"

The voices faded as they moved toward the common room.

"Clear," Alice whispered. "Up you go."

We climbed the narrow service stairs to the second floor, where Parker was waiting in the hallway, looking like a spy in a bad movie with a black beanie pulled over her purple hair.

"Targets acquired," she stage-whispered into her phone. "Proceeding to secure location."

"Is all of this really necessary?" I asked as she ushered us into my room.

"Absolutely," Parker replied, checking the hallway one last time before closing the door. "Mrs. Henderson has been on a rampage ever since she caught Jessica sneaking in that baseball player last week. We've got lookouts, decoys, and Bettie's ready with the 'urgent sorority business' excuse if needed."

She gave Flynn an appraising look. "Worth it though. Impressive, Tempest."

"Thank you?" I said, mortified.

"I'll leave you to it." Parker grabbed her overnight bag. "I'm bunking with Hannah tonight. Text if you need an extraction. And remember," she pointed to the wall we shared with the next room, "these walls are definitely not soundproof."

And with that parting shot, she was gone.

Flynn and I stood in the middle of my room, alone at last. The absurdity of the situation, the elaborate sneaking, the spy terminology, the entire sorority apparently invested in our privacy, hit us both at the same time, and we burst into laughter.

"Your friends are something else," Flynn said, wrapping his arms around my waist.

"They're ridiculous," I agreed, relaxing against him. "But effective."

"Very effective," he murmured, lowering his head to kiss me.

The laughter faded as our kiss deepened. Without breaking apart, we stumbled toward my bed, falling onto it in a tangle of limbs. Flynn's weight above me felt right, solid and warm as his hands explored my body with a gentleness that made me ache.

When his fingers found the hem of my sweater, he paused, looking into my eyes. "Tell me what you want or what you don't want, okay?"

I nodded, lifting my arms to help him pull it over my head. The cool air against my skin made me shiver, or maybe it was the way Flynn was looking at me, like I was something precious.

"You're so fucking gorgeous," he whispered, his fingers tracing the lace edge of my bra.

I reached for his shirt in response, needing to feel his skin against mine. He helped me pull it off, and I ran my hands over the sculpted muscles of his chest and shoulders, marveling at the strength there.

Flynn lowered himself to kiss me again, more urgently this time. His hand slid up my side, brushing the underside of my breast, and I gasped into his mouth.

"We'll take this slow," he murmured against my lips. "Whatever you're comfortable with."

"I want this," I assured him, though my nerves were a tangle of anticipation and anxiety. "I want you."

His smile was panty-melting as he reached for the button of my jeans. "We have all night, and I'm going to make good on that promise to make you tremble for me."

He remembered that? I wasn't about to tell him I was already practically vibrating from his touch and we only had our shirts off.

Just then, a sharp knock made us both freeze.

"Room check." Mrs. Henderson's voice called through the door. "All ladies present and accounted for?"

"Shit," I whispered, panic shooting through me. "Quick, under the bed."

Flynn dove for the floor, sliding under my bed as I frantically pulled my sweater back on. I flopped onto the bed and grabbed a book, flipping it open to the middle like I was reading it when the door opened without warning.

Mrs. Henderson stood in the doorway, clipboard in hand, eyes narrowed with suspicion. "Miss Navarro."

"Good evening, Mrs. Henderson," I said, hoping my voice sounded normal. "Is everything okay?"

"Just a routine check after that commotion downstairs." Her gaze swept the room. "Where is Miss Chen?"

"Studying with Hannah," I lied, praying she wouldn't notice the man-sized lump under my bed. "Big test on Monday."

Mrs. Henderson hummed skeptically. "I thought I heard voices."

"Just me on the phone with my sister," I said quickly and grabbed my phone, waving it at her. "Discussing spring break plans."

Her eyes lingered on the rumpled bedspread, and I silently cursed noticing the book in my hand was upside down. "Well, everything seems to be in order. Remember, lights out by midnight, please."

"Of course."

She gave the room one last suspicious glance before closing the door. I waited, counting to ten, mostly to calm my beating heart, before whispering, "She's gone."

Flynn emerged from under the bed, a dust bunny clinging to his hair. "That was close."

"Too close," I agreed, plucking the dust from his hair. We looked at each other and had to stifle the giggles, the tension of the moment breaking.

Flynn sat on the edge of my bed, pulling me down beside him. "Maybe the universe is trying to tell us something."

"That we have the worst timing ever?"

"Or that some things are worth waiting for." He brushed a kiss against my temple. "No rush, Tempest. We have time."

The passion of moments before had cooled, but in its place was something equally powerful, a tenderness that made my chest ache.

"But I'll be gone for... spring break next week. I'm off to LA tomorrow." I wanted to tell him why I was going to California, and I would, just not right now.

He grinned. "We'll have to meet up. I'm headed there on Monday. The Bandits want to show us around the facilities, trying to schmooze us before the draft. I'll have some free time after workouts and meetings."

What? He'd be in LA the same time as me? Now, I really should just tell him why I was going there. He probably thought it was to party like normal college seniors did. But what if the meetings with FlixNChill didn't pan out? I hated myself for still not being ready to tell him about my books. He'd done everything to try to gain my trust.

But a lifetime of hiding everything about myself from the world around me was a tough habit to break. Maybe if the meetings went well I'd finally be brave and tell him.

"It's a date," I said, surprised by how much I was now looking forward to seeing him outside of our regular lives.

Parker burst into the room, her hand firmly placed over her eyes. "Extraction team incoming. Put your clothes back on. Mrs. H found hot baseballer in his tighty whities in Jessica's room and she's on a mission to ruin everyone's love lives."

As much as I wanted him to stay, no one was safe when Mrs. Henderson was in one of those moods. "How do you feel about heights, Kingman?"

"I'm going out the window, aren't I?" he asked with a grin.

Parker peeked through her fingers, saw that we were

both mostly clothed, and then gave us a salute. "The donkey delivery system is still in place. Hope you've got rope skill, dude."

Flynn waggled his eyebrows at me and smiled wickedly. "I've got skills with ropes you haven't even seen."

Oh. My. Gawd.

Parker leaned over and whispered, "It's like he's right out of a certain romance novel, isn't it?"

Before I could respond, Parker shoved Flynn toward the balcony, and I followed, still a little dazed by the thought of Flynn doing naughty things with rope. Outside, he pulled me close for one last kiss.

"I'll text you tomorrow," he promised, then stepped over the railing, rope wrapped around one hand, ready to descend, "and we'll figure out LA when we get there."

"Be careful," I warned. "Mrs. Henderson is likely to patrol the grounds next."

"I'll channel my inner ninja." With a final quick kiss, he slipped down the rope and out into the night.

I had barely closed the balcony door when Parker jumped on me, eyes wide with excitement.

"Well?" she demanded. "How was it? Did you? Didn't you? Tell me everything."

"Nothing happened," I admitted, collapsing onto my bed. "Mrs. Henderson interrupted us before we could... you know."

"That cockblocking battle-ax," Parker groaned, flopping down beside me. "All that planning for nothing."

"Not nothing," I said softly. I hesitated, unused to sharing my feelings. "I really like him, Parker."

She propped herself up on one elbow, studying my face. "Oh my god. This is more than getting you laid by the hottest jock on campus. This is actually serious, isn't it? You're actually falling for him."

I nodded, unable to deny it. "Yeah, I am."

"The question is, are you brave enough to live your own romance novel?"

The next evening, I settled into my first-class seat, courtesy of FlixNChill. They had arranged everything, the flight, the five-star hotel, the meetings with my agent, and the executives who wanted to turn my books into a streaming series.

I should have been focused on the biggest opportunity of my career...life. This could change everything. Instead, my thoughts kept drifting to Flynn, who would be arriving in LA tomorrow for his meetings with the Bandits.

My phone buzzed with a text just before takeoff.

> Flynn: Don't have too much fun in LA without me. But do have dirty dreams of me tonight. You know I'll be dreaming of you.

If only he knew just how dirty my imagination was. Miranda Milan, the best-selling author whose identity was still a carefully guarded secret because she wrote smutty smut, had oh, so many dirty dreams, and they all currently starred a charming, flirty football player. The things I wanted to do with that man.

None of which I had any practical knowledge of.

Because Flynn didn't know the real me.

Almost no one did.

And that made me sad.

As the plane climbed higher, I wondered which version of myself would return to Denver when this was all over. Tempest the student, Miranda the author, or someone new entirely. Someone brave enough to let Flynn see all of me.

The captain announced we'd reached cruising altitude, and I reclined my seat, closing my eyes.

LA was waiting. Flynn was waiting. And for once in my life, I was stepping into the unknown without a carefully plotted outline to guide me.

A STORM OF SHAKESPEARIAN PROPORTIONS

FLYNN

The LA sun hit different.

I'd been to California before, bowl games, family vacations when we were kids, but something about stepping off the plane at LAX as a potential Bandits draft pick made the sunshine feel more significant. Like it was spotlighting possibilities.

"Not bad," Gryff said beside me, sunglasses already on, rolling his shoulders like he owned the place. "Could get used to this."

Dad grunted noncommittally, but I caught his slight smile. He was impressed too. Hard not to be with palm trees swaying against a perfect blue sky. Well, mostly perfect. Some clouds hovered on the distant horizon, but they didn't diminish the golden California glow.

"Coach Kingman, gentleman." A man in a crisp suit approached, Bandits logo pin gleaming on his lapel. "I'm Marcus Wilson, player relations for the Bandits. Welcome to Los Angeles."

"Thank you for having us," Dad said, shaking his hand with the firm grip he'd taught all of us.

Marcus smiled, all perfect white teeth. "The dynamic duo. We've been watching you. Very impressive college careers, gentleman."

My phone buzzed in my pocket. I resisted the urge to check it immediately, maintaining eye contact with Marcus as we exchanged pleasantries. But the moment he turned to lead us toward the exit, I glanced down.

> Tempest: Have you landed yet? Can't wait to see you.

A smile spread across my face before I could stop it.

"Something more interesting than the Bandits' welcome wagon?" Dad's voice was low but knowing.

I pocketed my phone. "Just Tempest wanting to know if we landed safely."

Dad nodded, a hint of a smile playing at his lips. "Good. You should make plans to see her while we're here. Better to have that settled so you can focus when you need to. The Bandits are putting on the whole dog and pony show for you boys."

Gryff threw an arm around my shoulder. "Kingmans can handle a girl and football at the same time. The boys have proven that this last season."

"Shut up," I muttered, elbowing him as Marcus led us to a sleek black SUV with tinted windows.

As we pulled away from the curb, Marcus launched into his pitch. "The Bandits are building something special. New coaching staff, state-of-the-art facilities, and a quarterback who needs protection." He glanced at us in the rearview mirror. "Having both Kingman brothers as the foundation of our defense on both sides for the next decade? That's the kind of dynasty move that wins championships."

A decade in LA. The words settled in my chest, heavy with significance. I gazed out the window at the passing cityscape, at the endless stretch of possibility.

With these few minutes in the car, I texted Tempest back quickly.

> Me: Just met our Bandits liaison. Very slick. Hotel looks amazing, but I'd rather be wherever you are.

I hit send before I could overthink it, then looked up to find us pulling into the circular drive of an upscale hotel near the stadium. From our vantage point, I could see the Pacific stretching toward the horizon, though those distant clouds seemed a bit darker now, creeping steadily closer to shore.

"Home for the next few days, gentlemen," Marcus announced as the valet opened our doors. "Dinner in a few hours. Tomorrow, we show you the future."

The Bandits' training facility was nothing short of spectacular. A gleaming monument to modern sports science, it made our college facilities look like a high school weight room. Everything from the recovery pools to the film room screamed elite-level commitment.

"This is where the magic happens," Coach Rivera, the Bandits' defensive coordinator, spread his arms wide as we entered the main practice field. "State-of-the-art everything. Best training staff in the league. And soon," he pointed at us, "two Kingman anchors for our future plans."

A row of lockers stood against one wall, temporary nameplates already in place. F. KINGMAN and G. KINGMAN side by side, just like always.

"Visualize it," Rivera said. "We want you to see yourselves here."

I ran my fingers across the nameplate. It felt real. Tangible. The culmination of everything I'd worked for since I was five years old tossing a football with Dad in the backyard.

"This," he said, pressing play, "is where you come in."

For the next hour, I lost myself in football talk, schemes, stunts, blitz packages. It was all fascinating, all exactly what I'd dreamed about. But part of me kept drifting to thoughts of Tempest. I was here to make plans for my future, but that also meant planning our evening together.

Because with every passing minute, I knew without a doubt I wanted her to be a part of it.

"You want to do some sightseeing or have some fun off the field while you're here?" Rivera asked.

I definitely wanted to have some fun off the field. "Sir?"

"Focus, son." He laughed. "I asked if you're planning to enjoy LA while you're here."

"I, uh," I hesitated. "A friend is in town too, so just some dinner plans."

"Lady friend?" Rivera grinned knowingly at Dad. "Beautiful city for romance, LA."

Dad nodded, surprising me with his casual acknowledgment. "I want the boys to be able to make the most of their time here, all aspects of it, so they can really see if they want to spend the next ten years here."

"Well, we definitely want you to have fun while you're here too," Rivera clapped me on the shoulder. "Tomorrow we really put you through your paces."

"Yes, sir," I nodded, already counting the minutes until I got to see Tempest.

"Still thinking of Denver?" Gryff asked quietly as we headed back to the car.

I hesitated. "I'm thinking about the best opportunity."

"This is it, bro." He gestured around us. "This is everything we've worked for."

I wasn't ready to think about whether everything I'd worked for was still what I wanted.

A couple of hours later, I'd met some of the biggest players in the League both physically and as players that I looked up to. Tomorrow we were scheduled to meet the owner. The Bandits were really rolling out the red carpet for us.

But tonight, we had the evening free. Neither Gryff nor Dad said a word when I flew out of the hotel to meet up with Tempest. Finally.

I spotted her immediately. A bright spot of color against the increasingly gray sky, waiting at the entrance to the beach path where we'd agreed to meet. The sight of her made my heart go all wobbly, warm and dangerously close to the emotional territory I usually avoided.

But not anymore. Not with Tempest.

"Hey," I called, jogging the last few steps.

Tempest turned, her smile breaking across her face

like sunshine. She wore a flowing sundress that accentuated her curves, her wild curls whipping slightly in the growing breeze. "Hey yourself."

Without thinking, I pulled her into a hug, lifting her slightly off her feet. She laughed, and the sound did dangerous things to my heart rate.

"How's your break been so far?" I asked, setting her down but keeping my arms loosely around her waist.

"Amazing." Her eyes sparkled with excitement. "Better than I could have hoped. How's everything going with the Bandits?"

"Impressive," I admitted, taking her hand as we started walking along the path toward the beach. "The facilities are insane. Gryff's trying to be cool about it, but I can tell he's impressed too."

We reached the sand, both of us kicking off our shoes. The beach was emptier than I'd expected, especially for a nice evening, though a few determined couples and families still lounged on colorful blankets or splashed in the waves.

"Those clouds are moving in fast," Tempest noted, looking toward the horizon where the dark mass had grown significantly since morning. "Maybe we should have picked an indoor activity."

"A little water never hurt anyone," I grinned, pulling her toward the waves. "Come on, live dangerously."

She hesitated only a moment before laughing and running with me toward the water's edge. The surf crashed around our ankles, cold and shocking against the warm evening air. Tempest shrieked as a larger wave splashed higher than expected, soaking the hem of her dress.

"You trying to get me all wet?" she teased, eyes sparkling.

"Baby, I haven't even started. You're going to be soaked," I challenged, reaching out to grab her up.

But she laughed and sprinted away. "Gotta catch me first, Kingman."

What followed was utterly ridiculous, and more fun than I'd ever had with any woman before. The two of us chased each other through the shallow surf, splashing and laughing like children. She let me catch her eventually, breathless and beautiful with droplets of seawater on her skin.

"You're mine now, Navarro," I said softly, tucking a wet curl behind her ear.

Something shifted in her eyes then, vulnerability replacing playfulness. "Maybe I am. Maybe you're mine. What are you going to do about it?"

The moment hung between us, weighted with possibility. I cupped her face in my hands, my thumbs tracing the curve of her cheeks. "First, I'm going to kiss you. Because it's all I've been thinking about for days."

She smiled at that, a soft, shy thing that made my chest ache. "And then?"

"Then," I said, lowering my head until our lips were a breath apart, "I'm going to figure out how to make this work, even if I end up in LA and you're still in Denver."

Her eyes widened slightly, surprise and something like hope flickering in their depths. "You've been thinking about that?"

"I've been thinking about nothing else," I admitted, the confession easier in the fading light with the sound of waves crashing around us.

In the distance, thunder rumbled, but I barely registered it as our lips finally met. This was a real kiss, deep and searching, her arms winding around my neck as I pulled her closer. She tasted like salt and sweetness, like everything I hadn't known I was looking for, hadn't known I needed. Everything I'd denied myself for too many years.

A louder crack of thunder finally broke us apart, and we looked up to find the sky had darkened dramatically. The few remaining beachgoers were hurriedly packing up, casting wary glances at the approaching storm front.

"Looks like we're in for some weather," I murmured, reluctant to break the moment but increasingly aware of the strengthening wind.

From a nearby blanket, a portable radio crackled. "...unexpected storm surge warning for coastal Los Angeles. Residents and visitors are advised to seek higher ground..."

"Maybe we should head back," Tempest said, though she made no move to leave the circle of my arms.

I nodded, pressing one more quick kiss to her lips. "Dinner first? I saw a cute place right up from the beach."

She smiled, lacing her fingers through mine. "Lead the way, Kingman."

Hand in hand, we trudged back up the beach as the first fat raindrops began to fall, each one a cold shock against my sun-warmed skin. The darkening sky and approaching storm should have felt ominous, but with

Tempest's hand in mine, all I felt was possibility stretching out before us, as vast and deep as the ocean itself.

"I think," Tempest said, peering out from under the restaurant's awning at the sheets of rain now pounding the beachfront, "we might have a problem."

What had started as a few threatening clouds had escalated with alarming speed into a full-blown storm. Wind howled down the streets, bending palm trees at alarming angles and sending beach umbrellas tumbling like colorful tumbleweeds. The restaurant staff had started boarding up windows as we approached, and closed their doors for the storm.

"We're closing early for safety," the manager explained. "The storm surge warning has been upgraded to an emergency."

I glanced at my phone, wincing at the multiple missed calls from both Dad and Gryff. A text from Dad flashed on the screen.

> Dad: Where are you? Let me know you and Tempest are safe.

I quickly texted him back letting him know we were together, near the beach, and safe.

We would be anyway. I grabbed Tempest's hand. "Let's try to get an Uber back to one of our hotels."

Water already pooled ankle-deep on the sidewalk, rushing down the sloped street toward the beach. The rain was coming down in near-horizontal sheets, the wind so strong it was difficult to stand upright.

Did California get hurricanes? I thought it was just earthquakes. What the actual fuck?

I tapped on my phone, but the rideshare app showed no available cars. "Everyone's trying to get to safety at once," I murmured, tucking Tempest under the minimal shelter.

"We have to find some place to get inside." Tempest shivered against me. "But I don't think we can walk. My hotel is at least two miles away. Where's yours?"

"Let's try finding somewhere closer," I said, my protective instincts kicking into overdrive. "There are restaurants and businesses all along this strip."

Tempest's teeth were chattering despite my arm around her shoulders. I needed to get her somewhere safe and warm, now.

The manager headed toward his car and I ran out into the rain after him. "Can we get a ride? We're really stuck, man."

"I gotta get home to my kids, but there's a small place, Inanna and Kur's Cabins, about three blocks inland," he said after a moment. "On higher ground. Old school place, separate cabins instead of rooms. Might be worth trying."

I returned to Tempest. "I have a lead. Three blocks that way, up the hill. Think you can make it?"

She nodded, determination replacing the fear in her eyes. "Let's go."

We half ran, half waded through the flooded streets, holding tight to each other against the buffeting wind. By the time we spotted the faded "Inanna and Kur's Cabins" sign, we were both soaked to the skin, water streaming from our clothes and hair.

The office was dimly lit, an elderly man wearing a rainbow Hawaiian style shirt and a twinkle in his eyes peering out as we approached, looking unsurprised by our bedraggled appearance.

"Hurry you two, get your butts in here." he said, opening the door. "Stranded by this storm?"

"Yes, sir," I nodded, water dripping from my hair onto the worn linoleum floor. "Any chance you have a room for us?"

Tempest shivered beside me and I was fully prepared to give over my life savings to this guy for a hot shower and some warm blankets for her.

The old man, Kur, according to his nametag, shook his head slowly. "My cabins are full up. But the people for number eight, haven't shown up yet, and I don't suppose their likely to in this weather." He eyed us appraisingly. "It's yours if you want it."

"We'll take it," I said, pulling out my wallet.

Kur handed over an actual key, not a keycard, attached to a massive wooden fob. "Power's gonna be spotty in this storm. Got extra blankets and lanterns in there. Might be a long night."

"Thanks," I said, handing over my credit card. "We appreciate it."

As Kur processed the payment, I called my dad real quick. "We're safe. Bunkering down at someplace called Inanna and Kur's Cabins."

"Take care of each other." The concern in his voice was evident. "You two are more important than any football team or meeting, understood? The Bandits will still be interested tomorrow."

"Yes, sir," I said, oddly touched by his immediate acceptance of us as a unit, a "we" that needed protection.

Kur handed back my card with a knowing look that I pretended not to see. "Cabin eight, up the path to the right. Highest point on the property. Should stay dry no matter how bad this gets."

We thanked him and stepped back out into the storm, my arm protectively around Tempest as we made our way up the waterlogged path. The cabin, when we reached it, was exactly as advertised—small, somewhat shabby, but mercifully dry and on solid ground well above the flooding below.

I unlocked the door, both of us practically falling inside as a gust of wind pushed at our backs. The interior was simple. A small bathroom, a chair in the corner, and a tiny table with a battery-powered lantern, and a little gift basket with a bottle of wine and some fruit and nuts.

And one bed.

One, barely bigger than my ass, bed.

"Home sweet home," I said, trying for levity as we stood dripping on the worn carpet.

Tempest's breath came out in a shaky laugh. "Could be worse."

As if on cue, the lights flickered, dimmed, and then went out entirely, leaving us in darkness broken only by occasional flashes of lightning through the curtained window.

"You were saying?" I murmured, fumbling for the lantern.

In the soft glow that followed, I could see Tempest's dress clinging to her curves, her hair plastered to her neck, her arms wrapped around herself as another shiver wracked her body.

"You need to get out of those wet clothes," I said, my voice rougher than I'd intended. "You're freezing."

"So do you," she countered, though her teeth were still chattering.

We stood frozen for a moment, the implication of our situation suddenly, acutely clear. One room. One bed. No dry clothes. And a long night ahead of us.

A particularly bright flash of lightning illuminated the room, followed almost instantly by a deafening crack of thunder that seemed to shake the small cabin. The storm was directly overhead now, wild and untamed, isolating us in our temporary shelter.

"Flynn?" Tempest's voice was small, vulnerable in a way I'd never heard before.

"Yeah?"

Her hair tumbled in damp waves around her face, and her eyes, when they met mine, held a mixture of trust and something deeper, more primal, that made my breath catch.

"Know any ways to get warm in a hurry?"

Did I ever.

MAKE ME TREMBLE

TEMPEST

"Tempest." Just my name, but the way he said it made my skin tingle. "I want you so fucking bad, but I want you to be sure you want to do this."

I wasn't sure of anything except that I wanted him, this connection, this moment, wanted to feel his skin against mine. I nodded. "I'm sure. I want to be with you. I want you."

He moved toward me slowly, like I was something precious that might spook. He stroked his knuckles down my cheek, his touch impossibly gentle. "I'm going to keep checking in with you every step of the way, and you tell me yes or no, or to stop, or even please, more. Okay?"

"Okay."

"Good girl. Now I'm going to kiss you until you go weak in the knees."

Ooph. He didn't even have to actually kiss me, I was already feeling a bit wobbly. Good girl? Was he kidding me with the words straight out of the pages of my dirtiest scenes?

But he didn't kiss me, he simply stared down at me with those dark and sparkling eyes.

"What are you waiting for?" The words were barely a whisper, and I wasn't even sure that was my voice breaking the silence.

"For you to tell me yes or no."

Oh. Holy cojónes. Why was the way he was asking for my consent so freaking hot? "Kiss me, please, kiss me."

"That's my girl." His lips met mine, soft and warm and perfect. Unlike our beach kiss, this one started slow, unhurried. His mouth moved against mine with exquisite care, as if he had all the time in the world to learn what made me sigh, what made me melt.

And melt I did. Right into a puddle of goo.

Sweet baby Jesus, what was my name again?

His hand bunched up one side of my dress, a thumb peeking underneath, barely caressing the skin of my upper thigh. He broke the kiss, brushing his lips across mine as I tried so hard to find where my breath had gone. "I want your dress off. I've been dying to see what you look like in nothing but a few scraps of lingerie."

I swallowed, then nodded. My bra and panties weren't exactly fancy lingerie, but they did match and had bits of lace on them. I'd picked them out special, just to feel sexy, not really knowing if he'd ever see them. Now I very much wanted him to see every stitch. "Take it off."

His fingers were warm as they slipped beneath the fabric, skimming up my stomach, over my chest and shoulders. Slowly, reverently, he unwrapped me like a gift, his eyes taking in every inch of exposed skin with such open appreciation that not once did I feel the urge to cover myself or hide from his gaze.

"You're better than every fucking wet dream I've ever had," he murmured, his voice almost awed. "So soft, and lush."

No one had ever looked at me the way Flynn did, like I was everything he'd ever wanted. Not like an afterthought or the ugly duckling, but like I was exactly right, exactly as I should be.

He dropped the dress to the floor, and I stood before him, bare and vulnerable. His eyes traveled over me, leaving heat in their wake. "I'm going to worship every inch of your body, my queen."

"Yes," I said, gaining courage from the desire in his eyes. "But first, it's my turn."

"God, you are such a turn on. Take your turn with me, sweet storm of mine."

My hands were clumsy finding the hem of his still-damp shirt. He raised his arms obligingly, letting me pull it over his head. Water droplets traced paths down his torso, and I followed their journey with my fingers, exploring the ridges and planes of him.

I could write sonnets about how gorgeous he was, a whole soliloquy to that vee of muscles at his waist, an ode to that tempting swatch of hair at his belly that dipped below his belt, the one that tempted me to touch, and follow it down, down, down.

He stood perfectly still, letting me take my time, though I could see the tension in his muscles, feel the restraint in his shallow breathing. My hands moved to his belt, fumbling slightly with the buckle. Flynn's hands covered mine, steadying them.

"No rush," he murmured. "We have all night."

Together we undid his belt, then the button of his jeans. I slid the zipper down, feeling him hard beneath the fabric. Heat flooded my cheeks, but I didn't look away. No, I pushed the wet denim down his legs, kneeling to help him step out of them.

The pure, unadulterated need on his face as he looked down at me on my knees in front of him gave me a surge of feelings I'd never in my life experienced before. I... I think it was a sense of feminine power. The knowledge that I was everything he wanted and more.

Only with him. He was the only one who I ever wanted to make me feel that way.

I ran my hands up his thighs, feeling the powerful muscles tense beneath my touch. The bulge in the front of his boxer briefs grew even bigger, and I bit my lip, staring up at him.

"You're shivering," he said, his own voice not entirely steady.

"I'm not cold," I admitted. "Just... nervous."

His expression softened. "Nothing has to happen, Tempest. Remember, you can say stop at any time. We'll crawl under those blankets and simply keep each other warm. We'll sleep or talk or—"

"What if I want something to happen?"

His eyes widened slightly, then darkened with heat. His hand came down to cradle my chin, his touch impossibly gentle. "Then we go as slow as you need. And you tell me what you want, every step of the way."

"I want to see you. All of you," I whispered. "But I've never..." I started, then stopped, embarrassment washing over me.

"I know," he said simply.

I wanted to look away, but I couldn't. I was captured in his gaze.

He brushed a strand of hair from my face. "You told me after our first kiss, and it doesn't scare me, Tempest. I told you I want to be the one who gets to do all of your firsts with you."

"Even if I have no idea what I'm doing?" That was definitely not what I wanted to be thinking about right now.

"Yeah." His thumb traced my lower lip, sending shivers down my spine. "It means you trust me. And trust like that is sexy as hell."

His words eased something inside me, a knot of anxiety I hadn't fully acknowledged. I did trust him, and he was trusting me in return. He was right. That was sexy as hell.

I slid my hands further up his thighs and reached for the waistband of his boxers. He didn't move a centimeter as I pulled them down his hips and then his thighs until he was completely exposed to me.

Okay, it's not like I hadn't seen a penis before. I watched plenty of... well, some people called it porn, but I called it research for my books. But seeing Flynn, so hard, so big, knowing it was because of me and what I was doing for him, made me ache in all the best ways.

I reached for him, but paused just before I touched. It was my turn to ask for his consent. "Can I touch you?"

His "yes" was nearly a growl, raw and eager.

I took him in my hand, wrapping my fingers around his cock. He was hot and hard and almost silky smooth. The sound he made when I stroked him sent a fresh wave of heat through me.

"Tempest," he groaned. "You're killing me."

"Good," I said, surprising myself with my boldness. "I want to."

I leaned into him, pressing my lips to his tip, darting my tongue out to taste him. Flynn's hand slid into my hair and he gripped a handful of it, sending ripples of heat through my scalp. "Tempest."

The harsh groan in his voice stopped me and I looked up. God, I hoped I wasn't already doing this all wrong. I was trying to remember how I'd written scenes like this and channeled my inner heroine.

"I'm the one who is supposed to be making you tremble, not the other way around." His voice did indeed have the slightest tremor to it. Because of me.

"Don't you want me to?" I licked my lips, full well knowing I was teasing him and I liked it.

"To suck my cock?" He said those words so easily, even if his voice was one hundred percent feral werewolf at the moment. "Yeah, I do. You have no idea how much. But one inch, hell, one millimeter into your mouth, and I'm going to come faster than some untried schoolboy."

"I want to see you come." I don't know who this inner wanton was, but I liked her and hoped she'd stick around. Before I got another word out of my mouth though, Flynn grabbed me up princess style.

Like, full-on, picked me up and took the three steps across the room. I was so shocked, I didn't even have time to squeal before he quite literally tossed me on the bed like I was some kind of fluffy pillow.

Then he crawled right up and over me, caging me under his body. "I have no doubt you're going to make me come, hard. But I have one more rule and I'm not willing to break this one."

I blinked up at him, finding it hard to do much more than breathe with all his attention, his barely contained sexual need, not mention all those muscles, focused directly on me. Somehow I found two words and plucked them out of the sweltering air between us. "What rule?"

"You come first. Always. Got it?"

If I hadn't already been on fire, and very wet, I would be now. I'd written about how the guys in my books had their minds go on the fritz because all their blood went straight to their dicks when they were turned on. I didn't expect it to ever happen to me. But hot damn if my pussy wasn't pulsing in time with my heart, and my brain had only the capacity to whimper, "Uh-huh."

"That's what I want to hear," he smiled and licked his lips. "Now I'm going to taste every single bit of you, and make you come for me."

But just like that first kiss, he didn't move, waiting for my affirmation.

"Please." The word came out breathier than I'd intended.

His lips moved to my throat, then paused. "I'm going to taste you here."

"Yes."

He didn't just kiss me, he scraped his teeth and then

tongue across my skin. Then his mouth moved down and hovered just above my bra.

"I need your bra gone."

I nodded, then remembering his need for verbal confirmation, whispered, "Do it, take it off."

The bra was unhooked and down my arms faster than I could blink, and his hand cupped my breast, his thumb brushing across my nipple. I gasped at the sensation, arching into his touch.

"Like that?" he asked, his voice strained.

"Yes," I breathed. "More."

He repeated the motion, watching my face as he learned what made me gasp, what made me press closer. When he lowered his head, his eyes held mine.

"I can't wait to taste this, Tempest."

God, the way he said my name, like a prayer, like a promise. "Yes."

His mouth replaced his hand, warm and wet, and I couldn't stop the moan that escaped me. His tongue circled my nipple before he drew it into his mouth, sending jolts of pleasure through my body. My hand found his hair, fingers tangling in the damp strands as I held him to me.

Flynn shifted, sitting back, leaving me exposed to his gaze. His eyes traveled over my body with undisguised appreciation. "You're so fucking delicious," he said. "Every inch of you."

I knew what I looked like. According to every magazine, TV show, and social media post, I was too round, too soft, too much in all the wrong places . But the way Flynn looked at me made me feel like I was exactly the right softness, the perfect amount of round, and exactly enough in all the right places.

He kissed his way down my body, brushing his beard down my cleavage, pausing at my stomach to kiss my belly button, nibble at the stretch marks on the curve of my hip, at suck on the soft flesh of my inner thigh. Each fresh territory came with him telling me exactly what he was going to do and I didn't even realize a dirty mouth could be the best kind of request for my consent to keep going. But it was and each of my answers only fueled his hunger.

By the time his face was at the very core of me, I was a wreck of anticipation. "Spread your thighs so I can fuck your wet pussy with my mouth and make you come."

I know I was supposed to agree out loud, but all I could do was comply with his demand.

He licked his lips and then his head was between my legs, licking, learning, tasting, teasing. Holy moly. I never would have guessed the tickle of facial hair on my inner thighs was a turn on, but whew, boy. I was telling Flynn never to shave his beard. Was beard burn on thighs a thing? I desperately wanted to find out.

When he finally licked across my clit for the first time, it made me gasp so loud, I clasped my hands over my mouth. But nothing prepared me for the way he looked up, watching my face as he brought me pleasure.

"Flynn," I managed, my voice barely recognizable. "I need—"

"Tell me what you need," he encouraged. "I want to hear you say it."

"I want you, inside of me," I whispered. "Please, I need more of you."

"Just as soon as you come for me, my queen." He pressed my legs wider and dipped his head back down, not just licking this time, but sucking my clit into his mouth, while pressing his fingers against my entrance.

There wasn't a rose toy or vibrator on the planet that had anything on Flynn Kingman's mouth and beard. I went from oh-that-feels-so-good to coming so hard I was seeing stars in seconds. My back arched, and my muscles locked. The only thing I could do was feel, feel the force of the orgasm that rocked through me until I was nothing but a mass of bliss and pure pleasure.

Flynn didn't let up until my body finally floated down from the high he'd just taken me to, and my muscles relaxed one by one. He crawled back up my body and wrapped himself around me, whispering, "You're a god damned goddess when you come. You did so well, and taste like a fucking dream. I can't wait to make you come on my face over and over."

Somewhere in the haze I found my voice, though it was a little rough. "Is that what they mean when the books say he whispered sweet nothings?"

He chuckled and held me tighter. "They aren't nothings. I mean every word."

"Can we do that again?"

His laugh was a little choked this time. "As many times as you want."

"What if I want something else? Something more?"

"Anything, love."

God, this was going to sound so corny. But it's what I wanted, more than anything else. "Make love to me."

He rolled away suddenly, and I made a sound of protest until I realized he was reaching for his jeans. He pulled out his wallet, extracting a foil packet.

He tore the packet open, his expression turning serious. "Tempest, are you absolutely sure about this? Because once we start, I'm not sure I'll be able to stop. Fuck, I don't mean that. I'll stop mid-fucking coming if you asked me to, but—"

I reached for him, pulling him back to me. "I don't want you to stop."

He rolled the condom on, then settled between my thighs, his weight supported on his forearms. I could feel him, hard and insistent, pressing against me.

His eyes searching mine. "Tell me if you need me to stop."

"I will," I promised. "But don't stop unless I tell you to."

He smiled at that, then kissed me deeply as he began to push inside. There was pressure, an unfamiliar stretching that bordered on discomfort but didn't quite cross into pain. I focused on his kiss, on the feeling of his body against mine, and then he was buried deep within me, our bodies as close as two people could be.

"Is this what you want?" he asked, his voice tight with restraint.

I nodded, adjusting to the newness of having him inside me. "Yes. Don't stop."

He began to move, his eyes never leaving my face as he watched for any sign of discomfort. The initial strangeness gave way to pleasure as our bodies found a rhythm together. He reached between us, his fingers finding my clit again, circling in time with his thrusts.

"Flynn," I gasped, my body tightening around him. "That feels—"

"Good?" he asked, his voice strained. "Tell me, Tempest. I need to hear you."

"So good," I managed. "Don't stop."

He moved faster, deeper, his control visibly slipping as pleasure built between us. I wrapped my legs around his waist, drawing him closer, wanting more of him.

"That's it," he encouraged. "Take what you need. Show me what you want."

His words, his touch, the feeling of him moving inside me, it all became too good. The tension that had been building shattered, and the orgasm hit me even harder than before. I called his name, my fingers digging into his shoulders as my body clenched around him.

Flynn faltered, buried his face in my neck, a groan tearing from his throat, and came right along with me. For several heartbeats, we remained locked together, our breathing ragged, our skin damp with sweat rather than rain.

Slowly, carefully, he rolled to the side, taking me with him so that I lay half-across his chest. His hand traced lazy patterns on my back as our breathing gradually returned to normal.

"Flynn—"

"I know it's too soon," he said quickly. "I know we haven't been doing this, us, for very long. But Tempest, I... I'm absolutely nuts about you. I've never felt like this about anyone before."

A short time ago, I would have thought that was a line. I would have put my walls up, and I definitely wouldn't have believed him. Instead, I searched inside my heart and said, "Me neither."

His smile could have lit up the darkened cabin. "Yeah?"

"Yeah." I settled back against his chest, listening to the steady rhythm of his heart.

Outside, the storm continued to rage, wind and rain battering the small cabin. But inside, wrapped in Flynn's arms, I felt safer than I ever had before. For the first time in my life, I wasn't hiding. Wasn't pretending to be someone I wasn't.

With him, I was just Tempest. And somehow, miraculously, that seemed to be exactly who he wanted.

"I want to tell you about something. Something important to me, about me." The words came easier in the dark, in the safety of his arms.

He shifted, his hand coming up to stroke my hair. "You can tell me anything."

I took a deep breath. He waited, giving me space to find the words. No pressure, no impatience. Just acceptance.

"I'm not just here on spring break. I was, am working," I said finally. "I was meeting my agent, and FlixNChill, because I write romance novels and they want to make them into a series."

There. It was out. The secret I'd guarded so carefully, revealed in the aftermath of the most intimate night of my life. I held my breath, waiting for his reaction.

Flynn's hand stilled in my hair, then resumed its gentle stroking. "Is that what you're always writing in that notebook? The one you slam shut whenever I get too close?"

I nodded against his chest, not trusting myself to speak.

"That's... cool as shit, babe." The genuine admiration in his voice made me look up. "You're already a published author? While still in college?"

"You're not... disappointed? Or weirded out?"

His brow furrowed. "Wait, they are dirty, aren't they?"

I snort-laughed and definitely blushed a little. "Yeah, I write pretty spicy stuff."

"Tempie, my girlfriend, writes dirty romance novels. I'm the luckiest man on the planet."

I was his girlfriend?

"Ooh," he said with a whole lot of excitement in his voice. "Does this count as research? Fuck, yeah. I am so down to get you inspired to write all night long."

Same.

BAGGACHOMC

FLYNN

*L*ight filtered through the thin curtains of the cabin, painting golden streaks across Tempest's adorable as fuck sleeping face. I'd been awake for nearly an hour, just watching her.

This moment felt... different. I'd woken up next to plenty of women before, but never with this bone-deep contentment. Never with this certainty that there was nowhere else I'd rather be.

I was so fucking in love with her.

This wasn't some fling, and I wasn't pretending it was only because she'd let me into her bed. I wanted into her heart too.

The plan had always been to feel nothing, attach to no one, protect myself. But I traced the curve of Tempest's cheek with my eyes, cataloging the constellation of freckles across her nose, and there was only this surprising sense of rightness.

Loving her wasn't scary. It was the easiest, most natural thing I'd ever done.

Her eyes fluttered open, confusion giving way to recognition as she focused on me. "Were you watching me sleep?" Her voice was husky with sleep.

"Guilty." I smiled, tucking a curl behind her ear. "You drool, by the way."

She gasped, hand flying to her mouth, and I laughed.

"I'm kidding." I pulled her closer, reveling in the warmth of her against me.

"Jackass." She pushed halfheartedly at my chest, but snuggled closer. "What time is it?"

"Early." I pressed a kiss to her forehead. "Storm's passed, but let's pretend it's still a freak hurricane outside so we can stay in bed."

She hummed contentedly, her fingers tracing absent patterns on my chest. I caught her hand, bringing it to my lips.

"Are you going to make me guess your pen name like I did with Burrito, or will you tell me, my sexy, mysterious author?"

A blush crept up her neck, but there was a hint of pride in her eyes as she said, "I don't think I could take your awful guesses."

"Come on. If it's not Amanda Hugandkiss, I give up." I already had at least half a dozen just as ridiculous guesses at the ready.

Tempest put her hand over my mouth. "It's Miranda Milan."

The name hit me like a linebacker at full speed. "Wait...like THE Miranda Milan?"

Her eyes widened. "You've heard of me?"

"Jules is obsessed with your books." I sat up, incredulous. "She made every Kingman in a ten mile radius scour bookstores when your last one came out because they were sold out everywhere."

Tempest's mouth fell open, then curved into a surprised smile. "Are you serious?"

"Completely. There's a group chat with Trixie's book club called 'Mint Milans' where they freak out over every single book." I accidentally let out a laugh at her stunned expression. "Tempest, do you not realize how big your books are?"

She shook her head slightly. "I mean, obviously I know they sell well, but it's hard to connect that with... real readers. Real people." Her fingers fidgeted with the edge of the sheet. "It still doesn't feel real sometimes."

"It's very real." I cupped her face in my hand and brushed my thumb across her lower lip. I kissed her softly. "And I'm more than happy to help with further research." I let my eyes travel down her body, still half covered by the sheet. "Got any positions you haven't written about that you wanna try out?"

She bit her lip. "I hadn't tried any of it until last night."

I kept my tone fun and flirty, wanting her to be at ease with me and everything we did together. "Then I volunteer as tribute. Use me and my body for all your research purposes."

"Research purposes, huh?" She was trying her best to be playful right back but I saw the flash of uncertainty in her eyes. "I'm not exactly... light. What if I hurt you?"

Aha. My girl wanted to try being on top. The thought of Tempest riding my dick, taking her pleasure at her will, had me hard in half a second flat.

I lifted her chin, making her look at me. "My queen, I'm a D1 athlete about to go pro. I've been training my body my entire life. I'm not some breakable toy. If I'm not man enough to have my girl ride me like a cowgirl, I don't know what I have all these muscle for."

"Umm, for football?"

"Football schmootball. Plus," I added with a wink, "it gives you all the control. You set the pace, the depth. I just get to lie back and enjoy the view."

A smile tugged at her lips. "For research purposes."

"Purely literary related," I agreed solemnly.

She laughed then, the sound warming me from the inside. "I suppose I should be thorough in my methodology."

I threw the sheets off and guided her over me, my hands sinking into the soft flesh at her hips. "Very thorough."

"Wait. Condom. I've always wanted to write the whole putting one on with her mouth, but it seemed so awkward. You have more, don't you?"

My laugh came out half bark, half shocked surprise. "Maybe we save that for later, because I only brought a couple and that sounds like it would take some practice. Which sounds fun and all, but—"

"But I'd rather use the one you have left so I can have my way with you." God she was so fucking cute and completely sexy without meaning to be all at the same time. She rolled off the bed and found my wallet in my jeans, pulling out the remaining condom. "But will you show me how to put it on you?"

She was going to be the death of me. What a way to go.

We got the condom on, and she straddled me once again, then looked down. She frowned, and pressed one hand against her soft, round belly.

"Wait, how am I supposed to...I can't see what I'm aiming for." She laughed and shook her head. "I mean... that's definitely going in a book."

I grabbed my dick in one hand and wrapped my other around the edge of her waist. "Let me do the aiming. You just feel your way around once you get there."

Tempest sank down onto my cock and it took all I had in me not to just thrust my hips up and start fucking her. Her expression was deliberate and thoughtful as she tested out the sensations. But her initial hesitation melted as she found a rhythm, and I lost my goddamn mind.

"Fu-uck, Tempest."

Confidence bloomed as she watched the effect she had on me. I kept my eyes on hers, letting her see exactly what she did to me, how beautiful she was above me.

"This feels incredible."

"That's it," I encouraged, my voice strained. "Take what you need. Show me what you want."

"I want to come like this," she panted, "but I don't know if my legs can take it. This is hard work."

She laughed, until I reached between us and pressed my thumb against her clit. "Slow down if you need to. I'll get you there."

"Flynn," she gasped, her head falling back.

I thrust my hips, filling her, rubbing my thumb over her clit, and recited DSU football stats in my head so I didn't come before she did. But she felt so incredible, looked even better with the wild abandon on her face, taking her pleasure from me, that I wasn't going to last more than about three more thrusts.

If I didn't find a way to push her over the edge and soon, I was going to break my golden rule of sex. What my romance writing sex-goddess loved was words. So I pulled out all the stops.

"Be a good girl and come hard on my cock." She moaned and I knew I was on the right track. Just a little more. "Come for me, Tempest. Give me that orgasm. It's mine now, you're mine now."

She gasped and her inner muscles squeezed around me so hard I lost my battle trying to make sure she came first. The way her entire body shuddered and shattered, the way she groaned out my name, was more than I could take. I exploded right along with her, the orgasm hitting with such intensity, I quite literally saw stars floating around my angel's head.

Afterward, she collapsed against my chest, both of us breathing hard. I held her close, my hands tracing the curve of her spine.

"Good research?" I murmured into her hair.

She laughed against my skin. "Excellent. Very... thorough. So incredibly informational."

"Happy to be your test subject anytime." I pressed a kiss to the top of her head, marveling at how right she felt in my arms, how complete.

A buzzing sound interrupted our little blissful afterglow bubble. We'd lost signal sometime during the storm. Both our phones went off at the same time.

"I guess the real world is back and has found us," I sighed, reluctantly reaching for my phone.

"Cell service must have just gotten restored," Tempest said, pulling the sheet around herself as she leaned over the edge of the bed to retrieve her own phone from her discarded clothes.

I had twelve missed calls from Dad, five from Gryff, and a string of texts ranging from concerned to panicked. I shot off a quick group message.

> Me: We're both fine. Heading back to hotel soon-ish.

Tempest was frowning at her own screen. "Eight missed calls from my agent. That's... unprecedented." She looked uncertain as she pressed call.

I busied myself checking my other messages while she spoke to her agent. The Bandits PR team wanted to reschedule our meeting with the owner.

"Gloria, I'm fine," Tempest was saying. "We found shelter... Yes, 'we'. I was with... a friend." Her eyes flicked to mine, a smile playing at her lips. "Of course I understand they aren't happy about that," she continued, her tone shifting to something more professional, more assured. "I will be a producer and maintain final say on that. I won't have them Hollywood white-washing or skinny-washing my heroines. It's nonnegotiable if they want the books."

I watched, fascinated, as she negotiated terms with the confidence of a seasoned professional. This was yet another side of Tempest I hadn't seen. Badass businesswoman, the successful author protecting her work. It was sexy as hell.

"Yes, email them over and I'll have my lawyer review

before signing." She hung up, meeting my appreciative gaze. "What?"

"Nothing." I grinned. "Just enjoying watching author Tempest in action. It's hot."

She rolled her eyes, but couldn't hide her pleased smile. "FlixNChill is sending over the contracts today. But they want the next book in the series ASAP. I'm on, like, chapter three and it's already overdue."

"What's it about?"

Tempest glanced up at me and turned fifty shades of pink. She huffed out a laugh and tried to look away, but I held her chin so she couldn't.

"Ooh. Something really dirty, then." Why were the sweet, innocent ones always the ones with the best imaginations? And by best I meant utterly kinky and wicked. "I love it. Tell me, Ms. Milan."

"I'm gonna make you sign an NDA first."

"All your secrets are safe with me, sweetheart." That may have sounded flirty, but I meant it sincerely.

She took a big breath and narrowed her eyes on me. "Do not read anything into this, Kingman."

"Who, me? I'm just a big dumb jock who doesn't read. So tell me." We both knew that wasn't even close to the truth. Although, I hadn't read a romance novel before, I was about to start.

Tempest looked up at the ceiling, finding it utterly fascinating. "It's a retelling of *Twelfth Night*."

She still wasn't looking at me. "And?"

One long exhale and a thousand darts of her gaze anywhere but at me, and she finally said, "With football players."

Oh ho-ho. "The play where not a single one of them actually takes the time to get to know each other so there's no way it was actually love, they're all just horny and should have just had one big orgy? That *Twelfth Night*, but with football players, oh, and there's twins too?"

She swatted my arm, but her laugh was warm. "Yes, that *Twelfth Night*. Why in the world is the only man I've ever had feelings for the one football player on the planet who actually knows anything about Shakespeare?"

My heart literally skipped a beat. Hell to the fuck yeah. She'd just said she had feelings for me. Out loud. I wasn't going to push on it though. I knew to take the win for what it was. For now.

"We should celebrate." I sat up, pulling her into my lap. "Let's do something fun tonight."

"Absolutely," she said. "But FlixNChill and my agent have been taking me to all these fancy restaurants, and you know what I really want?"

"Please say ordering in and a whole box of condoms to practice that putting it on with your mouth trick." Sounded like the perfect night to me.

"Good try." She smirked at me. "I want regular food. Burgers, or tacos. Let's see if these Californians can complete with our Mountain Mex."

"How about taco flavored condoms?"

We, in fact, got tacos that night instead of flavored condoms. Sadly, but also not, because it turned out Abuela had lived in LA as a young mother and knew exactly where to send us for really fucking good Mexican food. We ate a metric fuckton of every flavor taco we could at three different hole-in-the-wall places and one food truck.

"You two crazy kids want to go out on the town with me?" Gryff asked, then downed the remainder of his four hundredth birria taco.

There was something off about him tonight. "You good, bro?"

There was a pause before Gryff answered. "Nothing a night out won't fix. Just need to find someone to either be a rebound or break my heart again."

I didn't need twin telepathy for this one. This wasn't just shit talking. Something, or someone, had happened, and it had hurt my tough-guy with a mushy-gushy cinnamon roll of a heart brother. I'd kill 'em.

"You want to talk about it?" I asked carefully.

"Nope." The forced cheer in his voice was painful to hear. "Just want to shake my groove thang and make bad decisions."

"Fair enough." I knew better than to push. But I made a mental note to keep an eye on him tonight. Gryff had always been the more romantic of the two of us, falling faster and harder. Whoever this was had done a number on him.

Gryff nodded and then turned to Tempest. "Isn't clubbing a thing that young, beautiful, people do in LA? You up for some dancing till dawn, doll?"

"Sure. But maybe not until dawn. My bookish introverted heart really wants to be in bed by nine."

I liked the idea of in bed by nine, because I had other ideas of what to do that would keep her up all night.

"Come on, let's go shake that fine ass your mama gave

you." He jumped up on the picnic table bench and spun in a circle.

Tempest laughed at Gryff's taunt. "Fine. But you leave my mother out of this. She would definitely not approve."

"Good." I tossed our trash into the bin next to the food truck. "All the more reason to go. I'd like to show off my girlfriend tonight."

Her eyebrows shot up. "Girlfriend?"

"Yeah. My very sexy girlfriend."

A couple hours later we were showered, changed and in a town car on our way to some exclusive club my older brother's fiancé got us on the list for. Being the future first-round draft picks and the younger brothers of the Bowl winning Mustangs' quarterback, not to mention future brothers-in-law with the one and only Kelsey Best opened doors in a celebrity obsessed town like LA.

"Come on in, Kingmans." The manager greeted us like old friends, though we'd never met. "We've got a bottle-service booth ready for you."

Tempest squeezed my hand as we were led through the crush of beautiful people to a private booth.

"Is this normal?" she whispered.

"For LA? I think so." I kept her close, enjoying the envious glances she was receiving.

Gryff hit the floor right away and had men and women hitting on him in no time. I led Tempest out to dance and pulled her tight against me. She licked her lips and gave me the cutest little eyebrow waggle. Then proceeded to blow my mind with her dirty dancing skills, her curves moving in ways that made my mouth go dry and my dick eternally hard.

"You're staring again," she practically shouted against my ear over the ridiculously loud music.

"Can't help it." My hands slid to her hips, drawing her closer, pressing my lips to her ear. "Do you have any idea how beautiful you are? How every guy in this place is wishing they were me right now?"

She laughed, but I could see she didn't quite believe me. "Other way around."

"Trust me." I pressed a kiss to her neck. "I'm the lucky one here."

As I held her on that crowded dance floor, the bass thumping through us like a second heartbeat, I could see our future spreading out before us, game days and book launches, quiet nights and celebrations like this one. Successes and struggles, navigated together.

I wanted it all.

We hit three more clubs, danced our asses off, and when dawn broke, Gryff said he'd had enough of our disgustingly cute lovey-dovey-ness and went back to the hotel. Tempest and I found some hole-in-the-wall diner for breakfast.

"I'm never dancing all night ever again," Tempest groaned stretching her legs out, hiding her face in her hands as we waited for our breakfast order.

"That's what they all say." I slid her foot into my lap, popped off her shoe and rubbed it. "Here. This might help."

She leaned back and groaned, then reached for her water. "I can't believe your brother got us to close down the club."

I shook my head. "He's an all-in or nothing guy, and last night, he was definitely all-in."

"Must run in the family." Her smile was soft, knowing.

The waitress set down a carafe of coffee and a pitcher of water without being asked. Bless her.

I poured us each a cup, and caught sight of something on the screen of the restaurant's TV. The sound was muted, but the headline was clear. "MIRANDA MILAN'S BEST-SELLING SERIES COMING TO FLIXNCHILL."

"Tempest," I said quietly, nodding toward the screen.

She turned, her cup freezing halfway to her mouth.

The screen showed a glamorous shot of what must have been her book cover, then cut to some entertainment reporter. "...mysterious author may finally be unveiled as production begins."

Tempest's coffee cup shattered on the floor.

MEASURE FOR MEASURE

TEMPEST

The sound of ceramic shattering against tile echoed in my ears long after the actual noise faded. Time slowed as I watched coffee spread across the restaurant floor, dark liquid seeping between pristine white tiles. A server rushed over with a rag and dustpan, his mouth moving with apologies I couldn't process.

"I'm so sorry," I managed, the words feeling detached from my body. "I didn't mean to—"

"Hey, it's okay," Flynn's hand covered mine on the table, his touch warm against my suddenly ice-cold skin. "Tempest? Are you alright?"

I wasn't alright. I was drowning in panic, my chest so tight I could barely breathe. The television mounted on the wall behind Flynn was broadcasting my execution.

"...exclusive announcement about the adaptation of best-selling author Miranda Milan's sports romance series..."

The FlixNChill executive's face filled the screen, her

practiced smile revealing nothing about their plans for the "special reveal" mentioned in the teaser.

"Tempest," Flynn's voice broke through my spiral. "Talk to me."

I forced myself to meet his eyes, those blue eyes that had looked at me with such tenderness when I'd finally trusted him with my secret. Just yesterday, I'd felt brave. Today, that bravery felt like a terrible mistake.

"I need to...," I whispered, pulling my hand from his. "I'll be right back."

I practically ran to the bathroom, locking myself in the big stall as my shaking hands pulled out my phone. Gloria answered on the second ring.

"Tempest, thank god," she said, her normally composed voice tight with tension. "I've been trying to reach you—"

"They're going to expose me," I hissed, pressing my back against the cool tile wall. "That entertainment show is teasing some kind of special reveal about Miranda Milan. They're going to tell everyone who I am."

"It's worse than that." Gloria's words hit me like a physical blow. "There's been a leak. Someone talked. I've been on the phone with FlixNChill executives all morning."

My legs gave out. I sank to the floor of the stall, not caring about germs or appearances. "What? How? Who?"

"They don't know how it got out," Gloria said. "But they're in damage-control mode. They're worried you're going to kill the entire deal and that's the last thing they want."

My chest tightened painfully. Not just anxiety this

time—real, physical pain like someone was sitting on my sternum.

"The good news," Gloria continued, "is that they're willing to do just about anything to keep the deal on the table. They understand this wasn't how you wanted to reveal your identity."

I couldn't speak. Could barely breathe. The bathroom stall seemed to be shrinking around me, walls closing in.

"Tempest? Are you there?"

"I can't," I gasped, "breathe."

"Listen to me," Gloria's voice sharpened. "This isn't the end of the world. We can still control the narrative."

But I couldn't focus on her words. My heart hammered so hard I could hear it, feel it in my throat. Black spots danced in my vision. I hadn't had a panic attack this bad since last semester, before I'd started working with my therapist, before the animal sanctuary had become my refuge. Before Flynn.

"My family," I managed between gasping breaths. "My mother... she'll..."

"Tempest, maintaining complete anonymity has become more difficult the more successful you have become," Gloria said firmly. "We knew this day was coming."

I couldn't respond. My phone slipped from my trembling fingers, clattering to the floor as I hugged my knees to my chest. I was drowning, suffocating.

The stall door rattled against the lock. Then a voice, Flynn's voice, came from the other side.

"Tempest? Open the door, sweetheart."

I couldn't answer. Couldn't form words through the gasping.

"I'm coming in."

I heard a scraping sound, then his face appeared under the door as he slid beneath it, uncaring about the bathroom floor or the fact that he was in the women's restroom.

"Hey, hey," he said softly, immediately recognizing what was happening. He sat beside me, then pulled me onto his lap, wrapping me up in his arms. "I'm here. You're okay."

"Can't...breathe..." I choked out.

"Yes, you can," he said firmly. "Look at me, Tempest. Focus on me."

His blue eyes anchored me as he took my hand, placing it on his chest. "Feel that? Feel me breathing? We're going to do it together. In through your nose, out through your mouth."

He exaggerated his breathing, slow and deep, keeping my hand pressed against his chest so I could feel the steady rise and fall. "Like this. In... two... three... Out... two... three..."

I tried to follow, my first attempts shallow and gasping.

"That's it," he encouraged. "You're doing great. Again. In... two... three..."

Gradually, my breathing began to match his. The black spots receded. The crushing weight on my chest eased, though my heart still raced.

"Flynn," I whispered, embarrassment flooding me as reality returned. "You're in the women's bathroom."

A small smile touched his lips. "Yeah, well. Priorities."

"Someone will see you."

"Let them." He brushed a tear from my cheek. I hadn't even realized I was crying. "You're more important."

I leaned into him then, exhausted and shaking in the aftermath of the panic attack. I'd never had one this bad.

He held me, his arms strong and secure around me, one hand stroking my hair.

"I've got you," he murmured, "Just keep breathing."

My phone was still on the floor, the call with Gloria disconnected. I should call her back. Should explain the situation. Should do a dozen responsible things.

Instead, I closed my eyes and let Flynn hold me, let myself believe, just for a moment, that I wasn't alone in this.

When I finally felt steady enough to stand, Flynn helped me up, his hands gentle but sure. I splashed water on my face at the sink, avoiding my reflection.

"Someone at FlixNChill leaked my identity," I said hoarsely. "They don't know who, but it's out there now. It's only a matter of time before everyone knows."

Flynn's expression hardened, protective instinct flashing in his eyes. "That's some bullshit right there, babe. I'm sorry this is happening."

"I don't know what I'm going to do." I gripped the edge of the sink. The ringing in my ears started up again and—

"Hey." He turned me to face him, hands on my shoulders. "This might change how people see you, but anyone who doesn't like what you're doing can fuck off. I'll crush anyone who says a goddamned thing to you. Okay?"

"You don't understand," I whispered. "My family... my

mother... they don't know. They're going to find out from strangers that I've been lying to them for years."

What was I doing? I'd spent years carefully compartmentalizing my life, keeping my worlds separate. Then Flynn had come along, and I'd let down my walls. I'd told him everything. What if that had been the first crack in the foundation? What if letting one person in meant I couldn't keep everyone else out?

"I'm sorry I freaked out," I said, my voice still raw.

"Don't apologize," he said softly, pulling me into his arms again. "Whatever happens, I'll be there to help you through it."

The simple certainty in his voice nearly undid me. I squeezed him hard, knowing in my heart I'd been right to trust him. But he didn't understand the judgment, the chastising, the disappointment I was about to face. And even if he was there with me, holding me like this, I still had to suffer it all alone, inside my own damn head.

"I just... I've worked so hard to keep my worlds separate," I murmured. The thought of everyone finding out, of my family's reaction—"

"I get it," he said, though we both knew he couldn't fully understand. His life had always been public, his successes and probably even his minuscule failures celebrated openly. "But you don't have to face any of it alone. Not anymore."

And for just a moment, surrounded by the LA morning light streaming through the windows, I almost believed him.

They changed my flight back to Denver to go with the Kingmans. But the return felt like crossing a boundary, leaving behind the fantasy of LA where I could be both Tempest and Miranda, returning to reality where those identities had to remain separate. Flynn dozed beside me, his head occasionally dipping toward my shoulder. I couldn't sleep. Instead, I obsessively refreshed social media, searching for any hint that my secret was leaking.

Gloria texted before takeoff.

> Gloria Horne: Confirmed with exec team. They're containing it. Identity reveal NOT planned. All good. Breathe.

But I couldn't shake the feeling of impending disaster.

When the plane landed, Flynn suggested we visit Burrito Petito and Abuela. "Nothing cures anxiety like donkey therapy."

If anyone knew how to deal with celebrity drama, it was AbuelaNovela. Before she married Abuelo Leo, she'd been married a bunch of times, had two children, and divorced her no-good cheating husbands back when women weren't even allowed to have their own bank accounts. All while being a huge telenovela star and then starting her own career in Hollywood.

Burrito greeted us with his typical enthusiasm, braying loudly and pushing his velvety nose into my hands. Abuela watched from the porch, a knowing smile playing at her lips as Flynn scratched behind the donkey's ears.

"Mi amor," she said, embracing me. "How was your trip with your handsome footballer?"

"The handsome footballer part was good," I said, forcing a smile. "Really good."

"But something is troubling you." It wasn't a question. Nothing ever escaped Abuela's notice.

I was sure Abuela knew about my writing, but I'd never actually told her myself. I'd lied even to her, my biggest supporter in life. God, what was wrong with me?

She studied me for a moment, then patted my cheek. "You know, mi Tempestina, secrets are like seeds. Buried in the dark, they find a way to grow toward the light, no matter how deep you plant them." Her eyes twinkled. "Sometimes it's better to plant them in the open, where you can control how they grow."

My stomach clenched. "But even if I can control how they grow, it doesn't mean people won't stomp on them, tell them they don't belong, and make them feel small and ugly."

She took my hand in hers and shifted her attention to Flynn who was now taking selfies with the donkey. "That boy cares for you deeply. Your Abuelo Leo looks at me just the same way your footballer does you."

I followed her gaze, my heart aching with unexpected tenderness as Flynn looked up, catching me watching him.

"I care about him too," I admitted.

"Then trust him," Abuela said simply. "Trust someone besides your fabulously fantastic abuela with the truth of who you are."

"I already did," I whispered, and her eyebrows rose in surprise.

Before she could respond, Flynn jogged over, phone in hand. "I told you those sunglasses would look awesome on him."

For a few hours, surrounded by Abuela's cooking, Tio Pedro's stories while we ate, Flynn's laughter, and Burrito stealing all of the tortillas, I almost believed that everything would be okay. Almost.

When I returned to the sorority house that evening, the door to my room was locked from the inside. I knocked softly, then harder when there was no response.

"Parker? You in there?"

The lock clicked and the door opened just enough for Parker's purple-haired head to peek out. Her eyes widened when she saw me, then she yanked me inside, shutting and re-locking the door in one fluid motion.

"Thank god you're back. I thought you weren't going to be home until tomorrow," she said, immediately returning to her desk where three different laptops were set up, screens glowing with code I couldn't begin to understand. "I've been damage controlling all day."

"What?" My heartbeat accelerated. "You have?"

Parker swiveled in her chair, dark circles under her eyes revealing she hadn't slept much. "Someone posted that Miranda Milan lives in Colorado. Not your real name yet, but now the rumors are flying that she is a college student and they said there's a sorority connection."

My legs gave out and I sank onto my bed. I closed my eyes and imagined Flynn's arms around me and Burrito's fur beneath my fingers. When I could breathe again, I looked back at Parker. "How bad is it?"

"Could be worse," Parker said, turning back to her screens. "The source was anonymous, posted on some entertainment blog. I've been running interference, planting misinformation, making comments disappear, and tracking the IP addresses that seem most interested in the story."

I stared at her. "You can do that?"

She shot me an offended look. "Cybersecurity major, remember? This is literally what I'm trained to do, a whole-ass degree in keeping my roommate's secret identity as a smut-writing superstar under wraps." Her fingers flew across the keyboard. "I've already planted red herrings suggesting Miranda Milan is actually at Boulder, Fort Collins, and even Durango."

A lump formed in my throat. "Parker, I—"

"Don't thank me yet," she cut in. "I think the immediate fire is contained, but this is just the beginning. Someone knows, Tempest. Someone who was willing to talk."

Was there really someone at FlixNChill that was this adamant that revealing my identity was going to make the show a bigger deal? This had to just be a publicity stunt on their end. Maybe I wouldn't sign those contracts after all. Even if the deal was worth literally millions of dollars.

"And, I think you've got someone else on your side. There's a bunch of other accounts posting some crazy-ass shit that's kind of believable. Look." She pointed to a FaceSpace group for romance readers. "This Romance Reader Princess says she heard you're not from Colorado but every other place on the planet that starts with C. You've been Californian, Canadian, and even Cambodian today."

Huh. Okay, that was good, I guessed.

"And this person, Mint Milan, thinks you're a whole

group of literary fiction authors who were bored with their own genre and banded together to write and market the books."

Well, that was a weird theory.

"Although my favorite popped up in the Kelsey Best fan group and said she's the one writing your books and Penelope Quinn, better known as Bestie's Bestie, is hilariously not denying it."

Oh that was good. If the Besties joined the cause of thinking one of the world's biggest pop stars authored my books, I might actually be okay. For a while.

"I haven't dug deep enough to find out who they are, because I was too busy taking advantage of their rumor spreading skills." She took a long swig from an energy drink can. "But you should prepare yourself. Secrets this big don't stay buried forever."

I hugged my arms around myself. "Who do you think leaked it?"

"No idea yet. But I'm working on it." Parker's expression softened. "How was LA otherwise? You and Flynn hung out? Do anything else besides negotiate multi-million dollar deals? Is he going to sign with the Bandits? Oh my god, are you going to move to LA with him?"

"Whoa, whoa, whoa." I held up my hands, but a small smile broke through my panic. "I did hang out with him. He knows everything."

"Told you," Parker said smugly. "That boy is head over cleats for you. Wait. Everything? Like..."

"Everything." I allowed myself one moment to revel in the happiness and joy and... love I'd experienced this week before the utter catastrophe.

"Oh hells yeah. Finally," Parker said. "LA love story. Brilliant."

I leaned forward to look at her screens. "Do you think we're safe for now?"

"For tonight, at least," she said, her expression turning serious again. "Get some sleep. Tomorrow might be a different story."

But as I crawled into bed that night, my phone clutched in my hand, I had to swallowed down the worry that despite Parker's confidence, we were just delaying the inevitable.

The stares started the moment I stepped onto campus the first day after spring break. At first, I thought I was being paranoid. But three separate people in my lit crit class turned to look at me, then quickly back to their phones, whispering to each other.

Why couldn't this be the day I had Shakespeare and marketing with Flynn?

"Tempest," a voice called as I left class. I turned to find Bettie hurrying toward me, her expression grim. She grabbed my arm, pulling me into an empty classroom. "What the hell, Tempest?"

"What?" My heart hammered against my ribs.

She thrust her phone at me. The screen displayed The Dracarys, our campus news blog. The headline made my blood freeze:

**STUDENT AUTHOR UNMASKED:
IS KAT SISTER TEMPEST NAVARRO ACTUALLY
BEST-SELLING ROMANCE NOVELIST MIRANDA
MILAN?**

The article laid out the evidence with damning precision. They knew I'd gone to LA for spring break, which coincided with Miranda Milan's known trip to LA. It talked about how I was a lit major, and that my father was the long time DSU Shakespeare professor, which drew parallels to Shakespeare's influence on Milan's books. But most damning, they said they had an insider source who'd seen me in meetings at the FlixNChill offices.

"Is it true?" Bettie asked, her eyes wide.

"I—" The denial died on my lips. I couldn't lie to her face.

Bettie's gasp confirmed what I already knew, my non-denial was confirmation enough. "Oh my god, it is true. Tempest, why didn't you tell us? We're your sisters, your friends, your donkey sitters, and boyfriend sneaker-inners."

"I couldn't tell anyone," I said, my voice barely audible. "My family—"

The classroom door burst open. Two students I barely recognized entered, phones already raised.

"OMG. You're Tempest Navarro?" one called out. "Are you seriously Miranda Milan?"

Bettie stepped between us, pulling up the full force of her sorority president gravitas. "Not now," she snapped. "Back off."

But the damage was done. I could practically see the confirmation spreading across campus as I stood there, frozen in place. My secret, the one I'd guarded so carefully for years, was unraveling in real time.

"I have to go," I whispered to Bettie. "I need to—"

My phone vibrated in my pocket. Then again. And

again. A glance at the screen showed a barrage of notifications, texts, calls, social media alerts. But the ones that made my stomach drop were from my family group chat.

> Catalina: Tempest, why is there a reporter outside my boutique asking about my romance novelist sister?

> Ophelia: Wait, what?

> Freddie: OMG IS THIS REAL??

And then the one that sent ice through my veins:

> Mamá: We need to discuss this. I'll be calling tonight. Nonnegotiable.

I stumbled out of the classroom, barely registering Bettie calling after me. My carefully constructed world was collapsing around me, and there was nothing I could do to stop it.

By the time I reached the sorority house, Parker was waiting at the front door, her expression a mixture of panic and excitement.

"The house phone has been ringing nonstop," she said, pulling me inside. "Three different local news outlets, the campus paper, and I think someone from a publishing news website. Shit is going down."

"Everyone knows," I said numbly. "Everyone."

My phone buzzed again. Flynn.

> Flynn: Are you okay? Tell me where you are, I'm coming to you.

I stared at his message, tears blurring my vision. Part of me desperately wanted him there, wanted his strength as I faced the storm. But another part, the part that had been keeping secrets for so long, wanted to hide, forever, from everyone.

> Mamá: If you don't respond, I'm calling the university.

I looked back at Flynn's message, my thumb hovering over the screen. Did I want him to watch as everything I'd feared came true?

The phone trembled in my hand.

> Mamá: I'm booking a flight. Your father and I will be home tomorrow.

KINGMAN FAMILY GAME NIGHT TO THE RESCUE

FLYNN

The KAT house was surrounded.

I counted at least three news vans and a dozen people with cameras and microphones crowded near the front steps. Students clustered in small groups at the edges, smartphones raised, whispering as they recorded the scene. This wasn't just campus gossip anymore, this was a full-blown media circus.

I parked a block away and texted Parker.

> Me: Outside. How do I get in without the vultures or Mrs. H. seeing?

Her response came instantly.

> Parker: By the kitchen. Use secret knock. Three knocks, wait for the same, two knocks, wait for the same, one knock. A sister will let you in.

I circled around, keeping my head down, hoodie pulled up. Years of dealing with sports media had taught me how to move without drawing attention. Still, my heart hammered against my ribs. Not for myself, for Tempest. She'd spent years hiding her identity, carefully separating her worlds. Now those worlds were colliding in the most public way possible.

Parker was waiting at the service entrance, her expression grim.

"Thank god," she whispered, pulling me inside. "It's been insane. They started showing up an hour ago."

"How is she?" I asked, following Parker through the kitchen where several sorority sisters were huddled in strategy mode.

"Not good." She led me up the back stairs. "She's barely said a word since she got back from campus. The whole senior class is with her, but..." She trailed off, her meaning clear.

Parker did that same secret knock and someone opened the door, ushering me in quickly. The room was dimly lit, blinds drawn against prying eyes. Tempest sat on her bed, surrounded by her sorority sisters, their protective circle unable to shield her from what was happening.

"Flynn." My name on her lips was barely audible.

I crossed the room in three strides, crouching in front of her. Her face was pale, eyes red-rimmed from crying. I took her hands in mine, relieved when she didn't pull away.

"Hey," I said softly. "I'm here."

Her fingers tightened around mine. "They know," she whispered. "Everyone knows."

"Not for sure, and not everyone," Parker interjected

from her command center of laptops. "But those rats posted your student ID with links to your sorority profile and built a pretty convincing case connecting you to Miranda Milan. Once the first post went viral, bloggers ran with it."

She swiveled in her chair. "On the plus side, there are so many competing theories online now that there's reasonable doubt. This Mint Milan squad really came through with the misinformation campaign."

I had a feeling I knew exactly who that squad was, and I was buying them all flowers, or cookies or something later.

"My mother texted," Tempest said, her voice hollow. "She and my father are flying in tomorrow. She's... not happy."

The understatement was clear in her trembling voice. I glanced around the room, taking stock of the situation. The Donkey Sitters Club had mobilized impressively. Bettie was coordinating with campus security by phone, Alice was monitoring social media. Hannah had organized the whole house of girls to establish a perimeter defense. But this was beyond what they could handle.

This needed the Kingman treatment.

"We need to get you out of here," I said, reaching a decision. "Somewhere safe, and away from all this."

"Where?" She looked up at me, confusion mixing with the fear in her eyes. "The reporters are everywhere."

"Not everywhere." I pulled out my phone. "My family has dealt with this kind of media storm before. Trust me?"

She hesitated for just a heartbeat, then nodded. That

small gesture of trust hit me harder than a linebacker's tackle.

"Parker," I said, "can you pack a bag for her? Clothes for tonight and tomorrow?"

"On it." She moved with impressive efficiency.

I fired off a quick group text to the family chat.

> Me: Need help. Media storm at KAT house. Tempest exposed as best-selling author. Need extraction and damage control.

Dec responded first.

> Declan: On our way.

Then Chris.

> Chris: PR team on standby. Tell me what you need.

Hayes's name popped up next.

> Hayes: Willa and I can run interference and bring the claws if needed.

Then Everett.

> Everett: Pen's already drafting statements. Say the word.

My chest tightened with gratitude. This is what Kingmans did. We protected our own. And somewhere along the way, Tempest had become one of ours.

"My brother Declan is coming," I told Tempest. "He

was voted the meanest player in the league last season. No one will mess with him. We'll get you to my dad's place, regroup, figure this out."

She nodded, some color returning to her cheeks. "Thank you."

I squeezed her hands. "You don't have to face this alone. We've got you, babe."

Twenty minutes later, my phone buzzed with another text from Declan.

> Declan: Media dodge plan in progress. Four vehicles, three minutes. Back entrance to the KAT house.

I showed the message to Tempest. "The cavalry has arrived."

Her brow furrowed. "Four vehicles?"

"The Kingman convoy. Trust me, my brothers have done this before."

Almost exactly three minutes later, four identical black SUVs with tinted windows pulled up in sequence at the back entrance. Declan hopped out of the first one, expression all business.

"Just like we practiced," he said to me, then nodded at Tempest. "Sorry about the cloak and dagger, but we know this routine works when the media are hounding us. It's practiced, tried and true."

Tempest stared at the lineup of vehicles. "This is..."

"Excessive?" I supplied. "Welcome to the Kingman approach to problem-solving."

"Effective," Declan corrected. "We've got Chris, Hayes, and Everett each driving a decoy. Once you're in, we split in different directions. If anyone's watching, they won't know which SUV to follow."

Parker handed Tempest a DSU hoodie and baseball cap. "Add these over what you're wearing. Different silhouette from what the press has seen today."

I was impressed by how quickly Tempest adapted, pulling on the disguise without question. We made our exit in a carefully choreographed move, all four vehicle doors opening simultaneously, multiple people moving between them in a deliberate pattern of misdirection, before doors slammed and engines started.

I settled into the backseat of our SUV with Tempest, Declan at the wheel. The four identical vehicles pulled away in a synchronized dance, then split at the first intersection, each heading in a different direction.

"Nicely executed," Declan said, checking the rearview mirror. "No tails that I can see."

"You guys really have this down to a science," Tempest said, removing the cap now that we were safely away.

"Unfortunately, we've had plenty of practice," Declan replied. "The media circus around me and my fiancée got pretty intense last year. We had to get creative. We know what to do to help you out."

"Why would you all help me?" Tempest asked softly. "You barely know me."

The question caught me off guard. Didn't she understand by now?

"Because you're important to Flynn," Dec said simply, before I could find the words. "And because no one deserves to have their privacy ripped away without consent. We protect our own."

My phone rang. Jules.

"Dad just declared an emergency Kingman family game night. We're meeting at Cool Beans."

"Game night?" Tempest asked after I hung up. "Now?"

"Kingman tradition," I explained. "My mom wanted us to have something in our lives that wasn't playing football or watching football. After she...died, it was Dad's way of keeping us together when everything felt like it was falling apart."

"It's sacred," Dec added. "No excuses, no absences. And always viciously competitive."

"I don't think I'd be good company," Tempest said. "Not tonight."

I took her hand. "It'll just be family. No press, no pressure. Just people who care about you."

"But they don't even know me."

"They know you're important to me," I said. "That's enough."

She studied my face for a long moment, then nodded. "Okay."

Her acceptance surprised me. I'd expected more resistance, more retreat into the protective isolation she'd maintained for so long. Maybe she was finally realizing she didn't have to face everything alone.

Cool Beans Cat Café looked like an ordinary coffee shop from the outside, but inside, it was a sanctuary of comfort disguised as quirky charm. Cats lounged on custom-built perches and cubbies throughout the space, fairy lights twinkled from the ceiling, and the scent of fresh coffee and tea mixed with the subtle aroma of the homemade treats in the display case.

My entire family was already there, the café closed to the public for our private event. Willa's uncles, the owners, had created a Kingman-worthy spread of food and drinks along the counter.

I kept my hand on the small of Tempest's back as we entered, feeling her tense beside me.

"It's okay," I murmured. "They don't bite. Well, except maybe Jules, but only if provoked."

That earned me a tiny smile, the first I'd seen since this nightmare began.

Chris spotted us first, raising a hand in greeting as he disentangled himself from a heated debate with Everett over what appeared to be a Monopoly strategy. He approached with his easy quarterback confidence, the same way he'd greet a rookie on his first day of training camp.

"Tempest," he said warmly, offering his hand. "Good to finally meet you properly. Flynn won't shut up about you."

Before she could respond, a woman with glasses and a bright smile appeared at Chris's side. Tempest's eyes widened in recognition.

"Trixie? What are you doing here?"

Trixie laughed, stepping forward to give Tempest a hug that seemed to surprise her. "I guess I never mentioned that my fiancé is the quarterback for the Mustangs."

"You didn't," Tempest confirmed, looking between them with new understanding.

"And I didn't mention that I run a plus-size book club that meets right here," Trixie added with a significant look that made Tempest blush. "A club that happens to be very enthusiastic about a certain sports romance series."

Before Tempest could process this, we were surrounded. Hayes and Willa arrived with drinks, Everett dragged Penelope over for introductions, and Dad clapped a hand on my shoulder, giving me a nod of approval that meant more than words ever could.

"Mr. Kingman," Tempest began, but Dad waved her off.

"Bridger, please. And I'm glad Flynn brought you. Family belongs together during tough times."

I watched her face carefully at the word 'family,' saw the flicker of emotion cross her features. Her own family was likely bringing a storm of disappointment and judgment instead of solidarity and support. That really fucking pissed me off.

Trixie linked her arm through Tempest's, leading her toward a table where a striking blonde woman was setting up a board game with elegant precision.

"This is Kelsey Best," Trixie explained, seeing Tempest's wide-eyed recognition. "Dec's fiancée."

"The pop star?" Tempest whispered.

"The very same," Trixie confirmed. "And that's Penelope Quinn beside her—Kelsey's assistant and Everett's fiancée. She's also got about three million followers on her body-positive social channels."

I could see Tempest processing this information, trying to reconcile these celebrities with the casual family gathering around her.

"Can I steal my son for a minute?" Dad asked Tempest, who nodded, still looking a bit overwhelmed.

"You holding up okay?" Dad asked quietly, drawing my attention back.

"Me? I'm not the one whose privacy just got shredded."

"No, but you care about her." It wasn't a question. "That makes this your crisis too."

I ran a hand through my hair. "I just wish I could fix it for her."

"Some things can't be fixed, son. Only faced." Dad's eyes held a wisdom earned through all of our family's trials. Ones we always faced together. "You know, I suspected there was something special about her work when Jules wouldn't stop talking about those books. The way she described the writing—passionate, honest, fearless—sounded a lot like how you described Tempest."

I stared at him. "You knew?"

He chuckled. "I had my suspicions. Didn't matter either way. What matters is that she's important to you, which means she's important to all of us."

Across the room, I saw Tempest sink into a chair beside Willa, who leaned over to say something that made her shoulders relax slightly.

"I want to protect her," I admitted. "From all of it. The press, her family's so far shitty reaction, everything."

"You can't." Dad's hand squeezed my shoulder. "But you can stand with her while she faces it. You don't need to fight someone's battles for them. Just make sure they don't fight alone. That's what Kingmans do."

The wisdom of his words settled into my chest. I'd been thinking like a linebacker. Tackle the problem, eliminate the threat. But that wasn't what Tempest needed.

She needed what everyone needs when their world is

crumbling, someone to stand beside them in the ruins. And my dad was right. When our world had crumbled had fallen down around us seventeen years ago, the only way we'd made it through was the support of each other.

I rejoined the group as Willa was saying to Tempest, "I get it. I was completely overwhelmed by all of this at first too." She gestured around at the Kingman chaos. "I was just a barista when I started dating Hayes. But they've never once made me feel like I don't belong."

"It's a lot," Tempest agreed, her voice small.

"But a good lot," Willa assured her. "Trust me."

Jules appeared suddenly, plopping down on the arm of Tempest's chair with the casual confidence that only the baby of the family could possess.

"We need to talk," she announced, grabbing Tempest's hand in both of hers.

"Okay," Tempest took a deep breath like she was preparing for more unwelcome news. But I trusted my little sister. She wouldn't hurt my girl.

"I have a confession to make," Jules said, her expression suddenly serious.

Tempest tensed beside me.

"I've been Miranda Milan's biggest fan since the first book came out," Jules continued. "I've read each one at least six times—I can quote entire scenes from memory. I run three different fan accounts dedicated to your work."

Tempest's eyes widened. "You do?"

"And when all this started breaking today, I knew we had to do something," Jules continued. "So I rallied the book club. We've been flooding social media with competing theories about who Miranda Milan really is."

"What kind of theories?" Tempest asked.

Jules grinned mischievously. "That Miranda Milan is actually a collective of male ghostwriters. That she's a seventy-year-old grandmother in Maine. And my personal favorite, that Miranda Milan is actually Kelsey Best writing under a pseudonym."

"I heard about that one." Tempest visibly relaxed. "International pop stars probably don't have time to write romance novels though, do they?"

"She thought it was hilarious," Jules continued. "She's been dropping hints in her FaceSpace group all day that she has a 'secret creative project' just to fuel speculation. The more theories out there, the harder it is for anyone to be sure about the truth."

Tempest looked stunned. "Why are you doing all this for me? I mean, I appreciate that you're a fan, like, really, really appreciate it. But you hardly know me."

"Are you kidding? I know you through your words." Jules's expression grew earnest. "Your books got me through midterms last semester. The way you write about women taking up space in a world that wants them small. That matters. When I realized my brother was dating the author I admired, well, fate doesn't hand out coincidences like that every day."

I watched Tempest's face as Jules spoke, saw the dawning realization that her work had meaning beyond her own fears. That her words had touched lives.

"I don't know what to say," she finally managed.

"Say you'll sign my copies later," Jules grinned. "And say you'll let us help you through this. The Kingman machine is pretty unstoppable when we all work together."

Tempest looked at me, her eyes asking a question I couldn't quite interpret.

"Only if you want," I said. "No pressure. If you don't want us all up in your business, this can just be a night away from your problems."

She took a deep breath. "I'd be grateful for any help. Especially before tomorrow."

"What's tomorrow?" Jules asked.

"My parents are flying in," Tempest said, her voice catching. "They're... not going to be happy."

Jules squeezed her hand. "Then we'll make sure you're armed with a plan before you face them."

A shout from across the room drew our attention—Everett had apparently made a controversial move in whatever game they'd started.

"Come on," I said, standing and offering my hand to Tempest. "Let me show you how Kingman game night works. Spoiler alert. There will be shouting, accusations of cheating, and someone might flip a table."

Jules grinned and pulled out from behind her chair a worn green pillow embroidered with the words - *In this house we bleed green* - and held it high above her head. "And I'm going to win it all, because I've got the lucky pillow."

Isak, who'd just arrived with Gryff, whipped that pillow right out of Jules's hands. "Not for long, brat. You're going down."

Gryff gave Tempest a pat on the shoulder and said, "Welcome to the chaos, kid." Then jumped on Isak, taking him to the floor, wrestling for the pillow.

Tempest took my hand, a small smile playing at her lips. "Sounds like my kind of chaos."

The next hour unfolded exactly as I'd hoped. Game night worked its magic, pulling Tempest into our family's particular brand of competitive camaraderie. She even laughed when Chris accused Hayes of stacking the Scrabble tiles, and she formed an unexpected alliance with Kelsey during a particularly cutthroat round of Pictionary.

But I could still see the worry lurking behind her eyes. Tomorrow's confrontation with her parents cast a shadow over each moment of reprieve. I needed to do something more to help her feel supported and ready to fight her demons.

I sent off a quick text and then we stepped outside for air during a break between games. The night was cool, stars visible despite the city lights. I wrapped my arm around her shoulders, drawing her close.

"Better?" I asked.

"Your family is..." she began, then shook her head. "I don't even have words."

"A lot?"

"Amazing," she corrected. "You're lucky to have them."

"I know." I thought about what Dad had said, about not fighting her battles for her. "About tomorrow—"

"I'm terrified," she admitted, her voice small. "My mother has had my life planned since I was five years old. Academic success, prestigious career, everything proper and respectable. Romance novels are..." She trailed off.

"Beneath you?" I guessed.

She nodded. "In her eyes. She thinks they're unworthy

trash. And now everyone will know her daughter writes them."

"I'd like to be there," I said carefully. "When you talk to them. If you want."

She looked up at me, surprise clear on her face. "You would?"

"Of course." I brushed a strand of hair from her cheek. "You're not alone in this, Tempest. Not anymore."

She studied my face for a long moment, then nodded. "I'd like that." Then, more softly, "I need that."

The admission cost her, I could tell. She'd been independent for so long, shoulders bearing the weight of her secrets alone. Letting someone help wasn't easy for her.

"That's settled then." I pressed a kiss to her forehead. "Whatever happens, we face it together."

My phone buzzed with a return text from the message I sent a few minutes ago. The Kingman women were a force to be reckoned with, and I had a feeling Tempest's grandmother was the perfect addition to this night.

I showed Tempest the message, watching as surprise, then tentative hope crossed her features. "You invited Abuela to this craziness? She's going to love it. Abuela and the Kingman women together?" She laughed softly. "The universe doesn't stand a chance."

"No," I agreed, pulling her closer. "It really doesn't."

QUEENCON

TEMPEST

The door to Cool Beans swung open with dramatic flair. Every head turned as my grandmother made her entrance, resplendent in a flowing emerald kaftan with an honest-to-god feather-trimmed wrap draped around her shoulders. Behind her, Tío Pedro grinned, carrying what appeared to be several shopping bags.

AbuelaNovela never just arrived anywhere. She made an *entrance*.

"Mi Tempestina!" She threw her arms wide, her array of gold bangles jingling like wind chimes.

"Abuela," I whispered, relief washing over me as I crossed the room into her embrace. The familiar scent of her perfume enveloped me, a comfort I hadn't known I desperately needed until this moment.

"Shh, mi amor," she murmured against my hair, somehow knowing exactly what I needed to hear. "This is not the end. It is merely the beginning of a new chapter, yes? And who knows better how to write those than you?"

I choked on a laugh that was half sob. Trust Abuela to make a writing pun at a time like this.

When she released me, her eyes, the same deep brown as my own, scanned the room with the appraising gaze that had intimidated telenovela directors for decades. Her attention settled on Bridger Kingman, who had risen from his seat as she entered.

"Ah," she said, her voice carrying in that perfectly modulated way actresses of her generation had mastered. "You must be the father of these magnificent boys I've heard so much about."

Something passed between them, a recognition, perhaps, of two people who had shouldered the weight of raising families through both joy and tragedy. He gave her a slight nod, the barest hint of respect in the gesture, but I didn't miss it.

"Welcome to our impromptu family gathering, Mrs. Ramirez," he said, extending his hand.

"Estrella, please," she corrected, taking his hand in both of hers. "Any family that embraces my Tempest is family to me."

The tightness in my chest eased slightly at her choice of words. *Embraces*. Not judges, not tolerates. Embraces.

"So you're the fabulous AbuelaNovela?" Jules appeared at my side, practically vibrating with excitement. "I've got 'Corazón Dividido' added to my playlist. But Dad is a huge fan of the Agent Jaguar movies. He's kind of a movie nerd."

Abuela's eyes lit up with delight. "Ah, a young woman of culture. You must be Jules."

I glanced at Flynn, wondering exactly what he'd said

about his sister to my grandmother. He grinned and winked at me from across the room, and some of the day's tension melted away.

"Ladies," Kelsey Best said, rising gracefully from where she'd been sitting with Declan. "I think we need a little Kingman Queens conference. Pen, Willa, Trixie?"

Before I could process what was happening, the Kingman women plus my grandmother were forming a circle in the corner of the café, and I was being gently but firmly guided to join them.

The "queen conference" turned out to be exactly what I needed, even if I hadn't known I needed it.

"I think we can help with this media frenzy about your secret identity," Kelsey said, leaning in. The international pop star who had a freaking Bowl commercial was now giving me media advice. This day couldn't get any more surreal. "I've dealt with more media scrutiny than most people will see in ten lifetimes, and I've learned one crucial thing. You have to control your own narrative."

"Before others twist it," Penelope added. "I used to think hiding was the answer. But sometimes owning your story is the most powerful thing you can do."

"But how?" I asked, the question bursting from me before I could stop it. "People are so damn mean online. I don't even read my reviews anymore because they made me cry. My mother is going to be mortified. The school paper already has that article up linking me to Miranda Milan, and I—"

"Take a breath," Trixie said gently. "The world is always going to try to tell you how much space you're allowed to take up. Too loud, too quiet, too big, too much. But here's the thing, the only person who gets to decide that is you."

Tears pricked at my eyes and I blinked hard trying to hold them back.

"Your work matters," Willa added, her gaze steady on mine. "Do you know how many women have never seen themselves as the heroine? As worthy of love and happy endings? You're giving that to people."

"Practical advice time," Penelope said, pulling out her phone. "I've drafted three potential statements. One confirming, one neither confirming nor denying, and one requesting privacy during this time. We can tweak whichever approach you prefer."

My head was spinning. These women, who really didn't even know me, were rallying around me with a level of support I'd never experienced from anyone except Abuela, Abuelo, Tío Pedro, and Parker. And now Flynn. The few people I'd let see me. The real me.

"What I wish someone had told me earlier," Kelsey added, "is that you don't owe anyone access to every part of yourself, even when you're public about some parts. You get to decide which pieces of your heart stay private."

Abuela, who had been watching this exchange with bright eyes, finally spoke. "My Tempestina," she said, reaching for my hands. "When I was your age, women were told to be small, to be quiet, to be proper. When I chose to act, my own mother didn't speak to me for two years." She squeezed my fingers. "But here's what I learned. The only shame is in denying who you truly are."

The tears I'd been fighting spilled over. "I'm scared," I admitted, my voice barely a whisper. Scared that when the rest of the world, outside of the very carefully curated people I'd chosen to let in, would tell me I didn't belong, that who I was and what I had to offer wasn't what they wanted or expected of me.

That who and what I was would always be the ugly duckling and never the beautiful swan.

"Good," Abuela said firmly. "Courage isn't the absence of fear. It's action in the face of it. And you, mi amor, have more courage than you know."

Did I?

I wanted to believe Abuela. I wanted to be the woman everyone here thought I could be.

Trixie tipped her head and took off her glasses, studying me like I was, well, an open book. "And if you're not quite sure of your own bravery yet, you can do what I think most of the rest of us have done. We fake it, till we make it."

"Really? You're all so... confident."

The whole circle of women either, smiled or chuckled. But Abuela was the one who gave their response a voice. "The world's a stage, querida, and we are all merely actors, every one of us. Of course we have faked it a time or two."

That brought a round of giggles. "But not with the Kingman men," Trixie said and gave her fiancé a wave. He blew her a kiss and winked.

I could fake it. Just like these women did. Except for with Flynn. Trixie was right. I definitely didn't need to.

"Okay," Willa clapped her hands together. "Now that

we've solved the problems of the world once again, let's go wipe the floor with these boys. I've got twenty bucks on Declan flipping a table by the end of the night."

The Kingman Queens each gave me a hug and reassurances that they were all on my side no matter what I chose to do. I was completely overwhelmed by this outward and open show of support.

Abuela took my hand and kept me in my seat as the others joined the boys to set up the game night.

"Do you think I wouldn't recognize my granddaughter's heart in those pages?" Abuela asked, giving me no quarter. At my startled look, she laughed. "Oh, Tempestina. I've known since your first book. The way you nailed Catalina and her bossiness. The way you described the food that Ophelia, I mean Pheobe, makes for her hockey player in the second book? Pure Navarro. And your wise, fabulous grandmother giving love advice while making tamales? I believe I recognize that advice."

Heat rushed to my face. "Why didn't you say anything?"

"For the same reason you didn't tell me," she said simply. "You needed that part of yourself to be yours alone, until you were ready to share it."

I stared at her, processing this. "I thought everyone would be ashamed. Mamá is going to be so disappointed. Romance novels are—"

"Joy," Abuela interrupted firmly. "They are joy and hope and the promise that everyone deserves love. Even girls who look like us, who take up space, who have curves and opinions and don't fit into little boxes."

"That's why I wrote them," I admitted, the truth I'd never fully acknowledged to myself finally finding voice. "Because growing up, I never saw heroines who looked like me. Who felt like me."

"And now, thousands of girls all around the world do. Just like Latino men and Latina women saw themselves in the Agent Jaguar books your Abuelo wrote." Abuela's eyes gleamed with unshed tears and fierce pride. "Representation matters and you have made so many people feel seen, even as you have hidden."

Something shifted inside me, a weight I'd been carrying for so long I'd forgotten it was there. My writing wasn't something shameful. It was something powerful. Something necessary.

"I don't want to hide myself anymore. I need to face them," I said, the decision crystallizing with unexpected clarity. "Mamá and Papá, and the girls."

"Yes, you do." Abuela nodded approvingly.

I glanced across the room to where Flynn was laughing with his brothers, his entire face lit with joy. Something tightened in my chest, not anxiety this time, but a different, sweeter ache.

"I think I want Flynn there when I talk to them," I said. "Not to fight for me, but just... with me."

"Of course you do," Abuela said, as if this were the most obvious thing in the world. "Love is not about someone rescuing you, mi amor. It's about having someone who stands beside you when you rescue yourself."

Love. The word hung in the air between us. Was that what this was? This feeling that had been growing steadily since a baby donkey in dragon wings had brought Flynn Kingman barreling into my life?

Flynn looked up then, catching my gaze across the room. His smile softened into something more intimate, just for me. I made my decision.

Rising from my seat, I crossed to where he stood with his brothers.

For the first time since my secret had been exposed, I felt something other than fear. I wasn't exactly fearless, but I would fake it, and be brave.

"Ready to have a little more fun, babe?" Flynn led me to a table set up with something that looked like a complicated version of Candyland and Scrabble mixed together.

Flynn wasn't kidding when he said his family got competitive at their game night.

"They're cheating," Jules accused, pointing dramatically at Isak and Gryff. "There's no way they had two double word scores in a row."

"Maybe if you spent more time studying vocabulary instead of romance novels," Gryff shot back, "you'd have a chance against us."

"Do not start with me, Gryffin Kingman," Jules threatened, lunging for the family's lucky pillow. "I know where you sleep."

I couldn't hold back my laughter as Jules tackled her much larger brother, attempting to wrest the pillow from his grasp. The Kingman family game night was nothing like the reserved, intellectual games my parents liked to play. No, this reminded me of the summers at Abuela's villa in Mexico, getting into all kinds of trouble with the neighborhood children. This was full-contact, no-holds-barred competition, complete with trash talk, dramatic accusations, and the occasional physical scuffle.

And I was loving every minute of it.

"Your turn, Tempest," Willa said, passing me the dice for our current game, something involving dragons and complicated story quests that I was still figuring out.

I rolled, surprised by my own competitive surge of satisfaction when I landed on a prime trading space. "I'm making friends with the wolves and they become my allies, warding off all attacks on my village," I announced, placing my game piece with perhaps more force than necessary.

"Oh ho," Isak exclaimed, looking delighted at my aggressive move. "Girls, man. They run the world."

Flynn caught my eye from across the table, his expression a mix of surprise and delight. I realized I'd been holding back, not just in the game, but in so much of my life. Always trying to be smaller, quieter, more proper. The Tempest my mother wanted me to be.

But here, surrounded by this boisterous, loving family and my equally dramatic grandmother, I didn't need to be less. I could be *more*.

"That's my girl," Abuela crowed when I successfully negotiated a trade deal that left Trixie groaning in defeat. "She gets that ruthless nature from her Abuelo."

"It certainly wasn't from me," Tío Pedro laughed shaking his head. He always was a lover, not a fighter.

To my surprise, Abuela and Bridger Kingman had formed an unlikely alliance in the game, absolutely eviscerating all competition with their combined tactical skills. Watching them, I realized how much I'd compartmentalized my life. School Tempest, family Tempest, secret author Tempest, Flynn's girlfriend Tempest. All these separate versions of myself that I kept carefully isolated from each other.

I didn't want to live like that anymore.

Three hours and four hotly contested games later, I found myself the unexpected champion of the final round of a card game that involved bluffing and strategy in equal measure.

"Beginner's luck," Declan grumbled good-naturedly as I collected my winnings, which consisted of a pile of gummy bears that had served as betting currency.

"Natural talent," Abuela corrected, looking impossibly proud.

As the night wound down and people began gathering their things, I felt a strange sense of calm settle over me. Tomorrow would be difficult. My parents would be upset, disappointed, perhaps even angry. The campus gossip would continue, and the media scrutiny might intensify.

But tonight had shown me something important. I wasn't alone. I had Flynn, who had never once looked at me with anything but admiration and desire. I had Abuela and Tío Pedro, who had always embraced all of me. I had this extended circle of the Kingman family and their partners, who had welcomed me without hesitation.

And most importantly, I had myself—all of myself, the parts I'd been proud of and the parts I'd hidden away.

Tomorrow, I would face my parents not as the dutiful daughter desperate for approval, but as Tempest Navarro, best-selling author, college senior, and a woman who was finally ready to take up exactly as much space in the world as she deserved.

For the first time in my life, I wasn't going to make myself smaller to fit someone else's expectations. I was going to stand tall in the fullness of who I was, and that felt like the most revolutionary act of all.

CRASHING

FLYNN

I took Tempest back to my place after game night. No way I could I handle even a moment of her out of my sight. I would use every highly honed defensive tackle skill I had to smash anyone who even thought about approaching her or looking at her funny.

But sitting on my bed in my room, she was getting all up in her head without the distraction of my family chaos machine. I couldn't let that happen. So I used the skills the universe had bestowed upon me and what had been playful and new in LA had was deepening into something profound here, in the face of her fears.

I'd tried to be gentle, slowly undressing her, peppering her skin with soft kisses. But she'd wanted so much more from me.

"I need to feel something real," she'd whispered. "Something that's just mine."

So I gave her what she needed, losing myself in her until all the worry that shadowed her eyes was replaced with pleasure and connection.

Afterward, she fell asleep with her head on my chest, my arm around her, protecting her from whatever I could.

I put on a pot of coffee, leaning against the counter as I waited for it to brew. Last night she'd curled into me on my bed, vulnerable in a way I'd never seen her before.

The coffee maker beeped, pulling me from my thoughts. I filled two mugs. Mine with milk, hers with the cinnamon oat milk creamer I'd picked up just for her, and headed back to my room.

She was sitting up when I returned, her hair a wild tangle around her shoulders, wearing one of my t-shirts. The sight of her there, in my bed, in my clothes, hit me like a linebacker at full speed.

"Morning," I said, offering her the mug. "Thought you could use this."

"My hero," she murmured, accepting it gratefully. She took a sip, eyes closing in appreciation. "You remembered the oat milk creamer."

"I pay attention." I sat on the edge of the bed, giving her space even though every instinct wanted me to pull her close again. "How are you feeling?"

She sighed, cradling the mug in both hands. "Like I'm about to face a firing squad."

"Your parents can't actually execute you," I pointed out. "Pretty sure that's illegal in all fifty states."

That earned me a small smile. "You haven't met my mother. She is... intense, and she's going to hate you on principle for being a dumb jock who's corrupted her daughter into writing smut."

"First of all," I raised an eyebrow, "I'm pretty sure you were writing smut before I came along."

That got me a proper laugh. "True."

"Second," I continued, taking her hand, "I don't need your mother to like me. I just need to be there for you."

She gave me a wan smile. "That's the only reason I'm not having a full-blown panic attack right now."

The drive from my house to hers was only maybe twenty minutes, but because Tempest didn't say a single word the whole way, it felt like twenty-hundred hours.

Before we could get out of the car, the front door opened. AbuelaNovela stood there, resplendent in a deep purple pantsuit that somehow managed to look both elegant and slightly theatrical. She waved to us, gesturing for us to hurry inside.

"Mi amor," she greeted Tempest with a fierce hug. "Shoulders back. Remember who you are." Then she turned to me, reaching up to pat my cheek. "And you, handsome boy. Be ready to pull out those muscles."

With that cryptic warning, she ushered us inside.

Unlike when I was here for Abuela and Burrito's party, we were directed into a formal living room where the entire family had assembled. Catalina, sat beside a slender, elegant woman who could only be Dr. Luz Navarro. The family resemblance was striking, though where Catalina was all cool polish, her mother had a sharpness to her features, accentuated by her impeccably tailored suit and the severe twist of her dark hair.

Beside her sat Professor Diego Navarro, ever the very academic-looking distinguished, yet nerdy gentleman with salt-and-pepper hair and reading glasses perched on his nose.

Rosalind, who had this disdainful shrewd look on her face, sat on her mother's other side. Ophelia occupied an armchair near the window, while Freddie leaned against the fireplace mantel.

"Tempest," Dr. Navarro's voice cut through the silence. "I see you've brought your... friend."

"This is Flynn Kingman," Tempest said, her voice impressively steady. "My boyfriend."

Fuck yeah, I was. I stepped forward, extending my hand. "It's a pleasure to meet you, Dr. Navarro."

She regarded my hand with the enthusiasm of someone being offered a dead fish before briefly shaking it. "Indeed."

The professor rose, offering a firmer handshake. "Flynn. I've seen you play. You've made DSU proud out on the field."

"Thank you, sir."

"Let's skip the pleasantries," Catalina interjected. "We're here to figure out Tempest's... situation."

Tempest stiffened beside me. I placed my hand at the small of her back, a silent reminder that I was there.

"You mean my career?" Tempest asked, her voice taking on an edge I'd rarely heard from her.

Go on with your bad self, my queen. I wanted to fist pump, high-five, and cheer that she hadn't let their first play take her down. She was going to be a tough defender and I was here for it.

"Career?" Dr. Navarro scoffed. "Writing that kind of... book is hardly a career."

"Those books are bestsellers, Mamá," Tempest said. "They've been translated into fourteen languages."

"And yet you kept them a secret," Rosalind pointed out, her tone making it clear she thought this proved their shameful nature. "If you were so proud of this career, why hide it? This could cause those of us who want actual respectable careers a lot of trouble in the future."

"Because I knew this is exactly how you would react," Tempest shot back.

She needed a second to regain her composure, so I guided her to the empty loveseat, sitting close enough that our thighs touched. She was trembling slightly, but her jaw was set in determination.

"Do you have any idea," Dr. Navarro began, her voice dangerously soft, "what this has done to our family's reputation? Your father is a respected Shakespeare scholar. I am on the board of the Medical Association, your sister plans to be a lawyer. And now everyone knows our daughter writes—" She seemed unable to even finish the sentence.

"Romance novels," Tempest supplied. "I write romance novels, Mamá. With sex scenes. Between consenting adults. Who enjoy themselves."

I bit back a smile at her bluntness. It took everything I had in me not to proudly declare that I helped with the research for said sex scenes. Across the room, I noticed Freddie covering her mouth, eyes wide with what looked like delighted shock.

"This is precisely why I wanted you to pursue business," Dr. Navarro continued as if Tempest hadn't spoken.

"Or at the very least, if you insisted on literature, to focus on classics, on works of substance."

"My books have substance," Tempest insisted.

Catalina let out a derisive laugh. "Please. They're glorified bodice-rippers."

"Have you read them?" The question came not from Tempest, but from Ophelia, surprising everyone.

Catalina blinked. "Of course not."

"Then how would you know what they are?" Ophelia challenged.

"We don't need to eat garbage to know it's garbage," Rosalind snapped back on behalf of them both.

"Maybe you should read one before judging," Freddie suggested, straightening from her casual lean. "They're actually really good. The Shakespeare adaptations are super smart, and the hockey one made me cry. And you in particular, Cat, would identify with the heroine in book one. She's exactly like you. But happier."

The room went silent as everyone stared at Freddie.

"You've read them?" Tempest asked, looking genuinely shocked.

Freddie shrugged. "Yeah, all of them. I'm a huge Miranda Milan fan. I didn't know it was you until yesterday when the campus news broke, and then I was like, oh my god, my sister is my favorite author. That's so cool."

"Imogen," Dr. Navarro gasped. "You will not speak of this... embarrassment as if it's something to celebrate."

Who the fuck was Imogen?

"Mamá." Freddie's demeanor went from fun and casual to decidedly dark. "You will call me Freddie, or if you cannot, you may call me Fidele. But do not dead name me again."

Professor Navarro took his wife's hand. "You know better, Luz."

"Fine. I am trying. But I don't understand why you are supporting your sister's frivolity. You've worked extremely hard and have Olympic prospects. This isn't going to help."

"That's just dumb, Mamá," Freddie challenged. "Tempest is amazing at what she does. Her books mean something to people."

"They're smut," Rosalind interjected primly.

"They're romance," Ophelia corrected. "With some ridiculously hot sex scenes, yes. But they're also about women who look like us finding love and happiness. Do you know how rare that is? To see a heroine with brown skin, who isn't a size two, blonde, and bubbly?"

I felt Tempest inhale sharply beside me. I squeezed her hand, proud of the impact her work had clearly had, even on her own sisters without her knowing.

"I expect this kind of defense from Fidele," their mother said dismissively. "She's always been... rebellious. But Tempest, you were raised to aspire to more. I cannot understand how you could squander your education, your potential, on such frivolous content."

"It's not frivolous," Tempest said, her voice strengthening. "Romance is the top-selling genre in publishing. It's mostly for women, by women, about women. The stories are feminist, they battle against patriarchy, and misogyny. They've help women feel seen and valued."

"And they're making her rich," Abuela added with a not-so-subtle wink. "Very, very rich."

It wasn't like I was a millionaire or something. But it was enough to make writing a full-time career after college.

Dr. Navarro's lips thinned. "At least that's something. I don't want any of my daughters to have to worry about that. Money isn't everything. Don't you want to be respectable?"

"It's honest work that brings joy to others," Abuela countered.

"Joy?" Dr. Navarro stood, her posture rigid with anger. "Is that what we're calling it now? These books are nothing more than female wish fulfillment and sexual fantasy."

"And what's wrong with that?" Tempest challenged, rising to face her mother. "What's wrong with women having fantasies? With seeing themselves as desirable? With imagining a world where they get to be the heroine? Seeing themselves being with partners who treat them with respect, kindness, and honestly, the way Papá treats you."

The room fell silent. Even Dr. Navarro seemed taken aback by Tempest's fiery defense, and at the same time, showing how her parents have the love story many others were looking for.

I was fucking loving getting to watch Tempest standing tall, her face flushed with emotion but her voice steady. This was a side of her I'd glimpsed only in moments, like when she negotiated with her agent on the phone. Seeing her in full force now, defending her work

THE JACK*SS IN CLASS   353

and her passion, made my heart go all wobbly and warm with pride and something deeper, more profound.

"I think," the professor finally spoke, in a measured way that teachers used when explaining something that should be obvious, "that we shouldn't be so quick to pass judgment."

All eyes turned to him, the patriarch who had remained largely silent until now.

"Diego," Dr. Navarro began, but he held up a hand.

"I've read Tempest's—Miranda's—books," he repeated. "All of them."

Tempest looked stunned. "Papá? You have? Mamá said something about the first one, but she said you thought it was...silly."

"When a colleague mentioned a new adaptation of Taming of the Shrew set at an American university, I was naturally curious. It was quite good, actually. Clever modernization, maintained the thematic core while addressing the problematic, and frankly misogynistic elements of the original."

I felt Tempest trembling beside me, but this time I didn't think it was from fear.

"As a Shakespeare scholar," her father continued, "I recognize that he was essentially writing the popular entertainment of his day. His plays were not considered 'high art' at the time. They were meant to engage and entertain the masses, including plenty of ribald humor and, yes, sexual content."

"Diego." Dr. Navarro looked genuinely scandalized.

"It's true, Luz," he said calmly. "The idea that Shakespeare is somehow above the fray of popular entertainment is a relatively recent academic construction. In reality, he was writing for a broad audience, and his humor was often quite bawdy."

"Are you honestly comparing Shakespeare to—to—" his wife sputtered.

"To our daughter's work? In some ways, yes," the professor said. "Her adaptations show a real understanding of his themes and characters, reimagined for a modern audience. I found them quite insightful." He looked directly at Tempest. "You have a gift for storytelling, mija. I may not be that familiar with your choice of genre, but I cannot deny your talent."

Tempest looked like she might cry. "Papá..."

Dr. Navarro stood abruptly. "This is absurd. I expected better from you, Diego. Our daughter has embarrassed this family with her...her pornography, and you're encouraging her?"

"It's not pornography, Luz," Abuela said sharply. "It's romance. There's a difference."

"A meaningless distinction," Dr. Navarro snapped. "The point is that our daughter has chosen to sully our family name with this... trash. And I expect her to put an end to it. Immediately."

Outside, Burrito brayed, clearly sensing the sudden fucking drop in temperature. Tempest went rigid beside me.

"What?" she whispered.

"You will cease this Miranda Milan nonsense," Dr. Navarro said firmly. "You will issue a statement denying the rumors, complete your degree properly, and pursue a respectable graduate program as we'd planned."

"I will not do that," Tempest said, her voice quiet but firm.

"You most certainly will," her mother insisted. "I am still your Mamá, and I know what's best for you."

"No." The single word hung in the air between them. "I won't hide who I am anymore, Mamá. I won't pretend to be ashamed of work I'm proud of."

Dr. Navarro's expression hardened. "Then you leave me no choice but to—"

"Enough!" Abuela's voice cracked like a whip. "Enough, Luz!"

Everyone froze as Abuela rose to her feet, her eyes flashing with anger I hadn't seen before. Without another word, she stormed from the room, her heels clicking sharply on the hardwood floors.

The silence that followed was deafening. Tempest's hand found mine, gripping tightly.

A moment later, Abuela returned, clutching a stack of worn paperbacks. She marched directly to Tempest's mother and dropped the books onto the table in front of Dr. Navarro.

"Tell me, Luz Ximena Ramirez Navarro. Are you ashamed of these too? Are you ashamed of your papá's books? His writing career?"

"It's not the same. Papá doesn't write... filth."

"Perhaps," Abuela said, her voice dangerously quiet, "you should remind yourself of your own past before judging your daughter so harshly."

Her mother's expression shuttered. "I grew up and chose a responsible path." Her spine straightened. "As I expect you to do."

Tempest shook her head slowly. "I'm not giving up my writing. It's who I am, Mamá. Whether you approve or not."

"Then I have nothing more to say to you," her mother declared, rising to her feet. "When you're ready to be a Navarro again, to live up to the standards of this family—"

"You mean, *your* standards," Abuela corrected sharply.

"—then we can discuss your future," Dr. Navarro finished, ignoring her mother. "Until then, I suggest you consider very carefully the consequences of your choices." She turned to her husband, and when he didn't immediately back her up, she stomped away.

The professor looked torn, glancing between his retreating wife and his daughter. Then, surprising everyone, he bent to press a kiss to Tempest's forehead. "I'm proud of your talent, mija," he said quietly. "It takes your mother a while to adjust to changes to her expectations. I'll work on her."

With that, he followed his wife from the room, leaving a stunned silence in their wake.

Catalina and Rosalind exchanged glances, then rose in unison to follow their parents. Neither looked at Tempest as they left. But Freddie immediately bounded over to take their place on the couch.

"That was EPIC," she said, eyes wide with excitement. "Abuela bringing out Abuelo's spy novels and throwing them in Mamá's face? I did not see that coming."

"Freddie," Ophelia admonished, though she too had moved closer, perching on the arm of the loveseat next to Tempest. "Maybe not the time."

"Sorry," Freddie said, not looking sorry at all. "But

seriously, Tempest, it took Mamá a while to accept that I wasn't ever going to be the sweet daughter she wanted. You saw how she stumbled with my name today. But she's come around, and she will with this too."

"I don't know how you managed." Tempest grabbed her sister in a hug.

"Being true to yourself is hard sometimes. But I would have been your cheerleader, just like you were mine, if you'd told me. I still can't believe you're Miranda Milan. Can I get signed copies? Will you tell me what happens in the next one? Is it about the hockey player's brother? Because I have thoughts—"

"Freddie," Tempest cut her off, but she was smiling now, a small, surprised smile. "You really read my books?"

"Duh," Freddie rolled her eyes. "They're amazing. The scene in book three where the baseball player finally admits he's in love with the ice princess? I literally threw my Kindle across the room and then had to buy a new one."

"I've read them too," Ophelia admitted with a small shrug. "They're good, T. Really good."

I watched emotion well up in Tempest's eyes. She'd been prepared for unanimous condemnation from her family—this support, however small, seemed to hit her harder than the criticism had.

"I—thank you," she managed.

Abuela approached, gently taking Tempest's face in her hands. "You stood tall, mi corazón. I am so proud of you."

Tempest nodded, leaning into her grandmother's

touch for a moment before turning to me. "Can we go? I need to... process."

"Of course," I said immediately, standing and offering her my hand. "Whatever you need."

As we headed for the door, Freddie called after us, "Does he know about the scene in book two chapter seventeen? Because if he hasn't tried that move yet—"

"FREDDIE!" Tempest and Ophelia shouted in unison.

"What?" Freddie asked innocently. "I'm just saying, art should inspire life, you know?"

Oh, we were getting a copy of book two on the way home. That was for sure.

TAKING THE THRONE

TEMPEST

I pulled the baseball cap low over my eyes, shrugging myself down into Flynn's oversized DSU hoodie, and donning the biggest pair of sunglasses Parker could find in our room. I felt ridiculous, but my sisters assured me it was "peak celebrity undercover realness."

"You look like a hungover pop star avoiding the paparazzi," Hannah said, nodding approvingly as our group claimed the back corner of Cool Beans Cat Café. "Very on-brand for your new famous author status."

"I'm not a celebrity," I protested, though the past forty-eight hours suggested otherwise. My phone hadn't stopped buzzing with notifications since The Dracarys article broke, and according to Parker's surveillance, there were still two enterprising journalism students camping outside the KAT house.

"Tell that to the three news vans that were outside our house this morning," Alice said, setting down a tray of coffee mugs.

Flynn slid into the booth beside me, his arm settling comfortably around my shoulders. "No news vans followed us, so the decoy plan worked. We should be safe here for a while."

Across the café, Gryff and Isak had stationed themselves strategically at separate tables, pretending to study while actually keeping watch. Somehow, in the space of a few days, I'd acquired a security detail consisting of half the DSU football team and the entire KAT senior class.

"Okay, crisis management time," Bettie said, slipping into her chapter president mode. She pulled out a color-coded planner. "First issue, classes. You've got Shakespeare tomorrow with Professor Whitmore, then marketing, and your senior thesis meeting on Thursday."

I groaned, sinking lower in my seat. "I can't show up to Shakespeare. Professor Whitmore is likely having a cow over all of this. One of those really cute highland cows with the fluffy bangs."

"You mean the same Professor Whitmore, who emailed the dean to say, and I quote, 'I'm delighted to discover we have a commercially successful author in our midst,'" Bettie said, reading from her phone.

I blinked. "He what?"

"You're good for the English department," Parker explained. "Published authors equal prestige. They're capitalizing on your success faster than you can say 'liberal arts alumni fundraiser.'"

A large orange tabby cat chose that moment to leap onto our table, knocking over Hannah's empty cup before settling directly in front of me with regal indifference.

"See? Catticus Finch, Attorney at Paw recognizes

literary royalty," Flynn said, scratching the cat behind its ears.

Despite everything, I laughed. "My disguise isn't fooling anyone, is it?"

"Not even the cats," Parker confirmed cheerfully. "But we've got a plan. Operation Author Protection Squad is a go."

Parker did love a plan with a secret code name.

"Please tell me that's not what you're actually calling it," I said, already knowing the answer from the matching gleams in my sisters' eyes.

"APS for short," Alice replied. "We've mapped out routes to all your classes that avoid high-traffic areas. Thanks to your captain of the football team boyfriend, next year's captains of all the major sports on campus have volunteered as escort bodyguards, two per journey, rotating schedule."

I glanced up at Flynn, who gave me one of those confident I-got-you-boo chin bobs.

"I've drafted a statement for you to send professors," Bettie continued, sliding a printed paper across the table. "Brief, professional, acknowledging the situation while requesting privacy during this transition. The dean's office has already confirmed they'll support whatever accommodations you need."

I stared at them, warmth blooming in my chest. "You guys did all this for me?"

"Of course we did," Hannah said like it was the most obvious thing in the world. "That's what sisters do."

"Besides," Parker added, "this is the most exciting thing to happen at KAT since Jessica dated that guy from the band that got sort of famous for like three months."

"And the KAT alumni network has activated," Bettie added. "Maria Jimenez, who graduated the year before we pledged, works for a crisis PR firm in New York. She's offering pro bono consultation calls whenever you're ready."

"I don't know what to say," I managed, looking around at their determined faces. "Thank you doesn't seem like enough."

"You can thank us by signing our copies of your books," Hannah said, grinning. "We've all been reading them since the first book came out. Bettie just finished book three last night and cried for an hour."

"I did not cry for an hour," Bettie protested. "Forty-five minutes, tops."

Everyone laughed, and I felt something tight in my chest begin to loosen. This was what I'd been afraid of losing, this easy camaraderie, this unconditional acceptance.

"What about your family?" Alice asked gently. "How did your meet-up with them go?"

I exchanged a look with Flynn, who ran his hand down my back, giving me just that smidge of comfort I needed.

"Better than I expected, in some ways. Worse in others." I wrapped my hands around my coffee mug, drawing strength from its warmth. "My mom is... still processing. Her way of saying she's disappointed but not ready to disown me completely. Which is an improvement."

"She'll come around," Flynn said with more confidence than I felt. "Your dad knows what's up and he'll convince her. I'm sure."

"Papá's actually been texting me," I admitted. "And Freddie is already campaigning to be a character in my next book," I added with a small smile. "Ophelia too. Rosalind and Catalina are still firmly in Mom's camp, though."

"What about Abuela?" Parker asked.

I groaned but with a smile. "She actually called her agent to see about getting cast in the series."

"I like your abuela more every day," Flynn said, grinning.

Catticus Finch, Attorney at Paw chose that moment to headbutt my hand, demanding attention. As I scratched under his chin, I realized I was smiling...really smiling, for the first time in days.

"So what's next?" Hannah asked. "Did we miss anything?"

"I'm meeting with my agent this afternoon," I said, the smile fading slightly. "There are... complications with the FlixNChill deal. I need to sort those out before I make any other decisions. Anyway," I continued, "I need to decide if I still want to work with FlixNChill after this. The deal is incredible, but if I can't trust them..."

"Trust your gut," Bettie advised. "You've built this career on your own terms so far. Don't compromise now just because everyone knows who you are."

I nodded, gathering my resolve. "Okay."

I planned to harness that, the advice from the

Kingman Queens to take up space, and my inner Abuela-Novela for this meeting.

"Absolutely not acceptable," I said firmly, maintaining eye contact with Franklin Peters, FlixNChill's head of development. "You promised confidentiality throughout our negotiations. That promise was broken, which means all our previous terms are now void."

We were sitting in a private conference room at the Peachy Creek Four Seasons, where Gloria had arranged an emergency meeting with the FlixNChill executives. My agent sat beside me, uncharacteristically quiet as I took the lead.

Franklin looked profoundly uncomfortable. "Ms. Navarro, I assure you that FlixNChill takes this breach very seriously. Our internal investigation, well, we're still determining exactly how the information leaked," he hedged, adjusting his designer glasses. "These things can be complicated."

"What's not complicated is trust," I countered. This was not something I was willing to just let go in the name of being a good girl. "I want to know who compromised my privacy and that there will be consequences before I sign anything."

Beside me, Gloria suppressed a smile. This was not the meek, accommodating Tempest she was used to dealing with. But after years of hiding and the chaos of the past week, something had fundamentally shifted in me.

I was done being afraid.

"We understand your concerns," said Melissa Wong, FlixNChill's senior VP of content acquisition. She'd flown in from LA specifically for this meeting, which told me exactly how much they wanted this deal. "And we share them. The last thing we wanted was to jeopardize this deal."

"And yet, here we are," I said coolly.

Melissa exchanged a glance with Franklin, then leaned forward. "Ms. Navarro, Tempest, may I speak frankly?"

I nodded, bracing myself.

"Our preliminary investigation suggests this wasn't just an internal leak," she said, her voice dropping. "We believe someone close to you may have been involved."

The statement landed like a stone in still water, ripples of shock spreading through me.

"What do you mean?" Gloria asked sharply.

"We've tracked a message on our end that appears to have come from a Colorado number," Melissa explained. "It contained details about Ms. Navarro's routine, her writing habits, specific campus locations. It's information no one at FlixNChill would have had access to."

I felt sick. Someone I knew had betrayed me? An envious classmate? A disgruntled sorority sister? A family member?

"Someone who knew you were Miranda Milan?" Gloria asked, frowning. She knew how closely guarded I kept that information. Until Flynn, only three other people besides her knew. And I trusted them all implicitly.

"Or someone who figured it out and saw an opportunity," I said.

"We believe whoever called coordinated with someone inside our organization," Melissa continued. "We're close to identifying our internal leak. When we do, I personally guarantee there will be consequences."

"That's not enough," I said, finding my voice again. "I need more than promises."

"Which is why," Melissa continued smoothly, "we're prepared to offer you substantially improved terms."

All I'd asked for was a resolution to this problem, not more money. Whatever they were offering wasn't going to sway my decision.

She slid a folder across the table. "Additional creative control. Executive producer credit. An option on your next series, at your discretion. And a thirty percent increase in the overall compensation package."

Gloria reached for the folder, but I placed my hand on it first.

"And the identity of the leakers—both of them—before I sign anything," I added. "Or I walk away and take my books somewhere else. I hear Flamebird is very interested."

Franklin's face fell. "That may not be realistic—"

"It's nonnegotiable," I said firmly. "I need to know who I can trust."

Melissa studied me for a long moment, then nodded. "We'll find them. You have my word."

I opened the folder, scanning the revised terms. They were far better than what I'd initially been offered. The kind of deal authors dreamed about.

"I'll review these with my attorney and get back to you," I said, closing the folder.

"We look forward to your decision," Melissa replied, extending her hand. "And Tempest? For what it's worth, I've been a fan of your books since the first one. What you've created deserves to be celebrated. On your terms, of course."

As Gloria and I left the hotel, she turned to me with undisguised admiration.

"That," she said, "was masterful. Where has this Tempest been hiding all along?"

I smiled, thinking of Flynn, of my sorority sisters, of the Kingman Queens, and Abuela with her unflinching pride in who I was. "She was always there. She just needed to realize it."

"Well, I'm glad she showed up today," Gloria said. "Those updated terms are incredible. If they do identify the leakers as promised, I strongly advise accepting."

"I know." I glanced down at the folder in my hands. "But first I need to figure out who in my life would do this. Because that hurts more than any stranger at FlixNChill."

"Sometimes success brings out jealousy in the most unexpected places," Gloria said gently. "People you'd never suspect can resent what you've achieved."

As my rideshare pulled up, I thought about my family, my classmates, my friends. Who among them would betray me this way? And more importantly, what would I do when I found out?

My father was waiting on a bench in the park not far from our house. He stood as I approached, his expression unreadable behind his scholarly glasses.

"Mija," he said by way of greeting, offering a brief, awkward hug. "Thank you for meeting me."

"Of course, Papá." I sat beside him, suddenly nervous.

Despite the support he'd shown during the confrontation, we hadn't spoken one-on-one since everything happened.

For a moment, we simply sat in silence, watching ducks glide across the water's surface.

"I've been rereading your books," he finally said. "I enjoyed the *Much Ado About Nothing* adaptation."

I tensed, waiting to hear he thought it all went downhill from there. For criticism or disappointment.

He paused. "Your adaptation of Benedick and Beatrice's dynamic is quite inventive. Setting it in the world of college hockey has excellent parallels to the social hierarchies of Shakespeare's era."

I blinked, stunned by the scholarly analysis. "You're rereading all of them?"

He adjusted his glasses, a gesture I'd mimicked my entire life. "Of course. You wrote them. Now that I know they're yours, I can appreciate them on an entirely different level."

"But they're romance novels," I said, unable to keep the disbelief from my voice. "With... you know."

"Sex scenes?" A hint of amusement crossed his face. "I'm a Shakespeare scholar, Tempest. The bard wasn't exactly subtle about physical desire. 'The beast with two backs'? That's from *Othello*."

Despite myself, I laughed. "I know, Papá. I just never expected you to read my books, let alone talk about them like... like they're real literature."

"They are real literature," he said firmly. "Commercial fiction has just as much cultural value as the classics. It reflects and shapes contemporary values, explores human relationships, and connects with readers on a meaningful level."

I stared at him, this man who had shaped my literary education, who had always pushed me toward the classics, toward academic rigor. "Mamá doesn't see it that way."

He sighed, removing his glasses to clean them meticulously with his handkerchief. "Your mother... will need more time. She worries about appearances, about what others will think."

"About her daughter writing sexy books?" I couldn't keep the bitterness from my voice.

"About her daughter facing public judgment," he corrected gently. "She's seen how cruel the world can be, especially to women who don't conform to expectations."

I thought about that, about the protective fury that had colored my mother's reaction. Maybe there was something more complex at work than simple disapproval.

"Your abuela tells me you had a meeting in Los Angeles," he continued, changing the subject slightly. "With the people who want to adapt your books."

I nodded, still processing his words. "They've made an offer. A good one."

"And what about your football player? Does he figure into your future plans too?"

"It's possible," I admitted.

My father nodded approvingly. "Good. You should go where your work takes you, where your opportunities lie. You can live anywhere in the world and write your books."

"You think I should leave Denver?" I asked, surprised.

"I think you should spread your wings," he said simply.

"See more of the world than just Colorado and Oaxaca. Experience different places, different people. It will only enrich your writing. Perhaps even visit the home of the bard himself."

I considered his words, the implicit permission to go, to explore, to build a life beyond what had been planned for me.

"I've been spending time with your donkey," he added, unexpectedly.

"Burrito?" I smiled, picturing my distinguished professor father with the small, mischievous donkey.

"Yes. He's quite a good companion." My father looked slightly embarrassed. "I've been reading Shakespeare to him. We started with a *Midsummer Night's Dream* of course."

The mental image was so absurd and endearing that it made me love him even more. "Papá, that's adorable."

"Yes, well." He cleared his throat. "Unfortunately, I've discovered I'm somewhat allergic to him. Nothing severe, just some sneezing, itchy eyes."

"Oh no." I stifled back my giggle for my sweet papá who, despite the discomfort, was doting on my baby donkey.

"It's manageable with medication," he assured me. "And if you were considering taking him with you, should you decide to leave Denver, I would miss his company."

Somehow, I didn't think he was only talking about missing Burrito anymore.

"Thank you, Papá," I said softly. "That means more than you know."

That weekend I sprawled across Flynn's bed after a

marathon round of who could get who to come first. We were, of course, supposed to be studying and finishing our makeup work from time missed from classes recently.

But it had been my turn to provide him comfort, distraction, and fun. He'd been so good to me through this crisis, and I wanted to be there for him too.

Flynn smiled, but I could see the tension at the corners of his eyes. Tomorrow was the draft, the culmination of years of work, the moment that would determine where his career would begin. Where he would live. Whether we would be separated by half a continent or potentially living in the same city.

"You're nervous about tomorrow," I said, running my fingers up and down his chest, absently counting his abs. Who knew a person could have more than a six-pack?

"That obvious, huh?" He took my hand, his fingers lacing with mine. "Not about getting drafted. That part's pretty much guaranteed. It's more about where."

The unspoken question hung between us. He had a lot of prospects, because he was that good. At least a half dozen teams were gunning for him. But really, the real game was going to be between Denver and LA.

"I realize you could end up anywhere," I said carefully. "But have you decided what you want?"

Flynn sat up, his expression suddenly serious. "Honestly? I want to play pro ball. I want to go somewhere that values me, and if I get Gryff as a package deal, that would be amazing. I want to make my family proud." He paused, his eyes holding mine. "And I want you."

My heart stuttered. "Flynn—"

"I know it's complicated," he continued. "I know your

life is here, your family, your sorority, everything. But Tempest... these past few months with you have been the best of my life. Whatever happens tomorrow, I want us to figure out how to be together."

I leaned into him, my hand finding his. "What if you get drafted to Miami? That's on the other side of the country."

"Then we figure it out. Long distance, you visiting, me visiting. Or..." He hesitated, then forged ahead. "Or you could come with me."

The suggestion hung in the air between us, breathtaking in its simplicity and its complexity.

"My father thinks I should spread my wings," I said after a moment. "See more of the world than just Colorado and Oaxaca."

Hope flickered in Flynn's eyes. "Yeah?"

"Yeah." I took a deep breath. "But I don't want to make any decisions based solely on where you end up. That wouldn't be fair to either of us."

"I get that." He squeezed my hand. "But knowing it's a possibility... that makes tomorrow a little more exciting. And a whole lot less scary."

I leaned forward, pressing my forehead to his. "You, Flynn Kingman, afraid of anything? I don't believe it."

His smile was soft, vulnerable in a way few people ever got to see. "Only of losing the things that matter."

LEGACY

FLYNN

The Sports Network crew arrived, right on time and already lugging black cases of equipment up the walk like they were moving in. Dad opened the front door before they could knock, wearing his game day suit like the rest of us, and that calm, polite expression that meant he was trying not to scare the media.

I stood just inside the living room, watching as a guy with a boom mic followed two camera operators into the house. The Sports Network reporter they'd sent to talk to us about wherever we landed in the draft today glanced at me and grinned.

"You ready for the big moment, Kingman?"

I smiled like I wasn't vibrating at a subatomic level. "Born ready."

Which was a lie. I was mostly ready to puke.

Gryff wandered in from the kitchen with a slice of pizza in one hand and a stack of paper napkins in the other, like he hadn't even noticed our house was about to be turned into a live broadcast set.

"Hey," he said through a bite. "You saw? Three cameras on us."

"One for wide shots, one close on us, and a backup in case someone starts crying and they want the ratings. I hope someone cries," Jules said, appearing beside me with actual makeup on and a cute outfit. Dammit. My baby sister was growing up and I was going to have to prepare to beat any man who didn't treat her right with a sharp stick. If I was even here to see her grow up.

"I brought waterproof mascara." She batted her eyelashes at me. "I'm prepared for tears."

Tempest came into the living room wearing my DSU football sweatshirt over her dress. "Your Aunt June's been running around the kitchen muttering about coasters and camera angles. Is she always like this?"

"Welcome to Kingman family draft day," I said, wrapping an arm around her waist. I needed the grounding comfort she gave me right now. I didn't expect to be so on edge today. It's not like I didn't know exactly how this day was going to go. Get a call, get drafted, high-five, take pic in the new team gear.

Start a whole ass new life.

Tempest looked up at me, soft and warm and steady in all the ways I wasn't. "Excited?"

"Yep," I bluffed, because I was the confident cocky jock. Today, when my life was about to change forever, shouldn't be any different.

But my Tempest knew me better and narrowed her eyes at me.

I sighed and leaned into her even more. She was my

THE JACK*SS IN CLASS

rock when I didn't think I needed one. Wasn't I supposed to be hers? "I think I'll be okay when it's over."

She gave me a quick kiss. "Well, for what it's worth... you look like someone who's about to get picked first overall in a romance novel."

I laughed, actually laughed, and the camera closest to us immediately swung around.

Tempest froze. "Oh my god, was that on camera?"

"Nah, we're not rolling yet," the camera lady said. "But I wish we would have been. I know a lot of people who would love to hear you say that, Ms. Milan."

Tempest's eyes went wide for a moment, but then she smiled at the woman and nodded. "I'm still getting used to the idea of being in the public eye."

"You're sure you're okay with doing it today? We can strategically place you behind a whole defensive line of Kingmans if you don't want to show your face, babe." I smoothed a hand down her back and stared at the cluster of lights and wires now webbing across our living room.

"No, I'm sure. I'm faking it till I make it because I want to be here, with you. I'm happy for the entire world, or at least the ones who watch football, to be able to see how proud I am to be by your side. If they want to gossip about who I may or may not be, that's up to them."

I full well knew how much letting people see the real Tempest had cost her in the past couple of weeks. But she'd come out stronger for facing down those fears. "I'm the one proud to be by your side, my queen."

"Good god, you two. Get a room. No one on the Sports Channel is here to film a mushy gooshy Heartmark

Channel special." Isak pretended to wretch and I flipped him the bird while kissing my girl for the whole room to see.

The living room became chaos in a Kingman kind of way. Loud, overstuffed, full of bodies and snack plates and too many opinions on where to put the TV. Mom had never allowed us to have one in here. Said there should be one room in the house where football wasn't the focus. But all of us and the camera crew didn't fit into the home theater room downstairs, so Dad said he'd allow it for this one occasion.

Once Hayes, Isak, and Levi got everything hooked up, the League Draft lit up on the big screen, and Dad put the volume loud enough that the commentators' voices tangled with the laughter, the teasing, and it all felt surreal. Familiar and foreign all at once.

This was our house. Our team. Our family.

And it was all about to change while the whole world was watching.

I planted myself in the corner of the room like a linebacker on fourth down, trying not to show just how nervous I actually was. I'd never been good at sitting still, and this? This wasn't sitting still. This was sitting in a pressure cooker with every eye in the country waiting to see where I'd land.

Gryff sat next to me, calm as hell with his long legs stretched out and a plate of wings in his lap like this was just another Saturday. The only tell was the way he kept licking his lips, eyes flicking between the screen and his phone, like he was expecting it to vibrate at any second.

"You ready for this?" I asked under my breath.

He gave me that slow side-smile of his. "I was nominated for the Heisman, bro. I was born for this."

Cocky bastard.

I was proud of him. Of all of us. But it didn't stop the knot in my gut from twisting tighter with every second the clock ticked down. The Mustangs hadn't called. Not yet. They still could.

The Bandits were supposed to pick at sixteen. But they'd traded up to twelve. The pick was in, but they hadn't announced it yet.

Then Gryff's phone rang. He waggled his eyebrows at me and answered. Whoever was on the other end of the line said something, then Gryff smiled, and said, "Yep. Let's do it."

The Sports Network's coverage cut to the stage. The commissioner stepped up to the mic, flanked by two wide-eyed kids in custom jerseys. My entire family leaned forward like one collective beast.

"With the twelfth pick in the 2025 League Draft, the LA Bandits select... Gryffin Kingman. Safety. Denver State University."

The room exploded.

Screams, cheers, hands everywhere. Jules jumped on the couch, sobbing and laughing through it all. Aunt June hugged Dad so tight I thought his ribs would crack. Our agent, Mac Jerry, let out a sharp whistle and clapped Gryff on the back as the cameras on TV cut to our living room feed.

And me?

I clapped. I smiled. I hugged my brother.

But inside, I felt like I was falling.

I wasn't jealous. That wasn't it. Gryff deserved it, he'd worked harder than anyone I knew, played smarter than half the League already.

But everything was so fucking for real right now. Our lives were changing. In huge, enormous ways. Ways I thought I was prepared for. But inside I was a god damn wreck. What if I had to leave my whole family behind?

What if I didn't want to?

What if I wasn't okay without them?

What if they weren't okay without me?

This family was my everything, and only once in my whole life had we ever been broken up. And we were not okay after that. How could we have been?

"Flynn," he said, gripping the back of my neck. "They're gonna come for you next. I feel it."

I nodded, pretended to be excited.

The TV screen flickered. I heard someone shout, "Trade alert. Mustangs just traded up. They're picking number sixteen."

Every eye in the house turned to me. With a trade like that, right after Gryff just got drafted to LA, were the Mustangs making a play for me?

My stomach flipped.

There were three more picks before them, but none were teams who'd expressed more than a passing interest in me. The Kansas City Chefs, the New England Rebels, and Miami. I did have a call with the Hammerheads, but no one had pressed like the Bandits and the Mustangs. I was seventy-five percent sure I was going to either one.

The Chefs picked a quarterback out of Texas, and the

THE JACK*SS IN CLASS 379

Rebels grabbed a running back from Bay State University. Miami was up next, and then the Mustangs.

Then my phone buzzed.

Everything stopped. Not in the room—in me. I looked down. Unknown number. Area code... 213.

California.

Not Colorado.

I stood up, heart slamming.

Tempest was suddenly beside me, eyes wide. "Flynn?"

I answered, barely breathing. "Hello?"

"Flynn Kingman?" a familiar voice said. "Coach Reid with the LA Bandits. We're on the clock here and want you in black and silver. Are you in?"

My mouth was dry, my whole being was dry. My fucking soul was dry.

"Sir," I said, my voice just this side of cracking, "you said you're on the clock soon, but the Mustangs traded up to pick after the Sharks."

I could feel everyone staring at me, but my vision was going dark around the edges and all I could do was stare at Tempest, her pretty pink lips, her soft brown skin, the warm eyes I could get lost in.

Someone or several someone's in the room gasped and I heard some Kingman voice say, "Trade alert."

Coach Reid chuckled. "We just traded with the Sharks to move up. Word is, Coach Shenanigan was circling, but we're not giving him the chance."

The world blurred.

"We're about to make you a Bandit, son."

My knees gave out and I dropped back into the chair.

The TV thundered with the commissioner's voice.

"With the fifteenth pick in this year's League Draft, the LA Bandits select... Flynn Kingman. Defensive lineman. Denver State University."

The living room erupted into chaos—hugs, shouts, Jules leaping onto the couch and nearly taking out a cameraman with her flailing arms. Dad gripped the back of my neck, his eyes suspiciously bright.

"Both my twins," he said, voice rough with emotion. "Both of you to the Bandits."

I tried to process what was happening as cameras swung from my face to Gryff's, capturing the moment for all of America to see. The Bandits. Not the Mustangs. Not the family team where our brothers had built a dynasty.

LA, not Denver.

Chris was the first of my brothers to reach me, his quarterback arms practically vibrating with suppressed emotion.

"The damn Bandits?" he growled, but the ferocity in his voice didn't match the pride in his eyes. "Of all the teams in the League?"

"What can I say?" I managed, finding my voice, even if it sounded hollow in my head. "Their defense is—"

"Horseshit compared to ours," Chris cut in, but he was grinning as he pulled me into a crushing hug. "Congratulations, little brother. You better bring it on game day, kid. Don't you pull any punches with me. If you don't at least try to take me down, I'll kick your ass."

Jules launched herself at me, nearly sending us both toppling. "We're going to LA," she shrieked, as if she were the one who'd been drafted. "Do you know how many celebrities I'll meet?"

"Flynn, Gryff, how about putting on the hats and jerseys?" The Sports Network reporter appeared at my elbow, holding out the Bandits gear that had been handed to her. "We'd love to get the official shot of you two in your new colors."

My hands moved automatically, taking the jersey, black and silver, and sliding it over my head. Smile for the camera. Answer the questions. Yes, it's a dream come true. Yes, Gryff and I always hoped to play together. No, I hadn't expected the Bandits to trade up. Yes, we're excited for LA.

But underneath it all, a cold knot was tightening in my chest.

I felt Tempest's gaze on me, saw the slight furrow of concern between her brows. Across the room, Gryff laughed at something Dec said, but his eyes kept darting to me, that twin awareness telling him something was off.

The cameras kept rolling. I kept smiling. There was a hollowness to it all that I couldn't explain, couldn't understand. This was everything I'd worked for. Everything we'd dreamed about. Why did it feel like I was drowning?

It was nearly an hour before the main broadcast wrapped. The cameras still rolled, capturing B-roll of the family celebration, but the intensity had dimmed. Life continued around me while I stood in the middle of it all, strangely detached.

"You need some air, son?"

Dad appeared beside me, his expression carefully neutral. But his eyes—they saw right through me.

"I'm good," I said automatically. The same answer I'd been giving for hours.

"Sure you are." His hand settled on my shoulder, grounding in its weight. "Come help me grab some drinks from the garage fridge."

It wasn't a request. I followed him through the kitchen and into the garage, away from the cameras, away from the celebration. The door closed behind us with a soft click.

"You want to tell me what's going on?" Dad asked, leaning against the workbench, making no move toward the fridge.

"Nothing's going on." The deflection was instinctive. "I just got drafted. I'm moving to LA. Woo hoo."

"Flynn." Just my name, but the way he said it stripped away all pretenses. "You don't have to move to LA, or even play football at all if you really don't want to. I don't think that's what this is about though, is it?"

I ran a hand through my hair, dislodging the Bandits cap. "I don't know. I should be thrilled, right? First round. LA. Playing with Gryff. It's everything we wanted."

"But?"

"I know it's stupid," I continued when the silence grew too heavy. "Guys get drafted all over the country. That's the job. That's the dream. I just didn't expect to feel so..."

"Scared?"

The word hit like a tackle, knocking the wind out of me. But he was right. I was scared. Terrified, actually.

"Dad, I—" My voice cracked, and I swallowed hard.

"You can't help thinking that leaving will break something," Dad finished for me. "That you won't be here if something happens. That you'll miss parts of their lives you can't get back."

I nodded, unable to speak.

Dad moved to the mini fridge, pulled out two waters, and handed me one. A strange mirror of countless post-practice moments throughout my childhood.

"You were six when your mother died," he said, his voice steady despite the weight of the words. "Old enough to remember, too young to understand."

I stared at the water bottle, unseeing. I hadn't said anything about her. The night those policemen knocked on our doors and we found out she was never coming home. That was the last time I remembered really being scared.

This wasn't about Mom.

But she had left us and it did break something. She wasn't here when things happened. She did miss a part of our lives, and we would never get that back.

"You were broken," I said quietly. "We all were. But you were... It was like part of you went with her."

Dad was silent for a long moment. When he spoke again, his voice was raw with a vulnerability I'd rarely heard.

"You're right. Part of me did die with her. The part that believed the world was fair, that good things last forever, that love is safe." He took a deep breath. "But, Flynn, that's not the lesson I want you to learn from losing your mother."

I looked up, caught by the intensity in his voice.

"The lesson isn't to avoid leaving, or to avoid loving so deeply it could devastate you to lose it." His eyes held mine, unflinching.

The water bottle crumpled slightly in my grip.

"I've seen the way you hold back, the way you've held back with every girl," he continued. "Your no serious relationships, only date a girl for two-weeks rule isn't just about keeping things simple. It's about keeping yourself safe. About never risking what I went through when I lost your mother."

The accuracy of his assessment left me speechless. I didn't even know he knew about my rules.

"But son, life isn't safe. That doesn't mean we shouldn't try to live it to the fullest. If I'd played life safe all the time, I'd be the guy who sits in an office eighty hours a week. I certainly wouldn't have met your mother, wouldn't have all you kids, wouldn't have loved at all."

He stepped closer, putting his hand on my shoulder. "Your brothers aren't going anywhere, Flynn. Neither am I. Neither is Jules, or this house, or the life you've built here. Denver will always be home. But if you limit your life to what feels safe, you'll miss out on the greatest joys it has to offer."

"What if—" I started, then stopped, the fear too big to name.

"What if you lose someone again?" Dad's grip tightened. "You might. That's life. But I promise you, as someone who's been through the worst of it, the regret of playing it safe is far more painful than the grief of having loved fully."

The truth of his words settled into me, unlocking something that had been bound tight for too long.

"LA is waiting for you, son. So is the rest of your life. Don't let fear of what might happen keep you from everything that could be."

The knot in my chest finally to loosened. I blinked hard against the sudden burning in my eyes. "I miss her."

"I know. I miss her too. Every day. But Flynn, I wouldn't trade a single moment with her, even knowing how it would end." Dad pulled me into a hug, strong and sure.

As we pulled apart, I saw something in my father's eyes I hadn't noticed before. A strength that came not despite his grief, but because of it. He had loved and lost and somehow found the courage to keep going, to raise eight children alone, to build a life that honored her memory without being consumed by it.

"Now," Dad said, cracking a smile, "let's grab those drinks before they send a search party."

Back in the living room, the celebration had continued. Isak and Jules were arguing over the last of the nachos, which was so typical it almost made my heart hurt. I was going to miss this yes. But Dad was right. There was so much more I'd miss if I stayed.

Gryff caught my eye from across the room, a silent question in his expression. I nodded slightly, a wordless reassurance that I was okay. He understood, as he always did.

But it was Tempest I sought out, finding her helping Aunt May and June arrange plates on the dining room table for dinner.

"Can I steal her for a minute?" I asked my aunties, who both grinned and made a shooing motion.

"Go be all romantic and gross somewhere else," she said. "I've got this."

I led Tempest onto the back deck, the spring evening

cool but pleasant. The yard where we'd played football since we could walk stretched out before us, familiar and unchanging.

"How are you feeling about all of this?" Tempest asked, studying my face. "You seemed... somewhere else, after they announced your pick."

"I'm better now," I said honestly. "Just had to work through some stuff."

She nodded, not pushing, but her expression remained curious.

"It was about leaving. About what that means," I clarified.

"Your family," she said, understanding immediately.

"Yeah." I leaned against the railing, our shoulders touching. "It all kind of hit me that the last time our family was split up was when my mom died."

"Oh, Flynn." She took my hand and brought it up to her cheek, leaning into it. "I can't begin to imagine what that was doing to you."

"Dad helped me see it differently," I continued. "That leaving doesn't have to mean losing. That distance doesn't break what matters."

Tempest smiled, soft and understanding. "He's right."

"I've spent my whole life avoiding the kind of love that could hurt me if I lost it." I didn't really understand that until right now.

"But then you came along," I reached up to brush a curl from her face. "And suddenly two weeks wasn't enough. Suddenly, I was breaking all my own rules. I was falling for you, and it terrified me."

"Flynn—"

"Let me finish," I said gently. "I need to say this."

She nodded, her eyes never leaving mine.

"I've been scared of loving you the way I do, because what if I lose you? What if something happens? What if it all falls apart?" I took a breath, steadying myself. "And leaving Denver for LA felt like losing you just when I realized how in love with you I am."

THIS ABOVE ALL

TEMPEST

Flynn pulled back slightly, his hands framing my face. "I love you, Tempest Navarro. And whatever happens next, wherever I end up playing, that doesn't change."

My breath caught. We'd been dancing around these words for weeks, both of us feeling them but neither quite brave enough to say them aloud. Until now.

"Te amo, Flynn." I whispered, the truth of my love settling into my bones.

His smile was blinding.

He kissed me then, deep and tender, a promise without words. When we broke apart, he pressed his forehead to mine. "You're not worried about the distance? About LA?"

I wasn't. Because I was thinking about moving there too. Assuming this FlixNChill deal finally went through, and I had faith they'd figure out the leak, so it would happen, I'd been thinking it would work out great to be where the action was anyway.

"No. Not even a little." I gave him a sly little smile. "It won't be that far."

"You're right, just a quick plane ride."

"What if it was shorter than that? Like... a lot shorter."

"You buying some super-secret sneaky fast jet with your book money, babe?"

"No, but I was thinking I might...go with you. To LA." I'd just made a huge assumption that he wanted me to go with him. "I mean, we don't have to like, live together or..."

Flynn picked me up into his arms and spun me around like a Princess Barbie Ballerina. "Fuck yeah, I want us to live together. Having you there with me would make everything that much better. Please move to LA with me."

He set me back down on my feet and cupped my cheeks, searching my face. "Unless it's too soon. If you're not ready—"

Was this all too fast? Yes. Was I going for it anyway? Also, yes. "I do want to. I'm moving away from my family and starting a whole new life too, so it would definitely be better knowing I had you to come home to after a long day at... work? That sounds so weird to say."

The back door swung open and Gryff burst out, his eyes wide with excitement. "Hells to the yeah. We can have slumber parties, and midnight margaritas. I'm getting us all matching pajamas."

He grabbed us both into a hug and if my eyes weren't popping out from being bear hugged to death, they would at the thought of living with both Kingman twins. That hadn't quite fit into my future plans.

"Gryff," Flynn croaked out.

He released us, looked between us both and then

laughed so hard he snorted. "I'm just kidding. I'm not moving in with you two and getting your love cooties all over me. I'm fairly sure your shiny new domestic bliss and the way Tempest moans your name when you're making her come would severely cramp my style."

Oh, god. He'd heard that? But also, thank goodness.

"I just couldn't resist when I overheard." He laughed again.

"Why exactly are you out here torturing us anyway?" Flynn glared at his brother.

"Oh, right. I was just talking to Artie, since she blew me off for some super important rugby thing. And guess who just asked her to be their date for KATman?"

Flynn looked at me. "Your KATman?"

"Oh." Heat rushed to my face. "Yeah, about that. I've never gone before." I bit my lip. "If you wanted to go with me, that would be...cool or whatever."

A flash of concern crossed his face. "We have to go to LA for mini camp."

My heart sank. "Oh. Right. Of course."

Gryff put one of his hands on each of our shoulders, and leaned in like he was either commiserating or about to tell us something profoundly serious. "You two are the worst."

Flynn slugged him in the arm. But Gryff shrugged it off, likely having suffered something similar many times in his life. "KATman isn't until the following weekend. And you ruined the big reveal. Parker asked Aarti, and your very own KAT president, cutie patootie Bettie, asked yours truly. We're going on a triple date."

Gryff grinned, looked between the two of us, who were probably looking dumbfounded, and waved his hands like we were a lost cause. "Literally the worst."

But then Flynn gave me that patented flirty smile of his. "It's about time I get to see you all dressed up."

"It would be my first real dance," I admitted quietly. "With a real date."

His expression softened. "Tempest... you've never been to a dance? Not even prom?"

I shook my head.

Something fierce and protective flashed in Flynn's eyes. He pulled me close again, pressing a kiss to my forehead. "Then we're definitely going. And I promise to make it unforgettable."

Now I needed a dress. So when Flynn and Gryff headed off to LA for their mini camp, which sounded adorable, but apparently was going to kick their asses, I grabbed my friends and went dress shopping.

Which did not go great. After four stores which had only matronly mother-of-the-bride-style dresses in my size, we regrouped at a coffee shop.

"Don't give up yet," Bettie insisted.

I shrugged, trying to appear more nonchalant than I felt. "I should have realized sooner. This is worse than my quinceañera. We special ordered a dress because nothing in the stores fit right."

"You never thought you'd go to KATman," Alice reminded me gently. "How could you have planned?"

"Exactly. So maybe it's just not meant to be."

Parker plunked down beside me, eyes wide, holding

out her phone with an email open. "Tempest, did you just get me a job interview with FlixNChill's IT department?"

"More like strongly suggested they look at your resume. The rest will be up to you." I managed a small smile. "Because they have utterly failed at finding out who their leak is. And I was hoping you could, umm, help them."

Parker threw her arms around me in an uncharacteristic display of emotion. "You're the best roommate in the history of roommates."

I met her gaze. "I know I've been asking a lot of you lately, with all the donkey-sitting and boyfriend-sneaking and identity-crisis management, and well, I owe you."

"You don't owe me shit, sister." Parker spun around in her chair and it wasn't even the spinny kind. "I am going to hack the hell out of their systems and then they'll have to hire me."

We all frowned at her and she stopped spinning. "Uh, ethically hack whatever it is they ask me to so that they are very impressed and offer me a job." She cleared her throat. "That's what I said, and you didn't hear anything different."

Three days later, Parker burst into our room, her purple hair disheveled and her eyes wild with triumph.

"I finally got it. Well, almost, but I've got a great lead." She dropped my own laptop onto the bed. "Look at this."

I peered at the screen, trying to make sense of what looked like The Matrix displayed there. "What am I looking at?"

"Evidence." Parker's voice was vibrating with excitement. "I traced the digital breadcrumbs. Someone didn't just leak your identity, they've been monitoring your accounts for months. Like, since last semester."

"What?" Why would someone at FlixNChill be monitoring me way back then? We hadn't started talking to them until January.

"And I think whoever it is had actual access to your laptop. Because if they'd hacked in from the outside, I would have known." She shook her head, and I'd never seen Parker so upset. "I'm sorry, Temp, I should have caught it. But this was a serious inside job, man."

I grabbed her and hugged her tight. "This is not your fault. No way. This is a downright devious inside job."

But I refused to believe any of my sorority sisters would have betrayed me like this. They were all genuinely happy to find out I was Miranda Milan. No, the only people who were upset about it were my family.

Well, and Mrs. Henderson. She was so scandalized by the whole thing, she'd not only quit talking to me, she wouldn't even look at me. Even weirder, we hadn't had any surprise room inspections. Those had been her favorite thing to do all year.

"Could... could it have been Mrs. Henderson?" What did she know about hacking someone's email?

"She has access to the whole house and no one would blink twice if she went into anyone's rooms. She does love her room checks. But no way she did this on her own." Parker narrowed her eyes into her thinking face. "I have an idea."

She grabbed her laptop from the desk and typed away. Footage from the sorority house's front door camera popped up with a time stamp from last fall. "I know exactly what day you were hacked and this is a long shot, but maybe we can see if Mrs. H had any visitors that day."

"Unless they're wearing a t-shirt that says 'I hate Miranda Milan' we're not going to—"

Right there at nine twenty-four in the morning, when both Parker and I had a class last semester, was my sister, Rosalind, standing at the front door to the sorority house, looking over her shoulder while waiting for someone to answer.

Okay. It could be nothing. Dropping something off? But all she had was her regular messenger bag slung over her shoulder. Maybe she just stopped by to see me? Not that she ever had before. I waited to see if she left after finding out I wasn't home.

But Mrs. H answered the door and the two of them talked for a moment. Then Rosalind reached into her bag and pulled out a book, showing it to our house mother.

It was my first book. Even in grainy black and white, I knew that cover anywhere. It had changed my life. I froze. "She read my book?"

Their conversation continued, though we couldn't hear anything. But Rosalind went inside and no one looked happy.

My stomach churned with the bitter bile of betrayal. I didn't know for sure if she'd done it. In fact, I was still hoping it was just a coincidence. But I was going to find out.

Casa Navarro was quiet when I arrived. According to a text from Freddie, everyone else was out except Rosalind, who was studying. Law school and the internship she had this summer with the senator always took precedent over everything else.

I found her in her room, surrounded by case files and notepads filled with her neat, precise handwriting. She looked up when I entered, surprise quickly replaced by wariness.

"Tempest. What are you doing here?"

I closed the door behind me. "We need to talk."

"I'm studying." She gestured to her books. "Can it wait?"

"No." I pulled out a printout of the door cam footage showing Rosalind holding the book out to Mrs. Henderson. "It can't."

Her eyes flickered to the photo, then back to my face. "What's that?"

"Are you the one who leaked my identity to the press?"

Rosalind didn't immediately deny it. And that bile rose up the back of my throat. Instead, she carefully closed her notebook and set it aside.

"How did you find out?" she asked, her voice controlled.

I sat on the edge of her bed, studying this sister I thought I knew. "Why, Ros? Why would you do this to me?"

She was quiet for a long moment, as if choosing her words carefully. "Ophelia left a copy of your dumb book here last year, and I picked it up for something mindless to read." Her mouth twisted. "I didn't know it was yours, of course."

"Until you recognized Catalina in the heroine."

A flicker of surprise. "Yes. The way she could never be

wrong, that oh, so Catalina way of lauding her superiority around because she's the oldest. It was too specific. Too familiar." She shrugged. "So I started looking into Miranda Milan."

"And exposing me, without warning, without giving me any chance to prepare was a better choice than just talking to me about it?"

"You should have told us," she snapped back, her voice hardened. "You kept this whole secret life, this whole career, hidden from your family for years. Writing... that kind of content. It needed to be nipped in the bud. And I'm not the only one who thinks so. Mrs. Henderson always did like me better than you."

The anger I'd been holding at bay began to surface. "She's the one who let you into my room? No wonder we had so many random room checks this year. That was your fault, wasn't it? I was protecting myself and my work, and you were spying on me?"

"And never thought about how it might affect the rest of us?" She stood, pacing to her window. "I have a bright political career ahead of me, Tempest. Everyone says so. What do you think happens when the senator for finds out? Or when I run for office and have to explain that my sister writes porn?"

"So this was about your career? Your reputation?"

"It's about all of our reputations." She spun to face me. "You think Mamá's medical colleagues aren't gossiping about this? That Papá's academic friends aren't whispering behind his back?"

"My books are successful and they're not something shameful," I countered.

"Maybe not to you." Rosalind crossed her arms. "But some of us had to work our entire lives to build respectable careers. Some of us don't get to follow our passions and do whatever makes us happy."

The bitterness in her voice caught me off guard. "What are you talking about?"

She laughed, a harsh, brittle sound. "You did what you wanted, you pursued this... this writing thing that everyone told you was frivolous. While the rest of us towed the line and did what we were supposed to."

"I worked hard for my degree and the success I'm having in my career," I said, my voice quieter now as understanding dawned.

"So am I," Rosalind's composure cracked. "I've done everything right. Everything that was expected of me. I stayed at home and went to DSU for law school because that's the path to politics, which is what everyone has told me I should do since I was ten. Ten, Tempest."

"And is that what you want?"

She hesitated just a fraction of a second too long. "Of course."

That tiny pause told me everything. "Ros... if you don't want to be a lawyer or go into politics, you don't have to."

"Don't I?" She turned away. "Not everyone gets to buck the system. Not everyone gets to be the rebellious middle child."

The anger I'd carried into this room began to shift, making space for something unexpected...understanding.

"It's not too late to change your mind," I said gently. "To do something that actually makes you happy."

"Easy for you to say. You've already built your secret

career even if you don't seem to care what anyone else has to say about it."

By anyone else, we both knew she meant Mamá.

"Better than spending your life doing something that makes you miserable. To thine own self be true."

Rosalind turned to face me, her expression suddenly fierce. "Don't ruin my chances with your trashy romance novel scandal. That would be a real betrayal, little sister."

The attack stung, but I recognized it for what it was. Fear. Fear of disappointment. Been there, done that, got the scars.

"I hope someday you grow up and figure out you have to live your own life," I said quietly, "being true to yourself instead of living up to others' expectations. I spent too many years hiding who I was, and it was exhausting. I don't want that for you, Ros."

She stared at me for a long moment, something unreadable in her eyes. "I think you should go now."

I nodded. There was nothing more to say.

I made it all the way to my car before the emotional weight of the confrontation hit me. Tears burned in my eyes as I fumbled with my keys.

On the way back to the sorority house, I dialed Flynn's number. I needed to hear his voice. Tell him what happened.

Instead I blurted out, "We can't go to KATman."

"What do you mean we can't go?"

I just couldn't bring myself to tell him my own sister had betrayed me. His family was so damn perfect, and mine...just wasn't. So I'd said the only other thing I could think of.

"Tempest." Flynn's voice softened. "What's really going on? And don't tell me 'nothing'. I can hear it in your tone."

I sighed, relenting. "It's Rosalind. She's been spying on me, reading my emails, even had Mrs. Henderson searching through my things. She's the one who leaked my identity."

"What?" Flynn's expression darkened. "Your own sister did that?"

"To protect her future political career, she said," I confirmed, the bitter taste of betrayal still fresh.

"I'm going over there and Burrito and I are going to... well, we don't hit girls, but we will give her a very stern talking to."

"I'd love to see that," I whispered. "But honestly, I think she's hurting just as much as I am. She can't handle seeing me live authentically. I think I forced her to look at her own life, her choices. And sometimes that's too painful."

"You deserve to celebrate who you are, Tempest. All of who you are. The brilliant student, the best-selling author, the woman I love. Which is why we're absolutely going to KATman."

"But I don't have a dress," I sighed. "And I'm not sure I'm in a celebrating mood anymore."

"That's exactly when you should celebrate," he insisted. "When the world tries to make you feel small or wrong or not enough. That's when you put on something gorgeous and dance anyway."

His quiet determination warmed something inside me. "That's a lovely sentiment, but KATman is three days away, and I've tried every store in Denver."

"Trust me?" His voice shifted to something determined, almost secretive.

"I do," I said automatically.

Two days later, I returned to my room after class to find a large white box sitting on my bed, a gold ribbon tied around it. Parker sat cross-legged on her own bed, practically vibrating with excitement.

"It came about an hour ago," she said before I could ask. "With very specific instructions not to peek."

I approached the box cautiously. A small card tucked under the ribbon read "For my queen. For KATman and beyond. All my love, Flynn."

My hands trembled slightly as I untied the ribbon and lifted the lid. Inside, nestled in layers of tissue paper, was a dress that took my breath away. It was deepest black, trimmed with silver. The colors of the LA Bandits. The dress shimmered with subtle constellations when the fabric moved. The design was elegantly cut to flatter curves rather than hide them, with a neckline that would show just enough skin to be alluring.

"Oh my god," Parker breathed, peering over my shoulder. "That's a Rose Vond original. She makes clothes for royalty and pop stars and stuff. They're, like, impossible to get."

I lifted the dress carefully from the box, finding a smaller box beneath. Inside was a delicate silver necklace with a pendant in the shape of a crown that would nestle perfectly above my cleavage.

Tears blurred my vision as I clutched the dress to my chest.

"You have to try it on," Parker urged, already clearing space in front of our full-length mirror.

The dress fit perfectly, as if Rose Vond had somehow slipped into our room in the dark of night and measured me herself. The fabric flowed over my curves like water, the color making my skin glow. For perhaps the first time in my life, I looked at my reflection and saw not the girl who took up too much space, who didn't quite fit, but a woman who filled her space exactly as she was meant to.

KATMAN COUPLE GOALS

FLYNN

I checked my reflection one more time in the rearview mirror, straightening my tie. The designer Jules had connected me with, Rose Vond, had made me a matching suit to go with the dress she made for Tempest. I felt like frickin' James Bond in it.

The KAT house loomed ahead, lit up like Christmas with white fairy lights outlining the Victorian architecture. I grabbed the small box containing the corsage I'd ordered, a cluster of tiny white star-shaped flowers with silver accents that would complement the dress I'd given her, and headed up the walkway. Music and laughter spilled from the open windows. The excitement of KATman was in full swing.

The door opened before I could knock. Mrs. Henderson stood there, her thin lips pressed into a disapproving line. After finding out about her role in Rosalind's espionage, I had to fight the urge to tell the old witch exactly what I thought of her.

Instead, I channeled my most respectful, media-trained smile. "Good evening, Mrs. Henderson. I'm here for Tempest."

"Mr. Kingman." Her gaze traveled from my face down to my shoes and back up again, clearly searching for something to criticize. "You may wait in the foyer. The young ladies are still getting ready."

She stepped aside reluctantly, allowing me to enter the house that had become so familiar over the past few months. The foyer was buzzing with activity, KAT sisters in formal dresses, their dates in suits and tuxes, everyone laughing and taking photos.

I spotted Gryff by the staircase, looking sharp in his own classic black tux, chatting with Bettie. When he saw me, he broke into a grin.

"Look at you," he called out. Then in a really bad Sean Connery impression he said, "Shaken, not stirred."

"Says the guy who color-coordinated his pocket square with Bettie's dress," I shot back, noting the gold accent that matched Bettie's floor-length gown perfectly.

Bettie laughed, looking elegant and confident. "I told him it was required. KAT tradition."

"The things we do for beautiful women," Gryff said with an exaggerated sigh, though the way he looked at Bettie made it clear he didn't mind a bit.

"Speaking of beautiful women," I said, "where's my date?"

"Still upstairs with the finishing touches committee," Bettie explained. "You know how Parker gets with a makeup brush. Perfection takes time."

Parker herself appeared then, stunning in a violet dress that matched her hair, Artemis at her side in a sleek silver suit that complemented her athletic frame perfectly.

"Kingmans," Artemis nodded at me, then bumped fists with Gryff. "You clean up nice. Both of you."

"Not so bad yourself, Art," I replied. "Rugby season end well?"

I should know, because she and Gryff had eternal debates over which sport, football or rugby, was tougher. But I'd been a bit distracted this semester. Falling in love.

"National champions," she said with the casual confidence that had always drawn Gryff to her. I'd never been sure if there was something romantic between them or if they were truly just best friends.

The conversation flowed easily, but I kept glancing at the staircase, anticipation building. Mrs. Henderson hovered at the edges of our group, her hawkish gaze following our every move. I caught her whispering something to one of the chaperones, her eyes narrowed in my direction.

Then the room went quiet.

I turned toward the staircase and time simply... stopped.

Time, my heart, the world around us... all stopped.

Tempest stood at the top of the stairs, a vision in shimmering black and silver. The Rose Vond dress flowed over her curves like liquid starlight, the fabric catching the light with every breath she took. Her dark hair was swept up in an elegant style that left a few curls framing her face. The necklace I'd given her glittered at her throat.

She was breathtaking.

But it wasn't just the dress or the hair or the makeup.

It was the way she held herself, shoulders back, chin high, a small smile playing at her lips. Confident. Radiant. Taking up exactly the space she deserved.

"Wow," I breathed, not even realizing I'd spoken aloud until Gryff elbowed me in the ribs.

"Close your mouth, bro. You're drooling."

I ignored him, moving to the bottom of the stairs as Tempest began her descent. Our eyes locked, and the rest of the room faded away. There was just her—my brilliant, beautiful Tempest, the woman who had completely upended my life in the best conceivable way.

When she reached the final step, I held out my hand. She took it, her fingers warm against mine.

"You are... I don't even have words," I managed, my voice rougher than I'd intended.

Her smile widened, a hint of shyness beneath the confidence. "You look pretty incredible yourself, Kingman."

I fumbled with the corsage box, suddenly clumsy despite years of athletic training. "I got you this. I know it's kind of dorky and old fashioned, but I hope it's okay."

She looked genuinely touched as I slipped the delicate arrangement onto her wrist. "It's perfect. Thank you."

"Picture time," Hannah called out, herding everyone toward the grand staircase. "Let's get the whole Donkey Sitters Club together."

We assembled for photos—couples, friend groups, the entire senior class. Through it all, I couldn't take my eyes off Tempest. The way she laughed with her friends, the way she fit so naturally against my side, the way she glowed with a happiness I'd never seen from her before.

As we prepared to head out to the cars, Mrs. Henderson stepped forward, clipboard in hand.

"Young ladies, remember your curfew is two a.m. sharp," she announced, her gaze lingering disapprovingly on Tempest. "And I expect *all* of you to return to the house tonight. No... exceptions."

The implication was clear, and I felt Tempest stiffen beside me.

"Actually, Mrs. Henderson," Bettie stepped forward, her expression pleasant but her eyes ice cold. "We are grown-ass adults, and if we'd like to stay out all night long, or spend the night with our dates having wild passionate sex, we have every right to do so."

"Well, I never—" Mrs. H quite literally clutched the pearls at her neck.

"And we know what you did," Bettie added with all the venom of a pissed-off sorority president. "Helping Rosalind spy on Tempest, letting her into our rooms, going through our things. That was a betrayal of every KAT woman, past and present."

Mrs. Henderson's face flushed. "I was protecting the reputation of this house. The morals and standards that—"

"Were never yours to define," Alice cut in, joining Bettie. Hannah and several other sisters moved to stand with them, a unified front. "KAT stands for sisterhood and support, not judgment and betrayal."

"Which is why we're so pleased you've decided to retire at the end of this semester," Bettie continued smoothly. "The national board, especially Dr. Sterling, the president, was very understanding when we brought this to their attention."

Mrs. Henderson's mouth opened and closed like a fish out of water. "You can't—"

"We already did," Parker said, stepping forward. She put two fingers to her eyes, then pointed them at the house mother. "I'm watching you. Every digital footprint, every keystroke, every surveillance attempt. Don't even think about ever applying to be a house mother at any other sorority. Ever."

"Ladies," Hannah called out, as if laying their conniving house mother out flat was a regular Saturday evening event. "Our carriages await."

As we filed out the door, I squeezed Tempest's hand. "Your sisters are like the freaking mafia. Remind me not to get on their bad side."

She looked up at me, her eyes bright with unshed tears, but she was smiling. But Parker poked her head between us. "Yeah, no matter where we all are in the world after graduation as we spread our wings and fly out on our own into adulthood, just know, that, if you ever break our Tempest's heart, we will hurt you."

Bettie, Hannah, and Alice all stared me down. "Yes," Bettie said. "Like mailing you cow's tongues in Tiffany boxes just like the patron saint of badass women, Carrie Fischer did once."

I never, ever planned to break my girl's heart. "No horse heads in my bed?"

"No horses were harmed in the planning of your downfall, Mr. Kingman." Bettie looked at me like I was on crack. "Gross."

But Parker gave me an evil grin. "Oh, I'll do much

worse. Credit history schmedit history, Kingman. Remember that."

Okay, Parker was actually fucking scary. And it made me glad that Tempest had such loyal friends.

Outside, a line of limos waited to take us to the Peachy Creek Country Club. I helped Tempest into one of the cars, then followed her in, ogling her ass that was right in front of my face as she maneuvered her way into a seat.

"Did you know they were going to confront Mrs. Henderson?" I asked as we pulled away from the house.

Tempest shook her head. "No. But I should have. The Donkey Sitters Club doesn't mess around when one of their own is threatened." She turned to look at me, the passing streetlights casting a soft glow across her face. "Kind of like the Kingmans."

I laughed, reaching over to take her hand. "We do have that in common."

Peachy Creek Country Club was a sprawling estate right in the heart of Denver, its grounds meticulously manicured, the place looking like it was straight out of one of Jay Gatsby's infamous parties. The main ballroom had been transformed for KATman, soft lighting, floral arrangements in the KAT colors of black and gold, a live band on a stage at one end of the room.

We handed our invitation to the doorman and stepped inside, the sounds of music and laughter washing over us. Heads turned as we entered, whispers following in our wake. First-round League draft pick and recently revealed best-selling author. We made quite the entrance.

The next hour passed in a blur of introductions, drinks, appetizers, and dancing. I twirled Tempest around the dance floor, delighting in her laughter as I showed off the moves Jules had been mocking me for practicing. Gryff and Bettie joined us, along with Parker and Artemis, the six of us forming our own little group in the middle of the dance floor.

"I didn't know you could dance, Kingman," Artemis shouted over the music, executing a perfect spin that had Parker laughing.

"Full of surprises, aren't I?" I called back. "Not just a pretty face and incredible athletic ability."

"And so humble," Gryff added dryly, though his own moves were drawing appreciative glances from several nearby dancers.

The band took a break and played some upbeat pop song, then a more electronic dance song, and the energy on the floor intensified. Tempest moved with surprising grace and rhythm, her body swaying in a way that had me completely mesmerized. Seeing her having fun, her body in action, was something else entirely.

"You're staring," she said, her cheeks flushed from dancing.

"Can you blame me?" I pulled her closer, spinning her again just to hear her laugh.

When the song ended, she fanned herself with her hand. "I need a break and something to drink."

We made our way to the bar, where Gryff and Artemis were already waiting.

"Water for the dance queen," Gryff said, handing Tempest a glass. "You've got some moves too, Navarro."

"Just wait until Abuela visits us in LA and takes us out

salsa dancing." Tempest did a little salsa step. "You won't be able to move for a week."

We all laughed, and I felt a surge of warmth watching Tempest so relaxed and happy with my brother and his best friend, talking about our life together in LA. This was how it should be. Our lives intertwining, our people becoming her people and vice versa.

The band returned, and the singer's voice floated over the crowd. "Alright, couples, time to slow things down. Grab your special someone and head to the floor."

I held out my hand to Tempest. "May I have this dance, my queen?"

Her smile was soft as she took my hand. Back on the dance floor, I pulled her close, one hand at the small of her back, the other holding hers against my chest. She rested her head on my shoulder, fitting against me perfectly.

We swayed to the music, her curves pressed against me, her scent, that floral and uniquely Tempest smell, surrounding me. My body responded predictably. I glanced around, wondering if there was somewhere I could drag her off to have my way with her.

She pulled back just enough to look up at me, one eyebrow raised. "Is that a football in your pocket, Mr. Kingman or...?"

"Sorry, not sorry, babe." I pressed my lips to her ear. "You just... you feel really good. Wanna go find a coat closet and let me see what you've got on under your dress?"

To my surprise, she didn't tease me back. Instead, she

pressed closer, her lips brushing my ear. "I like knowing I affect you this way."

Jesus Christ. My body went from interested to fully at attention.

As if on cue, the music faded, and Bettie's voice came over the speakers. "Ladies and gentlemen, it's time for the moment you've all been waiting for, the crowning of this year's KATman."

Oh shit. I was about to have to get up on stage with a huge stiffy for the whole world to see. I tried desperately to think of anything unsexy. Coach yelling during practice, Isak's disgusting protein shakes, the time Declan's dog devoured my favorite cleats.

"You're thinking too loud," Tempest murmured, amusement in her voice.

"I'm trying not to embarrass myself in the middle of your sorority formal," I admitted.

She laughed softly and pressed her soft curves against the bulge in the front of my pants. "Maybe this will get you a couple of last minute votes."

THE CROWD CHEERED as the senior KAT class filed up on the stage with their dates, and I strategically placed myself behind Tempest. I wrapped my arms around her waist, pressing my hard on against her luscious ass. She gave a tiny squeak and whispered something about saving that for later.

God, I loved her.

"Our KATman candidates have been judged on charm, personality, dancing skills, and of course, their compatibility with their KAT date," Bettie announced. "We've tallied the votes, and we'll start with our runners-up."

I was genuinely curious about where I'd place in this ridiculous but endearing tradition. Competition was in my blood.

"Our second runner-up is... Artemis Ingvar."

Cheers erupted as Artie made her way to Bettie, accepting a small trophy and hamming it up for the crowd. Gryff wolf-whistled from beside us, making her laugh mid-bow.

"Our first runner-up is... Flynn Kingman."

I kissed Tempest's cheek. "Everyone is going to know exactly how hot I am for you now, babe."

A few titters and a couple of gasps sounded as I stepped out from behind her. But then someone stage-whispered, "If that's the runner-up, the winner must have, like, magical monster peen or something."

Everyone laughed and Bettie, being the smart woman she was continued the ceremony. "And this year's KATman is... Killian Kane."

A guy from the hockey team, that Hannah had started dating after the party that shall not be named, bounded onto the stage to thunderous applause, accepting the ridiculous crown and scepter with good-natured humor. I clapped him on the back as he took his place at the center, genuinely happy for him.

As we left the stage, Tempest met me at the bottom of the steps, wrapping her arms around my neck.

"Congratulations on your almost-victory," she teased.

"The only crown I care about is having the queen," I replied, bending to kiss her softly. Anything more and I would need to get a room like the onlookers were shouting at us.

The formal continued for another hour, but eventually couples began to drift out, heading to after-parties or back to campus. Tempest and I found Gryff and Bettie near the coat check.

"Heading out?" Gryff asked, his arm around Bettie's waist.

"Yeah," I nodded. "And don't come knocking until it's time to leave for the Dragon's Lair to do the captains' ceremony tomorrow. Tempest and I will be terribly busy."

"What's the captains' ceremony?" Bettie asked.

"It's a sacred tradition," Gryff replied solemnly. "The passing of the torch to next year's captains. Profoundly serious business."

Usually accompanied by a some kind of video game tournament. We were all ultra-competitive guys after all.

"Including the care and feeding of One-eyed Willie," I added with a straight face.

Tempest looked between us. "Who or what is One-eyed Willie? Please don't tell me you guys have some giant peen idol in the Dragon's Lair."

"The captains' mascot. A very distinguished, somewhat ugly, completely hairless cat who lives in the Dragon's Lair, and has been known to do his own bit of match-making of many a team captain over the years."

"You're joking," she said, though her expression suggested she wasn't entirely sure.

"Completely serious," Gryff confirmed. "One-eyed Willie has been overseeing the transition of team captains and helping to find and approve of their girlfriends or boyfriends at DSU for fifteen years. He's practically an institution. If any team captain brings a date to meet one-eyed Willie, you know it's serious."

"Somehow, this school gets weirder the longer I'm here," Tempest said, shaking her head with a smile.

We said our goodbyes and headed out into the cool May night. As the car took us back to campus, I said quietly, "You will come to meet Wille with me tomorrow, won't you?"

"That's seriously a thing? I find it completely adorable you big, bad bunch of team captains have a Cat Corleone you bring your girlfriends to for his approval."

"I nodded. "Yeah, it's a long-standing tradition. Almost as important as meeting the parents. Willie's going to love you, but not as much as I do. We're couple goals, babe."

Bringing a girl to the Dragon's Lair to meet Willie had never been on my radar, because I'd never intended to fall in love. Now I couldn't imagine the rest of my life without Tempest.

I wasn't the Flynn who'd started this semester, a cocky Kingman looking for nothing more than a fling, a round one draft pick to the Mustangs, and a solid, but hidden fear of change. My girl had changed all of that for me. She made me want to be the kind of man she deserved. Forever.

I kissed my girl, pouring everything I felt about her into it, my love, my hopes, my promises. When we broke apart, she rested her forehead against mine.

"Take me to bed and show me those couple goals, Kingman." she whispered.

I AM THE STORM

TEMPEST

Papá's arm was warm and solid around my shoulders as we walked from the English building, where the College of Liberal Arts had held its graduation ceremony. The midday sun beat down on the sea of emerald caps and gowns flooding the central quad, a kaleidoscope of colorful leis, honor cords, and beaming faces.

"I'm so proud of you, mija," he said, pausing to press a kiss to my temple. "Your speech was magnificent."

I flushed with pleasure at his praise. Being selected as the liberal arts student speaker had been a complete surprise—especially given the Miranda Milan revelation that had rocked campus mere weeks ago. But rather than hiding from the attention, I'd embraced it, writing a speech about finding your authentic voice in a world that tries to silence it.

As we approached the parking lot, I spotted Flynn leaning against his car, still dressed in his own cap and gown from the Business School ceremony that had ended earlier. The sight of him—tall, proud, undeniably mine—sent my heart into a familiar flutter.

"I'll see you both at the house," Papá said, giving my shoulder a final squeeze before heading to his car. "I promised your mother I'd help set up the bar."

As he walked away, Flynn wrapped his arms around me properly, lifting me off my feet in a quick spin that made my graduation cap teeter precariously.

"We did it," he said, his voice rough with emotion. "Four years of college, and we actually survived."

"Speak for yourself," I laughed, clinging to him. "I'm pretty sure part of my soul died during that British Modernism final."

"Oh please," he scoffed, setting me back on my feet. "You probably aced it while writing a steamy scene for your next book under the desk."

I smacked his chest lightly. "It was a boring guest lecture, not a final."

His eyes darkened with that familiar heat. "Still one of the hottest things I've ever seen, you writing a super filthy sex scene while looking all innocent and studious."

"Filthy? It was a perfectly tasteful scene about—"

"A filthy locker room shower after a game," he finished, eyebrows raised. "I read it, remember? I had to take an actual cold shower after."

I flushed, remembering all too well how that particular research session had ended. "Are you trying to distract me from my graduation party nerves with sex talk, Flynn Kingman?"

"Is it working?"

"Maybe." I bit my lip, studying his face.

He caught my hand, pressing a kiss to my palm. "Now, are we ready to go face your family? Or should we make a run for LA right now, change our names, and become beach bums?"

I laughed, though a part of me was tempted. "Abuela would hunt us down. She's been planning this party for weeks. And Ophelia has been cooking for days. Plus you'll get to meet my Abuelo today."

"Fair point. Never cross AbuelaNovela, especially when she's planning a party."

"Just be grateful she didn't commission an ice sculpture of you in your football uniform."

"Oh god, did she—"

"Almost," I confirmed. "I talked her down to a donkey ice sculpture."

"Well, now I'm kind of sad."

"I'm still nervous," I admitted. "But I'm not afraid anymore."

He lifted our joined hands to kiss my knuckles. "That's my girl."

Abuela had transformed the Navarro family home into something between a quinceañera and a royal coronation. Purple and gold balloons festooned every available surface. A massive banner reading "CONGRATULATIONS TEMPEST" spanned the living room wall, with "¡ORGULLO DE LA FAMILIA!" —pride of the family— emblazoned beneath it.

In the backyard, Burrito Petito held court near the ice sculpture, sporting a miniature graduation cap that kept sliding rakishly over one ear.

"¡Mi amor!" Abuela's voice carried across the yard as she spotted me coming through the side gate. She descended upon me in a swirl of fuchsia silk and perfume, clasping my face between her jeweled hands. "¡La graduada! ¡Qué orgullosa estoy!"

"Gracias, Abuela," I managed, before being enveloped in her embrace.

Ophelia had transformed the sprawling patio dining area into a gourmet buffet, showcasing the best offerings from her restaurant, Las Barditas. Elegant platters of empanadas, ceviches, and colorful salads were artfully arranged alongside traditional family favorites. A three-tiered cake, adorned with fondant books, a football, and a tiny donkey, commanded the center of the dessert table.

Freddie bounded over to me, grabbing me in a big hug. "Your speech rocked, T. I recorded the whole thing. Already has, like, ten thousand views."

"What? Freddie, you didn't—"

"Relax. Your fans love seeing the real you, T. Miranda Milan, giving an inspirational graduation speech about authentic self-expression? It's like catnip to them."

"Just keep the comments turned off," I reminded her. "I'm still not ready for that level of interaction."

I scanned the growing crowd for the family members I was most anxious about seeing. Catalina was near the drinks table, deep in conversation with one of Papá's colleagues. But Mamá and Rosalind were nowhere to be seen.

A familiar hand touched my elbow. "Looking for someone?" Papá asked gently. His knowing smile told me he already knew. "Your mother is inside, helping Aunt

Lucia with something in the kitchen. She was very moved by your speech, though she'd never admit it."

I nodded, unsure what to say. Since our blow out, things had been civil but strained between us. Mamá had stopped actively trying to get me to give up writing, but she hadn't exactly embraced my choice either.

"And Rosalind?" I asked.

Papá's expression tightened slightly. "Running late, apparently."

Rosalind had been making herself scarce ever since Abuela had discovered her role in leaking my identity to the media. No one had told the rest of the family yet.

Catalina approached, immaculate as always in her signature white pantsuit that somehow remained pristine despite the party chaos.

"There's the woman of the hour," she said, surprising me with a genuine smile. "Cum laude, departmental honors, and student speaker. Not bad for the girl who used to hide under the bed to avoid school."

"That was one time," I protested, "and it was because I hadn't finished my book report."

"Well, now you write the books that other students read while procrastinating writing their reports," Catalina replied smoothly. "Full circle moment."

Something in her tone made me look at her more closely. "Have you actually read my books, Cat?"

She took a deliberate sip of her drink. "I may have picked one up. For market research purposes only, of course. My clients are extremely interested in the crossover between sports merchandise and romance readers."

Coming from Catalina, this was practically a rave

review. I grinned. "Careful, Cat. That almost sounded like a compliment."

"Take it while you can get it," she advised, before her gaze shifted over my shoulder. Her expression cooled noticeably. "Heads up. Mamá alert at two o'clock."

I turned to see my mother emerging from the house, elegant as always in a tailored navy dress, her hair swept into a perfect chignon. She paused on the patio, surveying the festivities with an expression I couldn't quite read.

"There's my favorite graduate," said a warm voice behind me. Arms slipped around my waist and Flynn's chin came to rest on my shoulder. "Your mom's heading this way. Want me to create a distraction? I could get Burrito to eat the centerpiece."

I laughed, shaking my head. "I can handle this."

And surprisingly, I realized I meant it. After everything, the public revelation of my identity, the media frenzy, the initial family fallout, a conversation with my mother no longer seemed like the end of the world.

"Tempest," Mamá said as she approached, her voice carefully neutral. "Your speech was... well written."

Not exactly effusive praise, but coming from Dr. Luz Navarro, it wasn't nothing either.

"Thank you for coming, Mamá," I said, stepping forward to accept her brief, formal embrace.

"Of course I went. It was your college graduation." She turned to Flynn with a polite nod. "Flynn. Congratulations on your own achievement today."

"Thank you, Dr. Navarro," he replied, easy and confident beside me.

An awkward silence stretched between us until Mamá

cleared her throat. "Tempest, when you have a moment, I'd like to speak with you. About your plans."

And there it was. The conversation I'd been dreading all day.

"Actually," I said, squaring my shoulders, "now is good."

Flynn's hand found the small of my back, a silent show of support.

"I understand from your father that you've finalized your living arrangements in Los Angeles," Mamá began, her tone carefully controlled.

I nodded. "Yes. We found a house not far from the Bandits' practice facility. It's also near a great coffee shop that's perfect for writing."

She pressed her lips together, a familiar sign of disapproval. "And this is truly what you want? To leave Denver? Your family? Your academic prospects?"

"Mamá," I said, keeping my voice even, "we've discussed this. I'm not abandoning my family by moving to LA. And I'm not giving up on my career, I'm pursuing it. Writing *is* my career."

"A career that could end at any moment," she argued. "These trends, these... fads in publishing. What happens when people lose interest in your books? What's your backup plan?"

Flynn shifted beside me, and I could feel him restrain himself from jumping to my defense. But this was my battle.

"What was your backup plan, Mamá?" I asked quietly.

"That's different," she dismissed. "Medicine is—" Her

expression hardened. "Writing romance novels isn't the same as saving lives, Tempest."

"Tempest's books helped me through some of the darkest times of my life." The voice came not from me, but from Freddie, who had apparently wandered into our conversation bubble. She stood with her arms crossed, unusually serious for my typically exuberant sister.

"When I was figuring out who I was," Freddie continued, "when I felt like I didn't belong anywhere, I read your books. All these characters who were different, who took up space, who found love anyway? It mattered, T. It helped."

I stared at her, emotion tightening my throat. "Freddie—"

"It's true," she insisted. "And I'm not the only one. There's this whole thread on FaceSpace about how your books helped people accept themselves. Their bodies, their desires, their weird, messy hearts." She turned to our mother. "So yeah, maybe she's not saving lives with a scalpel, Mamá, but she's definitely saving them."

Mamá blinked rapidly, clearly thrown by this passionate defense.

Before she could respond, another voice joined the fray. "Are we having the 'writing isn't a real career' conversation again?" Rosalind asked, appearing with impeccable timing and a glass of champagne already in hand. "Because I thought we exhausted that topic already."

I turned to see my sister, immaculate in a structured dress that screamed 'future lawyer', regarding our little group with cool disdain.

"Rosalind," Mamá said, visibly relieved by the interruption. "I was beginning to think you wouldn't make it."

"And miss watching everyone pretend that writing smut is something to celebrate?" Rosalind replied with a tight smile. "Wouldn't dream of it."

Flynn's hand tightened on my waist, and I placed my own over it, silently asking him to let me handle this.

"Nice to see you too, Ros," I said evenly. "Love the dress. Very 'I'll be billing you for this conversation.'"

Her smile didn't reach her eyes. "Congratulations on your useless English degree, Tempest. I'm sure it'll look lovely framed above your desk while you write about fictional people having fictional orgasms."

"That's enough," Flynn said, his voice low but firm.

Rosalind's eyebrows shot up. "Oh look, the football player speaks. Shouldn't you be somewhere hitting your head against something?"

"Rosalind!" Mamá gasped.

"It's fine," Flynn said calmly. "I can hold my own. But I won't stand here and let you insult the woman I love on her graduation day."

The word 'love' hung in the air between us. It wasn't the first time he'd said it, but hearing it so openly declared, in front of my family, sent a warm rush through me.

"How noble," Rosalind sneered. "The jock defending his girlfriend's honor. Very romance novel, Tempest. Did you script this scene yourself?"

"What is wrong with you?" Freddie demanded, stepping forward. "Why are you being such a—"

"That's quite enough," came a commanding voice that

cut through the tension like a knife. Abuela strode toward us, resplendent in her fuchsia gown, a dangerous glint in her eye that stopped everyone mid-word. Abuelo Leo walked beside her In one hand, he held what looked like a weathered leather notebook, and in the other, an iPad.

"Mamá, Papá," my mother began, her tone cautious. "This is a family matter that we can discuss privately—"

"No, Luz," Abuela cut her off, her voice ringing with authority. "No more private discussions. No more secrets. This family has had enough of both."

She planted herself in the center of our small group, commanding attention the way she once commanded movie sets. Flynn's hand found mine, and I gripped it tightly, sensing the storm about to break.

"First," Abuela said, turning to my mother, "I have something for you, mi hija."

She held out her hand and Abuelo set the tattered notebook in her palm with reverence. Mamá's eyes widened with recognition, her hand automatically reaching for it before pulling back as if it might burn her.

"You kept it?" Mamá whispered, her composure cracking.

"Of course we did." Abuela pressed the notebook into her hands. "Parents always keeps their daughter's dreams, even when she forgets them."

Mamá opened the cover with trembling fingers, revealing pages filled with flowing script, the ink faded but still legible.

"What is that?" Rosalind asked, peering over Mamá's shoulder.

"This," Abuela announced to all of us, "is your mother's

romance novel. Written when she was nineteen years old, full of passion and drama and love scenes that would make a telenovela writer blush."

Mamá's face flushed dark red. "Mamá, please—"

"No, Luz. These children should know." Abuela's gaze swept over all of us. "Your mother once dreamed of being a writer too. Just like her Papá. She filled this notebook with stories of brave heroines who overcame all obstacles to find love. And she was good—incredibly good."

I stared at my mother in shock. "Mamá? You wrote a book?"

"It was a childish phase," Mamá said stiffly, though her fingers caressed the pages with obvious familiarity. "Nothing serious."

"Nothing serious?" Abuela scoffed. "You had real talent."

"And then Professor Collins told me it was trite, derivative, cliched trash," Mamá shot back, a flash of old pain evident in her voice. "That no publisher would waste time on it. That it wasn't respectable."

"And you believed him," Abuelo said softly. "You let a bitter old man kill your joy because you thought respectability was more important than happiness."

The revelation hung in the air between us. Mamá stared down at the notebook, her expression unreadable.

"And now," Abuela continued, her voice hardening as she turned to Rosalind, "you do the same to your daughters. You push them toward 'respectable' careers without asking what brings them joy."

Mamá still clutched her old notebook, staring at it as if seeing a ghost from her past. Papá watched her with gentle understanding, while Abuela surveyed us all with the satisfaction of a general whose battle plan had succeeded.

Mamá let out a shaky breath and her gaze met mine. "I chose the path that seemed more certain. The most respectable... and perhaps I've been too determined to see my daughters make the same choice."

The admission hung in the air between us, more powerful for its rarity. My mother was not a woman who acknowledged mistakes easily.

"I don't want that for you," she said, looking at each of us for a moment before continuing. "Any of you. I don't want you waking up at fifty-five, wondering what might have been if you'd followed your heart instead of your head."

Abuela raised the tablet she'd been holding. "Which brings me to the second matter. Rosalind, would you care to explain these emails?"

Rosalind's face drained of color. "I don't know what you're talking about."

"No?" Abuela's eyebrow arched dangerously high. "Perhaps I should read them aloud then. This one to the editor of The Dracarys campus paper. 'I have definitive proof that DSU student and KAT member Tempest Navarro is the trashy romance author Miranda Milan...'"

My heart stuttered in my chest. Hearing the literal confirmation of her betrayal felt like a physical blow.

"Rosalind?" Mamá's voice was sharp with disbelief. "You did this?"

Rosalind lifted her chin, though her lips trembled.

"Someone had to. She was living a lie and making us all look bad."

"It wasn't your truth to expose," Flynn said quietly, his arm tightening around my waist.

"You betrayed your sister," Abuela continued, her words cutting.

I found my voice at last. "I deserved to come out as Miranda Milan on my own terms, when I was ready."

"And when would that have been?" Rosalind challenged. "Another year? Five? Never? Better to come out now when we can mitigate the fall out."

"At what cost?" Abuela demanded. "The trust of your family? The respect of your sisters?" She shook her head, disappointment radiating from her. "In this family, we protect each other. We do not betray each other for our own agenda."

Rosalind's stepped back as if she'd been physically slapped. "What's done is done. I can't take it back."

"No, you cannot," Abuela agreed coldly. "And now you must face consequences. I've already spoken to my friend Senator Organa," Abuela continued, ignoring Mamá's interruption. "I explained that, unfortunately, you would not be able to accept the summer internship position in her office."

The color drained from Rosalind's face. "What? No, you can't—that internship is everything—"

"Was everything," Abuela corrected. "The senator was quite understanding when I explained that you would not be returning to law school."

"What? Abuela, why?" Rosalind whispered, her voice breaking.

Abuela replied firmly. "As the matriarch of this family, I am the keeper of our values. You betrayed your sister, and your family. That is not who we are, Rosalind. It is time you rethink your life choices and your place in this family."

Rosalind looked to Mamá for support, but found only confusion and disappointment. She turned to Papá, who had remained silent throughout the confrontation, but he simply shook his head.

"I've worked so hard," Rosalind said, tears finally spilling down her cheeks. "A law degree and that internship was my future."

"Was it?" Abuela asked, her voice softening slightly. "Or was it the future your mother imagined for you?"

The question hung in the air, heavy with implication.

"I don't know what you mean," Rosalind said, wiping angrily at her tears.

"I think you do." Abuela stepped closer, taking Rosalind's hands in hers. "I've watched you, mi nieta. I've seen how you flinch when people call you 'future senator.'"

Rosalind stiffened, but Abuela's gaze was penetrating. "You don't want to be a lawyer any more than Tempest wanted to. But instead of having the courage to choose your own path, you lashed out at your sister for finding hers."

Rosalind's composure crumbled completely, her shoulders shaking with silent sobs.

"I hate law school," she whispered, the confession torn from somewhere deep inside her. "I've always hated it.

But it's what was expected. What would make everyone proud."

Mamá made a small, pained sound, clutching the notebook of her own abandoned writing to her chest.

"Oh, Rosalind," Papá said gently, "we would be proud of you no matter what path you chose, as long as it was truly yours."

"Would you?" Rosalind looked directly at Mamá, her voice raw with years of unexpressed doubt.

Mamá stared at her daughter, then down at the notebook in her hands, tangible evidence of her own abandoned dreams. Something shifted in her expression, a realization dawning that seemed to age her and soften her all at once.

"Yes," she said finally, her voice steady despite the tears gathering in her eyes. "I would. Because I don't want for you what happened to me." She held up the notebook.

The sincerity in her voice seemed to surprise everyone, especially Rosalind, whose tears flowed freely now.

"I don't even know what my heart wants," she admitted.

"Then take the time to find out," Abuela said, gentle now that her point had been made. "But do not punish your sister for having the courage you're still finding."

Rosalind nodded, then turned to me, naked vulnerability in her expression. "I really thought I was doing the right thing. I was wrong and I'm sorry."

The apology was simple but I was going to need some time before I would be ready to forgive her. I would, in time, but Ros was going to have to do some groveling, and honestly, work to figure out who and what she wanted to be.

"I know what it's like to feel trapped by expectations," I said. "I spent years hiding parts of myself because I thought they wouldn't be acceptable. Trust me when I say, you won't be happy until you figure out who you genuinely want to be."

I had to admit that Abuela's particular brand of dramatic intervention had accomplished what years of tension and unspoken resentments could not.

Sometimes a family needed a little telenovela drama to find its way to the truth.

"Now," Abuela announced, clapping her hands together as if the matter was settled, "I believe we have a graduation to celebrate. Ophelia has made a beautiful spread of food, and the mariachi band is waiting to play. Tempest has achieved something remarkable today. She has graduated with honors and found the courage to live authentically. That is what we celebrate."

Following Abuela's directive to return to the celebration, Flynn leaned down to whisper in my ear, "Your grandmother is terrifying in the best possible way."

I laughed softly, leaning into his strength. "She gets results."

We sat down around the tables in the backyard, celebrated, and devoured Ophelia's food.

Mamá's gaze shifted to me, and I saw the struggle playing out behind her eyes, the clash between her lifelong expectations and her newfound understanding.

"I'm... adjusting to the idea of you moving to LA to be a writer," she said carefully. "But I cannot deny that your writing brings joy to others. Or that it clearly fulfills you in a way that any other career would not." She took a deep breath. "And yes, I will even admit that young man cares for you deeply. Even if his career involves an unnecessary amount of physical violence and likely TBIs."

Coming from my mother, this was practically a blessing.

"Thank you, Mamá," I said softly.

As she walked away, Freddie let out a low whistle. "Did that really just happen? Did Mamá actually support everyone's life choices in a single conversation?"

"I think Abuela slipped something into her drink," Ophelia stage whispered.

"I heard that," Mamá called over her shoulder, but there was a hint of amusement in her voice that made us all exchange surprised glances.

"Hey, can I come visit you guys?" Freddie asked. "LA has a great queer scene, and I need to scope it out before the Olympic trials."

"I'm coming too," Abuela announced, appearing beside our table with the dramatic timing she'd perfected over decades in telenovelas. "You know Los Angeles is where you're Abuelo and I met." She winked at me. "And someone needs to help you plan all the parties you'll host for the wives, girlfriends, lovers and partners of the Bandits."

Abuela loved a party. "I'm counting on it."

A commotion at the front of the house signaled the arrival of the Kingman contingent. Even from the backyard, I could hear Jules's excited voice, Declan's deep laugh, and the distinctive sound of Bridger Kingman calling for order like he was back on the sidelines.

"Brace yourselves," I murmured to my sisters. "Kingman family chaos incoming."

Flynn appeared at the patio door, grinning as he held it open for his family to stream through. Jules immediately made a beeline for Freddie, the two youngest siblings having formed a friendship based on their shared love of causing trouble.

Flynn tugged me away from the crowd, leading me to a quiet corner of the yard near where Burrito was now dozing under a tree, graduation cap askew.

"I can't believe you didn't mention your abuelo is Leo Ramirez," he said.

"I didn't think you'd care about the other kind of football."

"He's a legendary athlete. He and my dad are basically already bestie." He jerked his chin to where the two patriarchs were talking.

It was really nice to see our families blending together like this.

He wrapped his arms around me and nuzzled my ear. He whispered, his voice low and warm in my ear. "Did I tell you how hot I find your whole family rebel turned inspirational speaker thing?"

I laughed, leaning into him. "It feels like I'm finally becoming who I was always meant to be."

"I like who you're meant to be," he murmured, pressing a kiss to my temple.

"Even the parts that write smut about fictional athletes

having fictional orgasms?" I asked, referencing Rosalind's earlier jab.

A slow, wicked grin spread across his face. "Especially those parts. Though I do have some notes on technical accuracy for your next book."

"I bet you do." I wrapped my arms around his neck, rising on tiptoes to kiss him properly. "Maybe we should schedule a research session once we're in LA."

His arms tightened around me. "I've already blocked off my entire calendar for the foreseeable future."

It was a future I could hardly wait for. One where I got to write the best kind of happy ever after. My own.

EPILOGUE – WHAT STRENGTH I HAVE'S MINE OWN

TEMPEST

The September morning sunlight streamed through the kitchen windows of our Woodland Hills home, casting golden patterns across the granite countertops. Flynn stood at the stove, flipping pancakes with the same intense concentration he brought to studying play sheets. He wore nothing but sweatpants slung low on his hips, his hair still rumpled from sleep, his broad shoulders flexing with each movement.

I'd never get tired of this view.

"Stop staring at my ass and check if my phone is buzzing," he said without turning around. "Gryff said he had some last-minute adjustments to our ride today."

"Your ass is part of my pre-game ritual," I countered, but picked up his phone from the counter. "Nothing from Gryff. Just Jules asking if the Sports Network cameras ever show the family section, because she wants to make sure her makeup is perfect when they pan to her."

Flynn's dad and sister were flying in for the game and

scheduled to land in a few hours. I was anxious to ask Jules how her first semester of college was going.

Flynn snorted. "Tell her to focus on cheering, not preening. This isn't a fashion show."

I sent Jules a different, kinder message, then leaned against the island, sipping my coffee and soaking in the moment. It was all so... domestic, and I was loving it.

Flynn's eldest brother, Chris, gave us the house as Flynn's welcome to the big leagues gift. Which still absolutely floored me. He'd given one to Gryff too, right across the street. They'd said it was a family tradition.

Our house, still new enough that the phrase sent a little thrill through me, was the perfect blend of both of us. My colorful throw pillows on his sleek leather couch. My book collection filling the built-in shelves he'd insisted the place needed. Photos of both our families mixed together on the walls.

And outside, a backyard that would soon welcome an incredibly special donkey.

"Nervous?" I asked as Flynn slid a plate of blueberry pancakes in front of me.

He shrugged, but the movement was too controlled to be casual. "First official game as a Bandit. First time the fans paid actual money to see what I can do. First time playing where it actually counts in the pros."

"You and Gryff were literally born for this," I reminded him. "The Bandits are lucky to have both Kingman twins on their roster."

"Lucky or smart," Flynn grinned, some of the tension easing from his shoulders.

My phone chimed with an incoming FaceTime call,

the screen displaying "AbuelaNovela." I propped it against the fruit bowl and accepted.

"Buenos días, mis amores." Abuela's face filled the screen, resplendent as always in full makeup despite the early hour. "Are you ready for the big day?"

"Which one?" Flynn asked, leaning into frame. "My first real pro game or Tempest's book release on Tuesday?"

"Both, of course," Abuela declared, waving away the question. "They are equally important milestones."

The camera angle shifted wildly as Abuela adjusted her phone, then steadied on a familiar gray face with perked ears.

"Burrito," I exclaimed. "Hi, baby."

The donkey brayed at the sound of my voice, pushing his nose closer to the screen. Flynn laughed and waved.

"He misses you," Abuela said, reappearing in frame. "But the transport arrangements are all confirmed for next month. Your paddock installation is complete?"

"All done," Flynn confirmed. "The yard is officially Burrito-proof. Or at least, that's what the contractor promised. I have my doubts about any enclosure being truly Burrito-proof."

"He has grown into quite the little escape artist," Abuela agreed fondly. "Now go. Prepare. Conquer. We will be watching the game and sending all our energy."

After a long, very wet, extremely hot, very orgasmic shower, I sent Flynn off to the stadium, and got ready to attend my very first football game. Flynn had gotten me more Bandit's t-shirts, jackets, hats, and even some socks to wear than any one person needed in their lifetime. But I chose the jersey with his name and number and paired it with some jeans, and a cute pair of sparkly ballet flats.

The family section at Bandits Stadium was unlike anything I'd experienced before. Here, in this reserved section of luxury boxes, the families and partners of players were treated like minor celebrities themselves.

"Tempest, Over here." Vanessa Martinez, waved me over to where she sat with several other women. Vanessa's husband played tight end, and she'd appointed herself my unofficial guide to PAL life.

PAL I'd learned stood for Partners and Lovers, the Bandits' more inclusive version of the traditional WAGs, Wives and Girlfriends, designation. I'd been surprised and grateful for how welcoming they'd all been, especially once they'd realized I was Miranda Milan.

Jules, Artemis, and I headed over, while Coach Bridger went over to chat with Flynn and Gryff's agent, Mac Jerry.

"You all are just in time," Vanessa said as I slid into the seat she'd saved. "They're about to announce the starting lineup."

Beside her, Jade Wilson nudged my arm. "I finished your book last night. That scene in chapter seventeen? Girl. I had to take a cold shower."

I laughed, no longer embarrassed by such comments. "Wait until you read the next one. I had some very thorough research assistance."

"I bet you did," Jade winked. "Your man seems very... dedicated."

"Ew," Jules faux gagged. "Don't ruin Miranda Milan books for me with that kind of information.

"Speaking of," Vanessa interrupted, pointing to the field where the defensive starters were being announced.

The stadium erupted as Flynn's name boomed through the speakers. Number 50 jogged onto the field, helmet in hand, looking every inch the warrior heading into battle. My heart swelled with ridiculous pride. He might not be able to see me from the field, but I stood anyway, cheering as loudly as I could.

"The rookies usually look terrified," observed Priya Singh, joining our little group with her adorable baby. Her husband was the Bandits' star kicker. "Your man looks like he was born for this."

"He was," I agreed, watching as Flynn took his position for the national anthem. "Football's in his DNA."

"Just like writing is in yours," Priya said. "Anymore scenes like that one in chapter seventeen and I'm going to end up pregnant again. My hat's off to Flynn for being your research buddy."

"Oh gawd, it's never going to stop, is it?" Jules shuddered and stood up. "I'm going to get nachos and rinse my brain in cheese sauce."

I groaned as the women laughed. Somehow, in the past few months, I'd gone from hiding my identity to openly discussing my "research" with PALs I barely knew. The universe had a strange sense of humor.

"Ladies and gentlemen," the announcer's voice boomed, "please direct your attention to the jumbotron for today's 'Family Focus'."

I froze as our little group appeared on the massive screen. The other women waved, so I followed suit, and the camera zoomed in on me.

The crowd cheered—whether for me or simply because it was expected, I couldn't tell. But as the cameras lingered, I smiled and waved, embracing the moment instead of shrinking from it.

"You're famous now," Vanessa teased as the screen changed to find other player's families.

"Hardly," I laughed. "But it's still surreal sometimes."

"Get used to it," Jade advised. "Between Flynn's career and your books, you're going to be in the public eye a lot."

She was right, of course. In the months since graduation, I'd done more interviews, book signings, and public appearances than I could count. My fifth book was coming out in a few days, and according to my publisher, the pre-orders alone were almost a guarantee for it to hit several bestseller lists. FlixNChill was already casting on the series adaptation. And through it all, Flynn had been my steadfast support, just as I tried to be for him.

Different worlds, merging into one shared life.

As the kickoff soared through the air, I settled in to watch the man I loved do what he was born to do, surrounded by women who were quickly becoming loyal friends rather than mere acquaintances. Women who saw me as more than just "Flynn Kingman's girlfriend." Who respected my career as much as his.

For a girl who'd spent most of her life hiding, it felt remarkably like freedom.

Tuesday morning, I woke to the smell of coffee and the sound of Flynn's voice downstairs. Book release day. No matter how well received the rest of the books had been, I always had a niggle of nerves every time a new book came out.

It wasn't that I didn't think people would like it, but especially now that the public had an actual face to put with the name, this one in particular felt very... exposing.

I padded downstairs to find Flynn in a suit, phone pressed to his ear, gesturing animatedly as he paced the kitchen.

"No, we need at least five dozen," he was saying. "And make sure they're the special edition hardcovers, not the regular ones... Yes, I know they cost more, that's the point... Just get it done, please." He hung up, turning to find me watching him.

"Were you ordering books?" I asked, amused.

"Maybe." He grinned, that boyish smile that still made my heart skip. "The team wants signed copies for everyone. Including Coach, which is mildly terrifying considering what happens in chapter twenty."

I groaned, remembering the particularly steamy scene I'd written involving a coach's desk. "Oh god. I didn't think about that."

"Too late now." Flynn crossed to me, wrapping me in his arms. "Happy book birthday, by the way."

"Thank you." I accepted his kiss, then pulled back to study him. "Why are you in a suit at seven a.m.? Don't you have practice?"

"Later." He guided me to a chair, then pushed a mug of

coffee into my hands. "First, breakfast. Then I have a surprise."

"Flynn," I said warily. "What did you do?"

"Nothing bad," he promised, setting a plate of avocado toast in front of me. "Just a little pre-release celebration."

After breakfast, he handed me a soft but lightweight sweater and a pair of jeans, but added some silky lingerie for underneath and a pair of high heels to finish the look. Then he led me outside where a sleek black town car waited at the curb. The driver opened the door with a flourish.

"Your chariot, Ms. Milan," Flynn said, using my pen name with a playful formality.

"Are you kidnapping me?" I asked as he ushered me inside.

"Technically, no, since you're going willingly." He settled beside me. "Besides, kidnapping seems like a plotline for your next book, not this one."

Twenty minutes later, we pulled up in front of a the romance-only bookstore in LA. The windows were filled with displays of my latest novel, featuring the striking cover of twin football players with their backs to the reader, a woman's silhouette between them.

"What are we doing here?" I asked as Flynn guided me to the door. "The signing isn't until tonight."

"You'll see," was all he said.

Inside, the store was empty save for the manager, who greeted Flynn like an old friend. "Everything's ready, Mr. Kingman."

Flynn led me to a section, where an entire table had

been dedicated to my books. In the center sat a tower of hardcovers, arranged in a display that mimicked a football stadium.

"I wanted you to see it first," Flynn explained, watching my reaction. "Before the crowds, before the interviews. Just you and your work, the way it started."

Emotion welled in my throat as I traced a finger over my name on the glossy cover. "It's beautiful."

"There's more," Flynn said, guiding me around the display.

On the other side, someone had set up a small table with champagne, pastries, and a stack of congratulatory cards from my family, his family, and our friends.

"You did all this?" I asked, blinking back tears.

"With some help," he admitted. "Your sisters picked the pastries. Abuela selected the champagne. My sister made sure we got the space privately for an hour."

I laughed, wiping away a stray tear. "Our families really have merged into one unstoppable force."

"The Kingman-Navarro machine," Flynn agreed. "Terrifying in its efficiency."

We toasted with champagne, surrounded by my books and the quiet hush of the empty store. It was the perfect counterbalance to the public event that would come later —this private moment of appreciation for the journey that had brought us here.

"To my favorite author," Flynn said, clinking his glass against mine. "Who's finally taking up all the space she deserves."

That evening the bookstore was packed by the time we

arrived. A line of readers wrapped around the block, many clutching dog-eared copies of my previous books along with their recently purchased copies of the new one.

"This is insane," I murmured to Flynn as we slipped in through the back entrance. "There must be hundreds of people out there."

"Five hundred and twenty-seven at last count," came a familiar voice. "I had Artemis do a drone flyover to check."

I turned to find Gryff grinning at us, looking relaxed and California-cool in designer jeans and a fitted t-shirt that showed off the results of his pro football player training regimen. Beside him stood Artemis, drone controller and camera in hand.

"Surveillance seems excessive," I laughed, accepting Gryff's bear hug.

"It's not surveillance, it's documentation," Artemis corrected, snapping a photo of Flynn and me. "For posterity. And maybe extortion, depending on how the night goes."

Artemis had been Gryff's best friend since high school, where she'd played on the women's rugby team. When he'd been drafted by the Bandits, she'd followed him to LA, ostensibly to try out for the Olympic team, but we all suspected it was because neither could bear to be separated from the other. They shared the house across from ours, adamantly insisting they were just friends despite the obvious chemistry between them.

They were a romance novel just waiting to be written.

A bookstore employee appeared, looking slightly frantic. "Ms. Milan? We're ready for you whenever you are. The crowd is getting... enthusiastic."

I took a deep breath, smoothing down the deep purple dress I'd chosen specifically for tonight—the same shade as the DSU Dragons, a nod to where this journey had begun.

"You've got this," Flynn said, squeezing my hand. "I'll be right there in the front row, looking inappropriately turned on by my girlfriend talking about her dirty books."

"Flynn," I hissed, but it was only to hide the laugh.

"We'll keep him in line," Artemis promised, grabbing Gryff's arm. "Come on, Twin One and Twin Two. Let's go find seats before the two of you embarrasses us all."

As they headed toward the main event space, I caught Gryff's lingering glance at Artemis, the softness in his expression when she wasn't looking. So much longing, so much fear of ruining what they had. I'd seen that dance before—had performed it myself with Flynn. Someday soon, one of them would need to take the leap.

Maybe I'd need to draft their story next, to show them how it could end.

The event passed in a blur of readings, Q&A sessions, and signing books until my hand cramped. Throughout it all, Flynn sat in the front row, exactly as promised, his proud smile never wavering. Occasionally he'd catch my eye and wink, or mouth "that's my favorite part" when I read a particularly steamy passage.

During the signing portion, a young woman with curves similar to mine approached the table, clutching my first book like a talisman.

"I just wanted to say thank you," she said, her voice trembling slightly. "Before your books, I never saw heroines who looked like me getting the hot guy. It changed how I saw myself."

I swallowed the lump in my throat, remembering how I'd once felt the same emptiness, the same hunger for representation. "That's exactly why I write them," I told her, signing her book with extra care. "Because we all deserve to be the heroines of our own stories, no matter our size, shape, or what the scale says."

Later, after the last reader had left and the bookstore staff were clearing up, I found Flynn in deep conversation with Gryff and Artemis near the refreshment table.

"Ready to go?" he asked, slipping an arm around my waist. "The after party awaits."

"After party?"

"Just us," he clarified. "And these two moochers who invited themselves over to raid our wine fridge."

"Your wine collection is better than ours," Gryff shrugged unapologetically. "Besides, someone needs to help Tempest celebrate properly. You'll just try to get her to bed early for 'recovery' purposes."

"Recovery is important," Flynn argued with mock seriousness. "Book release is very taxing on the author."

"I'm right here," I reminded them. "And I vote for wine with friends, then early bed for... recovery."

Flynn grinned. "See? The author has spoken."

Back at our house, with shoes kicked off and wine glasses filled, the four of us sprawled across the living room. Artemis had connected her camera to our TV, scrolling through candid shots she'd taken during the event.

"This one's my favorite," she said, pausing on an image of me mid-laugh, Flynn watching me with unmistakable adoration. "Total romance novel cover material."

"Speaking of," Gryff said, examining my book's cover, "this seems remarkably familiar. Twins and a woman caught between them? Are you writing about us now, Tempest?"

I felt my cheeks warm. "It's *Twelfth Night*, not you specifically. Though I may have borrowed certain... personality traits."

"Should I be worried?" Artemis asked, arching an eyebrow. "Do I feature in this fictional love triangle?"

"You'll have to read it to find out," I teased.

Artemis snorted. "I've read yours, I know how it goes. Boy meets girl, boy meets boy, girl meets girl, obstacles arise, grand gesture, happily ever after. Real life is messier."

"Is it though?" I asked, glancing meaningfully between her and Gryff. "Sometimes the story writes itself, if you're brave enough to let it."

A weighted silence fell, Artemis suddenly extremely interested in her wine glass while Gryff studied the ceiling with unusual intensity. Flynn caught my eye, a silent laugh passing between us.

"To stories," Flynn said, raising his glass. "The ones we read, the ones we write, and the ones we live."

"To stories," we echoed, clinking glasses.

Later, after Gryff and Artemis had left, together, as always, but still stubbornly apart, Flynn and I stood on our back patio, looking out at the yard we'd designed with Burrito in mind. The donkey enclosure, the shade trees, the special gate that would theoretically prevent escapes.

"Did you ever imagine this?" I asked, leaning back against Flynn's chest as his arms encircled me. "When you were chasing a baby donkey across campus?"

"Honestly? No." His lips brushed my temple. "I definitely didn't expect to fall in love with the girl who wouldn't even look up from her book."

"I looked up eventually," I reminded him.

"You did." His arms tightened around me. "And then you saw me. Really saw me. Not just the football player or the Kingman legacy, but me."

I turned in his embrace, rising on tiptoes to kiss him. "Just like you saw me. All of me, even the parts I was hiding."

The night air wrapped around us, warm and sweet with the scent of jasmine from our neighbor's garden. Inside our home, signed copies of my books lined the shelves alongside Flynn's football trophies. Pictures of our families, Navarros and Kingmans and one special donkey, documented our journey from adversaries to partners.

Different worlds that had become one shared life.

"I have something for you," Flynn said suddenly, reaching into his pocket. "A book release gift."

"Flynn, you already did so much—"

He pressed a small box into my hand, and my heart stuttered. Not a ring box, but still small, still significant.

I opened it to find a key on a silver keychain shaped like a donkey.

"It's for the guest house," Flynn explained. "I had it

converted into a proper writing studio for you. Soundproofed, bookshelves, one of those fancy ergonomic chairs, a day bed... for research, the works. It'll be ready by the time Burrito arrives."

Tears pricked at my eyes. "You did that for me?"

"I did it for us," he corrected. "Because your writing is part of our story. And I want every chapter to be better than the last."

I clutched the key to my chest, overwhelmed by the gesture, by the life we were building, by how far we'd come from that first meeting.

"I love you," I whispered, the words still a wonder even after all these months. "So much."

"Love you more, Mi Reina." Flynn's smile was soft in the moonlight. "Always more."

Aww. When had he learned that endearment?

As his lips met mine, I thought of all the romance novels I'd written, all the happily-ever-afters I'd crafted for my characters. None of them compared to the story we were writing together. Messy and real and more beautiful than fiction could ever be.

The baby donkey in dragon wings had brought me more than just a man. He'd brought me to myself, to the courage to take up space, to live authentically in the full light of day rather than hiding in shadows.

Some might call it luck or coincidence. But I knew better.

It was exactly the kind of meet-cute that belonged in a romance novel.

And we were just getting to the good part.

Need just a little more Flynn and Tempest?

I've got a bonus chapter for you when you join my Swoon Zone email newsletter!

BookHip.com/RCXPFXL

A NOTE FROM THE AUTHOR

Buckle Up my friends, let's talk about how this book came into the world!

Whew boy, this was the longest book I've written to date. There was just SO MUCH to write about.

I'm not great at enemies to lovers stories because I don't actually like it when my characters are mean to each other. But *antagonists* to lovers? Hells yeah.

Remember the 1997 animated feature film *Anastasia*? (If not, Bridger Kingman demands you go watch it right now!) The way we watched Anya and Dmitri poke and prod at each other full well knowing they were going to fall in love had me swooning.

That's what I hoped to do with Flynn and Tempest. But you know I can't help but write a cinnamon roll golden retriever hero who falls first. The Kingman men will always fall first and harder.

I also wanted to take us to college for this story, because there is so much fun to be had in those almost time to be an adult years.

Remember Bettie, Alice, and Hannah at our fictional sorority of Kappa Alpha Tau? I'm giving a wink-wink nudge-nudge to my Theta sorority sisters with that one. IYKYK. Beta Gamma forever. (*holding up kite hands)

Sororities are so often portrayed as catty, bitchy houses of debauchery and scandal in the media, but I had the time of my life living in my sorority house. I wanted to portray the kind of amazing friendships, and a few shenanigans, that depicted what real sorority life was like for me.

This book is also a love letter to my English Literature degree. Yep… that ever maligned liberal arts degree. I've got one. I still hate Herman Melville, and find Shakespeare's history plays fascinating. But never once did any of my professors (not even my brilliant Shakespeare prof) ever let on that so much 'classic' literature was the popular, genre fiction…dare I say 'smut' of the day.

NEVER be ashamed for ENJOYING romance novels. They are so often maligned by people who've never even deigned to pick one up, just like in this story. If you want to know more about WHY the romance genre is so often denigrated by our world, I highly recommend - *Dangerous Books For Girls: The Bad Reputation of Romance Novels Explained* by Maya Rodale.

Down with patriarchy!

I spent a long time as a literature snob, and for that I'm horrified. Stories inform our world, they let us explore the world in a safe way, and we get to experience life through other's words.

And to that I end, I will say that I firmly believe that both reading and writing is, and has always been political.

I write my stories to express how I wish the world could be. Every book I write is a reaction to what's happening in the world I live in today.

That means I write about love is love, diversity, equity, inclusion, and accessibility, and everyone, no matter their skin color, language, religion, and/or gender identity deserving equal rights.

My readers have asked me to bring more diversity to the Kingman world, and it took me a lot of time and soul-searching as to whether I *should* write my main character from a different heritage than my own.

In the end, I could not, in this day and age, in good conscious write a whole series with only white people as the main characters. That doesn't reflect the world I live in, nor do I want it to.

Representation matters.

I worked very hard to respectfully write Tempest's character and the world she occupies, including working with my readers to give her as much authenticity as I could. But I know no matter how hard I've tried, it won't be perfect. If you feel I've done a disservice, you can tell me. I promise to do my best to learn, fix, and do better anywhere I can.

I don't presume to take the place of authors who are telling own voices stories. Please, please, read stories from authors who are writing from and about their own cultures. Support them.

Here are a few Latinx romance authors I've read and loved, and I think that you will too.

Leonor Soliz, Alexis Daria, Adrianna Herrera, Liana De La Rosa, Mia Sosa, Natalia Caña.

I'll continue to share more in my Swoon Zone email newsletter too.

There is a big chunk of this story about me exploring my own rush of success in the past two years. I worked hard, took lots of classes to learn the skills I needed, had some good timing, and good smattering of luck to be where I am today.

But as Tempest discovered, it's not all rainbows and marshmallows. I have absolutely loved being able to touch readers lives with my fluffy stories, but there has been my fair share of tears and stress too. I give as much as I can of myself, but I can't give as much as the world wants from me.

Not if I want to continue to create more stories for you to read. Just know I'm ever doing my best, and I love all my readers and fans so much for giving me this special shot at changing the world in the ways that I can.

Also… Yes, yes, I do think Netflix (aka FlixNChill) should turn the Kingmans into a TV series. #JustSaying #CallMyAgent

What's up next for the Kingmans? I think another twin whose had one too many broken hearts needs a good friend to help him figure out what love really means to him.

But how in the world are we going to have Kingman Family Game night when the boys are playing on rival teams???

I have faith that Bridger Kingman will figure it out.

Finally, know that a portion of the proceeds of this book will go to the Luvin Arms Animal Sanctuary.

Together, we're gonna save donkeys (and rooster, and cows, and pigs, and ducks, and geese!)

Luvin Arms is a 501(c)3 nonprofit animal sanctuary for abused or neglected farmed animals in Erie, Colorado. Their rescued residents include cows, pigs, turkeys, chickens, horses, goats, sheep, and ducks. These beautiful residents were rescued from horrific situations including abuse and neglect cases, factory farms, religious rituals, slaughterhouse-bound trucks, bankrupt farms, and more. They were left with nowhere to turn and would have been slaughtered if they hadn't been saved.

Extra Hugs from me to you,

—Amy

ALSO BY AMY AWARD

THE COCKY KINGMANS

*The C*ck Down The Block*
The Wiener Across the Way
*The P*ssy Next Door*
The Anaconda Downstairs
*The Jack*ss in Class*

ACKNOWLEDGMENTS

I owe a boatload of appreciation to my Spanish language gurus and diversity readers, Ashley De La Hoz, Valeria Lizarraga, and Elizabeth Mummey. You helped me make Tempest and the whole Navarro family the best that I could.

There's more fun in this book because of my trusted alpha reader, Heather Clark. I'm so glad you MADE ME be your friend, and it tickles me to no end how invested in the Kingman world you are. I'm lucky for that.

This career is hard, and my amazing mastermind friends, Lucy Lennox, Kaci Rose, and Hope Ford make it all a little easier, and a lot more fun. Looking forward to a lot more 7-figure digging with all of you.

I really look forward the author talks and days away from the computer at rando coffee shops around the Denver metro area with M. Guida, Holly Roberds, Parker Finch, and Nikki Hall. Y'all are my tribe.

I don't know that I would even be writing books, have this whole career, and understand how being my true authentic self leads me to success every damn time if it weren't for Becca Syme. My life are better because of you and your insights, and the way you gently push me to be better.

I'm so grateful you're there for me and all the other

authors who need help to be authors for life. Extra hugs for you.

I am ever grateful to my editor Chrisandra who somehow still loves me and my stories, even though I will suck at commas and deadlines forever. Sorry. (But only a little bit.)

Thank you to Ellie at Love Notes PR for for quite literally helping me make my dreams come true. I can't wait to continue to SLAY with you for a long time to come.

Huge thanks to Leni Kauffman for giving us another amazing cover. She makes us all feel beautiful with the way she draws plus size women (and the men who are soooo into them!) Thank you for helping me change the world one book cover at a time.

So many hugs to my chaos coordinator Kate Tilton. My author life would be such a tangled mess with out you. I appreciate you more than you know.

And to my Patreon Book Dragons - you are the reason I write books. I hope I continue to entertain you and make you proud. Your continual support means so incredibly much to me. You make me smile and happy cry when I read your comments on the chapters.

For my Swoonies, Flynn and Tempest's box with some fun swag is coming your way!

- Allie H.
- Amanda T.
- Amber I.
- Angie
- Anna R.

- Anne-Marie P.
- Annmarie B.
- Belinda M.
- Caitlin
- Cathy G.
- Chanel S.
- Charles F.
- Crystal R.
- Dawn J.
- Ember D.
- Emma M.
- Escalla
- Essence C.
- Ilona T.
- Irehne A.
- Janna G.
- Jennifer N.
- Jenny W.
- Jessica D.
- Jessica H.
- Johnna A.
- Judy R.
- JW
- Karla K.
- Kat V.
- Kathryn B.
- Kathy B.
- Katrina D.
- Kaylee B.
- Kelley M.
- Kiarra C.

- Kyndal N.
- Laura B.
- Laura P.
- Lauren K.
- Leanna B.
- Lydia K.
- Mackenzie B.
- Maria B.
- McKaylee E.
- Meghan M.
- Melissa E.
- Michelle A.
- Pam G.
- Tara V.

For my VIP Fans, signed books are coming your way!

- Amie N.
- Angelique A.
- Angie K.
- Arabella L.
- Ashley B.
- Barb T.
- Billy
- Brianna S.
- Cara-Lee D.
- Christin C.
- Christy B.
- Corinne A.
- Diana B.
- Emily J.

- Heather
- Heather L.
- Jen H.
- Jenna M.
- Jennifer L.
- Kara C.
- Kelli W.
- Kelly
- Kerrie M.
- Kristin A.
- Lis T.
- Lisa C.
- Melissa E.
- Melissa L.
- Nicole C.
- Rachael C.
- Robyn W.
- Sam B.
- Sara W.

For my Biggest Fans Ever, book boxes with so much hilarious donkey and football stuff and signed book are on their way. Thank you so much for believing in me.

- Alida H.
- Amy H.
- Ashley P.
- Cherie S.
- Danielle T.
- Daphine G.
- Dawn B.

- Hana K.
- Helena B.
- Kari S.
- Katherine M.
- Laura G.
- Lisa W.
- Mari G.
- Mashell A.
- Misty B.
- Orma M.
- Selena
- Tiffany L.
- Valeria L.

ABOUT THE AUTHOR

Amy Award is a curvy girl who has a thing for football players, fuzzy-butt pets, and spicy romance novels. She believes that all bodies are beautiful and deserve their own love stories with Happy Ever Afters. Find her at AuthorAmyAward.com

Amy also write curvy girl paranormal romances with dragons, wolves, demons, and vampires, as Aidy Award. If that's your jam, check those books out at AidyAward.com